REQUIEM

REQUIEM

...

Geir Tangen

Translated from the Norwegian by
Paul Norlen

MINOTAUR BOOKS
New York

MINOTAUR BOOKS
An imprint of St. Martin's Press

REQUIEM. Copyright © 2016 by Geir Tangen. Translation copyright © 2018 by Paul Norlen. All rights reserved. Printed in the United States of America. For information, address St. Martin's Press, 175 Fifth Avenue, New York, N.Y. 10010.

www.minotaurbooks.com

The Library of Congress Cataloging-in-Publication Data
is available upon request.

ISBN 978-1-250-12406-7 (hardcover)
ISBN 978-1-250-12407-4 (ebook)

Our books may be purchased in bulk for promotional, educational, or business use. Please contact your local bookseller or the Macmillan Corporate and Premium Sales Department at 1-800-221-7945, extension 5442, or by email at MacmillanSpecialMarkets@macmillan.com.

First published in Norwegian by MATA Forlag in 2016

First U.S. Edition: July 2018

10 9 8 7 6 5 4 3 2 1

REQUIEM

On the morning four days before the light went out, the journalist Viljar Ravn Gudmundsson stood proudly in the conference room, enjoying the atmosphere around him. Big smiles, hungry eyes, and arrogant laughter filled the room. This was how things should be.

"My God, Viljar! I don't know what you're giving your sources, but I want some of it. We're talking the Minister of Transport here. Pinned bare-assed to the wall with a nail gun. I'd gladly give half my liver to get my name on a story like that."

Although the arts reporter Henrik Thomsen was three heads taller than his colleague, his height did not noticeably add to his intelligence. Viljar looked up at him and could see remnants of caked sugar in his ample mustache.

"Believe me, Thomsen, you wouldn't have survived. There's a reason that you review concerts while I hunt predators in the corridors of power."

Viljar moved away from the burly man and stood at the outer edge of the room. Let the light shine on him. He deserved it. This was his hour. The moment when everyone's eyes were directed at him in respect and admiration. What he had done was unique in the 115-year history of the newspaper. To the other journalists and editors, the article represented months of ambitious investigative journalism. If that wasn't the whole truth, Viljar didn't care. This was his specialty. If the article came after a hundred hours of overtime or fell into his hands like a feather from the sky, it was all the same to him. He was sitting on a scoop, and he had the power of words.

What he wrote was the truth. That was how it was in Haugesund. Again and again, he had knocked the abusers of power down from their pedestals. As far as *Haugesund News* was concerned, a granite obelisk dedicated to Viljar Ravn Gudmundsson could be raised on the site of the paper's new office building, currently under construction.

The story he had presented to the news editors that morning had all the necessary elements for nationwide saturation coverage. That condition arises when all the major news organizations cover the same dramatic event at the same time, and the coverage is so extensive that it overshadows everything else in the media. Politics, abuse of power, celebrities, crime, and sex. All this in one and the same story, and it was little *Haugesund News* that was sitting on it. They had Viljar Ravn Gudmundsson, which gave them enough credibility to be heard in the national press.

At the age of thirty-seven, Viljar had long since acquired a reputation as one of the country's most trustworthy voices in the media. Job offers from the major media houses landed regularly in his inbox, but he ignored them. He was a weekend dad, and couldn't bear the thought of commuting to Oslo during the week. His twelve-year-old son, Alexander, lived here in Haugesund, and no job in the world could make him sacrifice the times they had together. Besides, there was no escaping the fact that Viljar liked to be comfortable. At the

regional newspaper, he had freedom. He came and went as he p
He wrote the stories that suited him best, and said no to assignments
he considered pointless. He played by his own rules, a free soul in a
free landscape. He dictated the agenda. He was the house anarchist,
following his own impulses to the great despair, and delight, of Editor-
in-chief Johan Øveraas.

When the story about Hermann Eliassen, the Minister of Transport and Communications, showed up a few days earlier, Viljar had
long been telling his superiors that he was working on a gigantic story
of unbelievable dimensions. Nonsense, of course. In reality he'd spent
most of his workdays planning a weekend in London with Alexander.
Fortunately, the departure had worked out to be on the very day he'd
been able to present the Minister of Transport's head on a platter for
the editors.

"People . . . Listen to me for just a moment!"

Editor-in-chief Johan Øveraas guided Viljar firmly up to a corner
of the room where the other journalists could gather around. Then
he took firm hold on his own hips, and Viljar observed with fascina-
tion that the editor's hands actually disappeared into his love handles.

"This story will hit the media elite in Oslo like a pint of Guinness
in a bubbling champagne party. This story will be a damned wet
blanket on Hermann Eliassen's chorus of admirers. We in the local
press who know the guy have waited a long time to see him dangling.
Bloody well done, Viljar."

The applause rang out in the small space, and Viljar Ravn Gudmundsson took plenty of time to enjoy the moment.

This was *his* story. He was invincible in this power play. The truth
was his steadfast squire, and no one could poke holes in this story.

Outside, the wind was rustling the old oak trees next to Lillesund
School. Exhausted leaves clung tightly to the sap of summer a little
while longer. Unlike the journalists inside, the trees knew that

everything comes to an end. The wind will strip the trees bare in violent gusts, spitting out the withered jewelry at a final resting place.

Seventeen-year-old Jonas and his lover were on a farmyard a dozen kilometers farther south. Without knowing it, through their impassioned looks and caresses, they had sealed not only their own fate, but Viljar Ravn Gudmundsson's too, the man who at that very moment was receiving a final pat on the back from his editor.

"Incredibly well done, Viljar. Go to London. Turn off your cell phone. Have a good time with your son. You deserve this. We'll take the story from here. In four days you'll be back. I can promise you a strong tailwind on the return trip, because here it will be very windy."

Viljar smiled slyly as he packed the most important things into his duffel bag. He looked through the photo material that would be used in the story on Eliassen one last time, and sent it on to the desk. The editor was still standing beside him when he was finished.

Viljar looked up at Øveraas with the customary mischievous gleam in his eye. "Windy? Isn't it always windy here in Haugesund?"

Four days later
Stemmen, Haugesund
Tuesday evening, August 31, 2010

Threatening clouds swept across the sky. Like a dark omen, they demanded their place in the blue hour between day and night. One moment the waters of Eivindsvatnet were bathed in a magical shimmer, and the next they were wrapped in a black, suffocating carpet of sulfurous air, accompanied by thunderclaps and violent downpours.

Jonas Ferkingstad was standing out on a small bridge known as Stemmen, built in 1907 over the dams at the entry to the recreation area around Eivindsvatnet. The spindly figure peered searchingly out over the edge.

His shoulder-length blond hair was plastered to his forehead, and ice-blue eyes were focused on an imaginary point out in space. In small flashes of light, when the clouds occasionally parted, he could see down over the stream on the lower side of the dams. From the bridge where he was standing down to the bottom of the rock-covered slope was perhaps ten meters. A thin, soaking-wet, burgundy-red cotton shirt was glued to his chest. His body was shaking. He cast quick glances up the hill, toward the walking path under Skjoldavegen, but mostly he looked out into emptiness.

Jonas straightened up when he noticed the person who came walking toward him. It was impossible to see the figure clearly, but Jonas knew who it was. For the longest time he'd had a slight hope that he could avoid having this reckoning. No denial or lying was possible here. No treachery and betrayal. Two people who both knew the truth, meeting alone. Neither of them needed to hide behind façades and masquerades.

For a long time they stood observing each other from a distance. The autumn wind whipped up crests of foam on the water, and another bolt of lightning slashed the sky. In the quick flash of cold light they saw each other. Naked. Unprotected. Alone. The next moment the darkness returned, and the thunderclap made the concrete bridge vibrate. Jonas stood waiting with slumped shoulders. He looked up at the person before him. Jonas longed to creep into that other person's arms. Just be there in that secure embrace and act as if nothing had happened. That it all was just a fata morgana. Unreal. Something that would disappear if you just blinked a few times. But it wasn't like that. Nothing could be made undone.

They stood like that for a short time while the water ran off them. Mutual powerlessness was reflected in their faces. Nothing was said, but after a while the other person reached out toward Jonas, who gasped for breath as he let himself be embraced. No words could describe the heartfelt sensation he felt then and there. Not happiness. Not relief, but something else. Something deep inside him that made him let go. All the pent-up feelings exploded like a geyser. Jonas could hear himself bawling against the chest of the person who was holding him, but he barely noticed it. Now it had to come out, all the pain.

Over the other person's shoulder Jonas sensed a shadow moving by the little boathouse. Two red kayaks that were lying along the wall of the boathouse clung to each other against the wind. He had seen them out on the water the past few days, but could not quite understand why anyone would want to be out in such weather.

The brief distraction made him inattentive. The embrace had become noticeably tighter, as if the other person was trying to squeeze the air out of him. Jonas tried to tear himself loose from the iron grip, but he didn't want to escape completely yet. Small sobs were still felt in his belly. Desperate, small whimpers that testified to what he had done. Jonas knew it was his fault. His and his alone.

The force in the arms holding Jonas was primal. Inhuman. His arms remained hanging limply down, only the strength of the other person kept his legs from folding up under him. Jonas was empty. He was a thin, fragile shell incapable of putting up resistance. He realized that this was a battle. A battle of life and death. It now occurred to him that the other person had not embraced him to give him comfort and support. Jonas gathered his last energy and tore himself loose from the paralyzing grip. He stared at his opponent with new eyes. He braced himself, but could feel how weak his body was.

Suddenly the scene on the bridge changed. A new flash of light. Another thunderclap. The larger of the two figures opened its mouth to scream, but all that came out was a hoarse whisper.

With calm movements one person took a powerful hold of the other, and in one quick motion a body was raised up from the ground and tipped over the railing of the bridge. The scream that followed cut into the ravine as the body fell down into the abyss. Then came silence. Even the raindrops fell soundlessly when it was all over.

Four years later
Media House *Haugesund News*
Monday morning, October 13, 2014

A solitary line flickered on the computer screen. *Text: Viljar Ravn Gudmundsson*. He blinked. His eyes were stinging. An hour of the workday was already history, but the only thing Viljar had accomplished was to write his name.

He raised his eyes and looked out toward Karmsundsgata: a tableau of cars in rain and mist. The architects behind the new media building in Haugesund must have thought the floor-to-ceiling windows would be inspiration for the worker ants in the open office landscape. The view, however, was just as depressing as listening to Metallica's *Black Album* played on a pan flute.

The space in the media building was brand new, but ten years in the same news organization had slowly bled the energy from the Icelander Gudmundsson. The joy of uncovering something that might make big headlines in the national media crumbled into an endless slog, where one day's sensation is yesterday's news. Nothing fades faster than newsprint.

He tried to straighten his back. Barely past forty and already crippled by endless hours in front of keyboard and screen. He looked around and noticed that he was the only one not working. The tapping from neighboring keyboards hammered in his ear canals like a thousand cockroaches across a parquet floor. The buzz of the voices of the other journalists irritated him to no end. Removing the old offices with doors that closed and replacing them with an open-office anthill was systematized cruelty.

Besides the quiet, the office chair was what Viljar missed most. The deep, sturdy design he'd had at his old desk was the kind you could lean back in. Complete support for your whole back. On a quiet day there was no problem taking a power nap if you wanted to. The new chairs were short and had the seat back shoved in against your lumbar region, creating the unpleasant sensation of a prolonged prostate exam.

Viljar exchanged a tasteless piece of nicotine gum for a pouch of snus and looked around again. The picture was the same, as always. Cubicle upon cubicle of workstations in groups of four, only separated by four-foot-high white blocks with a royal blue front, which mostly resembled overgrown external hard drives. The only break was a group of uncommonly ugly green sofas that sat like a bar setup in the middle of the space.

Editor-in-chief Johan Øveraas was standing by the sofas. Viljar observed him and noted with satisfaction that the boss was closer to retirement than he would ever get to heaven. Øveraas was everything a good middle manager ought to be in a corporate group like Orkla Media: unscrupulous, coldhearted, and morally stunted, but 100 percent loyal to management.

Øveraas noticed the eye contact and lumbered over to Viljar's little cubicle. "Bloody slacker! Not a damned day goes by without you sponging a few hours in the middle of the workday. Do you think I'm a complete idiot? Don't you think I see when people come and go in this building?"

Øveraas blew himself up like a balloonfish, but it was mostly talk. Viljar knew perfectly well what the editor was referring to. On Friday Viljar had left work with no explanation.

"Do I have to scratch you in a certain place to get you to react, or can you please answer me when I'm talking to you?"

His eyes were bulging and his complexion changed to indigo.

Viljar thought that the article Øveraas assigned to him on Friday would be taken care of by the weekend shift, but that wasn't the case this time. At the Monday morning meeting, the story had turned up again on his desk like a bad penny, and he had a deadline of noon to deliver.

In other words, he had three hours in which to write a main story of twelve hundred words, and a six-hundred-word sidebar on the Mental Health Association, which was dissatisfied with the treatment they got in their endless journey between emergency room, hospital, general practitioner, and psychiatry. This time they screamed and warned that seriously mentally ill individuals were wandering around the city because they were never caught up by the system.

Viljar looked at the editor indulgently. It was best to humor him so that he didn't explode like a rabid lemming. "Relax! I had a stomachache. Didn't want to infect the whole office here with the smell of shit. I'm working on the article now."

Øveraas stood there a few more seconds before in his customary manner he took his anger out on something material. This time it was two ballpoint pens that had to suffer as he swept them down on the floor, turned abruptly, and stomped back to the office island.

Viljar sighed, picked up the pens, and looked over the facts again in the article he was supposed to write.

Anemic. Boring. Uninteresting. Three words that were very precise, not only for the content of the impending article, but also for the task of writing it. Even so, one hour later it was mostly done. The text lacked soul, inspiration, and interesting literary flourishes. Such articles were what newspaper people called PCDF: politically correct dry fodder.

Viljar yawned, planting his shoes well down in the wall-to-wall carpet before, in a moment of thoughtlessness, he leaned backwards in the black chair. It was with a cry of distress that he managed to pull himself up as the chair lost its balance and threatened to send him flying. He looked quickly around to see if anyone had noticed, before with a dejected sigh he pressed Send without proofreading.

He was ready for the first smoke break of the day and grabbed the long gray topcoat he'd bought at Goodwill for a few bucks three years ago. The topcoat fluttered behind him as he walked through the corridor on his way to the elevator. One of the interns greeted him with a raised hand as he passed the lowest of the workstations. Viljar did not condescend to give the young upstart a glance. The interns were still beneath him in the work hierarchy, albeit just barely.

A colleague was standing in the parking lot outside the media house, smoking. Viljar went in the opposite direction and lit a cigarette. The only thing he hated more than politically correct dry fodder was colleagues making small talk. Viljar had more than enough problems of his own.

He suddenly had a guilty conscience as it occurred to him that he'd forgotten to check whether Alexander had arrived at school. Viljar thought back to the last time Alexander stayed with him. He assumed all was well, but Alexander was truant from school for several days. Viljar wasn't up to the responsibility of having a teenager diagnosed with ADHD living with him at times.

What am I doing wrong? We always had each other, and we loved being together. Now there's just an empty, wordless shell left. What the hell happened, really?

The ex—or "the witch," as Viljar liked to call her—had insisted that he take his share of responsibility from day one. In the past he could drop off his son on Sunday afternoons, but now when Alexander had turned sixteen, he showed up whenever he wanted to. His mother said it was a natural development, and Viljar didn't care to protest, even if it made his life even more of a mess.

The cigarette breathed its last sigh and fell to the ground as Viljar slowly made his way back to the office. A sour odor of tobacco smoke trailed behind him down the corridors. A couple of nonsmokers wrinkled their noses demonstratively as he passed. Viljar couldn't have cared less. He dampened the worst smoker's breath with another stick of nicotine gum when he saw that Øveraas was standing ready by his cubicle yet again.

"If I docked your pay for those fucking breaks you take every day, your monthly salary would be pitiful, Gudmundsson." The editor was standing with his hands firmly planted in his spare tire.

"And if you compared the number of words I contribute to the newspaper to what the other reporters produce, you'd see that I should have a pay raise. A story always has several sides, Øveraas. You ought to know that, since you call yourself an editor."

The corpulent editor-in-chief's face again turned noticeably redder. "Damn it, it's not about length, Gudmundsson."

"No, like I said . . . You ought to know that."

Viljar laughed and pushed his way past the editor, who now showed all signs of losing control. Fortunately he was also speechless. Øveraas turned on his heels, kicked at a potted plant, and left the field before war broke out.

If Viljar had had an office door, he would have slammed it behind him. Instead he put on his headset. He looked with dismay at the dreariness outside the windows. For hour after hour, he could sit and stare at the drops trickling down the panes. In the steam on the glass, the rain formed an undulating latticework. People huddled up under the rain-heavy sky by the 7-Eleven on the other side of Karmsundsgata before they ran toward waiting cars.

He pulled an old T-shirt from the drawer and dried his hair to keep drops of water from dripping down on the keyboard. Then he tossed the T-shirt under the desk. He updated his email in-box and noted in the corner of his eye that it was full of incoming messages. He started deleting them. Mostly these were ads and meaningless notices from management.

Viljar had to concentrate to avoid deleting any important email. Finally he had three messages left. An appointment from the Helse Fonna clinic, one from the betting pool at work, and an email from a man whose name he didn't recognize. Probably a reader who wanted to point out something that was wrong or omitted in one of his articles. He sighed. That was the worst thing about this job. Constant comments from readers who didn't seem to have anything to do other than write complaints. Often the same readers again and again. He opened the email.

Viljar felt the pain in his chest after a few seconds. Noticed that it was getting harder to breathe. The room swayed. Shooting pains in his face made him gasp. He got up from his chair and started wandering aimlessly around the office area. Breathed deeply in and out as he'd been taught by the psychologist. Tried to think about something else. Right now that was difficult. Viljar nodded with effort at a colleague before he loosened an imaginary tie and turned back to the desk and the computer screen. He stared at the text. The letters flowed together as a drop of salty sweat ran down into his eye. He wiped it away and read the email again.

Attn.: Viljar Gudmundsson

I am writing to you because I know that you are an honorable man. A man who will condemn what I am in the process of doing, but at the same time is capable of understanding my indignation and frustration over a legal system that no longer functions.

We have laws that are supposed to protect us against people who take what they want, and not an unkind word shall be said about those who admit their guilt and take their just punishment. It is the others I want to put the spotlight on. Those who even in the hour of judgment avoid punishment and get away. They are the hyenas of society. Cowardly, greedy, and evasive. They deserve the punishment I shall give them. I will be punished myself for my actions. This I will take with head held high when the time comes. Until that happens, people will die by my hand. Guilty people who each in their own way avoided their rightful punishment.

In today's society, fewer and fewer people think of anyone but themselves. The sense of solidarity is dead. The spirit of collective work is gone. Loyalty to employers is a foreign word. People steal from the hand that feeds them.

One of these greedy people is a woman. She is convicted of gross embezzlement and disloyalty in service. She has no previous record, but this has not been deemed an extenuating circumstance. The punishment will be effectuated tomorrow, Tuesday the 14th of October.

10/13/2014

Stein Åmli

UL7-1

Viljar stuffed a fresh portion of snus under his lip. Felt the prickling in his fingers and toes. Again he took a deep breath before slowly letting it out again. The familiar darkness settled like a lid around the gray matter of his brain. Would he have to relate to this too? The letters radiated from the computer screen. Aversion radiated from Viljar. For a moment he considered deleting the whole message. Use the defense mechanism he knew best. "Avoidance syndrome," the psychologist called it. "The majority of problems we worry about are completely unfounded," she had tried to convince him. He felt reasonably certain that this particular email did not belong in that category. A single click, and the problem would be out of his hands. *No. It isn't like that.*

Deep down he had no faith that this was a genuine threatening letter. No one writes such things. Nonetheless, there was something in the email that made him feel anxious. He dried his clammy hands on his pant legs. The email was as if lifted out of a bad crime novel. The classic "judge" who takes the law into his own hands, and who defends his actions to a journalist. A worn-out cliché that would have made any editor refuse the manuscript before the end of the first chapter.

The "pronouncement of judgment" had the marks of being jotted down in five minutes without particular inspiration. Maybe that was why the hairs on his neck stood up? It was unimportant that it should appear like a court document. It was as if the email was written because it had to be, not because the author had a need to express himself. In many ways this frightened Viljar far more than an indignant threatening letter would have.

He quickly searched on the name "Stein Åmli." Of course it produced little or nothing. Various offers for purchase of stone, crushed rock, and gravel in the town of Åmli was the closest he got to a hit. *Fictional* name.

He knew that if he went to Øveraas with the email, the dollar signs in the editor's eyes would roll like a one-armed bandit on the Danish ferry. His ring finger lingered one last time on the Delete key in the right corner of the keyboard before he pulled his hand away. He needed to hear what Ranveig thought about this pile of shit. He climbed out of his chair with a hunched back that invited neither company nor small talk. He noticed that people kept their distance.

Ranveig Børve saw the black look in Viljar's eyes several seconds before he was standing beside her. It was always that way with Viljar. He kept his distance on good days, and came sneaking up on her on bad ones. Once when she was at the food festival in Stavanger, she bought a T-shirt for him that said THERE'S ALWAYS SOMETHING. He wore it often at work, and obviously hadn't caught on to the sarcasm.

It wasn't easy to be fond of Viljar, but Ranveig was. She was ten years younger than he. He was her mentor when she started as a reporter at the newspaper. Back then he was passionately engaged with a gleam in his eye and a master at creating news where others saw only short articles. Now it was the other way around.

Something had happened. After a long sick leave four years ago, he had come back a shadow of himself.

No one really knew what had taken the spark of life out of the Icelander, but the rumor mill at the media house was an insatiable troll.

Ranveig put on a smile under her long, blond bangs and twirled around on the office chair. "Hi, Viljar. Finished with that DPS thing that made Øveraas delirious that you hadn't done?"

Viljar plopped down in the chair that belonged to the cubicle next to hers. He waved away the question, set the paper he had with him on her desk, and tapped it with his index finger. "What do you make of this? It landed in my in-box a few minutes ago."

Ranveig drew her bangs behind her ear with her index finger and guided the pen over the sheet of paper while she read. Several times she stopped and looked inquiringly at Viljar, but he stopped her from saying anything, and she kept reading.

"This is bullshit," she said. "This is some joker who wants us to completely lose our heads, and bring out the extra bold font we used during the TERRA case."

Viljar seemed relieved, but he still had a panicked look.

"You're not taking this seriously, are you, Viljar?"

"No, of course not, but I just can't give it to Øveraas. He'll get a little horny and stagger around with a hard-on the rest of the day if he sees that email."

Ranveig laughed out loud and leaned over toward Viljar. "Yes, like that time Arsene Wenger came to town to buy Håvard Nordtveit for Arsenal," she whispered, laughing like a naughty child.

Viljar nodded and smiled. He picked up the paper and looked inquiringly up at Ranveig. "Seriously . . . What do I do with this?"

Ranveig studied the pen in her hand as if it held all the answers. "Email a copy to the police, and forget about it. Nothing will happen, and if it does, strictly speaking it's a police matter, isn't it?"

"Obviously. You're completely right."

He leaned over and gave her a quick hug. Ranveig was completely dumbfounded, and responded to the squeeze with a fumbling gesture.

"Nice. Let's do that then," she said, conjuring away the embarrassed mood between them with a forced smile.

Ranveig didn't want to say it, but there were many things that didn't add up with that email. This was Haugesund, not a bad episode of *Criminal Minds*. She hoped her gut feeling was wrong, and that this was the last they heard from Stein Åmli.

Requiem: Introitus

I look into her eyes. Dark green. Sparkling. A flirtatious twinkle when she sees it's me. Her mouth forms an impudent little smile. She doesn't hesitate, pulls off my coat and drops it on the old linoleum floor from the early seventies. The floor is in keeping with the unmodern, poorly maintained apartment. Rita Lothe is considerably livelier in bed than she is in interior design, you might say.

As she tears garment after garment off us with practiced movements, I look around the apartment. I notice details. An old, well-stocked liquor cabinet in yellowed pine beside the corner sofa. A laptop computer totters on the armrest of a worn black leather armchair. I don't yet know if the computer is password-protected. I spy about for her cell phone. It's crucial that it turn up in the course of the night. Her breathing has shifted gear. She's horny. I let her keep fumbling with her own buttons while I study the door to the balcony and the area outside. Big enough, I determine as she sighs contentedly and closes her lips around my dick.

My head is aching intensely as we're catching our breath twenty minutes later. I massage the tender area behind my left ear, and realize that exertions like this make the pain worse. It feels like tiny shudders along the nerve pathways, like rhythmic jolts, and I get a strange metallic taste in my mouth.

I know what awaits me. I've known it a long time. Glioblastoma multiforme . . . Sounds beautiful, doesn't it? Almost like a kind of tropical flower from a botany text.

Some will no doubt maintain that death is beautiful. In ancient Greece, Death was depicted as a handsome and attractive boy, and on gravestones, he was depicted as a gentle and good divine guardian with downturned torch and a wreath in his hand. I can refute all the beauty. Death is lonely, dark, and terrible. Sometimes painful too. As with me. Glioblastoma multiforme, or malignant brain tumor if you wish, is not recommended if you're someone who takes three Tylenol at the first hint of a hangover.

Every single waking hour of the day it screams for my attention from its source in the area behind my left ear. I know it's there, and what it's up to. I still have time. Several weeks, perhaps even months, if fate wishes it.

Rita comes out of the bathroom. Freshly showered and decked out. *What's the point?* A hint of jasmine brushes past my nostrils. She sits down beside me. Raises the glass of red wine and drinks greedily. I empty my glass in a flowerpot every time she leaves the room on some little errand or has her attention directed somewhere else.

I fetch my backpack from the hallway. Open it and take out a bottle of red wine I brought along. She twitters contentedly from the couch. I open it, and set the bottle beside her glass. It will barely have time to breathe before it's empty. I take out a glass and pour myself a cognac from the liquor cabinet. Renault Carte Noire—VSOP. *Her taste buds must have died long ago*, I think as I let the golden-brown fluid rotate in my mouth. It tastes cloying and dead. In that respect, suitable for the setting.

Benzodiazepines are found in many forms, several of which are easily soluble in water or other liquids. The drawback is that most of them produce a bitter aftertaste that is difficult to conceal. In a bottle of red wine, four sleeping pills will give the wine a slightly unfortunate aftertaste. Worth noting if someone hasn't already had so much to drink that anything at all slides down. Rita does not show the slightest sign of displeasure as she drinks the way she usually does. Steadily bigger gulps and more frequent refills. I feel calmness spreading in my body. This is the only awkward note in the score. The bitter aftertaste. Now it's only a matter of waiting.

Her gaze is blurred now. She snuffles, yawns, and talks nonsense. The plan is a masterpiece. My *Requiem aeternam*. The composition is neatly categorized in six rows at home on the desk. Six names. Six death sentences. Six movements.

Everything must be exactly as it is described. This is a magic mirror. One step to the side, and the illusion disappears. A forgotten trifle is enough for the table to turn.

I look up at the dim light from the chandelier. The corners in Rita's apartment have crept into semidarkness. An image of my life. I was in the room, but the light never reached me. A life that almost became something great. I've decided to step out of the shadows now. The thought thrills me. That everyone will get to see. The completion of the masterwork, like a final movement in one of Mahler's symphonies.

I am the Maestro. I look at my hands. They are not shaking.

Rita is in the middle of her *Confutatis maledictis*, without even knowing it. It amuses me that she is lying less than an arm's length away from me with her mouth in a blissful grin. She does not suspect that the hourglass is about to run out.

In a little flash of unvarnished self-insight, I see myself as I really am. The stroke of a crow's wing. I *must* believe in this. *I* am the masterpiece itself. A coincidence made it so. I had a revelation. A chance to compose my own requiem.

I carefully close the eyes of the slumbering sinner beside me and spray a bandage with crystal clear fluid from a bottle on the table. I place the rag around her nose and mouth. She whimpers and is about to wake up. I count down the seconds, and little by little she falls asleep. All pain disappears. I am pure.

Pain is weakness leaving the body, I think contentedly, and close the final door to the life I once lived.

Fjellvegen, Haugesund
Tuesday morning, October 14, 2014

Low-lying fog rolled in over the town on the strait of Karmsund. Fall was in the air. Sea fog, a damp, clammy blanket that slowly squeezes the life force out of you. As the 8:20 flight from Oslo cut through the cloud cover over the apartment buildings, the passengers could barely glimpse the top floors, and something blinking blue and red on the ground.

"Tell me, Lotte, why is it necessary to send out multiple police officers every time some depressed idiot takes the shortcut out of their problems?"

Chief Inspector Lotte Skeisvoll with the Haugesund Police Department looked dumbfounded at the newly minted constable sitting beside her in the car. The two colleagues were en route from the police station by Smedasundet. A patrol had called for assistance to the high-rises on Fjellvegen.

Christian Hauge was clinging to the steering wheel. The way he drove did not correspond with his attitude toward the mission. Full sirens and blinking blue lights through the roundabouts by *Haugesund*

News. A small black e-Golf stopped in terror, halfway up on the median, after they passed. Lotte concealed a smile.

The response concerned a suspicious death. Although perhaps it wasn't very *suspicious*. A woman had in all likelihood jumped from the balcony of one of the apartments and ended her life on the asphalt strip between the building and the lawn, but a death was always counted as suspicious until it could be concluded that it was either from natural causes or a suicide.

The young man eased up on his driving a little when they had passed Spannavegen and the traffic was lighter. Lotte cocked her head in irritation and straightened the police radio in the holster on the dashboard. It was not in line with the car stereo alongside, and such details bothered her.

"Is it really necessary to send more than one patrol?" The driver glanced quickly at her before turning his eyes back to the road again.

"And if it turns out that the victim hasn't done this on her own?"

"Well, then the officers in the patrol car can call in the rest of the team from the station. We could save a lot of money that way."

"Exactly," she answered.

That one word was dripping with sarcasm. Lotte went through the routine description in her mind once more instead. Quickly ran through all the details she had to recall when she arrived at the grayish white colossi that had stood watch over the City of Herring since the dedication in 1969. A historic marker of a time when every self-respecting city built high-rise apartment blocks.

Thirty years old was young for a position as chief inspector and investigator with the police. She had all the right courses. Nonetheless, it had seemed like an eternity before an opportunity opened up.

The constable stopped the car in the parking lot in front of the high-rises. The woman should be on the front side of the north block. As Lotte opened the car door, she heard voices from the crowd that had gathered. She silently hoped that the first patrol had sense enough to cordon off the area around the dead woman's body, and she bet that they had a bit more professionalism than her teammate of a constable. She was greatly relieved when she saw the officer with seniority at the police station round the corner there to meet her. Lars Stople had a whole lifetime behind him as a policeman, and he could no doubt have risen in the ranks if he'd had any interest in that worth mentioning. A wise, deliberate, and balanced guy who never behaved provocatively. His main area of responsibility was preventive work among the youth of the city, but by his own wish he also kept patrolling as part of his duties. He stroked back his smoothly combed gray hair and addressed Lotte.

"Hi, Lotte. We've cordoned off and started talking with witnesses over in that corner."

Lars Stople nodded toward a small plateau by the parking garage and a small white transformer station. A handful of people had gathered and were rubbernecking, like a clump of curious giraffes.

"The majority came after the rumors started to fly, but there are a few we need to question more closely," he said.

She could see that Stolpe's partner, Knut Veldetun, was talking with one of them.

"Tech?" Lotte looked inquisitively at Lars.

"Don't know. Assume they're on their way. I asked for that anyway. Besides myself and the two EMTs that checked her, I don't think anyone has been inside the barricades."

"Do we know who she is?"

Lars Stople looked down at his notes, shook his head slightly, and cleared his throat. "Not for sure. A resident, potentially renting 7B, and in that case we're talking about a fifty-seven-year-old woman by the name of Rita Lothe, but we haven't been able to check that out yet. We've prioritized keeping people away from the body."

"Okay. Nicely done, Lars. Will you lead us over there?"

Stople showed her the way under the police barricades and around the corner to the front of the block.

"The woman was discovered by a resident in one of the apartments on the first floor when he was going out on the terrace to have a smoke," Stople explained. "That was a little over half an hour ago. Knut and I were on the scene ten minutes later."

Lotte peeked at her cell phone and could see that Stople's information tallied. They had received the emergency call at 08:05 hours. Now it was almost 08:45.

It wasn't so strange that the woman hadn't been found earlier. The combination of autumn darkness and morning fog has a tendency to conceal most things. She took the red notepad out of her uniform jacket. In neat handwriting she noted the time and events in separate headings, before she turned the pad over and wrote questions for the CSIs on the form she had prepared in the back. Facts on the first page, loose threads on the last. That was how it had to be. A single question found its way down onto the paper.

Time of death?

The woman was in a twisted position, and even at a distance, Lotte could see that there were major injuries to the body. The dead woman was dressed in a mint green skirt, thin skin-tone pantyhose, and black stiletto boots. The face was crushed to the point of being unrecognizable. In an area around the head, there was a sticky brownish gray mass, and red bone splinters stuck out from the jaw. Teeth that had been knocked out in the collision with the asphalt were lying around the smashed mouth. Lotte felt the nausea as a surge in her abdomen.

"Well . . . What do you say? Homicide or suicide?" Lotte addressed the young police constable.

Christian Hauge squirmed. "Uh . . . Didn't you say in the car that it was suicide?" She noted with contentment that he was blushing.

"No, I didn't say that. I said that it was 'suspected.' You managed to work out the theory about suicide fine all by yourself. Now let's pretend you're the only policeman on the scene. Homicide or suicide?"

The constable looked over at Lars Stople, but got only a shoulder shrug in response from the old fox.

"It's either an accident or a homicide," he said, looking up at Lotte with a self-confident expression.

"I see, why is that?"

"She has a crushed skull, so she must have landed flat or head-first. People who jump out of a window or from a balcony to commit suicide land on their feet ninety-nine percent of the time. If she'd jumped, she would have had major injuries to the legs, hip sockets, and pelvis. Here it's the head and shoulders that are crushed."

Lotte looked at her police constable and was unable to conceal her surprise. "Jesus . . . You're impressive. Now, probably what you're saying is a modified truth, and bones are broken regardless from such heights, but here the injuries to the upper body are so extensive that I'm leaning toward the same conclusion as you."

She cast an irritated glance at Lars Stople, who was clearly suppressing a laugh.

Lotte knew that she deserved to be led by the nose. The young man actually had a point. She looked up toward the balcony on the seventh floor. The fog meant that she could sense only the outlines that high up, but she saw that the railing was high enough that it would take a lot to fall over it by accident.

Lotte found her way to a vacuum deep inside her awareness. An imaginary space emptied of all feelings. Only ice-cold cynicism. Bare blue walls. Full daylight, but no windows. This was a technique she had learned from her mentor at the police academy. To move into a space where nothing could affect her emotionally. In that space, she could work without taking notice of anything other than the details. Inside there, seeing crushed faces, sticky brain mass, or maltreated body parts had little effect on her. In that space, she could observe mistreated children, worm-eaten corpses, and fat maggots creeping in and out of body openings.

She leaned down toward the crushed face of the dead woman. It was so damaged that she could not be identified solely on the basis of that. One eyeball was knocked out of its socket and hanging in shreds, while the other was closed. It was a woman approaching sixty, so fifty-seven could be right. She had short-cut mahogany-dyed hair. Lotte could see remnants of hair dye by the hairline. She had makeup on, and the clothes suggested some kind of festivity.

Some dress up to be a beautiful corpse, but very few choose to jump from tall buildings, she thought dryly.

Lotte was a bit taken aback when she noticed an acrid smell from the bloody face. She put her nose all the way down by one cheek. "It's ether."

Lars Stople mumbled, but the words reached Lotte nonetheless. She frowned and looked skeptically at the old policeman. "Yes, a damp cloth with ether puts a person out of the running in a few seconds. The odor is very recognizable, and it stays behind a little while post-mortem. The ether fluid itself vaporizes in seconds, but the air particles always attach to the skin and persist longer."

Lotte nodded thoughtfully. So the woman must have been anesthetized when she was helped over the railing.

She looked up the apartment block once again. *Who does such a thing?* she thought sadly. The killer evidently didn't care to camouflage it as a suicide. Then you don't use ether. Lars kept his eyes to one side of the woman. Unlike Lotte, he was unable to look right at her.

"Yes, that was why I called in the death to you. I recognized the odor from when I had an appendectomy. Ether was used as an anesthetic in the past."

Lotte straightened up, turned toward the other police who were standing around her, and began giving orders. "No one gets past these barricades, except the crime scene investigators when they arrive. From now on, this is their scene. Set up outer barricades too from the main road and around the block. Start questioning witnesses immediately. Knut, you'll take responsibility for that, since you've already started. Take my constable with you."

Then she addressed Lars.

"Find out whether this is the woman who lives in 7B. Locate the super, and get ahold of extra keys if her place is locked." Lotte took out the phone that was vibrating in her pocket. Looked at the display and knew she had to take it, even if she was at the scene of a probable homicide.

She walked away from the others and answered curtly. "Yes, what is it, Anne? I'm in the middle of something extremely important here."

Lotte could hear her sister, five years younger than she, breathing heavily on the other end. Her voice was sluggish, as if there were delays in the communication between her brain and vocal cords. The usual.

"Seriously? You never have time for me, damn it. Isn't what I'm dealing with, like, serious enough? Your fucking cop buddies have brought me in, *again*!"

Lotte noticed how heavy wisps of fog were slipping in under the jacket of her uniform. She shivered. She also felt how irritation was building up inside her, but she was able to control herself. Her sister had no one else since they lost their parents in that frightful railway accident at Åsta. She called every single day. Every single day with new problems, or simply to tell Lotte off. Today it was probably a little of both, judging by the introduction.

Lotte had asked the others at police headquarters again and again to be a little tactful when they had to bring Anne in, but it didn't seem like they cared about that anymore. Anne was a drug addict, and she wasn't handled with kid gloves despite her family background.

"What did they get you for?" Lotte asked, even if she knew exactly what the answer would be.

"Nothing! They don't have a damned thing on me. I haven't done anything, and what I had on me was for my own use. That cocksucking cop cunt can't even weigh a gram right."

"How much, Anne?"

"Forget about that! You don't believe me either. Forget it!" she roared, and hung up.

Direct hit. Lotte remained standing with a pounding heart. Knew she shouldn't care, that it was the high and the abstinence that were talking, but it was *Anne* who said it. It was her mouth that pronounced the words. Her little sister she was so incredibly fond of. The words lingered inside her, making her feel that she'd failed. Then her gaze fell on the woman lying in front of the building, and she closed the door to her guilty conscience.

She would have to see what she could do for Anne when she got back to the police station. For the time being, there was another woman who demanded her attention. A dead one.

Ranveig Børve had just ended a conversation with Viljar over by his workstation and was on her way back to her own, when she felt someone tugging on her skirt.

"So, how are things with the Dragon?" Henrik Thomsen asked sarcastically when Ranveig turned around. Thomsen, who himself had the nickname "the Butcher," sniffed his way to any chance to take people down a notch. As usual, he was gossiping with one of the sows from the marketing department, which had been moved up into the editorial offices. Now he stretched his two-meter-long body and moved unpleasantly close to Ranveig, who quickly took a step back.

"The Dragon?"

"Yes, you know . . . The Icelander over there. Irritable, dangerous, smoke coming out of his jaws, all that." Thomsen showed a disrespectful smile toward the office. No one seemed to notice his witticism.

Ranveig met his gaze. "Oh . . . Is that because you have so many nicknames that you've starting giving your colleagues the same treatment?"

Ranveig didn't wait for an answer. Just turned on her heels and walked toward her workstation.

"You're so disagreeable today," Henrik called. "PMS or what?"

Ranveig stopped, turned around, and showed him her middle finger before she sailed into the Ingress conference room, which was like an island in the office landscape. A small, encapsulated space, which despite the floor-to-ceiling windows north and south seemed claustrophobic. The room was sparsely furnished with a spindly, tall plastic table and wobbly light-green barstools. Not designed for comfort, but for lightning-quick meetings that everyone hoped would be over as soon as possible.

The episode between Thomsen and Ranveig had not escaped Viljar. He hummed contentedly to himself, but felt cold. Each day was like a viscous substance where he was forced to tread constantly to keep his head above it. It was always like that. No variation, no inspiration, no unexpected high points.

His psychologist, Vigdis Nygård, was ready to put him on sick leave that day, but he wouldn't let her. His job was the only thing that kept him on his feet.

"You show no joy in what you do," she said the last time they met at Café Espresso on Haraldsgata. "You're uninspired, burned out, and you don't like the people you work with. Your boss is no fan of yours, and your articles are so dry and boring that no one can bear to read them anymore. Are you sure this is the right niche for you?"

Viljar sat there for a whole hour, looking out at the stream of people on the pedestrian street after she left the café in favor of Saturday shopping with her husband and children. Getting a piece of her mind like that was not something he handled particularly well. Yet he knew she was right.

The workday moved along at a snail's pace, and Viljar transformed one news item after another into small blocks of text. Outside the window there was still no inspiration to be had.

Yesterday's drizzle was replaced by thick, dirty fog. He straightened up and forced himself to focus on the text. A few seconds later came the rescue. Editor Johan Øveraas was standing in the middle of the office landscape with his phone in one hand, gesturing. He ended the call and pointed at Viljar.

"You have to go out on a story, Gudmundsson. We've received a tip."

"I see, what's it about?" He was relieved to get out of the futile task he was occupied with.

"Get yourself up to the high-rises. The police are already there. Apparently there's a lady who has fallen out of one of the apartments." Øveraas was eager now. His flab jiggled as he shifted back and forth on his feet.

"The hell I will, Øveraas. You know I hate fatal accidents. We talked about that at the employee review. I don't write such things." He challenged the boss with his gaze.

The editor was no longer shifting his balance. Now he took a wide stance and braced himself. "You have to move that arrogant, self-righteous ass of yours up to the high-rises right now. You will write what I say you're going to write. It's been years since you could dictate what you wanted here in the building. Your job is dangling like the dingleberries in your ass hairs! Believe me, Gudmundsson. You don't want to challenge me on this one!"

He lowered his voice and adopted a threatening undertone. "I am longing for something I can get you on! The next board meeting has redundancy on the agenda, just so that's said."

Øveraas struck his hand against the wall of one of the vacant cubicles and roared at curious heads that were sticking out from their workstations.

"Pull your heads back in and work!"

The heads ducked back into the cubicles as quickly as they had come out. Only Thomsen had stood up and continued to follow the scene.

Viljar knew that he was not particularly popular with Øveraas. The feeling was mutual, but he had never thought it could actually cost him his job. He pulled on the gray topcoat that was hanging over the chair, took his notepad and phone, and shuffled out of the office with bowed head. Right now the fog outside was preferable.

Henrik Thomsen came to meet him in the corridor. "Was that you Sauron was screaming at?"

Thomsen was smiling under the bushy handlebar mustache. The cultural journalist's comparison of the editor and the evil ruler in *The Lord of the Rings* was well known in the building. Viljar stopped short, stretched, and stood on tiptoe, sticking his head as far as he could up into the face of his tall colleague without giving him a French kiss.

"Why don't you go over to your corner and beat off to the websites that always disappear like dew in the sun when anyone passes your screen!"

Henrik Thomsen stepped back. Without any more wisecracks, he let Viljar past.

Four years earlier . . .
Ådland Meetinghouse, Karmøy
Monday, August 16, 2010

ABRAHAM was printed in shiny gold letters on a blue background on the banner in the very front of the hall in Ådland Meetinghouse. Jonas Ferkingstad looked up at his father, who was busy hanging up the banner for the congregation. It was put up and taken down again before and after the weekly prayer meetings.

The name of the congregation was not coincidental. They wanted to go back to the source. A direct connection between God himself and man. The members promised fidelity to the text as it was written, and they shared the view that the other congregations were becoming secularized by a sinful global society. The word of God was adapted to the world outside. That was not the way it should be.

Jonas had a desire to spit on the crucifix on the wall, but didn't dare. Not when his father was in the room. He felt imprisoned. Books had vanished from their house. Only the Bible remained. Bare walls with an occasional crucifix or relief were all there was to see in his childhood home. His parents disappeared into the silence.

He stopped playing soccer and put his marching band uniform

on the shelf. Not because he had to, but because it always involved discussions. Quiet, low-pitched discussions he was doomed to lose. For what could be more meaningful and noble than dedicating your life to the Lord? His father underscored the point every time by referring to the fact that he himself had cut back to a 70 percent position as senior executive officer at the courthouse, simply to be able to serve the Lord and the Holy Scripture.

Jonas left his father to his work. He went out on the steps and tried to draw in the taste of summer on the west coast of Norway. It was raining and he got wet, but he didn't care. The rain washed the treacherous tears that came more and more often when he was forced to attend such prayer meetings. To start with, he had managed to close out the annoyance. Pretended that what was happening to him was actually just his imagination. Another reality. It was no longer that way, and he couldn't hide. The truth was breaking out.

He was looking forward to the weekend. Membership in the Center Party Youth was his refuge. There he could spend time on something other than futile wandering through the writings of the Old Testament. He got to attend meetings several evenings during the week, and on weekends there were seminars, courses, and various other gatherings in the county organization. Those were his moments of freedom, fractions of time when he could just be himself.

The moment Jonas caught sight of Fredric Karjoli, who was a year older, in the doorway to the meeting room of the Center Party Youth a year ago, the truth was carved in stone. Deep down he'd known it was like that. But he'd always believed that God would show mercy on him and let him find the right way. Then and there, he could almost hear God's ironic laughter ringing in the little meeting room.

Jonas again dried rain and tears from his face. He looked out over the gray, windswept landscape while he thought about the old Yiddish proverb his father had referred to many times. Slowly, as if he were an old man, he got up from the steps and looked up toward the cross under the ridge of the roof on the meetinghouse.

That's how it is, Dad . . .
Man makes plans, and God laughs.

Fjellvegen, Haugesund
Tuesday midmorning, October 14, 2014

Viljar was standing outside the police barricades, where half the city seemed to have gathered. In the throng he saw Øystein Vindheim, one of the few friends he still had after his problems the past few years. A tall, lanky guy with a pigeon chest and square glasses. The friendship was very off and on, and months might pass between the times they met.

"Do you know what happened?"

Øystein shook his head weakly, adjusted his glasses, and leaned down toward Viljar's ear. "Even though I work at the library, I don't know everything."

Øystein laughed quietly and tapped his friend on the shoulder. Viljar let the wisecrack pass and concentrated on what was going on right before his eyes. You didn't need to be a detective—or a librarian, for that matter—to understand that someone had fallen from one of the balconies in the high-rise.

The nausea made itself known in his upper abdomen when he saw the technicians in the white crime scene suits bending over the body.

It was like that every time. It created unpleasant associations with that Tuesday when everything changed. *The Jonas case* . . . His personal "Black Tuesday," he thought, in a reference to the day the American stock exchange on Wall Street crashed in 1929.

Viljar closed his eyes and tried to close out all impressions. Knew that Øveraas would see right through him if he suddenly got "sick" after their argument earlier in the day. His pulse calmed down somewhat. The mush in his throat loosened up bit by bit. The stabbing pain under his rib cage when he saw the stretcher being rolled past gradually subsided. Øystein Vindheim patted him on the back as he turned to leave. Good friends didn't need words to understand or console. As a rule, the friendship was in the silence between them.

In the background Viljar heard that Hans Indbjo was talking away on his phone. As usual, he was broadcasting live on Radio 102.

A tragic accident has occurred in Haugesund this morning. A woman fell from her balcony in the high-rises. As you heard before the musical interlude, Radio 102 is on the scene, and we are now covering the event live here from Fjellvegen. The police have started their investigations, and we promise to return with more as soon as it becomes clear what happened.

Viljar shook his head. The media house's own radio channel was a firmly entrenched corn that was impossible to get rid of. Worst of all was that parasite Hans Indbjo. If anything happened, no matter what, Indbjo was *live* from the scene ten minutes later. He was a gold mine for the owners of the media company, but a tragedy for humanity.

Viljar noticed that there were more police at the scene than usual. He tried to find someone to interview, so that he could get away from there as quickly as possible. If it was an accident, it would be a short back-page story. There was a clear policy about such things at the newspaper. They should take the family into consideration. With a "personal tragedy," a short article would be enough. Why Øveraas had been so eager to send out a reporter and a photographer on a matter like this, he really didn't understand. He dismissed the thought and directed his attention to a familiar face that was moving around on the lawn and talking with the technical team. Viljar smiled. Lotte Skeisvoll was just what he needed. Concise, honest, and always by the book.

He was about to wave to her when he became aware that the radio journalist had taken up position right beside him.

"It's great that something is happening," said the radio man while he dug his hands deep down into his pants pocket and rocked up and down on his toes like a minister at the altar.

"Uh . . . Has something happened?" Viljar asked peevishly.

"Don't try that, Gudmundsson. I know that you newspaper people are just as focused on striking while the body is warm as I am. I just get there a little faster, and that's why I have to bear the brunt."

Indbjo was grinning from ear to ear. The short-statured Asian pushed his glasses all the way up to his eyeballs. He was adopted from Vietnam in the late seventies and since then had been overprotected until he turned thirty. After he started at the radio station, he had broken all boundaries for how you behave in the public space.

"There is some difference between striking while the body is warm, as you say, and conducting a full autopsy in public before the family has been informed of the tragedy."

Viljar looked down at Hans Indbjo. He was barely 165 centimeters tall, and it didn't help much that he was rocking on his toes. With what could be perceived as a defiant look, he met Viljar's gaze.

"A few years ago, you and I were much alike, Viljar. I actually looked up to you back then. Took you as a role model."

Viljar concealed a smile while he demonstratively bent his knees a little to offset the difference in height. He stroked the shoulder-length blond hair away from his eyes and tried to sound like he was interested in what Hans Indbjo had to tell. He mostly had a desire to shake the little pest.

"You showed people out there that a wretched journalist could make a difference. Mean something. Be something more than an anonymous bell sheep that acts like everyone else."

"Cut it out, Hans! What *you* do is call out every single little incident in this town as if it were a sensation. There isn't an ounce of finesse or delicacy in what you do. Journalistic success isn't measured in decibels or capital letters." Viljar was boiling.

"Now I've heard everything," Indbjo answered with a snort. "Viljar Ravn Gudmundsson, the city's most arrogant asshole, lectures me on ethics and morality."

He was still smiling, but turned away and called the radio station again.

Viljar was relieved to escape having Indbjo at his heels, so he waved to attract Lotte Skeisvoll's attention. She was still on the phone, and pointed with her free hand toward an area at the end of the lawn right by the day care center. Viljar obediently ambled over and took out his notepad. One minute later, Lotte ended the call and turned in his direction.

Lotte Skeisvoll was a mystery. Short, slender, dark, and with an aura of unassailability. She radiated a slightly stiff and blank façade of power and professionalism. The black pageboy hairstyle was combed in a side part. Her nut-brown eyes were nailed firmly onto Viljar when at last she was standing before him.

"What's happened here?" he asked.

"We have a woman who fell from the balcony on what we think is the seventh floor, and naturally enough died from the fall."

"Name?"

"We're waiting on that until the family is informed, Gudmundsson. I can say this much, that we have a reasonably certain identity. She's in her midfifties and resides here in town."

"Do you think this is a personal tragedy or an accident?" Viljar was hoping for the first. In that case, he didn't need to ask any more questions.

"For the time being, the police consider this a suspicious death, and we've called in assistance from forensics." Lotte Skeisvoll let the words vibrate in the autumn air.

Viljar looked at her with tired eyes. He guessed that it would be a long day. "Suspicious?"

"Yes, we consider this suspicious. There are traces on the woman that indicate that she was subjected to a criminal act. We obviously can't draw any conclusions yet, but we've initiated an investigation."

She stopped a moment before she added, "And you won't get any more details from me now, Gudmundsson. I expect that you won't release the name, even if it's a simple matter to check out whom it concerns. Okay?"

Viljar could do nothing other than nod in confirmation. Had this been in his previous life, he would never have given in. He would have hung on to Lotte like a monkey on her back the rest of the day. Now this truly had become news, and he hoped Lotte had sense enough not to make the same comment to Hans Indbjo. Then the name of the victim would be on the airwaves before lunchtime.

Viljar followed the routine. Called in to the editorial office and asked them to send more people. He sent a brief text message to the photographer, who he could see was busy outside the barricades. The procedure was simple. With homicide or major accidents, extra staffing was called in. After this was done, Viljar felt completely exhausted.

Maybe the psychologist is right? That I don't have it in me anymore. That I ought to find something else to do. Something a little solitary and isolated where I don't have to relate to people?

Viljar took his thoughts with him back to the car. He decided to wait until the rest of the pack from the newspaper was on the scene. Turned on Radio 102 and heard the voice of Hans Indbjo spewing out the latest news from Fjellvegen.

We interrupt the music to give you the latest news about the death at the high-rises. If you've just tuned in, a tragedy has possibly occurred in our city today. A woman was found lifeless on the ground in front of one of the high-rises. Detective Inspector Lotte Skeisvoll with the Haugesund Police underscores to Radio 102 that it is too early to see whether this concerns an accident or if it is a personal tragedy we have witnessed this morning.

Viljar laughed out loud. He had a sense for Lotte Skeisvoll.

Rita Lothe's apartment, Haugesund
Tuesday midmorning, October 14, 2014

The last steps up to Rita Lothe's apartment on the seventh floor went slow as molasses. Lotte had chosen to take the stairs. Her head had to be reset after talking to the press. Every single detail in the apartment could be the difference between whether the case was solved or not. She had to be sharp.

The damp air outside left a musty, clammy odor in the stairwell. Lotte felt a physical surge of antipathy and despondency when she caught sight of the red-and-white police tape set up in front of the door to the woman's apartment. Lars Stople had been the first man in, after the superintendent had opened the door for them.

A technician met her at the door and gave her the white overalls, plus blue plastic booties that she pulled over her shoes. Stople remained standing in the doorway to keep watch. He gave her a friendly pat on the shoulder before she went in.

The whole apartment was shabby. Probably not renovated since the early seventies, Lotte observed. In the hall was an ancient brown floor covering. The wallpaper signaled the same era. Garish contrasts in orange, brown, and dark green, put together in psychedelic patterns, screamed at her. Here everything was like when Dr. Hook ruled the charts. She stopped and wrote down observations on the notepad. Felt extremely irritated that she had left the red and blue pen in her uniform pocket before changing. *Now everything will just be a mess.* She tore off the sheet and put it in her pocket. Borrowed a mechanical pencil from Lars. She would have to rewrite later.

She registered in passing that the pictures on the wall were exclusively old family pictures from a vanished time. She withstood the compulsion to straighten the pictures, which were hanging crooked, and instead took out her pad again.

Inheritance? Check the apartment's ownership history, she wrote, and added *fully furnished* when she caught sight of the gaudy orange and white pillows on the dark green sofa in the living room.

Faint clicks from the digital cameras and rustling in the crime scene suits were the only sounds. At regular intervals, flashguns lit up an otherwise dark, poorly illuminated living room. The technicians worked in silence. An old, well-stocked liquor cabinet in yellowed pine stood alongside the corner couch. *Borrowed, rented or owned?* she noted on the pad. The three-seater sofa had once been green, but the tooth of time had ravaged it. On the right side, both the cushion and armrest were worn down so that a flap of foam stuck up between the white threads.

On a flaked teak coffee table were two wineglasses and a cognac glass. The latter was barely touched, if you assumed the customary two centiliters. There were obvious marks of dark red lipstick on one of the wineglasses. The table otherwise offered an assortment of sweaty cheese and dry crackers. A wine bottle on the floor was half empty, while an empty one was at the foot of the couch, where the woman had probably spent the evening. On a little corner table was a worn copy of a crime novel by Unni Lindell. Lotte picked it up and looked at it. Inside was a bookmark from the library. The stamp showed that the book should have been returned several weeks ago.

Romantic evening for two. With whom? Lotte drew two lines under the question. The bottom line got a little crooked, so she turned the pencil, erased it, and using the novel as a ruler, redrew the line. Perfect, she thought. *Unni Lindell has always been upright.*

Lotte took it as a given that Rita Lothe had been visited by a man. Only the one glass had lipstick marks. She was taken aback. *It's not like me to draw conclusions so quickly.* Something was picking at her subconscious, but she was unable to pin it down. Lotte took out the notepad again and wrote down her thoughts.

She raised her eyes and looked in the direction of the balcony. Got a warning look from one of the technicians when she tried to go past him. The technicians didn't say anything, but she understood the sign. The balcony was not a cleared area for her yet. That was where Rita had been lifted over the edge and sent headfirst toward the asphalt. Instead of taking the forbidden steps out onto the balcony, she remained standing in the middle of the living room for several minutes. Soaked up all the impressions.

She slowly turned around her own axis, caught up details from walls, floor, and interior. Occasionally she took notes. An outsider would have wondered about the episode in the apartment. A skinny girl with dark, almost Goth eyeshadow twirling around herself in slow motion. The two men in the room paid her no notice. They'd seen it before, and they knew that right now they were invisible to her.

"There's blood on the doorframe."

The older technician raised his head and looked at her inquisitively. "Where?"

Lotte pointed toward the balcony door. An almost invisible dark stripe right over the door handle. They probably would have discovered it themselves when they got over there, but it was nice to have it pointed out. The technician nodded and showed a thumbs-up.

"I need five things from you," Lotte said after a few seconds of silence in the room.

The two technicians stopped what they were doing and looked over at her. She was still standing in the same place and held their gaze while she slowly went through point by point.

"One: There is a laptop hidden under the sofa. It should be secured and the contents checked for all communication. Two: All three glasses on the coffee table should be checked for prints. The contents should be analyzed. The same applies to the wine bottle under the coffee table, cognac bottle in the cabinet, and all opened bottles in there too. Complete toxicology check. Three: There is a piece of cheese left on the plate farthest to the right. It's been bitten, and we can see tooth marks on the upper edge. Four: On the floor by the right side of the armchair there are some drops of transparent fluid. Probably water. Check it regardless. Five: Her handbag is in the third row of the bookshelf, stuffed in over the books. It should be emptied out, and all contents checked and secured as evidence. The bag with contents should be ready on my desk in the morning."

Lotte did not wait for a response. She turned around quickly like a guardsman and left. The two technicians looked at each other and shook their heads in resignation. Lars was waiting in the hall. She went all the way over to him, straightened his uniform tie, and smiled cautiously.

"This apartment is as sad as the decade it was furnished in," she said while she pulled off the plastic slippers.

Lars Stople looked at her in feigned amazement. "The seventies? . . . A fireworks display of color, nudity, emotion, experimental highs, and political idealism. You think that's *sad*?"

She took off the hood and blew back the dark fringe that settled like a wing in front of her eyes. With a gleam in her eye she whispered, "Chaos, Lars. Complete, boundless chaos. Everything is hanging crooked, and nothing matches. That sort of thing is just sad."

Media House *Haugesund News*
Tuesday afternoon, October 14, 2014

The workday crawled to an end. Viljar had written, interviewed, double-checked, and proofread. The article on the death in the high-rises had been sent to the desk. Everything was done, but he felt no satisfaction. When death pounded on the door, it was as if he were locked inside a cold, damp cellar. His thoughts took over and lowered him down into an endless darkness where all cries were an echo of what had been. The keyboard went on autopilot. There was no connection between the flying fingers and the mind that found itself in the blue-black depths.

Far back in his awareness, another, even darker thought had started to stir when he talked with Lotte. *Could this have anything to do with the email I received?* To start with, he'd dismissed that. It would only disturb the article he had to write, but now that the article was delivered, the thoughts came trickling in.

He was interrupted by editor Johan Øveraas stopping by his workstation. "Look at that, Gudmundsson. Busy at work today. I'll be damned if it wasn't time."

Viljar didn't bother to turn around and only answered with a little grunt. When Øveraas stood there in silence, he felt compelled to stop his work to see what the burly man wanted this time. Øveraas was smiling. Not ironically, the way he usually did. A genuine smile.

"Two things, Gudmundsson. First I want to apologize for my outburst earlier today. I shouldn't bawl you out while I'm standing in an open office landscape where other employees overhear what's being said. That was unprofessional. Now that it happened, I meant every word I said."

So much for that apology, thought Viljar.

"And the second thing was?"

"Huh?"

"The second thing, Øveraas. You said there were two things."

"Ah . . . I must have blanked out. Secondly, I wanted to praise you for the article you just delivered. Extremely well written. Thorough work."

Johan Øveraas started to go toward his own office, but turned around again after a few steps. "So the police think it's a homicide?"

"When Lotte Skeisvoll goes so far as to use the phrase 'suspicious cause of death' to the media barely an hour after she arrives at the scene, then it must be quite an obvious homicide."

"Do we know anything else?"

Viljar knew that this was the point where he ought to tell about the email he'd received, but he chose to ignore that. "No more than what's in the article. We'll have to see what turns up tomorrow."

Johan Øveraas stood expectantly and looked searchingly at Viljar, as if he was waiting for something. When Viljar showed no sign of wanting to expand on his answer, he nodded curtly and went on. As the door to the editor's office closed, Viljar's hands started shaking. He fished out three sticks of nicotine gum and chewed them frantically until his hands gradually calmed down.

Not long after that, his cell phone vibrated. He picked it up and looked at the display. It said BLOCKED in shining letters. He answered.

"Gudmundsson, *Haugesund News*."

"Hi, Viljar. Lotte Skeisvoll here."

"I see. . . ."

"Can you come on down to the police station? We need to talk with you." Lotte's voice was cool and firm as always.

"May I ask what this is about?"

"You can ask, but you won't get an answer," the policewoman said, hanging up before he had an opportunity to protest.

The police building clung firmly to the edge of the pier by the sound. The entry to the white brick building could be mistaken for the entrance to a charming hotel, but the facilities for those who spent the night here were probably a bit more Spartan than in the city's other overnight accommodations.

Inside the police building, the climate control system was done for the day. It was hot, clammy, and smelled of closed-in sweat. Viljar was sitting alone in what he assumed was a provisional interview room. *Maybe this is just an office?* The spindle-back chair he was sitting on was hard and angular. He looked around to find the typical "glass wall" where the police could follow what was going on in there from outside. Viljar realized that there were disappointingly few similarities between movie clichés and real life.

The door opened and Lotte Skeisvoll came in with two cups of coffee. She sat down across from him and pushed one paper cup across the table. Viljar raised the cup in a toast.

He turned his attention to the police detective. She was in civilian clothes, but could just as well have been wearing a uniform. A tightly buttoned beige blouse. Just ironed. Black trousers with a crease. Straight posture and a tight face.

Lotte read the formalities on a small digital recorder and then placed it with geometric precision at the origin point of the round table between them. Studied the recorder and waited a moment before throwing out her hands in an inviting gesture to Viljar.

"Tell me," she said.

"Tell you what? You were the one who brought me in."

"And you're the one who sends us emails about impending homicides," she replied dryly.

"Ah . . . Now I understand."

Then it was as Viljar had feared. The police had started to connect the two incidents.

"Do you believe that email has anything to do with the murder of Rita Lothe?"

"We don't believe anything. And if we believe something, we won't talk about it to the press. We only tell you what we know. Since we don't know anything yet, we're asking you to tell us a little more about this email. When did it arrive? Were there other recipients besides you? What made you assess it as serious enough that you wanted to send it to me personally? Have you received other emails? Who at the newspaper office has been informed about the email? In brief . . . Tell me."

Viljar told her to the best of his ability. About the email, about how he thought that this was probably a joke, about the conversation with Ranveig and what they had agreed to do.

"Your editor doesn't know anything?" Lotte asked with surprise.

"No, not yet, but if any more arrive, yes . . . Yes, then I'll have to. . . ."

Lotte nodded in confirmation. A little gleam of recognition appeared in her eyes. "This means, if I understand you correctly, that there won't be something about a mentally ill person who has chosen to inform the public about his exploits through *Haugesund News* in tomorrow's edition?"

"Not tomorrow, no."

Viljar wished he could promise that would also apply from here on out, but he knew Johan Øveraas better than that.

"Great. Then we have some time before the wolves are let loose."

Lotte stopped. Placed a pen with millimeter precision in line with the recorder. Studied it thoroughly before she raised her eyes. Looked at Viljar. Hesitated a moment.

"Why did he send the email to you?" she asked while her gaze kept him from looking in another direction.

Viljar straightened up in the chair. "What do you mean? Why? I have no idea."

Viljar noticed that the sweat glands under his arms were starting to work in high gear. It felt like he was sitting in a Turkish bungalow with no air-conditioning.

"I mean what I'm asking. Why did he send the email to you?"

"I must disappoint you, Lotte."

Viljar breathed in calmly before he continued. "I have no idea why he, or she, chose just me. There are many people who want to give me trouble because of things I've written about them, but I'm not the one who's the victim here."

Lotte studied him a long time. Tried to let the silence bring out more answers. When that didn't succeed, she continued.

"Great. You say he *or she*, but isn't it clear from the email that it's a man who's the sender?"

"No. Apart from the fictional name and a Gmail address he *or she* has created for this purpose, I don't find anyplace that shows that this is a man."

"That adds up in a sense, but he uses the phrase 'I am an honorable man' right at the start of the email."

Viljar asked Lotte to wait a moment. Fished out his phone and opened the email program in the Outlook app. The sender had said that it was *Viljar* who was "an honorable man," not himself. Viljar was quite sure of that.

The phone pinged just as the email program opened. The little dispute between them soon became insignificant. At the top of Viljar's in-box was a new email from the same sender. All thoughts that this had been a bad joke were crushed like an annoying beetle under a shoe. He waved Lotte over to his side, and they leaned closer to the phone.

Attn.: Viljar Ravn Gudmundsson

I assume that I have your full and total attention this time. You have today been witness to Rita Lothe's passing. It was not tragic, as it surely will say in the obituary, simply just. Your investigations will undoubtedly confirm this.

We have laws that are supposed to protect us against people who take what they want, and not a bad word shall be said about those who admit their guilt and take their just punishment. It is the others I want to put the spotlight on. Those who even in the hour of judgment avoid punishment and get away. They are the hyenas of society. Cowardly, greedy, and evasive. They deserve the punishment I shall give them. I will be punished myself for my actions. This I will take with head held high when the time comes. Until that happens, people will die by my hand. Guilty people who each in their own way avoided their rightful punishment.

In contemporary Norwegian society, one would think that a woman's human value was worth more than it actually is, but women's protection from the law in assault cases is still equal to nil. Very few rapists are punished for their actions. The burden of proof is put on the woman, not on the assailant.

One of these sexual offenders is a man. He is convicted of rape of at least one, and probably several, innocent women. He has a previous record, but not under this section of the law. The punishment will be effectuated tomorrow, Wednesday the 15th of October 2014.

10/14/2014
Stein Åmli
JN3-5

Requiem: Kyrie

I am content. I lie down, check that I have the right position. One that gives me the support I need. Perfect . . .

Twilight comes creeping in now that evening is here. Heavy, drooping trees block out the light. Suffocate hope. The birds are expectantly quiet. The endless night is waiting. Not for me this time. Someone else is marked. In my mind, there is a shivering sense of peaceful pleasure.

I know that the score is painfully precise down to the slightest detail, but there is always a danger that some quirk or other will slip in and ruin the composition. It hasn't happened yet, and it was with childish delight I shredded the papers that concerned Rita Lothe a few hours ago.

Now I know that I am capable of completing the masterwork. Lifting her over the railing and letting her go was like releasing a paper airplane from the balcony. I felt an intense happiness when I heard the body hit the asphalt. I actually thought I would feel anxiety, fear, and regret, but it was just happiness. A bubbling, effervescent delight.

For a while I started to get a little nervous that it would take too long before she was found, but when the morning rush set in, it wasn't long before with some satisfaction I could hear the first sirens heading toward the high-rises.

All that remains in me is a tingling sensation. A numb apathy in my body. For the time being, I am on schedule. I repeat the two admonitions I've written in the notebook. "Don't get too eager" and "Don't lose focus." I've read so much criminology that I know it's easy to move ahead too fast when you've succeeded the first time, or that you lose focus in exactitude and precision. I feel I'm ready, but I force myself to wait.

The lean-to I've made for myself is concealed from the house, the road, and the forest path. I have camouflaged it to the best of my ability, even if strictly speaking that's not necessary. A hiker would have to go very far off the path to stumble across this hiding place. If it wasn't for what will happen early tomorrow, I could probably stay hidden until winter without a single confused soul stumbling across it.

From the lean-to it is only a few steps over to the lookout post. From here I have a clear view down to the house, and I see a big enough area of the forest path to have control of people who might be in the vicinity. The dogs are securely chained. In the relevant time frame, there won't be anyone passing by. Maybe a jogger, but even that is highly improbable at six thirty in the morning.

I take out the gun. Rub the telescopic sight one more time with the cloth. Put it to my eye and look. The white house stands alone down in the hollow. Pretentiously modernistic. Right now, a family of five is living in the house. Tomorrow there will be only four. I hardly give a thought to the children, but I sense that I don't particularly care.

The slightest problem in the preparations was acquisition of the silencer. Silencers are easy to get ahold of for hunting rifles that are registered. Most hunters have such things these days, because it doesn't scare off other animals, it dampens the recoil and reduces the spurts of flame, which can be blinding when you see them through a telescopic sight at dusk. The only problem is that you have to turn in the gun to thread the barrel so the silencer can be screwed on. That takes a week.

The gun is my own hunting rifle. A Lakelander 389, standard. There are thousands of them registered by name in Norway, and probably just as many unregistered. Ideally it should have been a completely different rifle, a Märklin rifle with 16 mm Singapore ammunition. But they don't really exist. Even a master can do faulty research. An insignificant little bump in the road.

The first heavy raindrops let go over me, and I crawl carefully back to the lean-to. Take out the phone and set it to wake me at 5:00.

I'm ready! Everything is ready. . . .

All that's left is to wait for the royal stag.

Haugesund Police Station
Tuesday afternoon, October 14, 2014

Lotte scraped the chair backwards, picked it up, and set it neatly against the end of the table. Her gaze glided rapidly over the group.

She quickly went through the dry facts in the case before she picked up the notepad and double-checked that she had covered the most important things.

"Everything I've said until now is sorted in the folder in front of you. As you see, it is in chronological order with color codes for follow-up. If you need more detailed information along the way, contact me."

Someone laughed quietly when he saw the system in the folder; a low-pitched murmur filled the room. Lotte cleared her throat.

"We are quite certain of our case. This was a homicide. Toxicology tests will show that ether and sleeping pills were used mixed with alcohol. We have found traces of both at the crime scene. Other injuries are secondary as a result of the fall." She looked over at Åse Fruholm, who represented forensics.

Fruholm had been part of the police corps technical unit so long that she was viewed as an institution. Her thin, stringy hair was slicked down in a short, severe hairdo. Frightfully out of date, but in that sense it fit well with the rest of her style. Her wardrobe had a worn, thrift-store cut about it. On the other hand, there was nothing to say about her professional integrity. Her word was law.

Lotte looked up from her notes for a moment before she continued. "As you all know, inhaling ether leads to almost immediate unconsciousness, and the substance was used as an anesthetic in surgery in the past. Maybe you can help me with some supplementary information here, Åse?"

Åse Fruholm cleared her throat as she stood up. Her clothes hung on her as on a spindly scarecrow. When she frowned, her face could be mistaken for a topographical map, a result of decades of chain-smoking. Her voice rasped as she finally started to speak.

"*Ether* is the common name for the chemical substance diethyl ether. It is a clear fluid with a boiling point of 36.5 degrees Celsius. It has a strong odor and is highly flammable."

Lotte followed Fruholm's specifications carefully and made diligent notes on the pad in front of her.

"Inhalation of ether fumes will cause unconsciousness and painlessness, also generally known as anesthesia. Ether fumes produce a relatively stable anesthesia, and can be given, with reasonable safety, even under primitive conditions."

Police Chief Arnstein Guldbrandsen shook his head and threw out his hands. "Where the heck did this guy get ahold of *ether*?"

Åse Fruholm smiled at Lotte, as if the two shared a secret, rolled her eyes a little, and cleared her throat lightly before she answered.

"At a pharmacy, Guldbrandsen. It's sold over the counter in half-liter bottles."

Arnstein Guldbrandsen loosened his tie, something he almost never did of his own free will. He looked thunderstruck. "The pharmacy sells it over the counter? Why in the world do they do that? What in the name of God would people do with an anesthetic in their medicine cabinet?"

Åse smiled indulgently at the police chief. "Butterflies, Arnstein. Entomologists use it to anesthetize butterflies and other insects that they catch. So with the use of larger quantities, they can do the same with people," she added.

Åse Fruholm sat down again, and Lotte took the floor.

"We have to check the pharmacies in town. There can't possibly be too many people who've bought that sort of thing. I'll put a constable on that task after the meeting is over. Now, however, there is something quite different that's burning here."

She pushed her bangs behind her ear and made a brief pause to prepare herself to break the news to the rest of the team.

"So, Rita Lothe was killed, but what you don't know yet, is that we were warned in advance."

Lotte registered some raised eyebrows before she continued.

"Yesterday morning, the journalist Viljar Ravn Gudmundsson at *Haugesund News* received an email from a person who calls himself Stein Åmli. The name is an alias. The person in question maintained in the email that he will execute an unknown number of individuals who in his opinion have performed criminal acts without being punished for them. Gudmundsson didn't take this too seriously, and we didn't either until we checked on Rita Lothe's past."

Lotte made a theatrical pause to be certain that she formulated herself correctly. She raised her eyes from the tabletop, straightened her blouse, and tried to find a point over the heads of the others that she could focus on. She had learned that useful trick at a course in speech and debate techniques.

"In the email, Åmli hinted that he wanted to kill a woman who committed embezzlement, but who was not punished for that. A search in our registers shows that Rita Lothe was indicted for embezzlement of seventy-four thousand kroner from the till at a shoe store, where she was manager for a one-year period from 2002 to 2003. She was acquitted by the court because it could not be proved that it was her. In theory, a number of other employees could have helped themselves from the cash register in that same time period. Lothe nonetheless lost her job as a result of the indictment, and has been on disability ever since."

Lotte handed out a printout of the email and the indictment against Rita Lothe. She let those present read through all the documents before she continued.

"The person in question who committed the murder of Rita Lothe cares little about hiding traces. In Lothe's apartment we found a whole series of fingerprints that don't belong to her. All identical, and most likely the perpetrator's. It has also come to light that Rita Lothe had sex shortly before the murder. We have a quantity of biological traces that obviously have been sent for DNA analysis. Normally, when a killer leaves many traces behind him, we're talking about murders that are committed in affect. That is hardly the case here. Very few people go around with a bottle of ether in their pocket without intending to use it. Why the perpetrator chooses to proceed so carelessly is a major mystery. At any rate, we can be reasonably confident that we won't find him in our registers. If that were to happen, the case would be solved tomorrow."

Lotte concluded the session by reviewing some photos that showed bruises under the armpits of the victim, pictures from the apartment, and various other details that they'd found at the scene.

"One very unpleasant and quite important detail remains." She breathed in deeply before she dropped the bomb. "Gudmundsson has received a new email. Today, while he was being questioned." Lotte clicked on the next image in the presentation, and a slightly blurred image showed the text that had popped up on Viljar's cell phone an hour before.

A dark silence settled on the room, and the faces around the table wilted.

Inner Pier, Haugesund
Tuesday evening, October 14, 2014

The mood along the city's wharf promenade was in glaring contrast to how Viljar felt. Here the city's residents were celebrating noisily at the outdoor restaurants lined up like domino tiles. Viljar, however, was standing with both feet in a bad crime novel. The half-dead journalist in him would have rejoiced, but Viljar Ravn Gudmundsson had lost the spark. More than anything, he wanted to get under a blanket and hide from everything that was annoying. What he needed least of all now was such a demanding case. The emails were sent to him, and Lotte had asked the justifiable question: "Why?"

Viljar had no idea, but a thought had crept in under his skin while he sat at the pier. A thought that made the hairs on his neck stick up like hog bristle. *Black Tuesday.*

He stood up and walked with his gaze stiffly fixed on the cobblestones in the direction of Ranveig Børve's home. Paid no heed to the pouring rain or the stoop-shouldered people walking along the row of boats by the sound.

Ranveig lived on Risøy, just to the right across the Risøy Bridge in the city center. The bridge was a connection point between the mainland part of Haugesund and the island that housed some of the city's key companies. The enormous blue factory hall at the Aibel shipyard, a well-known landmark, loomed in the background.

Somewhere the city officials had gotten the idea that the bridge could be illuminated in the evening, and a violet tinge gave the city a gaudy, urban hipster aspect.

Ranveig and her husband, Rolf, had settled down in an old white Swiss chalet when she came back to town after her studies. Since then the couple had renovated the house from a neglected dump into a modern residence for a family with small children. They had paid just over a million kroner for a house that now would sell for five times that much. Rolf was a robust and energetic handyman, and Ranveig had a good eye for the small details.

The doorbell was the kind that echoes in every room, and doesn't fade out until a generation has passed. A short time later she was standing in the doorway. Somewhat surprised—this was, after all, the first time Viljar had shown up without an invitation.

Ranveig was a revelation. Even like this, in workout clothes and with her hair in a tousled bun, she radiated a sensuality that made him tingle inside. It was her eyes. They sparkled with life and promised amazing moments he would never get to experience. Not with her anyway. Viljar apologized and asked if he'd come at a bad time. He could have spared himself the polite phrases, because Ranveig's astonished expression was quickly transformed into a big, open, and genuine smile.

"No, no, how nice. Come in," she said, calling up to Rolf that it was Viljar who had come to visit, and that they were sitting in the room with the open fireplace. She told him that Rolf was busy putting their six-year-old daughter to bed.

Viljar hung up his topcoat on a massive stand that took up half the width of the hall, before he followed Ranveig to the room with the fireplace adjacent to the living room. Both rooms had panorama windows from floor to ceiling with an amazing view toward Smeda-sundet. Without asking, Ranveig poured fresh rose hip tea for both of them and took out sugar and lemon. Coffee or beer was evidently not an alternative, Viljar noted.

She made herself comfortable in a soft purple armchair across from him and looked him over. "Have you been out and had a couple of beers, or what?" Ranveig smiled slyly.

"Does it already show? Only three pints at MM," Viljar defended himself.

"Three pints on a Tuesday evening in October when you're not on vacation?"

Viljar hemmed and hawed a little. Felt that it was unpleasant to drag Ranveig into the muck he was standing in, but he needed an ally.

"Got another email this afternoon. Same sender. This is not some-one who's messing with us, Ranveig. He even confessed to the murder on Fjellvegen today."

Ranveig was about to drink from the teacup, but set it down again untouched. "The woman who fell out of the high-rise?"

"Yep. She evidently got help on the journey, and now he's announc-ing the next man out."

Viljar fished out his phone to show her the email, but Ranveig stopped him. He looked at her with surprise. There was something in her eyes he was unable to interpret. Instead Viljar put a portion of snus under his lip while he patiently listened to what she had to say.

"Damn it all, Viljar! You have to go to the police with this, not come to me to chat." She looked at him sternly.

Viljar quickly told her about the interview with Lotte Skeisvoll at the police station, and that he was there when the new message arrived. Viljar gave the phone to Ranveig so she could read it. She wrinkled her nose as if he were handing her a pair of stinky gym socks.

"As you see, it's almost a copy of the previous email. Apart from the admission at the start and the new 'judgment' at the bottom, he has simply cut and pasted what was there last time."

Ranveig nodded and finished reading.

"Same style as last time. No energy. No nerve. No passion. How eager are you to get your message out when you can't be bothered to write a new one, but just cut and paste?"

Ranveig looked up from the phone and set it down on the table. "It may be that this is exactly what he wants us to see. He is making the whole thing into such an obvious and poorly executed crime cliché that we'll realize there is something else altogether behind it."

"Okay, I see that. Let's say you're right. . . . Why bother to do this at all then, if it's not to put the police on the wrong track?"

The question remained unanswered in the air.

Ranveig had picked up the phone again and was squinting at it. "Do you see at the very bottom of the message? The letters and numbers." She gave him back the phone.

Viljar had noticed that, but hadn't given it any thought.

"'JN3-5' . . . Well . . ."

Viljar tried to think through whether anyone used such footers in emails or other correspondence, but couldn't think of anything.

"Either it's a fixed email signature, and in that case it means a lot, or else he has written that in deliberately. This may be important, Viljar!"

They were interrupted by the patter of bare feet on the parquet floor. Six-year-old Victoria came a little hesitantly into the room. She stopped a moment in the doorway before with a pretend sad face she went over and sat on her mother's lap.

"Daddy's mean!"

Victoria tried her best to sob. Rolf was standing by the door, following the episode goodnaturedly. A bushy beard hid a little of his smile. He was dressed in green wool clothing from top to toe. Ranveig must have noticed the question mark on Viljar's face, because she cleared up the mystery at once.

"Rolf actually just stopped by the house to pick up something. He's on a deer hunt with his buddies, but was captured by the little princess here."

Rolf kept a safe distance from the girl and showed Ranveig by resting his cheek against his hands that the girl wouldn't go to sleep. Ranveig sent him an air kiss.

"Daddy won't let me sleep with the dollhouse in bed."

Ranveig smiled and tousled her daughter's wild curls. She kissed the child on the cheek and pulled her next to her. Let the girl cry out her crocodile tears. When the last sob had quieted down, Ranveig set Victoria down on the floor. Stroked her hair carefully while she looked her in the eyes.

"Daddy is nice. Do you know that he's the one who bought the dollhouse? He paid all the money. Then maybe it's not so strange that he's afraid it will fall off the bed and get broken, right? Will it be okay if the house sits on the shelf so you can see it from your bed? Do you think you can fall asleep then?"

Victoria nodded and dried the tears with the back of her hand. She took Rolf's hand, who had now come over to his daughter.

"Night, Mommy. Night, strange man."

"The strange man is also a journalist, Victoria. He writes too. Just not as good," she whispered into Victoria's ear, who giggled.

Ranveig looked longingly at her daughter, who was now hanging over Rolf's shoulder on their way up to the child's room. Then she turned her attention back to Viljar. She looked at him inquisitively.

He took a sip of tea before he continued talking.

"You know what, Ranveig, let's leave that part with the letters and numbers for the time being. I'm not very good at those kinds of puzzles." Viljar paused for a moment. "I had a slight ulterior motive in coming here. . . . You have access to the work network from home, don't you?"

She nodded in confirmation. As a cultural journalist, she often had late evening assignments to turn in after the desk at the newspaper office had left for the day. For that reason, Ranveig could connect to the internal network by means of Citrix keys and submit finished articles from home.

"I thought we could do a quick search in our own archives to see if we get any hits on rapists who were acquitted here in town. This guy who calls himself Åmli has produced one anyway, and I doubt that he has access to better search engines, so long as he doesn't work at the courthouse or with the police, I should note."

Ranveig shook her head dejectedly. "Fair enough, but even if we find old articles about rapists who've gone free, we never use names, only age and gender," she objected.

"That's true, but the murderer has the same problem too. He's probably picked out someone who made his story public. We print such things occasionally, when the victim or the one who's indicted steps out with their name and picture to get their side of the case covered in the media."

"You make it sound like the newspaper is a kind of public pillory."

Viljar broke into a faint smile at Ranveig's naïveté. "Call me conspiratorial, but don't you mark your articles with names when there are scandals going on? Image tags that only you can see, and not the reader?"

Ranveig sighed. She understood what he was getting at. In cases involving better-known persons, they usually tagged public figures with cases that the general public knew nothing about. In that way, they could quickly locate background material and images if other media were not so reserved as themselves.

"Perhaps our murderer is going after a slightly better-known face this time. Then he will force the press to see him, and write about him. That's what he really wants."

Ranveig looked like she was cold. She pulled her mauve cashmere sweater tighter around her and crept into the chair in a kind of lotus position, but with her arms tightly coiled around her upper body. She did not seem convinced, but did as he said this time too.

"Okay . . . Search terms?"

"Try 'rape' and 'acquitted.'"

Ranveig did that, and a whole series of documents appeared on the screen. The majority were nondescript short articles about anonymous rape cases from Haugaland District Court. There was little to be had from the pictures. Heaps of illustration photos, but no faces. They tried further with various search combinations, but with no luck.

Viljar sat there in his own thoughts. An old case had started to murmur in the back of his mind.

"Fine, I understand you're tired, but can you make one last search?" She nodded in confirmation.

"Search on 'Claussen' and 'exonerated.'" Ranveig turned quickly toward Viljar.

"Oh, damn it!"

She wasn't known for using strong language, but once Ranveig did, there was something big going on.

Sure enough. This time both articles and images showed up. Shipowner's son Christopher Claussen was known as a man about town, and seven years ago one of his many festive after-parties led to his being taken into custody, accused of having raped a woman while she was asleep. The case got major coverage, not least when the old man, Sigfred Claussen, told about how he felt having his own son be accused of such a thing.

Sigfred Claussen was normally extremely media-shy, but this time he had fully supported his party-happy offspring. The indictment of Christopher Claussen was dropped in district court because the police only had evidence that he'd had sexual intercourse with her, not that it had happened against her will. The poor woman didn't have a ghost of a chance against Claussen's hired suits.

"I don't understand why I didn't think of this case sooner. Claussen was previously convicted of drunk driving, and that fits completely with the profile the murderer draws. Someone who has been acquitted after having raped at least one woman, but probably more, and who was previously convicted in court in another case."

"Several women?"

"For sure! Claussen's parties are widely known, and it's probably more usual than not that he ends up in a hotel room with one of the partygoers. He totally ignores his family, but it seems as if his wife gives him permission to carouse," Viljar added.

He patted Ranveig on the back, took his topcoat down from the coatrack in the hall, and was out the door before Ranveig had collected herself to so much as say goodbye.

Norheim forest, Karmøy
Tuesday night, October 14, 2014

The air was heavy and raw. Static. Clammy. Heavy black clouds lay like a lid over the house, which clung to the crags above the Norheim forest. Viljar got the taxi to stop, paid in cash, and made his way quickly through the pretentious villas at the top of the ridge. Here they were lined up in rows, and not a single one for under five million kroner. This was Haugesund's answer to the mansions on Holmenkoll ridge in Oslo.

Strictly speaking, Norheim forest was not part of Haugesund. It was in Karmøy municipality, but Viljar didn't know anyone who lived here who saw himself as a Karmøy resident. The area on the north side of the Karmsund Bridge was characterized as the "mainland side" of Karmøy. A strange and unnatural division of the municipal boundary between Haugesund and Karmøy. Most other places started the boundary of an island when you drove across the bridge.

Christopher Claussen and his family lived here, well isolated from the other villas in the development. He'd had a massive modernist villa built a few hundred meters into the popular recreational area.

How he got permission from the municipality was still a mystery, but wicked tongues drew a parallel to the fact that at the same time Claussen Shipyards chose to locate their main office in the Norheim industrial area, that too within the boundaries of Karmøy municipality.

In his new white villa, the Claussen family could be left alone for the most part, with the exception of an occasional person who strayed from the hiking path. Claussen's lot basically had forest around it on all sides, but the shipping magnate's son had enough trees removed in front of his living room windows that he had an amazing view toward the sound.

Viljar had no plans to seek out the shipowner's son and his family, but he wanted to go up to see if they were actually at home. The family often traveled to more southerly climes, and several times before, he'd made needless trips to Norheim forest when he'd been in search of a comment in connection with cases he was working on. If Christopher Claussen was the perpetrator's next victim, it would be nice to know in advance if he was home or not.

In principle, Viljar thought that it was best to leave it to the police to check out Christopher Claussen, but curiosity got the upper hand. Besides, Viljar wasn't sure that the police would buy his assumption that it would probably be a more known face that would be removed this time. According to the email, the "judgment" would not fall until tomorrow, so it shouldn't involve particular risk to approach Claussen's residence right now.

It was pitch dark in the forest around the villa. It was as if every single tree and every single stone crept closer and squeezed him into a space without doors and windows. He saw nothing, could feel only the gravel that crunched under his running shoes. His heart rate increased, and he had to struggle the whole time not to panic. Fear of the dark had actually come to him as an adult, along with all the rest.

All that had led him into the office of the psychologist Vigdis Nygård late one autumn day in 2010. Now, four years later, the fear was just as intact. Just as present. Just as paralyzing.

As Viljar left the path, he thought he heard a movement in the bushes right behind him. He stopped short. His gaze flickered frantically back and forth. The dark swallowed everything that was more than five meters beyond him. The adrenaline rush had given his anxiety a jump start, and he had to force himself to think rationally. His heart was pounding. His throat tightened up. He got goose bumps on his upper arms. A faint, monotonous piping sound was vibrating deep inside his ears. Symptoms of anxiety. He knew them all too well.

"There's no one here," he said to himself again and again. However, the creeping sensation would not let go of him. He sensed someone there in the bushes. Someone who observed him with increasing interest, but who clearly did not intend to make himself known.

"Hello?"

Viljar whispered toward the invisible someone a few meters away. Nothing happened. He hyperventilated. Put his hands like a bowl around his mouth and tried to breathe more slowly. Ordered himself to calm down. There was no one there. He was alone. The sounds he had heard were either from an animal, or else it was the anxiety once again playing a trick on him.

After getting control of his breathing somewhat, he started to work his way forward in the heather and brush that led toward the back side of the house where the entry door was. The whole time with the same feeling that there was someone three steps behind him. Two steps back . . . Again and again he turned his head. His gaze flickered. He didn't see a thing. Just an all-encompassing darkness. Nonetheless . . . He didn't want to walk in the main way, because that was visible from the house, and Viljar knew from experience that the two watchdogs who were leashed outside were a breed you couldn't bring

into Norway without someone knowing someone who knows someone. There was a reason that they were always chained with carabi-
ners to a thick ship's anchor. This anchor was bolted and welded firmly
to a beam according to all the rules of the art. Not even the Fenris
wolf could tear itself loose if it was chained here. Claussen's dogs, on
the other hand, seemed strong enough.

He tried to be quiet as he approached the area where the dogs kept
watch. Even if he didn't go past them, they would notice the sounds
from the forest and create a commotion. At a little opening between
two birch trees, he discovered that the dogs were gone. Either the
family was away, or else the dogs weren't chained up. The latter alternative made Viljar look behind him yet again. In the corner of his
eye, he seemed to notice a slight movement in the branches; the de-
ciduous trees quivered. Viljar stopped completely and held his breath.
There's no wind.

The thought that there might be two full-grown Argentine mas-
tiffs off leash in the forest made his legs almost buckle under him.
Viljar no longer had control of his own body, or his muscles, his
breathing, his heart. Everything was out of control. He had to move
on. It couldn't be the dogs. Even Claussen wouldn't let two such killing machines wander freely on the hiking path around the property.

Viljar knew of a small rise behind the house where he would have
a free view into the backside of the villa. He struggled laboriously up
to this high point in the terrain. The whole time, he was on guard.
Looked behind him. Stopped. Tried to lower his breathing rate and
pulse. If there was someone out there, Viljar could just as well have
come with an entire Tyrolean band in tow. It wasn't sound discipline
that occupied him most there and then. Anxiety was his worst enemy.
It made him see and hear things. He thought he saw outlines of human
forms everywhere in the terrain, *but there's really no one there, right?*
The sounds made him start. *Is it possible? Are there imagined*

*sounds? Does hearing have a center for fata morganas? If not, then
I am definitely not the only one here in the forest.*

Every ten seconds, there was a new sound. Rippling and rustling
in brush and heather. The fear paralyzed him and made it hard to
focus on anything else.

At last he lay down in the heather on the ridge. Decided to lie there
completely still until the chaos he felt inside himself subsided and
opened up for the real senses. The true sounds. The ones that were
really there. The harmless sounds. For almost ten minutes he lay like
that until he dared to raise his upper body and support himself on
his elbows. Viljar could note with satisfaction that there were both
lights on and people in the house. That this was an extremely irrational thought, inasmuch as the family was in mortal danger, did not
occur to Viljar as he lay in the heather looking down toward the house.
His own fear was more than enough for him.

He forced himself to dismiss the anxiety. Viljar refused to let these
self-inflicted intrusive thoughts take control one more time. If he did,
he knew from experience that they would come again and again,
stronger each time. At times he had let it go so far that he was unable
to go out in public for days. He saw ghosts in broad daylight. It was
basically Ranveig who managed to bring him back to life after such
episodes. She had a particular ability to say the right things. *Life is
what happens between the waves,* she'd said one time, and in a
strange way, those words seemed to help. It was about relaxing and
letting the waves come. They always pass, and always come back.

Suddenly he was certain. Something was terribly wrong. There
was someone else nearby. Behind him. Very close. A sudden sense of
danger, no time to react. The fear and pain struck him like a tsunami.
Every single nerve in his body sent frantic alarm signals to his brain,
and his breathing reflex stopped. He realized, as he started to black
out, that it was all over.

Five years earlier . . .
Eivindsvatnet, Haugesund
Friday, July 17, 2009

redric stroked his hand across Jonas's naked back. Jonas pushed the hair away from his face and cast a glance up at the friend by his side.

"He's gay, did you know that?"

Jonas looked up and caught the teasing eyes of Fredric Karjoli. "And so are you, Fredric. So what? Is that supposed to mean something?"

"Yes. It does. There are secrets that everyone knows, but no one tells. The fact that Hermann Eliassen, the Minister of Transport and Communications, is homosexual is that kind of secret. The only one who would be shocked if the minister came out of the closet would be Eliassen himself."

Jonas couldn't help smiling. He had unmasked the minister the first time they met at a seminar on new road projects in Rogaland.

Fredric didn't say anything for a while. He looked out over Eivindsvatnet. Wrapped in darkness, as if the answer were waiting in the depths out there. Nighttime swimming had become a ritual for the two friends this summer. Concealed by the dark of night, they could give themselves to each other.

"Actually, then it means everything, Jonas." Fredric moved his gaze from the water and down to his friend's naked body. He let his fingers play with a solitary water drop that was running down Jonas's back. He noticed that he had goose bumps.

"Everything? How's that? Is it supposed to help us that we have the same orientation? He's gotten lost in the closet. He's rooting around in a Narnia he's not coming out of, and we're not exactly open either, are we?"

"I am."

Jonas sighed and hoisted himself up on his elbows. Took Fredric's hand and stroked the back of it carefully. "Yes, maybe you are. But *we* are definitely not open. You know my family. Just thinking the word 'homo' is a sin. Thoughts are just as sinful as actions in my world. You know what will happen if they find out. For them, it would be a lesser sin if I were a child murderer. That can be forgiven, Fredric. What we're doing is not an isolated sin in their minds. It's a lasting condition of total damnation. Besides, I don't see why this secret could help us. The party isn't exactly known for pressing queers to their chest and embracing them."

"It's Eliassen who picks candidates for the youth campaign New Voices. If we get in, we'll have a lot of safe spaces. Weekend trips. Seminars. Courses. We won't need to hide. Besides that, it's a brilliant opportunity to rise in the party. Before we know it, they'll put us in the county leadership in Stavanger, or in Oslo. Think about it, Jonas. We'll be able to move away from this godforsaken place. Get you away from your crazy family, like your uncle always says."

Jonas smiled and looked teasingly at his friend. "Godforsaken? Dad should hear you. He would have a heart attack. But seriously . . . How can this help us be two of the ones chosen?"

Fredric got an introspective expression on his face. It was as if it closed up for a few seconds. The answer was deep inside. He poked in the sand. Let the question hang unanswered in the air, before he shook off the final remnant of uncertainty and let the words fall.

"We can seduce him."

Bleikemyr, Haugesund
Tuesday night, October 14, 2014

L otte was wakened from a light slumber by the sound of the phone. Fumbling feverishly on the floor beside the bed, she cursed before she finally found it. As she answered, she realized that another work-day was already about to begin. The only thing to do was to get dressed. She could sleep some other time.

Down at the police station fifteen minutes later, she was met by the night-shift desk officer. A strange fellow with an enormous chest and pipe-stem legs. He looked like an aged version of Johnny Bravo.

"When did this happen?" she asked as she walked slowly by the side of the disproportional constable who had wakened her.

"About ten thirty," he answered curtly.

Evidently not a man with a need for long explanations. She reached over and brushed a little dandruff from his shoulders. He looked at her with surprise, but didn't say anything.

"What was he doing up in the Norheim forest at that time of night?" Lotte said that mostly to have something to say. At the same time, she looked feverishly around the room for something she could wipe her hands on.

"You're the one who's the investigator here in the building. Not me."

The constable was undoubtedly the moody type, and Lotte gave up on further conversation. She was shown to one of the holding cells, where another man was sitting. Someone who knew a bit more about why she'd been dragged out of bed than the constable did.

Viljar looked up at Lotte like a subdued puppy when she burst into the room, closely followed by the desk officer who had locked him in the cell. Lotte threw out her arms in frustration.

"Thanks a lot," she said sarcastically.

"Thanks?"

"Yes . . . Thanks for waking me up when I'd finally managed to close my eyes after a hell of a long day."

Lotte stood with her back to Viljar as she said that. Didn't want him to see that the black top she'd pulled over her head as she was leaving was buttoned wrong. Satisfied, Lotte looked up after having corrected the faux pas and became aware of a moping Johnny Bravo who had just gotten an eyeful. She thought he'd left the room as soon as they came in. Viljar was talking behind her, and she turned on her heels.

"Oh . . . I understand. Sorry."

She heard Viljar say that, but she suspected that he didn't mean it. In his mind, it was probably the police who should apologize, she thought. Lotte looked down at the report she'd been handed by the on-duty officer. Viljar was arrested under dramatic circumstances in the Norheim forest. A police guard they had placed in the area had observed a suspicious figure approaching the house of the Claussen family. According to the report, Viljar had the wind knocked out of him when the body of the overzealous policeman landed on top of him, and he'd shouted about miscarriage of justice and police brutality as he was transported back.

Lotte looked at him. For a long time.

"Tell me," she said suddenly.

In contrast to last time, Viljar evidently understood what it was she wanted to know. He described what he'd been doing and thinking after the interview. The stop at Café MM, the visit to Ranveig, and at last the trip to the Norheim forest.

"So you want me to believe that you took the trouble to tramp around in the forest in pitch darkness simply to see whether the Claussen family was at home?"

"Yes, really. I meant to warn you first, but I didn't want to bother you."

The last words from Viljar were hung out to dry and testified to particularly poor judgment.

"Is stupidity a separate subject in journalism school?" she shouted, pounding a clenched fist on the table in front of him.

The sudden outburst made Viljar jump in his chair, and his shoulders sank. He quickly straightened up. "Not stupidity, but vigilance and curiosity," he answered dryly.

She looked at him in shock, and with modest movements she righted an empty plastic mug that had fallen over during the outburst. She rubbed her eyes. The tiredness made her unprofessional. Made her lose control.

"So you mean, in complete seriousness, that making yourself a suspect in a homicide case isn't stupidity?"

She stopped and stared at Viljar to see if he showed any form of reaction. He did. He looked nervous, worried. His gaze wandered while he chewed his nicotine gum frantically.

"You do understand, Viljar, that we have a rule of thumb here in the building where investigations are concerned. If a face shows up one time in an investigation, it's probably a coincidence. If the person in question shows up two times, it's suspicious. The third time is a pattern."

"And now I've shown up for the second time," said Viljar.

"Third," she corrected him.

"Third . . . What the hell is that you're saying?" He looked at Lotte in amazement.

"That's right. You are the recipient of the emails, and you're crawling around in the woods by the house of someone we think may be the killer's next victim. In addition, you've shown up in Rita Lothe's calendar. We have actually had a police patrol on the lookout for you all evening."

Viljar didn't understand a thing. He just shook his head and looked blankly out into space. Lotte did not change her expression. She tried to wait him out, but after a little while she gave up that technique.

"In Rita Lothe's apartment we found a good old-fashioned pocket diary. I didn't think they still existed, but the lady evidently parked her life sometime in the seventies. Your name is in it on three dates. All neatly decorated with a heart around them."

"It's not me. There must be another Viljar. Damn it all. I'm not a complete idiot. . . . She was almost sixty, and I recently turned forty. You realize it wasn't me, don't you . . ."

Viljar was talking like a waterfall now. At last Lotte raised both palms toward him to stop the flow of words.

"Great. As soon as I've checked your story with Ranveig, I'll release you, but tomorrow Kripos will arrive, and then you have to expect more questions. Is that understood?"

She stood up, straightened the wrinkles on her blouse, and gave him a stern look before she took out her phone to call Ranveig Børve. Five minutes later, Viljar was a free man.

The rain that had been threatening the past few hours pounded against the ground as Viljar stopped to fish the tobacco pouch from his pocket. He had sought refuge under the overhang at Victoriahjørnet on Haraldsgata. The interview was buzzing in the back of his head like mental background noise. He was unable to put his thoughts aside. He must have been placed in this drama on purpose by someone who wanted to hurt him. That he himself made matters worse by tramping around like a drunk festivalgoer in search of an after-party, he had to rack up to stupidity. It was self-inflicted.

He tossed away the cigarette in a manhole cover on the street and took out the box of snus. Suddenly he became aware of a shadow in the corner of his eye. A man who crossed the street, stopped suddenly, and looked with apparent interest at the window display at Norli Bookstore. The distance was too great for him to see who it was in the dark.

How many people stop to study new book titles in a downpour like this? Viljar started to walk. At the corner of the next block, he turned his head again and could quickly determine that the man was following him. Viljar smiled.

"If you're a suspect, I guess you have to expect that sort of thing," he told himself. *You will have a wet and boring night if you're going to surveil me,* Viljar thought, making his way home to sleep.

Haugesund Airport, Karmøy
Wednesday morning, October 15, 2014

The approach to Haugesund Airport felt like an exercise in air acrobatics. The Norwegian plane with Thor Heyerdahl emblazoned on the fin bumped through the air pockets as *Kon-Tiki* did on the Pacific Ocean a half century earlier. The Kripos investigator Olav Scheldrup Hansen felt like an explorer facing unforeseen hazards as he clung to the armrest and looked out into an unbroken, seemingly endless layer of white clouds. Finally the cloud cover changed from white to gray. Morning fog was certainly not an uncommon phenomenon in Haugesund in the fall. For that matter not the rest of the year either, he'd been told.

The airplane landed with a heavy thud without any advance warning. After a few seconds of sudden braking, the investigator happily noted that the pilots had found their way to an airstrip in the sea of fog. He let go of the armrest and exhaled.

Olav had received a brief update by email from the police chief in Haugesund, and an introduction to the nature and extent of the assignment from his own department head. The ticket was ordered in his name, and Olav's objections against flying were met with a shoulder shrug. Haugesund did not have time to wait for him to cross the mountains by bus.

The information about the case was seriously lacking, and he hoped that did not mean poor police work had been done so far in the investigation. Fortunately the Kripos director had assured him that the district's best detective was leading the investigation. In other words, a practiced old fox with many years behind him in the corps. Olav himself had recently turned fifty, and had spent the last fifteen years in his position at Kripos. He enjoyed great respect as an investigator, was in demand as an instructor and lecturer at the police academy, had written two technical books about investigation tactics, and could basically dictate to his bosses as he wished.

The only drawback was that he was sent out at odd intervals to the periphery of Norway to assist in homicide cases. He felt most at home in Oslo, and had little liking for being buckled into an airplane seat. Sunny Oslo with its eighteen degrees was replaced by gusty fog and seven degrees Celsius. He regretted not having brought his duffel coat along.

A short, narrow Jetway led to the arrival hall: a small area the size of an average Norwegian living room. Here a baggage carousel wound around at one end of the room while the other end was reserved for families and friends who were meeting their loved ones.

Among the three in attendance stood a tall colt of a police constable with a sheet of paper in front of him where HANSEN was written in marker. Olav was sharp enough that he probably would have picked him out anyway, because the man in question was in uniform.

Ten minutes later, Scheldrup Hansen was sitting in the passenger seat of a marked patrol car. A rattling Volkswagen Passat, with sausage wrappers and empty pop bottles where he was supposed to put his feet.

Olav was silent, and fortunately the constable wasn't particularly talkative either. He nodded off in the seat, and half asleep registered that they were driving over a big bridge before the urban development began to take shape as they approached the center of Haugesund. The investigator's mood rose a notch or two. Haugesund was certainly not completely out in the sticks anyway. He knew it had a population of about thirty-five thousand, and that the city actually had one of Norway's better soccer teams, but he had nonetheless pictured a tiny urban core with scattered development in the surrounding area.

At Haugesund Hospital, they turned down into the city and drove through some empty city streets. Shortly afterwards the police car parked outside the police building by Smedasundet, and the constable jumped out to help him with his baggage. Olav took that as a sign that they hadn't found a hotel room for him yet. Two minutes after he had reported in at the counter, Lotte Skeisvoll appeared. He remained seated, looking stupidly at her and her outstretched hand far too long before he reacted. That she was the leader of the homicide investigation turned everything he'd planned upside down. He recognized her at once, and it was not a heartfelt sight. Probably not for her either, but she was cleverer than he in concealing it.

Lotte Skeisvoll was the youngest cadet he had advised at the police academy. She had come in as a whippersnapper who thought she knew everything from day one. As he remembered her, she was so long-winded that she would probably take a year explaining evidence to come to the conclusion that an egg needed nine minutes in boiling water to be hard-boiled.

There's really only one thing to do here, thought Olav as he finally stood up and took her hand. He had to use all channels to take over control of the case. All other outcomes would lead to an aimless investigation where nothing happened, nothing got done, and no one took chances to follow up leads before they turned ice cold. He didn't expect that in the ten years since Lotte Skeisvoll graduated she had become any less pedantic and detail-oriented.

Olav could not avoid noticing that Lotte Skeisvoll had to struggle not to start laughing during the first meeting. His thoughts went back in time a few years. Back when he first made the acquaintance of this lady from West Norway. This know-it-all. The young woman who always raised her hand and tried to instruct him, when he was the one who was the lecturer. Olav felt annoyed. If he knew her right, she'd been looking forward to this day for ten years. . . .

Haugesund Police Station
Wednesday morning, October 15, 2014

Lotte observed the investigation group. This was the team that would solve the murder of Rita Lothe and hopefully manage to stop the killer before he could strike again.

She had noticed the obvious distrust on Scheldrup Hansen's face when she met him in the hall an hour earlier. She knew very well that he could not stand women like her in the police department. That is . . . He could certainly tolerate *women*, but it was probably worse with women who thought and acted like typical women. Hansen was sharp, quick, decisive, and goal-oriented. She herself was detailed, in search of evidence, cautious, and precise. Both ways lead to Rome. She was clear about that, but she had longed to be able to prove to Olav that her methods worked just as well as his. Her arrest percentage could not measure up to the instructor's, but where percentage of convictions was concerned, she gave him a run for his money.

Lotte cleared her throat to show that it was time to start the meeting. She introduced each of the members in the investigation group in alphabetical order, and she noticed in the corner of her eye that Scheldrup Hansen's patience was already about to run out. He rolled his eyes and demonstratively smothered an occasional yawn. Lotte reluctantly set the preinstalled interval on the PowerPoint presentation to a faster mode.

"I'll give you fifteen minutes to read through the papers on the table. There is a detailed description of what we know about the murder of Rita Lothe so far, and also a number of other interesting details that may be related to the case."

Exactly fifteen minutes later, Lotte opened the floor for discussion, but immediately regretted that she hadn't taken firmer control.

"We have to stop thinking like a flock of clucking hens at a sewing circle," said Scheldrup Hansen without anyone else having said a peep, fixing his eyes on Lotte as he said it. "We have to prioritize our forces and put money on one horse at a time. Based on what I see and with my experience from a number of previous cases, I have an idea about what we should and what we absolutely should not do in a situation like this.

"To start with the latter. We should drop long, meaningless meetings where everyone sits and tosses out their theories. That leads nowhere. I know it sounds brutal, but you have no experience with these kinds of homicide cases, and the certain death of an investigation is when the police start spending more time on coffee parties than on investigation."

He paused to take a sip of coffee, but raised the palm of his hand toward Lars Stople when he was about to say something. Scheldrup Hansen continued.

"I definitely think we should focus on what is closest at hand. The answers are almost always in those nearby things. We are going to find Rita Lothe's killer by pulling on the threads of her love life. Lotte evidently thinks that this journalist Gudmundsson is a peripheral character, but I think it would be sloppy police work not to examine him more painstakingly. His name turns up everywhere. I'm not saying he's the man we're looking for, but it's not a coincidence that he's involved. Journalists have enemies. Check his previous cases. Has he made some big mistake or exposed someone who may have motive to get revenge on him?

"In addition, we should not remove him from the list of suspects. The way I read the documents, we're talking about a journalist with previous high status who is no longer doing so well. Suddenly he himself is in the center of a 'murder mystery.'"

Olav made quotation marks with his fingers.

"We mustn't overlook that he may be trying to create a good story for himself that can get him back on his feet as a journalist. It's every journalist's wet dream to get a murderer in his hands who wants to use the newspaper as a mouthpiece. Now the thing is that this wet dream is and will remain a dream, because the killer doesn't really want to be seen or heard. That happens only in movies and TV series. I hate to disappoint you, but this is Haugesund Police Station and not the final season of *The Bridge*."

Olav looked into four sets of inquisitive eyes. He sighed before he continued the monologue.

"Don't tell me you haven't seen *The Bridge*?"

He rose from his seat while at the same time holding up his palms again. Everyone in the room had given up long ago, so no one interrupted him.

"Now we'll shadow this Viljar Ravn Gudmundsson. If nothing else, this will prevent him from creating more trouble that ruins things for us."

He turned toward Lotte.

"Now, Lotte, can you give those of us sitting here various tasks that can help get this investigation on its feet?" Lotte straightened the tablecloth in front of her. Caressed the smooth surface. Needed time to gather her thoughts before she spoke. Scheldrup Hansen would undoubtedly be a harder nut to crack than she had imagined.

Beate Fredriksen stretched her body like a kitten. The bed linens embraced her in a soft morning greeting. The sun made its way through the gaps in the blinds, and narrow streaks of light tickled her face. She lay quietly and listened. Quickly picked up familiar sounds from Disney Channel in the living room. So Sander was up anyway. Beate heaved a sigh. Her father had gone to work and once again turned over the kitchen to a six-year-old. There was probably a mess everywhere. She refused to let the irritation ruin the peace and contentment she felt under the warm duvet.

As Beate turned in bed, she picked up a faint odor of perfume from the clothes she had thrown off before she went to bed. She pushed it away. Couldn't bear such smells in the morning. She was alone the whole day with little Sander and her sister, Julie. It was planning day at school, and her fourteen-year-old younger sister would probably sleep well into the afternoon, if she knew her right.

When she opened the bedroom door, she noticed that Julie was already up. The sounds from the shower meant that she'd dragged herself out of bed abnormally early this morning. Beate could only dream of a drop of hot water. Instead of starting the day by hammering on the bathroom door and arguing with the fourteen-year-old inside, she grabbed a bathrobe and pattered out into the living room.

"Sissy!" Sander leaped up from the little red TV chair and ran to meet her as soon as he caught sight of her in the doorway. She got a warm and long hug from the little boy. He was still in his pj's, and his chalk-white hair stood straight up in a serious tangle on one side. Beate quickly noticed that her clean white bathrobe now had two sticky brown spots from an affectionate chocolate nougat mouth. She laughed and hoisted her brother up in the air.

"You little brat! Have you been eating nougat bars? It's not Saturday today, is it?"

Sander looked at her with precocious eyes before he came up with the world's best explanation. "Sissy, uh . . . It's a day off today. And all days off are Saturdays."

Beate laughed again, tousling him lightly on his bed head.

She set him down on the chair and went over to the kitchen counter. Noticed the mess made by little brother. Sighed a little, but decided that it evened things out a bit that her father had made coffee before he went to work, and for that reason she could pour herself a cup before she started cleaning and other housework.

She was brought up that way. She had never known anything else. Her mother, the author Sandra Borch Fredriksen, was a nomad in the desert. She swept into the oasis only occasionally for a refill of water. Otherwise they saw little of her, except on the TV screen. Beate was the eldest and the one who had to take on the household duties while her father was at work.

With coffee cup in hand she padded out into the hall and took out a pair of worn blue Crocs. She wanted to enjoy this morning time with the local newspaper, which hopefully was on the front steps. Dreadfully unmodern for a seventeen-year-old who had access to a horde of Mac computers, iPhones, and iPads in the house, but this had become her silent protest against the rich man's life they lived here.

"You're just soooo retro," Julie said to her again and again. Her sister had not inherited a single gene of the rebellion against the family wealth after her mother had a breakthrough with her crime series. In the beginning it was just fun, but after the books had been made into TV series, and even had amazing success internationally, her mother more or less disappeared from their lives. For her little sister, life was a bottomless source of delights that they had every right to take advantage of. Beate cast a glance at Julie's phone, which was on top of a heap of dirty clothes outside the bathroom. The display showed 9:40.

The newspaper carrier wasn't usually there until ten o'clock at the earliest, but it didn't hurt to check.

When she tried to open the door, something was blocking the entry. Beate was surprised, but after a few attempts to slip through the cracked-open door, she gave up and instead put all her weight against the door itself. The front door finally gave way, and she stumbled forward. As she fell, she embraced what was lying on the steps. A scream immediately rose up from her belly. Her body tensed and she felt her feet starting to shake. She stared at what had once been the back of her father's head, but which now was a crater of blood, bone fragments, and brain mass. The scream didn't reach her throat before she was on her feet again and had backed into the hall. Her scream echoed in the walls, as she was unable to take her eyes off the ghastly sight.

Before she knew it, she heard a small child's feet come running. Sander called to his sister repeatedly while he ran the short distance from the living room to the hall. The boy stopped short at her feet. His desperate cries were strangled as if someone had used the remote control Mute button on him. The next few seconds seemed like an eternity of silence for Beate. A little sob broke the silence before the boy turned his face toward his sister's paralyzed body.

A sound behind them took their eyes off the gruesome sight. Beate did not turn around. She knew who it was. The word was only whispered, but it could just as well have been screamed out by Julie's mouth.

"Daddy?"

Viljar's apartment on Austmannavegen, Haugesund
Wednesday midmorning, October 15, 2014

Hell had broken loose in the media house. The devil was heartily present in the form of editor Johan Øveraas, but the sinner had not shown up to take his just punishment. Viljar Ravn Gudmundsson had not appeared at work, and in the mingle area on the second floor, Øveraas had his hands full pacifying three police constables who'd been sent to the newspaper offices to get the journalist. Ranveig Børve had evening shift this Wednesday, but the editor had duly depicted the chaos and annoyance for her when he called her at ten thirty. He was furious and ordered Ranveig to track down Viljar as soon as hell.

She tried to explain that she was alone with Victoria and had no time to do detective work, but was met with a tirade of abuse that made it clear that Øveraas knew about both emails and the conversations she'd had with Viljar about them. The editor saw her actions as directly disloyal, which for that matter she could not dispute.

In rapid sequence her daughter was placed with Grandma, a café visit with a girlfriend was postponed, and her husband had to cut short his deer hunt and pick up Victoria as soon as he could.

As if that weren't enough, she got a flood of abuse when she explained to Rolf that she and Viljar had kept something important concealed from management. He had every right to be annoyed—after all, in the end it was his hunting trip this affected.

She parked the car by the Opel Building on Karmsundsgata and went by foot the last stretch up to the top of the Austmann high-rises. Five rectangular blocks in a line each with sixteen apartments bathed in the sun in the grassy areas along Austmannavegen in the south part of the city. As Ranveig rounded the corner on her way to Viljar's stairway, she noticed two police cars outside the entry. She hurried over to them and knocked on the window of the car in front. A young, dark police constable appeared behind the rolled-down window after a few seconds. His facial features were sculpted, and he had a becoming cleft in his chin. He looked inquisitively up at her.

After Ranveig had introduced herself and explained what she wanted, the policeman shook his head firmly. "No one's going up there now. We're waiting for permission from the city attorney to enter the apartment by force. We know he's there, he was standing in the bedroom window a little while ago, but he won't open the door." The policeman who had introduced himself as Knut Veldetun was about to roll up the window again, but Ranveig stopped him.

"He won't open for you, but he will for me. Call Lotte Skeisvoll. She knows me well," Ranveig said with a smile. "And I'm sure she'll agree that I should try to talk with him."

Veldetun scrutinized her and hesitated before he entered the number to the detective. After a moment, he handed the phone to Ranveig.

On the stairs, Ranveig encountered a familiar face. Alexander was sitting on the bottom step with his hands laced around his knees. He was staring straight ahead apathetically.

"Dad won't answer the door."

Ranveig noticed that she became sad and angry at the same time. Now that old chain-smoker would just have to straighten up. She patted Alexander on the cheek, asked him to go home to his mother instead, and went past him up the stairs.

Ranveig didn't ring the bell. She knocked lightly and started talking to Viljar through the locked door. Without expecting any reaction from the other side of the door, she started to tell about what had happened this morning, and that he ought to open for her if he didn't want to get in even deeper. That Alexander was sitting like a banished latchkey kid in the stairwell. He didn't answer, but after a while, she heard a single click in the lock. It was open.

Once inside, she understood how wrong things were with Viljar. Stuffy enclosed air. Dirty clothes and mess all over the floor. Dust bunnies the size of tomcats danced in front of her feet. Old pizza boxes in stacks in the hall. The place hadn't been cleaned for weeks. That Viljar clearly was no longer taking care of himself was perhaps not apparent at work, but here it couldn't be concealed. *What the hell? He has a son living in this pigsty?* thought Ranveig while she stepped over the most toxic areas. Viljar shuffled ahead of her to the living room dressed in little other than a pair of shabby jogging pants. *This is a man in decline.* He tossed some dirty underwear and wrinkled jeans off an armchair and indicated with a hand gesture for her to sit down there. Ranveig felt uncomfortable, but she did so anyway.

Viljar looked out the window. What he was looking at she didn't know, but she assumed it was the police cars below. He turned around and looked at Ranveig.

"What the hell is really happening out there?" His gaze was defiant. She didn't move an inch.

"Strictly speaking, I should probably ask you that, shouldn't I? You're shirking work, don't answer the phone, don't open the door for the police, lock your son out . . . Need I say more?"

Viljar sighed and sank down into the brown leather three-seater. He rubbed the back of his hand against his forehead and stared vacantly ahead. In the background, Ranveig saw that Alexander had come in the door, and then went into what must be his room.

"I have no idea, Ranveig. I woke up early today with dark clouds in my head. Tried to get up, go to the bathroom, and get ready, but I had to give up. I couldn't bear work today. An hour later, Øveraas called and left a hysterical message on my voice mail."

"I know all this, Viljar. Forget about it! Why didn't you get dressed, and why don't you open up for the police? You don't need a master's degree in psychology to suspect that you have something to hide when you behave like that."

Viljar regained his defiant gaze. Looked sternly at her. Didn't say anything, but after a moment fished out a cigarette butt, which he meticulously lit. Blew out the smoke before he looked back at her.

"Anxiety!"

"*Anxiety* . . . What do you mean?"

"I have anxiety, Ranveig. I go to a psychologist, but it doesn't go away. Dark, hellish, shameful, paralyzing, creeping anxiety. It's so simple, and so damned difficult. Hiding under the covers like a little kid . . ."

Ranveig looked at him. Studied his face. This explained a lot.

She stood up and went over to him.

"Don't touch me, please. . . ."

She took her hand away from Viljar's shoulder, but stood there. "Listen, about Alexander. Does he live here full-time now?"

Viljar shook his head and explained to her that he still lived with his mother, but that he was here for an occasional overnight.

"You can't let it look like this. . . ."

He waved her away with a stifled expression. Clearly not something he wanted to discuss now. She would have to bring it up again later. This no longer worked. After a little while, Ranveig went over to the window and raised the blinds. Without asking Viljar, she waved the police up.

"Tell the police the same thing you told me," Ranveig said.

That was an order, not a suggestion. Viljar simply nodded in response. Put out the cigarette meticulously in the overfull ashtray, fished out a snus pouch, and waited obediently to be picked up. Ranveig found a bucket and some rags in the closet. Someone had to do something here, and that wasn't going to be Viljar for a while.

Rommetveit, Stord
Wednesday midmorning, October 15, 2014

The autumn air was raw and chilly. At Rommetveit, some of the trees had a streak of yellow. Lotte had noticed it before, that trees were just as individual as people. Autumn came to all of them, but not at the same time. Lotte observed Johannes Fredriksen with interest. He looked back with a disinterested gaze. Not so strange, because he was dead. The bullet that had penetrated his skull was embedded in the wall. On the way out of the back of his head, it had taken a lot of blood and brain mass with it that stuck to the white wood wall.

She opened her notepad and paged up to the green tab. Notes for crime scene investigations. A new, clean page awaited her. Quickly she noted the most obvious. The perpetrator was a good marksman. The place where the body was found was undoubtedly the same as the crime scene. Based on the fact that rigor mortis had already started to set in, the killing must have taken place early that morning. Lotte Skeisvoll also noted a number of details that might give rise to speculation. The car key in Johannes Fredriksen's hand indicated that he was either on his way out to the car or had just come home. He was supposed to be at work in Leirvik at seven o'clock, which hadn't happened. He was dressed in a nice gray suit of the Riccovero label. Becoming blue tie of the same brand. Tiepin with the logo of the car dealership where he worked as a salesman. Shiny polished shoes.

"He was on his way to work, and then we can conclude a probable time of death between six thirty and six fifty," she said out loud. No one heard her. She was completely alone inside this barricade. Olav Scheldrup Hansen was standing a short distance away, talking with Beate Fredriksen, Johannes Fredriksen's eldest daughter.

Rommetveit was bathed in sun this morning, but down here in the woods, the sun had not yet taken hold. Chilly fall air bit into her cheeks. The house was isolated down in a hollow with birch forest at both ends. A narrow gravel road led down to the house and was a shortcut from the hiking path a few hundred meters farther up.

Lotte had brought her team with her to Stord as soon as she got the news. Johannes Fredriksen had been on their very long list of possible victims. Lars Stople came up to the barricade tape while she crouched and studied the exit wound.

"You have to do something, Lotte."

"What do you mean?" She looked inquisitively up at the old fox. He nodded toward the area outside the barricades, where Olav was standing.

"That guy from Oslo is taking over all control here."

"I know that," Lotte replied with a sigh.

She leaned a little closer to Lars and whispered, "He's a handful, but he does have a little weight in cases like this. Besides, he's only been here a few hours. Let him have at it."

"That doesn't mean he's always right. He asks the witnesses leading questions, and he commandeers the rest of us as if he's the one leading the investigation. I don't even bother to ask if he clears these things with you first."

Lotte's eyes narrowed. She'd had a suspicion about this all morning, because constables disappeared left and right before she had talked with them about what they should do. It wasn't exactly uncommon that Kripos took control when they were going to support local police, but what Scheldrup Hansen was doing approached mutiny. She decided to have a serious talk with him when they got back to Haugesund later in the day.

It was a good two hundred meters to the nearest neighbor, which was a small farm. Lotte had already checked whether anyone had seen or heard anything this morning, but no one had. This was despite the fact that the farmwife had been out working in the cow barn at the time the shot must have been fired.

The Stord sheriff's office had called Haugesund very quickly after they learned of the victim's shabby record. What triggered that wasn't what Johannes Fredriksen had been convicted of in his youth, but rather what he'd been acquitted of in 2006. The year before, he had been accused of rape by a seventeen-year-old girl aboard a pleasure boat during the Sildajazz in Haugesund. Originally the rape accusations also concerned the girl's female friend, who had been at the same party on Fredriksen's boat, but she retracted her testimony before the case came to court. Without the friend's testimony, the case was hard to win for the offended girl. Word against word seldom leads to a conviction when there is no other evidence.

Lotte stood there a long time, looking into a vacuum in which none of the others were present. Lars took care not to disturb her. After a while she nodded three times, as if she were having a conversation with someone inside the vacuum. She stood parallel to the doorway, looking up into the woods where she thought the shot must have come from. Gave a sign to Lars that he should follow her and went up toward the slope about a hundred meters from the house. She looked carefully ahead of her while she walked, to assure herself that there were no tracks in the area, but she doubted that the murderer had taken the risk it would involve to go down to check that the job was completed. This shooter knew when he hit the mark. Besides, the ammunition was a safeguard. The hole in the forehead was not very large, while the exit hole was a crater. "Expanding ammunition," Åse Fruholm had determined as soon as she looked at Fredriksen.

It wasn't difficult to find the place where the killer had been positioned. He hadn't bothered to remove traces. Here it was almost as if the man was simply out on a walk and took a quick pee break. A blue backpack was tossed into a thicket. A paper plate and plastic utensils were left by the side of the pack. A partly hidden lean-to contained a green sleeping bag, a sleeping pad, and a half-empty bottle of Coke. A Nesbø book was found by an inflatable pillow. A little Mag-Lite flashlight had evidently served as a reading light.

"He spent the night here," Lars Stople said behind her.

That was obvious, but she refrained from commenting on that.

"Hmm . . . and he's not at all afraid of being caught. If this goes to court, we're going to have so much biological evidence that the case will practically prosecute itself."

"And what is he telling us by doing that?"

Lotte turned around and looked at Lars Stople with curiosity in her eyes. The old policeman was sharper than many believed.

"Tell me. . . ."

Lars stood in thought for a moment. "I think there are two possibilities, Lotte. Either he's indifferent to what he leaves behind because he thinks we'll never find him. That is, he intends to keep himself completely above suspicion. Regardless, he won't be found in the conviction register."

Lars stopped and studied the area around them a moment before he continued.

"The other possibility is that he's not afraid of being caught. He knows we'll find him at last, and he has no plans to deny the criminal acts. It may actually be that he wants to be caught and get credit for what he's done. Then we're dealing with someone who has lost contact with himself and his surroundings."

"We know one more thing." Lotte challenged the older police constable with her gaze.

"Yes?"

"We know that Olav Scheldrup Hansen is on the wrong track when he wants to tail Viljar Ravn Gudmundsson. If it had been him, he wouldn't have put himself in the center of the investigation while leaving behind hundreds of clues, true?"

Lars Stople smiled wryly and nodded. "Have you ever doubted that, Lotte? Hansen may have solved however many cases, but he's a loose cannon on deck. Any idiot hits the mark now and then if he shoots wildly in all directions."

Lotte chuckled. She appreciated the old constable more and more. They moved quickly down the terrain and waved Åse Fruholm over to them.

Four years earlier . . .
Room 306, Rica Maritim Hotel, Haugesund
Thursday morning, August 19, 2010

Blood was dripping from the broken bottle Jonas was holding. Dark drops were soaked up by the wall-to-wall carpet. Broken shards of glass crunched as he shifted his weight from one leg to the other. Jonas did not notice the pain. He kept his gaze locked on the man in front of him. The man shielded his face with his hands. An irrational reflex, as his throat and chest were both far more vulnerable points. Jonas swiped a sharp edge of the broken bottle across the man's left nipple. A piece stayed stuck like a barb. The man whimpered.

A thin stream of blood ran from his chest down onto the white sheet. Jonas didn't say anything. Everything was said. There were no more words that could wound him.

The room at Rica Maritim Hotel was sterile and bare. Stripped of soul. Cold colors. Blue bedspread, white bed linens, gray curtains, lemon-yellow walls. Jonas was cold. Naked, he had goose bumps from the draft from the window. His hands held tight around the broken bottle. Pressed it carefully in toward the man's throat.

The man moaned and tried to push himself back in the bed.

Jonas took hold of his hair and pulled him brutally back. The man screamed as he collided with the headboard. Jonas pressed the bottle against his throat again, and this time a piece of glass slid into the soft tissue on his throat. The man lay there without moving a muscle.

"Shut up and lie still!"

Panic shone in the man's face. His chest was rising and falling faster now.

The adrenaline rush gave Jonas tunnel vision. His heart was galloping in his chest, and he noticed that he was hyperventilating. His eyes were swimming.

He tried to get back to the volcano that raged in him when he realized that Minister of Transport and Communications Hermann Eliassen had tricked him. He felt nausea building up at the thought. The transition between blind fury and a paralyzing contempt for everything he'd been forced to go through. Thought back on all the times he'd forced himself to pretend as if desire and admiration had driven him into the arms of this man. All the times he had cried, vomited, and injured himself. A whole year of broken promises about participation in the trainee program for New Voices. A whole year of lies. A whole year of disgusting sexual services.

"It will be too close to take the two of you into the program, too personal. . . ."

The words still resounded in the room long after they were said. Jonas noticed that most of all, he wanted to drive the bottle farther into Hermann Eliassen's throat with full force, but something stopped him from doing that. There was something pitiful and sickly about the politician. Killing a naked, defenseless man he'd been kissing and caressing half an hour earlier no longer seemed tempting. He took a deep breath; it felt as if his lungs were about to burst. He decided at the same moment, and acted.

He threw the bottle with full force at the wall so it exploded.

Couldn't care less that the racket would make those in the adjacent room pound on the door or call the front desk. It would be over then regardless, and Jonas did not intend to remain at the scene, even if it definitely was Eliassen who had the most to lose by being found bloody and naked in a hotel room with a seventeen-year-old boy on top of him.

When Jonas met a security guard in the elevator five minutes later, he was dressed and calm. Moved politely to the side as the guard ran out. Jonas entered the elevator and pressed the button for the first floor. Knew that it would take time for the guard to make his way into Eliassen's room, and that the only one who could expose his involvement in what had happened was the Minister of Transport and Communications himself. But he was, and would remain, as silent as the grave.

iljar Ravn Gudmundsson felt every single nerve ending and muscle fiber in his body protesting. He'd been waiting for hours in a small office. The room seemed airtight. Since the policemen picked him up at the apartment three hours earlier, little had happened. He knew he should call Øveraas, but his job was probably history regardless. Ranveig had mentioned that the police thought he was suspiciously very involved in what had happened. This was actually dead serious. Viljar was about to leave the room for a smoke break when Lotte Skeisvoll suddenly appeared, along with a world-weary gray suit in his fifties with sad and mournful eyes.

The two police investigators pointed to tell him to turn around and go back into the room. Viljar sat down in the same chair in which he'd spent the last few hours. The man with the Saint Bernard eyes quickly took control, which surprised Viljar a little. He thought Lotte would ask the questions.

"Why weren't you at work today, and why didn't you answer the door when the police came to get you?" The man talked quickly and rationally in a monotone, robotic voice. From East Norway, Viljar decided.

"I was sick and didn't feel like talking with anyone. I didn't have any unsettled business with the police either."

"Have you ever heard of obstructing an investigation?"

Viljar snorted and shook his head. "Yes, you can report me then."

"Where were you between six o'clock and eight o'clock this morning?"

"I was at home in my apartment sleeping. Or that is, I tried to get up at seven o'clock, but gave up. I was too sick to go to work."

"What illness?"

This was an unpleasant question. He didn't want to tell about his anxiety.

"Stomach flu. Diarrhea. The runs. Call it whatever the hell you want. . . ." The corners of Lotte's mouth quivered a little, but the man from East Norway didn't seem to be affected.

"Maybe it's time that you start taking this seriously, Gudmundsson. There's been another homicide. Can anyone verify that you really were at home between six and eight today?"

Viljar took in the new information. Felt how the anxiety came creeping back . . . Forced it away. He had the world's best alibi, and they ought to know it. Communication within the force was clearly very poor here.

"I don't know the name of the police constable, who by the way should probably take a course in how you stay unseen during surveillance, but you sent a man after me when I left the police station last night. I assume that your log will show who was on duty last night, and who can thereby document that I was in my apartment the whole time from when I came home at one thirty until you picked me up."

Lotte stopped Olav's series of questions with a brief hand gesture. She leaned forward and looked Viljar in the eyes.

"A detective, Viljar? Why do you think we put surveillance on you?"

"I don't know," Viljar replied. "I just saw that there was a man following me from the police station all the way home. I figured it was you who'd sent the guy after me. . . ."

Who the hell would have followed me if it wasn't the police?

"We had a police constable follow you. That's true, but it was only to make sure that you didn't go out on new adventures. He turned around as soon as you went inside." Lotte looked extremely serious, while the little gray suit was very amused.

"Does this mean you don't have an alibi, Gudmundsson?" Olav Scheldrup Hansen sneered openly as he said it.

Viljar shook his head. He understood less and less of this. He had twisted himself into a fishing net. "You can believe what you want, but it wasn't me. Would I have sent idiotic emails to myself, in order to carry out killings that I've alerted myself to? Do you understand how sick that sounds?"

"Do you understand how sick the man who is doing this is?" Scheldrup Hansen was still sneering.

"Fine. You can take all the tests you want on me." Viljar pulled out a strand of hair and held it in front of the detective.

Scheldrup Hansen took the strand of hair. Curled it between his fingers and started up again. "Be quite certain that we will check you out in every conceivable way. With as many biological traces as this murderer leaves behind him, there is actually a slight possibility that they are placed there to mislead us. If you were to go free on finger-prints and DNA, that doesn't mean that you're beyond suspicion.

"So, how long have you known Rita Lothe?" The Kripos investigator was evidently not done.

Viljar sighed heavily. "How many times do I have to tell you? I have nothing to do with this, and I've never met Rita Lothe."

"There you're mistaken, Gudmundsson." Olav fished out a print-out of a photograph.

When Viljar saw the picture, he instinctively recoiled so quickly that the chair scraped along the floor, and he let out a whining sound.

"What the hell!"

It felt as if his heart had stopped, as if it had suddenly come loose from its moorings and fallen down on the floor in front of him. In panic he glanced at Lotte. She met his gaze. Resolute. Hard. Her eyes had a decisiveness that frightened him. Viljar turned slowly around back to the picture.

He could not believe what he was seeing. Now he was truly scared. He felt the nausea spurting up his throat. Did not want to look, but the photograph was like flypaper. Viljar could not get out a sound. He put his hand in front of his mouth, so the contents of his stomach wouldn't come up.

"I found this picture on Rita Lothe's Facebook page."

The picture showed Viljar and Rita sitting close to each other while they smiled into the camera. Both clearly very drunk.

"This was uploaded a week before the murder. Do you want to change your explanation?"

This was evidently news to Lotte Skeisvoll too. She looked at the interview leader with raised eyebrows. Viljar could not for the life of him remember either when or how that picture was taken. Festive mood evidently, but they looked like a couple. He didn't answer Scheldrup Hansen's question, simply shook his head.

"The woman has written your name several times in her calendar. You maintain you don't know her, but then you are entwined with the murder victim on a picture taken quite recently. You lack an alibi for both murders, you try to avoid the police, and you find yourself in the vicinity of a possible victim number two the night before the second murder. To me that's enough circumstantial evidence that I no longer believe you."

The investigator droned on in the same monotonous voice, not taking his eyes off Viljar for a moment.

It was boiling inside Viljar's head now. He needed air. Air and a smoke. Lotte did not come to his defense. She sat looking down at her notes. Almost seemed as if she had given up completely.

"We're going to hold you overnight, Gudmundsson." Scheldrup Hansen looked at him and got back the fawning smile he'd had at the start of the interview. "Until we've checked out your movements the past few days, and gone through your computer, we are keeping you in custody."

He stood up and left Viljar and Lotte.

Lotte looked amazed, to put it mildly, but after a few seconds it was as if she had collected herself. She stood up suddenly. Turned toward Viljar and raised her index finger at him. It was shaking.

"You stay here, Viljar. You damned well better not move!"

Lotte slammed the door to the little office, while the darkness took full control over his fragile mind. He collapsed on the chair, and for the first time in four years, the tears came.

Haugesund Police Station
Wednesday afternoon, October 15, 2014

The cell walls were creeping in. Viljar could see that, centimeter by centimeter, they were moving closer to him. He sat on the lowered bunk with his legs curled up under him in a kind of seated fetal position. He knew purely logically that concrete walls don't move, but they were doing it anyway. . . .

The first ten minutes of confinement, the panic attack had torn him to shreds. Made him hammer on the cell door and shout all the oaths and bile in the world against the society outside. Pathetic. Gradually he calmed down enough to sit on the bunk, but the anxiety still pursued him in waves. Viljar's nerves were frayed and he jumped every time there was the slightest sound from outside.

There were no windows. Only bare walls painted in a shade of blue that most resembled the shirt color of a police constable. It was a myth that blue instills peace and harmony in people.

"Myth busted!" he said out loud in English, imitating the voice of Jamie Hyneman in the series *MythBusters*.

The gallows humor helped a little. The blue walls were still creeping.

Viljar was in a cold sweat. His brain was uninhabited. Every time he tried to capture bits of what had happened the last few days, anxiety came washing over him again, and it took several minutes to collect himself. Concentrate on breathing normally. Convince his own brain that the pain in his chest wasn't dangerous. Vigdis had taught him these techniques to better handle the hyperventilation and anxiety, and he'd gotten more skilled at pushing away the heavy thoughts that produced the attacks. Now it was in vain.

"Can you stand still, damn it!" he shouted at the walls. They could crawl, but evidently they had no ears. Viljar threw his arms around himself as he sat on the bunk. Understood his own madness, but was unable to do anything about it. All reason was blocked. In his delusion, he even thought he could hear a grand piano from the police building on the floor above. He was a powerless witness to the fact that his own mind was crumbling.

In a final attempt to understand the insanity, Viljar started talking out loud to his own anxiety. Vigdis had said he could try this trick. It seemed a bit far-fetched, but right now it was sink or swim. . . .

"Come on then," he said to the anxiety. "I'm not afraid of you. You're not dangerous." He fixed his gaze on a spot on the wall in front of him.

"You are just feelings. This is a farce. Come on then," he said again.

Little by little, Viljar noticed that the paralyzing panic was starting to leave him. Ecstatic that the method seemed to work, he used stronger words and more energy every time he talked to that point on the wall.

"Go to hell! I don't want you here, you miserable parasite. Go away!"

He noticed with astonishment that the anxiety was receding. He ordered the walls back in place. Focused intensely on rational and reasonable thoughts. It was frightfully delicate, but Viljar somehow or other managed to collect himself. The piano music stopped.

Why do I find myself in this situation? He asked himself that question, revealing a completely new perspective. *It's not a coincidence,* he decided.

I'm here because that's what the killer wants.

Someone was trying to pin the guilt on him by placing him in the middle of the beehive with both hands full of honey. He had to get out, and made a silent prayer to higher powers.

Ten seconds later, the cell door opened. . . .

Requiem: Sequentia

I am satisfied. Every slightest sequence is going as expected. The piece has started to take shape. Not a single false phrasing. Small changes in the composition here and there. A kettledrum instead of a cymbal. I enjoy the feeling. Not killing, that's just a necessity, but creating . . .

It's lovely to see the various instruments come in at the right time. How they overlap one another. That people act predictably. Every single little movement, every choice they make, is part of the creation, and it works. I smile at the evening sun. I've found myself a cozy little nook on the terrace. For the moment, the pain is only a dull grumbling in the background. I relax with a beer and a good book. I've mowed the lawn. Suddenly it strikes me that I've done it for the last time. New delight. It's important to be happy about the things at hand. This day has been liberating.

Right from when the day started with a dull crack at Stord and until I sat down out here in the autumn sun.

The third row of information and preparatory material is packed in the bag beside me. The next step is unpleasant. The first two have gone playfully easily, and I've had reason to keep myself at a proper distance from it all. Observing but not participating. Seeing the investigators inspect the corpse of Rita Lothe was a rush. I was walking on pillows of air in all the excitement. I was seen but ignored, exactly as I'd foreseen.

The same thing today. Only small changes. All the uproar around my journalist is a challenge, but it amuses me. They've found the link much faster than I thought. But now it remains to be seen whether they find the actual context in time.

Tomorrow and the next day will be a test of whether I have the spine for this. I think about Jonas. Steel myself. If the work is to be completed, I must go through this part of the process too. At the same time, the risk of making a mistake undoubtedly increases now as I take a step out of my comfort zone. So far, it has all been a game. An exercise to see whether I am capable of going further. Challenging my own limits. Enter into the artwork and become a part of it.

Now days are coming when the whole orchestra will go into action. With each instrument that steps out of the silence, the pressure on me increases. They have to see me. Feel me. Be me.

It will be spectacular. I revel in the thought of what the newspapers are going to write after the third one is found. They will see it then. Someone will understand. They must actually understand it. That's the point. It can't be helped that I myself will become visible in the approaching process. My worry is not essential in this connection. This is much bigger than I, and so much greater than the pain I cause myself by executing what the script says. . . .

It's time to go into the hall. It's time to make myself visible and vulnerable. It's time to swing the hammer.

Maestro . . .

Haugesund Police Station
Wednesday afternoon, October 15, 2014

Olav Scheldrup Hansen closed the door to his temporary office and plopped down in the creaking chair. The adjustment mechanism was stuck, and it was set too high, so he sat there dangling his legs.

"What is it with women and their need for control?" he asked himself. He could not understand why Lotte got so angry about the picture he set out during the interview. It was circumstantial evidence that Viljar Ravn Gudmundsson and Rita Lothe were acquainted, but she evidently thought that such confrontations should be approved by her first. That he had ordered the arrest of Viljar was clearly not okay either, which proved what he had thought all along: Lotte Skeisvoll was a long-winded stickler, and if he let her get her hands on the rudder, the ship would founder.

Lotte would have to accept that she couldn't steer this boat alone. The team she had selected actually spoke for itself. Most of them were as sluggish as the last kilometer of an Ironman course up a mountainside.

When the laptop was finally finished with all the start-up functions,

Olav started work by checking up on Viljar Ravn Gudmundsson a little more thoroughly than the Haugesund folks had managed so far. He was a hundred percent certain that the man was hiding something. He'd seen it on several occasions during the interview. The question was what, and why he was wrapping the net around himself. Apart from the shot itself that killed Johannes Fredriksen at Stord, it was all amateurishly performed. The killer did nothing to hide his actions.

Rita Lothe's Facebook profile opened quickly because he had searched for it less than an hour ago. The profile contained only five photos, all of recent vintage, and only one where Viljar Ravn Gudmundsson figured. Olav called up Lars Stople and ordered him to check the profile for Rita Lothe's family. The account had only been set up in August, and included only seven status reports and a friend list of fourteen persons, none of them family. What was even more remarkable was that she had ignored a series of friend requests, far more than she had accepted. If the profile was genuine, this indicated that this was a lady who wanted to be private on Facebook, but still had a public profile where anyone had access.

Olav then turned to Johannes Fredriksen, but he evidently had no profile at all on social media. The investigator sighed and scratched his thinning head of hair. He took out the papers the team had collected about Viljar Ravn Gudmundsson in the course of the day. He would just have to read his way to the answers the old-fashioned way.

The papers told little or nothing that led the investigator toward what Gudmundsson was trying to hide. His history as a journalist was interesting enough. Impressive work in uncovering scandals and skulduggery that the police wouldn't have managed to figure out without his help. But somewhere along the way, he had evidently gotten tired. After the revelations that made him a national celebrity in 2010, there was little to find other than boring articles. It seemed like Gudmundsson was on autopilot. *Can there be something in that case with the Minister of Transport and Communications?* He called his department in Oslo and asked to have all the papers concerning the Hermann Eliassen case sent over. At the same time, he confirmed that Eliassen was still in prison. *Maybe there's another connection to the same case?*

Further along in the documents about Gudmundsson, he became aware of a detail that caught his attention. Earlier in the day, one of the constables had conducted a routine interview with the editor of *Haugesund News*. In the interview it came out that Gudmundsson had been ordered by newspaper management to seek psychiatric help in the winter of 2010. The journalist had been irascible and unstable for some time and was starting to be a strain on the work environment. A few minutes later, he had the editor on the line. The conversation that ensued gave Olav everything he needed. Editor Øveraas was a plainspoken monkey who clearly did not have much use for his journalist. At the media house, Viljar was a dead man careerwise.

Olav packed up his things on the desktop. Took the notepad and a pen with him. He was happy to confront Gudmundsson. He rounded the corner and passed Lotte Skeisvoll's office. It was empty. Just as well, because he had no intention of dragging her with him anyway.

After asking for directions in the corridors, he made his way to the holding cell and got a constable passing by to unlock it. When the door opened, Olav stood there like one big question mark. It was empty. He turned to the constable and asked if they had other cells for suspects. The constable shook his head.

"Only the drunk tank, but we don't put folks in there who are suspects in other cases."

The Kripos investigator stomped back to his office, but was stopped on the way by the city attorney, Synne Lie.

"Is there something wrong?" she asked with a fake smile.

It didn't suit her. He looked at the pencil-thin figure in front of him and let all his frustration out on her. "Hell yes, there's something wrong. Someone or other has let Viljar Ravn Gudmundsson out of the cell!"

Synne Lie cocked her head and looked at him like a little sparrow waiting for bread crumbs. "I was the one who signed the release papers. At the request of investigation leader Lotte Skeisvoll. She expected that you would come to me, and asked me to tell you that the reason for the release was that all physical traces point toward a different perpetrator. She also asked me to remind you that making arrests is not one of your duties. You're here to assist the investigation, not lead it."

Viljar's apartment on Austmannavegen, Haugesund
Wednesday evening, October 15, 2014

There are days with bad karma. When every choice you make leads to a downward spiral. Breaking out of that spiral seems impossible. Everything you say, everything you do, sends you further down toward the abyss. It was not until Lotte Skeisvoll unexpectedly showed up at the door of his cell and let him out that he was able to make the turn. He looked at her inquisitively.

"Wasn't I put under arrest?"

"No, it must be a misunderstanding." Lotte did not let her facial expression reveal the reason for the sudden reversal.

"All suspicions removed?" Viljar knew the answer, but asked mostly to complain.

"I can promise you that we are going to be a pimple on your ass in the days to come. If you think about changing the channel on your TV at home, I want a written application in triplicate. You're not out of the picture, but next time you're sitting in a cell, it's because I say you should be."

Viljar had spent the hours in freedom the way he had thought in the cell. Searched out places he knew had video surveillance, kept track of receipts from stores, talked with the neighbor in the stairwell on his way into the apartment. For the first time in a week, he also called his father. Counted on the phone being traceable. No one would get him without an alibi more than once. He still felt the feeling of terror from seeing the cell walls approaching, and his hands were still shaking as he sat peacefully on the couch. Viljar put a sachet of snus under his lip and fired up a fresh cigarette.

An hour after he came home, a police constable brought back his computer. Viljar started on the excavation work that lay ahead of him.

He quickly searched Rita Lothe's public Facebook profile. The picture of him and her was actually the last one that had been posted. He stored the pictures from the profile in a folder. Copied the status updates, and noted the names of the Facebook friends.

Viljar began by studying the surroundings in the picture. Behind him and Rita, he could see black leather barstools around a mahogany-colored hexagonal bar. Round globe lights in the ceiling, dark wallpaper or paint on the walls. Farther back, he could barely make out a Winchester-style sofa set. Viljar smiled and nodded in recognition.

"Bestastuå," he said out loud to himself. The nightclub had a reputation for being a "flea market" for worn-out old ladies seeking fresh pastures, but Viljar still had a hard time seeing that they were happier after their nocturnal escapades.

He knew that he'd been at the nightclub only two times so far this year. Once in connection with a sponsor party for FK Haugesund in March. The other time a few weeks ago, when Henrik Thomsen insisted that he and Øystein Vindheim go with him after they met by chance at Café MM on a Saturday night. Viljar had protested, but after a while they let themselves be dragged along by that idiot.

Viljar opened his online bank account and searched back until he found entries from the bar at Bestastuå. September 20, he noted. It was a Sunday. The entries were listed with the times 12:30 A.M., 1:03 A.M., 1:47 A.M., and 2:22 A.M. Steadily larger amounts. It was evident that he'd been on a spending spree toward the end.

He remembered very little.

The arrival and the first drink together with Henrik were there, but after that . . . ? Viljar remembered dancing at the disco, and he vaguely recalled a dispute with a massive guy who claimed to be a policeman out in the smoking area, but no Rita Lothe. He wrote down on his to-do list that he had to talk with Henrik and Øystein about this.

Viljar started checking out the friend list for Rita. He quickly determined that they had no friends in common, and the fourteen friends she had were all unfamiliar to him, apart from two local celebrities that "everyone" in Haugesund was friends with on Facebook. Radio journalist Hans Indbjo obviously, and the TV 2 personality Ragnar Håtveit. Most of the others had private profiles, and he didn't get as far with the search as he'd hoped.

Viljar was suddenly struck by a suspicion. He looked at the status updates. Not a single friend had posted an "R.I.P." or similar message after her name was published earlier today. None of the fourteen friends. No one from the family, who he knew were out there, had written anything. This didn't add up. When people die, very little time passes before the whole Wall is spiced with hearts and final greetings to the deceased. This could not possibly be Rita Lothe's real Facebook profile. But the picture of him and Rita was genuine. *Someone is trying to make me a scapegoat*, thought Viljar.

His train of thought was disturbed by sounds from out in the hall. Viljar froze.

The door to the apartment opened, and he heard a thud, as if something was thrown on the floor. Viljar was on his feet in a bound, but stopped abruptly when he saw the figure in the hall.

"What the hell! Are *you* here now?"

Viljar looked at the ungainly body standing with stooped shoulders in the doorway. It was as if legs and arms had decided that the boy would play professional basketball, while the rest of his body struggled hard against it. Alexander's gaze wandered. An uncertain look crossed his face before he assumed his usual sullen expression.

"You don't want me here now either, maybe? Are you hooking up with someone?"

Two-part question. One part made Viljar want to open his arms to give him a hug, while the other provoked him so that he wanted to give the boy a good tongue-lashing. The result was neither. He stood there like a post and stammered out what was supposed to be a clear message that Alex wasn't allowed to talk to him that way.

Alexander looked around and wrinkled his nose. He drew his fingers through his greasy black hair and shook his head. Since his hands were at head level anyway, he could just as well squeeze a pimple.

"My God, Dad. You need to get some Polish cleaning help or something. Seriously! That woman you work with had to clean up here after the cops left. Fucking embarrassing."

Viljar looked at the boy in despair. This was no place for a sixteen-year-old. Ranveig was completely right about that. According to the agreement, his mother should have Alex on weekdays and Viljar on weekends. They'd arranged it that way because she often had weekend shifts in the kitchen at the nursing home. Necessary extra income to pad the meager returns from the hairstyling salon she ran at home. But the past year, Alexander had more or less thumbed his nose at all agreements and came and went as he pleased.

The high-rise apartment reeked of smoke and old sweat, even though Ranveig had cleaned the worst of it. She had stacked empty pizza cartons in the corner of the hall. The clothes were lying where he'd stepped out of them the past few days.

The boy looked at his father and shook his head once more. "You'd think you were the one with ADHD, not me. Don't you ever clean up when I'm away, or what?"

The correct answer would have been no, but Viljar declined to confirm his son's assertions.

"Listen up, now. You can't just stroll into my living room and throw a lot of abuse at me. I damn well don't accept that. I can stand living in this mess, and you should be at your mother's now."

The boy just stood there by the sink with his back to his father without saying anything.

"I can't take any more of that fucking bitch!" he screamed suddenly, throwing a half-full glass of milk at the wall with full force.

Viljar cowered and knew he had to do something. Say something. He sat down on a chair. Alexander's shoulders were shaking. A long time passed without anything being said or done. Viljar wanted to get up. Go over and hug the boy who was standing there. Instead he stayed seated. In no condition to seize the moment.

Alexander turned and walked calmly toward the doorway to the living room. He wiped away what must have been tears with the sleeve of an oversized hoodie.

Viljar tried to hold him back by taking hold of his arm. "Listen. Now, you clean up that mess you made. There are shards of glass all over the floor."

His son drew his arm back, turned around quickly, and shoved his father. "Don't touch me! Clean it yourself. It's completely disgusting in here anyway! Why should I care when you don't?"

Alexander slammed every door that he passed on his way to the little room that Viljar tried to convince himself was completely adequate for an adolescent. Seconds later "The Eternally Damned" by Einherjer boomed from worn-out speakers.

Viljar sighed and tried to return to the thought he was having before Alexander stomped in.

Who is trying to nail me to these killings?

If he had any enemies who were willing to go as far as this, then somehow or other, they must be connected to the Jonas case.

Reluctantly, Viljar took his eyes off the screen. He wouldn't get anything else done until he had put his thoughts in order, and right then and there, that was an impossibility. Alexander had turned up the volume on the stereo to max in pure defiance. Viljar entered Hilde's number. He had to call her, even if it was unpleasant. She had to see about coming and getting Alex. His fingers trembled over the numbers on the display. He had to concentrate to hit them right. The cooperation between the two of them could hardly be called good. He steeled himself against the tirade of accusations that usually came before he had finished the first sentence. There were days when he was completely convinced he'd had a child with the Antichrist.

Four years earlier . . .
Torvastad, Karmøy
Friday midmorning, August 20, 2010

Jonas looked quickly around him, like a deer that catches the scent of the hunter in the bushes. Knew that no one could see them in here, but felt the fear even so. *What if . . .* He could not allow himself that. Could not even finish the thought.

Jonas let himself be embraced by the outstretched arms. Felt his pulse rate rise as he lay his head next to the hollow of Fredric's throat. He drank in the aroma of a fresh and spicy cologne. Enjoyed the tingling feeling along his spine as the beard stubble scraped his cheek. Fredric stroked his back with one hand while the other kept a firm hold around his waist.

There was still summer in the air. Almost twenty degrees Celsius, and the sun broiled against Jonas's brown thighs. He loosened the tense grip a little and let his hands stroke the muscles along his friend's back. Carefully he let one hand glide down under the denim shorts and noticed that Fredric was getting short-winded. With tender and careful kisses, he moved from the neck and down along Fredric's chest.

He stood up and pulled Fredric next to him again. Kissed him. Affectionately at first, then more greedily. He could both see and feel the desire in Fredric now. In this one moment, nothing else existed. No worries. No fear. No regret. No shame.

Hermann Eliassen was history. Everything that had happened in the hotel room in Haugesund the day before was swept away.

His friend took his face carefully in his hands. Pushed it gently away from him and studied it. With his thumb he stroked Jonas from his nostrils and in under his eyes. He shifted his head a little and gasped as Jonas took a firmer hold around his rear end. Fredric always got a mischievous gleam in his eyes when he got horny. Jonas knew this, and loved it. The lust bubbled up in him, but he controlled himself. Wanted to enjoy the moment. Keep the wonderful feeling of bare arm muscles holding him tight. He bit Fredric on the earlobe and whispered loving words. Stroked his free hand across the suntanned chest and stomach. Brushed teasingly over his shorts at regular intervals. He could see that Fredric was on the edge of losing control. He was breathing heavily against Jonas's neck, and he felt his friend's heart pounding against his chest.

When he loosened the button a little later and pulled down the zipper, it was if all the energy was released from Fredric's body. He clung to Jonas and gasped for air.

Jonas let it happen, and didn't care if he got soiled. This was pure and lovely. Not dirty like the day before. Here there was balance. Two people who had sincere feelings for each other. He stroked Fredric across his back and let himself be thrown into a wave of pleasure as his friend gradually allowed him to release everything that had built up inside him the past twenty-four hours.

A branch that snapped in the grove made him wake suddenly. His heart turned a somersault, and he looked in panic from side to side.

Suddenly he felt certain. Someone had been standing in the forest watching them.

Uncertainty and fear took hold in him. For a brief moment everything had just been a sea of delight. What was happening between him and Fredric was one thing. If that was discovered, it would no longer be bearable for him on the island. He knew how his father would react. . . . Something else altogether were the consequences of what he'd done the day before in the hotel room. He hadn't thought for a second that he was also putting his friend in danger. It was only in the hours afterwards that he understood what concentric circles in the water his choice had entailed.

For all Jonas knew, this could be the end. The end of everything fine and beautiful they had together. From here on, there were only denials, playacting, and lies. The die was cast. There was no way back. Nothing could be made undone.

Haugesund Police Station
Thursday morning, October 16, 2014

Lotte saw that Olav Scheldrup Hansen was ready to confront her the moment she rounded the corner on her way to the conference room. He was in a wide stance by the door, puffing himself up. Dressed in a suit as always, and the little that was left of his hair on top was combed back. Lotte raised her cell phone to her ear as she walked and acted as if she were talking to someone. As she approached the Kripos investigator, she pointed at her phone while she walked right past him.

The entire investigation group was gathered, waiting obediently for her to start the meeting. She ended the fictional call and waved Scheldrup Hansen to his place. He tried to take the floor as he was sitting down. Lotte simply raised her voice louder than his.

"We'll wait a little for open discussion, Olav. There's a lot on the agenda today, but the city attorney has asked to speak first to explain some structures and chain of command for us as a team. Synne, can you do that right now?"

Synne Lie stood up and took the floor. In extremely clear terms, she accounted for what the various roles in the team involved. She was crystal clear about the chain of command. No one should do anything at all on orders from anyone other than the investigation leader, and Lotte, for her part, must clarify everything that concerned arrests, house searches, interviews, and confiscation with her. Synne made a dramatic pause after the word "arrests" and looked straight at the Kripos investigator.

Lotte's deliberate move this morning had its effect. Olav Scheldrup Hansen was off balance and had lost the room. She was a little unhappy that she indirectly corrected him in public, but realized there was no other way if she was going to regain control over the team and the investigation.

"And who do we go to if we are in sincere disagreement about which way the investigation is going?" Scheldrup Hansen put on a scornful sneer to be sure that everyone got the sarcasm.

"Then you come to me," said Synne Lie. "I will listen to your objections. Last time I checked the papers, Kripos was asked to *assist* the investigation, not lead it."

The attorney looked at him with a mild and friendly expression as she said that.

Lotte was about to start the review of evidence when the phone vibrated in her pocket. She looked quickly at the display and then asked the group to take a five-minute break. She had to answer this.

It was Anne. Lotte cursed to herself on the way out of the meeting room. She had completely forgotten to deal with her sister's problems, and now she knew there would be a new round of accusations and reproaches about how little she cared about her. It didn't turn out that way. There was a calmer version of Anne today. The problems she had on Tuesday were already forgotten. Heroin has that effect. New problems always show up that overshadow the old ones.

"Lotte . . . Do you have time to see me today? I want to talk with you about something important."

It was always something important.

"I'm terribly busy until lunch, but maybe after that," Lotte said, so her sister wouldn't think she didn't want to.

She had a perennial guilty conscience that she wasn't supportive enough, even though she knew that giving drug addicts too much support to lean on only helped them stay in that life. The only motivation an addict has to get out of the hell of heroin is that it really is *hell*. If you give them money, food, consolation, a job, and a roof over their head, there's no point in quitting.

"After that is fine."

Lotte noticed that there was a tenderness in her sister's voice she hadn't heard in a long time. Maybe this *was* important.

"Great, Anne. I'll try to be there in a few hours, but I can't promise an exact time. Okay?"

Lotte breathed out after the call, pressed the mental button that suppressed her guilty conscience, and went back into the meeting room.

"First item on the agenda is the crime scenes. Lars, you have the lead there?"

Lars Stople got up from his chair, but in contrast to most in the new century, Lars still swore by flip chart and marker. He turned to a blank page and wrote down the main points while he talked.

"We are undoubtedly dealing with a man who does not have the slightest intention of concealing his tracks. It has actually occurred to us that there are so many traces at each crime scene that they may be put there to mislead us. We have fine-combed both Rita Lothe's apartment and the ridge behind Johannes Fredriksen's house in Stord.

"We have good fingerprints that don't match Rita Lothe's on a wineglass that had been used and a cognac glass in the apartment. The same print is found on the Nesbø book and on a plastic glass we found in the forest at the other scene. In other words, there is no doubt that the same person has been at both places.

"Besides the fingerprints, we have biological material. We will get a complete DNA analysis of the killer. However, we don't expect to get hits in the database when this analysis is finished."

Lotte got up and went over to Lars. Straightened one leg on the flip chart so that it stood right. She cleared her throat nervously and turned back to the constable. "Did we get any results from the pharmacies?"

"Unfortunately, no. That lead is dead. He must have bought the anesthetic somewhere other than in town. We expanded the search to the neighboring municipalities, again without result."

"Fine. Is there anything else that can link us to who the perpetrator is, Lars? As I understand it, we have enough on him to get a conviction once he's found?"

"That's right. It's probably as simple as what we talked about yesterday. Either he intends to stay completely beyond suspicion, or else being arrested is utterly inconsequential to him."

Lars paused, but continued when Lotte indicated with a hand gesture that he should say something else. "Yes . . . So . . . The rest of what I have to say is pure speculation. Based on the crime scene investigations, we choose to conclude the following." He wrote four points on the flip chart.

"First, we choose to believe that this is a man. In addition to the obvious fact that Rita Lothe demonstrably had sex a short time before she died, we also have other circumstantial evidence. Short strands of gray hair that don't originate from Rita. For that matter, we found the same in the sleeping bag at Stord. The size of the fingerprints from both places shows that this concerns a person with large hands. Finally we include the fact that it takes a certain amount of physical strength to lift an unconscious person weighing seventy kilos over a balcony railing. Everything indicates that it is a man," Lars concluded the first point.

"Second, there is a lot that indicates that the man resides in Haugesund or in the immediate area. Both of the killings happened in our district, and the emails have gone to a local journalist.

"Third, we think that the man is over forty. Here we are far from certain, but we have a few indications. Some of the hairs we found are gray, as I said. Now, obviously men can turn gray at a young age, but the majority have passed forty before that starts to happen. At Stord, there were pans left behind and some food scraps that are not typical everyday fare for younger people. In addition we found cigarette butts in the lean-to at Rommetveit. Not commercial cigarette butts but hand-rolled. That too is a dying art. Basically it's older people and drug addicts who still swear by loose tobacco.

"The fourth and final point is the emails, and I think you have the best overview of them, Knut. Isn't that right?"

Knut Veldetun stood up and went over to the projector. He put a flash drive in the corresponding machine and then opened a PDF copy of the two emails.

"As you see, both emails have the same sender. The address steinamli@gmail.com is fictional. Or more precisely, the person behind the email address is fictional. It is registered in the name of Stein Åmli, and he set up the email account three weeks ago. No activity at the address before Monday morning, when the first email was sent."

Knut cleared his throat and took a sip of water before he continued.

"Everyone here knows how easy it is to set up an email account, so we won't dwell on that. Hope it's okay with you, Lotte, that we assume this person is using a false name?"

Lotte nodded in response at the same time as she heard a heavy sigh from her right side. Scheldrup Hansen's patience was evidently at the breaking point. Knut Veldetun indefatigably kept talking.

"What is more interesting, however, is what Google's experts have helped us with. They've shared their information with us, which has given us some interesting results. For one thing, we know where both emails were sent from."

Several on the team looked up now with interest.

"The first email that Gudmundsson received was sent from the recreational club the Old Slaughterhouse here in Haugesund on Monday at 08:05 hours. The other from Rica Maritim Hotel on Tuesday at 16:02 hours. We have obviously checked out both places, and we've questioned the staff. So far without any results, but I got the obvious answer from one of our IT people here in the building. He asked me to check whether these places have open wireless networks. 'Guest networks.' "

Lotte interrupted him. "So that means that the man who sent the emails wasn't using computers that are at those two places, but brought his own?"

"Yes, either that or a smartphone or tablet. Probably he hasn't even been inside the building. It's very easy to connect to Wi-Fi networks from nearby, for example in a car. Neither of these places has video surveillance, unfortunately; otherwise, we could have looked for parked cars in the relevant time frame."

Lotte took the floor again. "We'll choose to let the email lead rest for the time being. Pick it up again if more emails arrive. What else do you have?"

"Well . . . Not much, I'm afraid."

Knut turned off the projector and went to sit down. Lars Stople had the floor again.

"The codes at the bottom of the email, have you found anything out there?"

"No. I'm working on it, but for now these are just meaningless numbers and letters. At least we can rule out any of the usual coding tools. We've checked that."

Lars Stople wrote a fifth and final point on the flip chart.

"There is one thing I've personally had some thoughts about, which seems like a natural place to start to poke around." He made a dramatic pause, breathed in, and continued.

"I think we're talking about a man who has an occupation where he has greater access to information than ordinary citizens. I've tried myself, and it's just impossible to work your way to the acquittal of Lothe and Fredriksen on the internet or by searches in old newspaper articles. The killer must have direct knowledge someway or other of both cases, and perhaps also has access to old court decisions."

Lars stopped a moment before setting out his hypothesis for the others.

"I think—and I underscore that these are only speculations—that the man we are searching for works in the police, in the legal system, in the media, or at a law firm. It's in such places that you can find the information he's made use of."

Olav Scheldrup Hansen had not said a word during the session. Now was the first time they heard his voice.

"Listen, what a great team. An eternity of truisms, and not a single time was the name Viljar Ravn Gudmundsson mentioned. Oh well . . . I can agree that perhaps he's not a killer, but in that case, someone out there is having a strangely good time pasting his name on everything that happens. What enemies does he really have? Eliassen, for example? I've checked him out, and I've just had it confirmed that he's still in prison, but can there be others with a connection to that scandal? Or is Eliassen so powerful that he can pull strings from behind bars?"

Olav Scheldrup Hansen threw out his hands.

"With Stople's method of elimination, we are thus down to about a thousand potential killers in this district, I would think. But the elephant in the room is named Gudmundsson, and no one seems to want to see him. Can someone please order white canes for us from the equipment warehouse? God knows we need them."

When the third death sentence landed in Viljar's in-box, he was deep into the news articles about the double murders. It was unpleasant to write about a case in which he himself was involved. A complete breach of good journalistic practice, which the editor completely ignored. In addition, Johan Øveraas had asked him to write about it in a personal reportage form. *"A journey into the darkest corners of the murder case,"* he'd said. Viljar was on the verge of strangling the editor, but this was not the day to pick a fight.

Drawing yourself into the case in this manner, where you would lead the reader through the events as a kind of guide, was not only morbid and disrespectful, but also like placing your head on the block for serious criticism. Viljar could not protest, however. He had to go along with it.

He looked through what he'd written. There was a fact box that summarized the course of events, structured by time. Two other fact boxes presented the murder victims. Facsimiles of the two emails that he himself had received. A personal running text of over two thousand words, where he described his experiences. Obviously written in the first person to increase the drama. There were big photos from both crime scenes, and the headline was the type that figuratively speaking compelled the reader to read the story itself: MY MEETING WITH A MURDERER.

Calling the emails a "meeting" was stretching the rope to the breaking point, but the editor wanted it that way. The newspaper was sitting on a case where they had every element in play to be the premier source, and they would show the national press that in the Friday edition. They were in possession of considerably more information than the Oslo newspapers *VG* and *Dagbladet* could dream of, and now it would be published under the biggest headlines possible.

Ranveig had been given very unusual orders in the editor's office the day before, and now she was loaded down with work that went far beyond her actual job description. Viljar could not understand why Øveraas absolutely wanted to use her for this when they had fully ambulatory news reporters available. But that was the editor in a nutshell. When Øveraas didn't find some object or other on which he could exercise physical violence, forced labor was a good substitute to show who ruled the roost.

Ranveig was tasked with the more serious bits of the assignment. Talk with the police, check facts, arrange interviews with relatives or acquaintances, plus a short side article where a media-savvy psychiatrist could explain what made people commit such actions.

Ranveig had more than enough material to fill a whole day's work, but Viljar knew that she also had a story she had to write about a "love of reading" campaign at the Haugesund Public Library. Øystein had told him that on the phone last evening. Viljar had a suspicion that she would never give that story to Thomsen. He hadn't written a feel-good story since the North Rogaland Symphony Orchestra performed Haydn's *Creation* in the mideighties.

Viljar's suspicion was confirmed when Ranveig and Øystein Vindheim waved to him as they passed his workstation a few minutes later.

The articles on Viljar's screen were definitely not material for a journalism prize. They were speculative, right on the borderline of being true, and a mishmash of facts, assumptions, and descriptions that did not resemble anything he had once been known for. To be on the safe side, and in order not to have the police on his neck, Viljar sent a copy of what he had written by email to Lotte Skeisvoll. Not completely according to the guidelines in the newspaper, but she deserved to be updated.

Viljar had a sickeningly sweet taste in his mouth. He knew he would get massive criticism by media critics for the mishmash he had written. He looked up and caught the eye of Henrik Thomsen. The guy was smiling broadly, and gave him a thumbs-up. Viljar ignored the arts reporter. *I still have some distance to go before I reach the bottom of the barrel as a journalist*, Viljar consoled himself.

It was while Viljar was sending the email with all the attachments to Lotte that there was a ping in his in-box. His heart rate quickly shot up, and he noticed the reluctance to open the email come toward him like a monster wave. Nonetheless, he chose to plunge in once again. He had to know.

Attn.: Viljar Gudmundsson

    So far, my dear Viljar, everything is going according to plan. The state is the law-giving power. I am both judge and executioner. It is most practical that way. Your role is to assume the responsibility you have as the fourth estate. That of reporting . . . So far you haven't done that, Viljar. That disappoints me. You force me to make use of stronger means in order to get your attention.

I am writing to you because I know that you are an honorable man. A man who will condemn what I am in the process of doing, but at the same time is capable of understanding my indignation and frustration over a legal system that no longer functions.

We have laws that are supposed to protect us against people who take what they want, and not a bad word shall be said about those who admit their guilt and take their just punishment. It is the others I want to put the spotlight on. Those who even in the hour of judgment avoid punishment and get away. They are the hyenas of society. Cowardly, greedy, and evasive. They deserve the punishment I shall give them. I will be punished myself for my actions. This I will take with head held high when the time comes. Until that happens, people will die by my hand. Guilty people who each in their own way avoided their rightful punishment.

Every year dozens of people in Norway die as a result of being killed by persons who drive a car, motorcycle, or boat in a state of intoxication. Again and again, we see guilty parties set free because it cannot be proved who was sitting behind the steering wheel. Other times, blood tests have been taken too late to be able to prove use of intoxicants. These are people who are not willing to take responsibility for their actions. They get away because society gives them a chance to do so. Not even when innocent people die by their hand are they willing to come forward with the sin. I despise such people.

One of these persons is a woman. She is hereby convicted of having caused another person's death after having driven in a state of intoxication. She has no previous record, but that will

not be seen as an extenuating circumstance here. The punish-
ment will be announced to her and effectuated tomorrow,
Friday, 10/17/2014.

10/16/2014
Stein Åmli
GS8-1

Viljar felt sick as he read the message. Now he was addressing Viljar even more familiarly. It was clear that he was following what happened, because he had included the fact that *Haugesund News* had kept silent about the emails so far.

This man had to be stopped, but he was driving things at such a tempo that Viljar felt like a stenographer, capable only of recording what happened without getting an overview. It was going too fast.

"Look at that, Gudmundsson. . . . Are there more emails on the way, or what?"

A sense of unease crept down the back of his neck. Viljar hurried to close down the window on his laptop. He tried to collect himself before he turned calmly toward the uninvited guest. "What the hell are you doing in here, Hans? Aren't your offices at the other end? We have more than enough to handle with getting a crowd of salespeople up our asses without you starting to sneak around our legs too."

The radio journalist smiled sheepishly. "Is saying hi to old friends no longer allowed?" Hans Indbjo put emphasis on the word "friends."

"We're not in agreement on much, Hans, but we can agree that we're not particularly fond of one another, right?" Viljar fished out a smoke and stood up. He wanted to get Indbjo away from his workstation as quickly as possible.

"Listen, I'm going out for some air in ten minutes. Most everything is about the double murderer. The way I understand it, he contacts you personally in advance. You couldn't consider answering a few questions for broadcast?"

Viljar looked down at the shrimp in front of him. "What idiot has pumped you full of nonsense now, Hans? You mustn't believe every acidhead who calls your tip line."

"I don't believe anything. I know. My source has never lied to me, and the person in question isn't doing it this time either. Besides, we're part of the same media company. It's actually the point, that we should share news in here. We've talked about that several times, and if you disagree with me, I can bring it up directly with Øveraas."

Viljar stared hard at Indbjo for a moment, as if with pure mental force he could get the man to dissolve and disappear. "In that case, I have only one comment to Radio 102's listeners, and you can quote me if you want. . . ."

Indbjo eagerly pulled the recorder out of his pocket and turned it on. After that, he took about half a minute for a dramatic intro to the question before he put the microphone up to Viljar's face.

"What is your comment to our listeners about this case, reporter at *Haugesund News*, Viljar Ravn Gudmundsson?"

"Go to hell!!!"

Viljar roared into the Dictaphone and saw to his delight that drops of spit had landed on Indbjo's eyeglasses. He could only wish it were a live broadcast and not recorded.

Rådhusplassen, Haugesund
Thursday afternoon, October 16, 2014

L otte Skeisvoll looked at Viljar indulgently. Now he wouldn't have
to drag himself to a meeting after the third email showed up.
People should stop complaining about police response time, thought
Viljar. They were sitting on a bench on the square at Rådhusplassen.
Rainwater flowed between the cobblestones in glistening seams.

"So you mean the whole case is a conspiracy against you personally, is that what you're trying to say?" Lotte Skeisvoll barely
concealed her skepticism.

"I don't mean anything, Lotte. I'm just mentioning it. It's a hypothesis, not the answer key." The journalist turned his gaze downward and splashed in a little puddle with the sole of his shoe.

"Great, Viljar . . . Let's assume you're right. Someone is trying
to pin you as the perpetrator in this case. Then there are two questions that crystallize here. Who could conceivably do such a thing, and
why?"

Viljar quickly looked up at her. Let his gaze keep wandering to

Olav Scheldrup Hansen, who was sitting beside her, but lowered it again at once.

"I don't know. . . ."

Lotte sighed. This wasn't the first time Viljar had answered with those three words.

"You've cobbled together a brilliant conspiracy theory, but you don't know anything when it comes to person and motive. What is wrong with you? Do you have a fucking martyr complex?"

Viljar stared stiffly ahead of him, wrapped in a cloak of aversion. He could see people hurrying in and out of cars down by the KM building. *People know so little,* he thought.

"He wants me to do something. . . . You see it in the emails. It's as if he wants to make me an accessory. He's giving me a stage role that I have to play."

"Viljar . . . *Who* is doing this, and *why* is he doing it? Unlike you, I work with things like this on a regular basis. Motive is the central concept in any criminal act. All investigation is about finding or supporting a motive for the deeds. No one would have thought of making you a scapegoat without having a *motive* for doing that."

Viljar shook his head. Picked nervously at the paint on the wooden bench. He did not answer her.

"What you are *really* saying is just as stupid as if you called a soccer fan in the middle of the night to inform him that today two teams, the names of which you don't know, played a match someplace in the world, but you don't know what the score was. Do you get what I mean, Viljar? What you're saying to us has absolutely no value unless you can connect it to a name or a motive."

Lotte stood up abruptly, intending to leave, but Viljar stopped her.

"The codes are different, Lotte."

"Huh?"

"The letters and numbers at the bottom of the emails are different each time."

Lotte sat down again, rubbing energetically on a little speck that had settled on her yellow rain jacket. Her mouth was taut.

She seemed stymied.

"Haven't you seen that before now, Viljar? I guess there's not much left of the investigative journalist you once were. We've had our hands in that flower bed since the second email showed up."

She was about to stand up again when Scheldrup Hansen suddenly perked up and put his hand on her shoulder.

"May I ask you a couple of questions, Gudmundsson?"

He looked at Viljar, who nodded cautiously without looking up from the tips of his shoes.

"Tell me about the Eliassen case. If we're going to search for a revenge motive, we ought to start there."

The question had an immediate effect. It was as if the stoop-shouldered figure was tightened up by a corset. He looked in panic from side to side before he finally was able to meet the gaze of the policeman in front of him.

"Hell no!"

Olav Scheldrup Hansen held him in his gaze a little while longer. "Hell no that you don't want to talk about it, or is it the thought that Eliassen may be involved that makes you react?"

Viljar did not reply.

"How long have you had mental problems?"

Viljar opened his mouth a couple of times to answer, but closed it again. With trembling hands, he took out a box of snus and managed to get a portion under his lip. A few seconds later, he seemed to have regained his composure.

"What do you mean by mental problems?"

Scheldrup Hansen sat slightly turned on the bench and looked right at Viljar. "I shall mention at random . . . Anxiety, depression, aggression, persecution mania, suicidal thoughts, isolation . . . Are those familiar concepts to you?"

Viljar did not answer the question. Just sat with his arms limply by his side staring out at nothing.

The investigator continued to ask questions about Viljar's mental health, about episodes that had occurred, about sudden changes in his life. He still got no answer. After a few minutes, he gave up, and the two police detectives got up and left.

Viljar stayed behind on the bench for several minutes after they had gone. He knew of only one person who had that much information about him, and that was his psychologist. Now Vigdis had betrayed the trust he had placed in her. *Can a psychologist do such a thing? Turn my life over to the police?*

Haugesund Public Library
Thursday afternoon, October 16, 2014

Ranveig was listening with half an ear. Øystein Vindheim babbled like a brook about the approaching library campaign when they arrived at the library. With impressive enthusiasm, he brought out placards and banners. The story would have a maximum of half a page in tomorrow's paper, but the passionate librarian had already laid claim to two hours of her valuable time. He was pleasant, amusing, and sociable, but Ranveig had soon had enough.

The photographer had finished his part of the job and was long since at work on his next assignment. She, on the other hand, was being held hostage. The campaign that Øystein had evidently spent the greater part of the fall planning was about increasing the love of reading among those who sat plastered to the screen and watching endless TV series. He wanted to "reintroduce" the reading nook in the living room. Vindheim clearly thought that the hegemony of cell phones, flat screens, and tablets had taken over. Ranveig was not sure this kind of library campaign would make a major difference, but she smiled and was positive.

After yet another long-winded monologue from the librarian, she felt the need to stop him. He got puppy-dog eyes.

"I'm sorry, but I've been assigned to write some stories for tomorrow's paper about the two killings. I assume you've heard about them?"

The librarian nodded understandingly but didn't say anything.

"That's the way it is for us journalists when such things happen, everything piles up."

She felt the need to excuse herself further. Always unpleasant to have to cut off pleasant folks who were just sincerely engaged in their projects.

"I understand perfectly what you mean. It's like that for us too on busy days. It's just terrible about these murders."

"Yes, I really don't understand what drives a person to do such things. You have to be pretty messed up to throw a lady out of the seventh floor in a high-rise."

Øystein Vindheim nodded. "Such things only happen in books," he said, opening the door courteously for Ranveig.

"Yes, I don't know if it even happens there. This case is very strange," she added.

Ranveig turned in the doorway to shake the tall librarian's hand. He smiled.

"Then you don't read much crime fiction, that's for sure. In *Man of Darkness* by Unni Lindell, that very thing happens. A woman is thrown out of a high-rise."

Ranveig smiled at the bookworm in front of her. She liked him. "Discussing crime books with a librarian isn't an exercise I would emerge from intact, so I'll have to take your word for it," she said, shaking his hand.

"Will the article be published tomorrow?" he called after her when she was halfway down the stairs outside the public library. She confirmed it with a thumbs-up while he waved back.

Ranveig had less than two hours at her disposal to write three articles. She realized that it would be impossible to do that within office hours. She would have to work overtime from home. Fortunately, her husband and child were on a visit with the grandparents in Grinde. She had the whole house to herself.

She threw her bag over her shoulder and hurried toward Rådhusplassen. The rain poured down without her noticing that she was soaked through. Low-pressure systems came in from the North Sea in an even queue from the end of August to the end of April. The only break was a monthlong period with strings of Christmas lights that fluttered in the wind. She smiled at her city when she thought about it. It smiled whimsically back.

At home in the house in Risøy, she settled down on the chaise longue with the laptop. She got out the Citrix key with the passwords to the office network and opened the text program. On the coffee table was a freshly brewed pot of chai, and she had even indulged herself in a hundred-gram chocolate bar from the store on the way home. She had divvied it up into squares, which she placed in a little glass bowl alongside.

She was about to start writing when she became aware of something in the corner of her eye. The bookshelf was chock-full of crime novels that she never read. It was Rolf who was the crime lover of the two of them. She could see the title from where she sat. Unni Lindell was one of his favorites. To be sure, he'd never said that—they never discussed that kind of literature—but she had cleared the books from her husband's nightstand countless times.

Man of Darkness was at the far right on the shelf. She set the laptop down on the couch and took the book down from the shelf. The cover was gloomy. In the foreground was a young girl in a flowery summer skirt, but the shadow behind her toward eleven o'clock was of a big and powerful man. What was apparently idyllic was thus overshadowed by a threatening darkness. Ranveig felt that she was shivering a little. Didn't like such books.

Why can't people write about more pleasant things? she thought while she paged to the start of the book. Read a few pages and quickly understood the descriptions because the woman in the story lived on one of the top floors in an apartment building. She continued browsing to the inevitable and felt herself getting cold and clammy by turns. Øystein Vindheim was quite right. Such things happened in the world of books too. After having read a little more, she understood that it wasn't going to stop with this murder, and she let Cato Isaksen live his fictional life in peace. There was more than enough death and misery for her during the day.

Ranveig leaned back with the laptop in front of her and worked intensely to finish the articles. While she worked, a thought about the case was forming in her mind. She thought she remembered something, but she had to talk with Viljar to check if it was right. She picked up the phone to call him. Noticed at once that it was on silent, and she hadn't noticed that he'd tried to call her three times. She sighed dejectedly and entered his number. At the other end, only voice mail waited.

"Hi, Viljar. See that you called. Guess I had the phone on silent. Can you call me back? I think I've found out something important where the case is concerned, but I have to check with you first. I've put the sound on now."

The last piece of information perhaps she could have spared herself, but she always felt so awkward when she had to leave a voice message.

Haraldsgata, a street in Haugesund
Thursday afternoon, October 16, 2014

In the summer, the sidewalk tables outside Café Espresso in the middle of Haraldsgata worked like flypaper for the streetwalkers of the city. Calling it a sidewalk café was perhaps a stretch for the four wobbly tables on the cobblestones, and it could not be denied that the remaining population of the city, the part with money to spend, avoided that route when half the tables were occupied by shabby-looking drug addicts with a pack of angry, drooling dogs by their side. But in October, it was rather short on customers.

Good Lord, is it really six years ago already!

Lotte shook her head. She could see the ailing figure sitting alone outside the café from far off. Bent over the little table. Not bothered by the rain that was splashing down. The years after Anne was swallowed up by the street had flown by. Just like the death of her parents. It simply happened, and then it faded out in history. Sometimes Lotte found herself thinking that she'd forgotten them completely. Weeks might go by without her thinking about them, and as time passed, she struggled to remember their faces and voices.

Her sister, on the other hand, she did think about. Every single morning, every single day, every single evening . . . *Where are you now? Are you alive? How have you debased yourself today? Are you cold? Are you in pain? Do you think about me?* . . .

The questions were grinding in her head. She knew that she could never let go of Anne. Even if Anne were to die, she would demand her place with Lotte.

Lotte had long since lost track of how many hours she had spent at the emergency room with a tattered sister there was nothing wrong with other than the consequences of living a life on the street. Every time, the same thing. Her sister was stressed, shaking, cursing, and aggressive. Lotte the opposite. As an addict, Anne was prejudged in all situations. She was looked down on, moved to the back of the line in the waiting room, viewed with suspicion by the staff and other patients, and rejected by doctors who never took her problems seriously. The list was endless. The whole thing was shameful and degrading.

She shoved the thoughts away as she approached the café. Lotte looked around to see if she could catch sight of any of the other street people, but for once they were nowhere to be seen. She would much prefer to take Anne inside where it was warm, but knew it was impossible, and instead pulled her raincoat tighter around her.

"Did you chase away the rest of the gang?" Lotte asked as she plopped down on the chair beside her sister.

"Yeah."

Lotte looked at Anne and smiled.

"I got a deal with Ingjerd at the café. I can sit here if the dogs and the rest stay away. There was no problem working it out." Anne remained quiet a moment and looked down at the cobblestones. "Listen, it was a pretty long time to wait. You don't have any cash on you?"

"No, damn it, Anne. You know perfectly well I'm not giving you money for the shit you're on."

To Lotte's great amazement, Anne smiled at her. It was amazing to see that smile again. Even if it lasted only a few seconds. The explanation for the smile came quickly.

"I pay for that stuff myself. You know that. You were so late that I got hungry. Ingjerd gave me a little something to eat if I promised to pay when you came."

Lotte was relieved and fished out a fifty-krone note from her wallet.

When Anne came back a few minutes later, she seemed a little more restless. Lotte was very aware of such small changes in Anne. Knew they could mean trouble.

"Something wrong . . . ?"

Anne looked quickly around her a few times before she answered. "No. Nothing. I've just gone sober for a few hours, and I'm starting to feel it a little. Could have taken a little, but I don't want to talk with you when I'm high. Then you never take me seriously."

Lotte raised her eyebrows. When her sister of her own free will chose to stay sober for her sake, for once she had something important on her mind. There was little doubt of that.

"Do tell. . . ."

Anne cleared her throat slightly and moved a little restlessly in the chair. Then she jumped right in. "I need money, Lotte, but not for what you think. Not dope. Not dope debt either."

"Oh, well . . . If it isn't dope or debt, what is it then? You get enough from welfare for food and lodging, I know that." Lotte looked at her a little sternly, actually without wanting to, but it was a bad habit she'd picked up from countless interviews.

"I want to admit myself, Lotte. Be clean for good . . ."

This was the first time. The first time Anne had expressed a wish for a different life than the one she was living. Lotte was speechless a moment, but finally cleared her throat and got out a few words.

"Seriously . . . ? You're not joking now? You want out?"

Anne looked at her. "Yes, I do. Really. I'm fucking tired, Lotte. But it's just that the public programs have at least a full year waiting period, and I don't have that long."

"Don't have . . . ? Are you sick?"

"No. It's something else, but forget about that. It's not really that important. What does matter is that I want out, and I want out now, not in a year. But that costs money, and I don't have it."

"Great. How much are we talking about?" Lotte knew enough about the system that she didn't want to hear the answer, but she had to ask.

"Seventy-five thousand."

Anne looked down at the table while she said that. Lotte knew that this was hard for her sister. She had made a big point again and again of how well she managed without her help.

"That's an awful lot of money, Anne. If you get yourself on the list, something may turn up before a year has passed. Good Lord, half of those on the waiting list will die of an overdose before they get started."

"Yeah. That's just it. People die."

Anne's words flew like an iron rod through Lotte's belly. That was exactly what happened. People died in line because they couldn't bear to wait any longer to get help. But seventy-five thousand kroner was far more money than Lotte could conjure up from her bank account when she didn't have a house she could use as collateral. Consumer loans at 18 percent interest were not an option. She would have to arrange this some other way.

"Great, Anne, but what do you get for the money then?"

"A place now. Tomorrow if I want. Detoxification. Treatment.

Follow-up. Therapy. Six months including all treatment, room, and board. And standing offer of six more months if I'm still unsure whether I can manage it."

"Jesus . . ."

Lotte didn't know that her sister even knew such terms, and now she was using them as naturally as if she'd been a trained social worker. It sounded almost too good to be true. A part of Lotte rejoiced and most of all just wanted to embrace Anne. Another part held back. An addict short of money would do anything at all for it, and seventy-five thousand was a lot of money in those circles. Besides, the health statistics from such treatment centers were mournful reading. Few succeeded, even among those who completed the stay.

"So where is this place, Anne?"

"It's called Vangseter, and it's in Jevnaker due north of Hønefoss. I know two people who've gotten completely clean after being there. Much better setup than the state-run centers. I can pay you back too. I'll get a job."

"Who in the world would give you a job now, the way your life has gone?" Lotte realized that she was unnecessarily coarse, and quickly got an answer in response.

"You don't believe me, damn it!" She leaned over the table and hid her head in her hands.

Lotte apologized and stroked her sister's hair to show that she was sincere.

Anne gave her a good, long hug before Lotte left her fifteen minutes later. Her sister promised to cut down on the doses in the future.

Four years earlier . . .
Kvalsvik, Haugesund
Sunday evening, August 22, 2010

Fredric shoved his friend so he lost his balance and had to support himself on a stone next to where they were sitting. The flat rocks glowed as the sun made a brief assault. A final intense embrace before the ball of light drowned in the sea.

"You're out of your mind. Do you realize what you've done? Do you have any idea?"

A seagull drifted toward them and didn't turn aside until it was so close, they could have grasped it with their hands. It emitted a long screech as it passed, clearing the roofs of the houses in the development behind the lookout point. The screech made Jonas raise his eyes. He could see that Fredric had tears in his eyes.

"I don't understand why, Jonas. It's one thing that we thought we had an airtight plan and it fell apart. That's terrible, but what you did was pure stupidity. Everyone's going to realize it's us. You understand that, don't you?"

"No, Fredric, they won't realize that. We're not the only ones. He has others."

Fredric turned his head slowly toward Jonas. The mistrust shone in his eyes, and he laughed nervously. "Stop fooling around, Jonas. This is actually not funny."

"Eliassen said so himself. Tossed it out as if it were something trivial. That perverse pig still has a few more in his club."

"Damn him!"

Fredric got up in one quick motion. Stood with his back to Jonas and his face toward the sea. He repeated the oath, even louder this time.

Jonas let him stand alone a few seconds before he took courage, stood up, and put his arms around him from behind. "I couldn't let that asshole get away with this. Use us for a whole year, and then shove us aside when the decision came."

For a long time they stood there looking at Røvær, which slowly slipped into evening shadow. Beyond it they could barely make out the outlines of the island of Utsira. The last bit of Norway before the sea enveloped the horizon.

"After what you did at the hotel, no one is going to believe you. Eliassen is going to portray you as crazy, violent, and unpredictable."

"No."

"No? You left him at the hotel in a pool of blood with any number of cuts. It's a marvel he hasn't already reported you, and that you're not rotting away in a dungeon."

"Think a little further, Fredric. He didn't report it. Ask yourself why. The answer speaks for itself. If he's going to tell what happened in there, he also has to admit that he had a visit from a seventeen-year-old boy in a hotel room at six o'clock in the morning. The same applies now. For Hermann Eliassen, the best defense is to deny that anything happened."

Fredric shook his head. Kicked loose a tuft of grass that had hidden between two stones.

"With a case like this, Hermann Eliassen is politically dead in the Center Party. It won't help to deny it. I'll go out with my story anonymously. The journalist can use you as an extra source if he's unsure. Eliassen is definitely not going to disclose our names. It's not in his interest what we're saying is actually true."

"You've got someone who wants to write about this?"

Jonas smiled for the first time in ages. He took a firmer hold of Fredric's shoulders, while the color of the sky changed to slate gray. "I've got Viljar Ravn Gudmundsson at *Haugesund News* to write about the situation. The only thing to do is get out the spade. Eliassen is already a dead man."

Media House *Haugesund News*
Thursday afternoon, October 16, 2014

Jonas . . .

That name had been a sticky mass in Viljar's subconscious ever since the first email arrived. It was several years since the day Jonas stood at Viljar's door and delivered the fateful letter, but he remembered every slightest detail from the meeting. His clothes, the smell of new-mown grass, the torrential rain, his sorrowful eyes.

Everything was there. Razor-sharp high-definition images in his memory. The intense, brief meeting that had turned existence on its head.

When Viljar got the first email on Monday, Jonas came to mind at once. *Could this have anything to do with that old case?* To start with, he had dismissed that. The thought was too unpleasant, but now he was forced to check up on it. There was only one place to start probing.

The workday was over, but Viljar couldn't bear to go home yet. He had to dig things up in the archives about the old case, and then it was best if the media building was empty of anyone other than security guards and those who worked at the desk. Radio 102 was buzzing in the background. It wasn't often Viljar felt the need to listen to the radio station's programs, but this particular day, he had to keep track of Indbjo, and whether he saw fit to spread the news about Viljar's involvement in the murder case. Strangely enough, this hadn't happened. Hans Indbjo had not yet leaked the news about the emails.

Besides, the media sharks in Oslo would have called if they'd got wind of this. Ultra-bold fonts would be used, and the inevitable consequence of such saturation coverage was new front-page stories and more new front-page stories with follow-up, rehashing, and ever more wide-ranging theories. Anything that could create fear and panic was gold. It sold newspapers.

Viljar went into the elevator after having a puff outside in the parking lot. While he ambled toward the workstations, he thought through how he could best approach the Jonas case again without stirring up the still-smoldering embers too much. He knew it would be difficult, but he couldn't just ignore it.

As he rounded the corner and the office landscape opened before him, he got a surprise. On the chair in front of his computer sat a clearly bewildered editor. He got up immediately when Viljar approached, but no quicker than Viljar was able to see what Øveraas had been up to. Clearly uncomfortable with the situation, Øveraas chose to attack rather than apologize.

"Yes, that's the way it is, Gudmundsson. You've stuck your peter into a hornet's nest. You damned well have to accept that I keep track of you."

What the editor said seemed strange, awkward, and artificial.

"Great, I'll take that," Viljar said calmly. "But what's the real reason for you snooping in my computer?"

Øveraas got a look of panic in his eyes. Anyone could see that his brain was searching feverishly for something ingenious that could rescue him from this awkward situation. It failed. . . .

"I just said that. Have to make sure you're doing your job." Viljar chose to let him get off with that paper-thin explanation.

He directed the editor away from his station with a servile gesture. Fortunately, Øveraas waddled off. That was the most important thing.

The desire to get started on tracking down threads in the Jonas case disappeared as quickly as the dope peddlers on Bytunet when the police come around the corner. He took out his cell phone and saw that Ranveig had called. Pressed the Callback button, but the monotone ringtone at the other end was quickly replaced by an equally monotone voice mail. He would have to try later. Viljar packed up his things, pulled on his topcoat, and left. Assured himself one last time that the computer was turned off.

On his way to the parking lot, he took out his keys but suddenly became aware that he didn't have his cell phone in his pocket as he usually did. Viljar stopped and checked his other pockets, but decided that he'd probably left it behind at his workstation. He was about to go back in again, when he was witness to a scene at the other end of the parking lot. The arts reporter Henrik Thomsen was leaning over and talking with a person through a car window. They were too far away for Viljar to see who it was, but he didn't need to. The car was a familiar sight. It was Hans Indbjo's rattletrap.

Seconds later, Thomsen rounded the car and got in on the passenger side. How that burly guy found room in Indbjo's little Fiesta was a mystery.

I'll be damned, thought Viljar. *Is that Laurel and Hardy babbling together? Then it's not so strange that Indbjo has information he absolutely should not be in possession of.*

Haugesund Police Station
Thursday afternoon, October 16, 2014

Olav Scheldrup Hansen did not see himself as a sensitive man. This investigation group, however, did the most navel-gazing of any he'd experienced. No matter where he turned, he met only narrow-mindedness and resistance. He was evidently seen as a fifth wheel. A burden.

It was only twenty-four hours since he'd arrived in town. With his baggage full of good intentions and an open mind, he had entered the arena, but Lotte Skeisvoll chose to thwart him. She clearly also had the rest of the group siding with her in this silly power play.

Olav was deliberating whether he would be able to reestablish a certain symmetry in the investigation. Since the whole investigation group appeared to dance to Skeisvoll's tune in everything, he would have to win their trust little by little. Get them to see and understand why he was a Kripos investigator, while Lotte Skeisvoll was still scurrying around in the corridors at the local police station.

After the third email, things got hectic. They knew they had a maximum of twelve hours to stop the killer from striking again, probably less. Lotte sent the flock of sheep in all possible directions and commanded Olav to go through the registers to track down previous drunk drivers who had been acquitted in court. He'd been brought in from Oslo to assist with investigation tactics, but then was assigned to carefully read old court documents. A clerical task anyone at all could have done. He figured she did it to set an example for the others, and he would make damned sure to humiliate her at the next crossroad.

Searching for reported drunk drivers was an easy matter. The digital search tools at the police building were good, and the majority of reports concerned men. What was far more difficult, on the other hand, was sorting out who had been acquitted. To get to that, he would have to pull out every single court document after entering the case number. This was a process that repeated itself for every single case, and it took an eternity every time.

The list of women was already rather long when two hours later he'd gone through all judgments back to 2006. Olav felt like an idiot. The work he was doing was completely meaningless. They would have a list of at least twenty names before he was done. It was completely impossible to try to protect the killer's next victim based on such a list. There were far too many names. The more he thought about it, the more convinced he became that he'd been assigned this slave labor to be kept away from the actual investigation. Irritated, indignant, and a little angry, he put a stop to this monotonous work and instead started to make an investigation chart, where he laboriously plotted in all the details about the two murders. He emailed the list of names he'd found to Lotte Skeisvoll. She could do whatever the hell she wanted to with it. This was a waste of resources.

After all, human life is at stake, and it doesn't help to count to a hundred after someone's been shot, he thought.

Risøy, Haugesund
Thursday evening, October 16, 2014

Ranveig's plan to go to bed early was in vain. The thoughts grinding in her head wouldn't leave her alone. There might be a connection between the emails that they had overlooked. If that was correct, it would give the police a completely different angle on the investigation. She considered calling Lotte Skeisvoll, but wanted to confirm her suspicions first. Everything would have been much simpler if Viljar had just picked up the phone. After yet another fifteen minutes of sleeplessness, she gave up. She sighed heavily, put her feet on the floor, and pattered out into the darkened living room. Ranveig warmed up a cup of tea on the Tassimo machine. The tea was supposed to be a natural sedative, but in previous attempts, the effect had been absent. She hoped for a miracle this time.

She found the book by Unni Lindell and reviewed the descriptions of the first murder in the story. Ranveig did not like what she was reading. That people could be so vicious and vengeful was beyond her comprehension.

On the other hand, neither did she understand why people liked reading about horrible acts or watching movies and TV shows where murder and violence were the main elements. She had never had this morbid compulsion, but she also realized that among her own social circle, she was sadly alone in thinking that way. Most everyone she knew reveled in blood, killing, rape, and spectacular methods of torture in their free time. Yet they would never be able to do something like that to others. *That's where the wrong connection is.*

She turned on the ceiling light and opened the blinds. It was dark outside. A couple of party-loving neighbors had evidently had a pre-party in the apartment next door. They laughed and hollered as they locked up and started strolling toward a night of drinking at the restaurants by the pier. One of them waved up to her where she stood at the window. She waved back. Didn't recognize him, but he smiled at her and hollered. A moment later, it occurred to her why. She was standing buck naked in front of the picture window. Ranveig quickly stepped back and threw a white bathrobe around herself.

She curled up at one end of the couch with her legs under her and the teacup in her hands. Both hands . . . Tea should be drunk that way. With both hands around the cup the way a bird wraps its wings around a newly hatched chick. Why she had acquired this peculiar habit, she didn't know, but it was harmless enough.

She fell asleep like that a few minutes later. The teacup rested snugly between her hands in her lap.

Torvastad, Karmøy
Thursday night, October 16, 2014

The flames roared toward the night sky. Complaining woodwork crackled and sparked. An inferno. The firemen shouted and ran past each other to connect hoses to the nearest hydrant. One of the beams in the old house was about to give way, and you could see that the south wall was leaning heavily toward the chimney. The house had long since reached flashover, and couldn't be saved. Nonetheless, the firemen worked as if lives were in danger. A large crowd of people had lined up behind the provisional police barricades. Nothing attracts more local tourism than fires. A quiet congregation present at what deep down they fear will happen to them. That everything they own will be consumed by the flames. Also standing right behind the barricades was a camera team from TV Haugaland, while a photographer from *Haugesund News* slipped past the barricades to get better angles.

Lotte Skeisvoll looked up toward the house, which seemed about to collapse at any moment. She had no business there. It was completely pointless. Nonetheless, she stood there as if in a trance and followed the ravaging of the flames.

"You don't need to be here, Lotte, we've got everything under control. The house was vacant. The smoke divers were inside before we arrived. André Ferkingstad hasn't lived here the past four years." Knut Veldetun placed a friendly hand on Lotte Skeisvoll's shoulder.

She nodded absently, but stood there anyway.

The house wakened sad memories in her. She still remembered that fateful Sunday in August four years ago, when the Ferkingstad family was torn to shreds by an incident that was on the front page of every newspaper in the country for several days.

Lotte turned and started to trudge down the road. Fatigue was pounding in her temples. She stopped alongside the previous occupant of the house. As was the case four years ago, she was unable to look him in the eyes. There was something implacable in his gaze that always made her turn away.

"I'm sorry about this," she said, kicking into the gravel in front of her a little.

André Ferkingstad did not say anything at first. It was as if he were looking into a dimension that no one else saw, holding the back of his head as if he had a kink in his neck. Suddenly he woke up. André took Lotte's hands and smiled.

"It doesn't matter. It was high time that God let this pool of sin turn to ashes."

Lotte straightened up, pulled back her hands, and continued walking toward the car. On the way, both the *Haugesund News* reporter and the always irritating Hans Indbjo tried to get her to stop, but she ignored them. They would have to make do on their own.

Inside the car, she rolled the window down a little so she could see and hear what was going on. Couldn't take her eyes off the fire. Suddenly all the beams gave way at the same time, and the wood structure collapsed onto the foundation in a ball of sparks.

With amazement she saw how Ferkingstad stood with his arms

over his head, clapping his hands. *That guy needs to be checked for insurance fraud—you'd almost think he set it himself,* she thought as she let the car roll down the gravel road. In the rearview mirror, she saw Ferkingstad shake his fists one last time before getting into an old Toyota Corolla that was parked along the road.

Risøy, Haugesund
Thursday night, October 16, 2014

Ranveig was wakened by a buzzing sound on the coffee table. The display on the vibrating phone showed that it was Øveraas calling. She wondered what he wanted so late as she answered the call.

"Ranveig?"

"Hmmm . . ."

"Listen, I hope I didn't wake you, but I need you to check something out for us."

"Now? It's . . ." She moved the phone away from her ear to check the clock on its screen. "It's almost eleven thirty, Øveraas. Isn't there anyone on duty you can ask?"

"You know Murphy's Law, Ranveig. Anything that can go wrong, will go wrong, at the worst conceivable time. Thomsen's in Stavanger. Went to cover some performer or other at the concert hall there. Don't remember who. Must be something special, because he was quite excited. Stiansen is on vacation, and I sent the evening reporter and photographer out on a house fire at Torvastad half an hour ago."

"Okay . . . What's so important that it can't wait until tomorrow? The newspaper's on press, isn't it?"

"Best on the net, Ranveig. Don't forget that. We've received two tips independent of each other that Stein Vikshåland is dead. The police won't confirm that—but they never do, of course, when it's a celebrity. The tipsters say that he was found at home. He doesn't answer the phone or messages from us either, which I have never experienced before. The guy is so media-fixated that he has the newspaper on speed dial."

Stein Vikshåland was perhaps Haugesund's biggest celebrity. In two scandalous books that each sold close to a hundred thousand copies, he attacked the entire Norwegian cultural establishment with a frankness that was borderline unethical, revealing and extremely provocative all at once. In a microsecond, Vikshåland went from being a cipher to a regular on almost all the TV talk shows. He was portrayed up, down, and in the middle of every newspaper, magazine, and TV station in the country. Appeared in every celebrity context, and was hated by everyone. Nonetheless, he was in constant demand by the media. If you wanted to sell magazines and newspapers or get higher viewer ratings, you had only to use Stein Vikshåland in one angle or another.

Ranveig had to think. This was the last thing she'd expected. True enough, Stein Vikshåland was a man about town who made other celebrities seem like Boy Scouts, but that he would drop dead now was extremely surprising. He was only in his early forties. Regardless, Ranveig realized that this really was news that couldn't wait until tomorrow. Øveraas was not exaggerating.

"You said at his home? Are we talking about his little writer's shack up in Tømmerdalen, or the *See and Hear* Palace on Salhusveien?"

Vikshåland's villa got that nickname after the magazine *See and*

Hear had the longest "at home with" story ever from the housewarming party. Seven consecutive pages.

"And you call yourself a cultural journalist? Everyone knows the guy never stays in that luxury mansion. It's just for show."

"I know that, Øveraas. But you said there were tipsters, and it's not certain they know the same things we do."

"Okay, but it's in Tømmerdalen. One of the tipsters mentioned that in particular. Can you drive up there in a hurry, and then call me when you know anything more?"

Ranveig answered affirmatively and quickly got dressed. She wasn't concerned that her clothes might not match tonight. She tossed the bag with the camera and telephoto lens over her shoulder, snatched up her keys, and left the house.

Tømmerdalen, Haugesund
Thursday night, October 16, 2014

Ranveig eased the car in between a rusty Toyota Corolla and a newer Audi at the Kiwi store in Skåredalen. Once it was out on social media, news like this spread like chlamydia at a senior class party, and she didn't want to be blocked in by ambulances, media people, and curious residents who "just happened" to be in the area.

It was pitch dark, and leaden rain clouds raced to get the best seats over the city. Ranveig glanced up to assure herself that the rain wouldn't start for a while yet. She was not eager to stand there soaking wet, interviewing the hoi polloi in the middle of the night.

As she rounded the bend on foot on her way toward Skåredalen School, she suddenly realized that something didn't add up. Not a single car was visible anywhere close to the driveway to Vikshåland's house up on the hill. There was no one there. No ambulances, no journalists, no spectators. She sighed when she realized that this was a wasted trip. Even so, she continued walking the two hundred meters up to the little house he had inherited from his parents. The house looked abandoned. All the windows were dark, and mail was starting to pile up in the green box. If the tip was true, it must mean that the death had occurred on Salhusveien, after all.

She took out her cell phone and called Øveraas.

"Øveraas, *Haugesund News*."

"Ranveig here. Listen, I'm up at Tømmerdalen now, and there's not a soul here. No souls who've left their body either, as far as I can see," she added dryly.

"No? That's strange, because there's no one on Salhusveien. I checked up on that after I talked with you."

"Looks like someone wanted to play games with us tonight."

Ranveig lost her patience. If she hadn't been tired a few hours ago, she was now. She just wanted to go home and crawl under the covers. Preferably before the neighbors came home from the bar and hosted an after-party.

Øveraas started talking again. "Listen, Ranveig . . . I think you can pack up. Doesn't seem like there's as much to this as it appeared. Sorry, but . . ."

She ended the call with the editor and put the cell phone in her bag again. The wooden house from the early seventies loomed over her like a silent witness. She felt exhausted and alone out here. Even though it was only fifty meters to the nearest house, and the twisted little gravel road leading up from the school was all that separated Tømmerdalen from urban life.

The gravel crunched under her shoes as she took the first steps away from the property of the exhibitionistic author. She herself had not minced words in her descriptions of him. "Narcissist," "agitator," and "ruthless fortune hunter" were all insults she had pulled out of her hat when she reviewed his latest book, *From Hotel Caesar to Skippergata*. A mishmash of loose assertions about named cultural personalities' dealings with representatives of organized crime, involvement in prostitution, drug use, and paid junkets. The book strayed as far from ethical norms of journalism as you could, but the protagonist hid behind the idea that the novel was a mixture of fiction and reality. Which was which, he refused to clarify. For that matter, Ranveig didn't think this was the worst thing about the novel, but the compulsion Vikshåland had to reflect himself and his stunted values in anything and everything was nothing less than nauseating.

She tossed her head as she left the property, as if to remove any particles of Vikshåland's personality that had settled like imaginary dandruff on her shoulders. There were not many people she was capable of hating, but that man brought out the worst in her. He was the personification of the egotistical, navel-gazing society that Norway was in the process of becoming.

As she turned one last time toward the house, she saw it. Not only saw, but heard too. A slight flash of light from the back side of the house, and the unmistakable sound of a stone that thumped against a wall. She stopped and crouched down behind a bush. There was someone behind the house. The flash of light had been from a Mag-Lite, and the last time she checked, only one species in the animal kingdom had mastered the use of such a tool. In other words, this was not a cat or a passing deer. She was less certain whether the person in question was aware that she was on the other side. A few seconds later, the light flashed again. Two times now, and the width of the beam revealed that the person had moved closer to the east corner of the house.

Ranveig sat quiet as a mouse, but could feel her heart pounding under her blouse. The fear that rushed through her body was a primitive instinct. The same instinct that in its time had made the human race the most viable of all animal species: fight or flight. For millennia it had made humans in danger fight enemies or run for their lives. Ranveig had no plans to do either. She wanted to see who was lurking behind Vikshåland's house. There was a good chance it was another overeager journalist. Other media might have picked up the tip too.

When she heard the sound of shattering glass a moment later, she was no longer so certain. Plenty of journalists were willing to intrude far into the private sphere of celebrities, but breaking and entering was a bit too much. She had barely completed the train of thought before she saw the beam of the Mag-Lite create a reflection down in the cellar of the house. The unknown person must be on his way in. Ranveig got up carefully from her hiding place and ventured toward the corner of the house. She moved the way she had seen soldiers do in movies, bent over with cautious, quiet steps.

Up at the corner of the house, she caught her breath for a few seconds before she peeked around the corner. All the alarm bells in her body reacted at the same time when she looked right into two eyes and a smiling mouth. She had expected that the man was in the cellar. He wasn't. He was standing barely an arm's length from her, waiting. A scream of terror was on its way up her throat, but it was efficiently smothered by a heavy and precise blow to the skull. In a fraction of a second, all her sensory impressions disappeared, and the pain from the blow could barely reach the nerve center in the brain before she was unconscious.

When Ranveig came to half an hour later, she understood that she had made a major blunder. The man who had struck her down had probably been waiting for her the whole time.

Why is he doing this? Has he gone completely crazy?

She recognized him the moment she stuck her head around the corner. The experience was surreal. This man should not be here. The astonishment was perhaps the main reason she didn't manage to react before the blow came.

Ranveig was furious.

I'll be damned if he'll break me, she thought before she realized that she was tethered tightly to a beam that made it physically impossible for her to put up resistance against anything whatsoever. Her head, hands, and feet were all tied with zip ties so that he could actually do whatever he wanted with her. Her mouth was covered with duct tape. She tried to scream, but all that came out were desperate howling sounds. The thought of what he might come up with made her nauseated. The fear came when she realized the connection.

Panic started to spread, and the anger and resistance she had felt a few seconds ago were replaced by new fear. She wanted to wipe away the tears that welled up at the corners of her eyes, but couldn't move a muscle. As her vision gradually became more and more blurry, she saw the familiar male figure come walking toward her. He had discovered that she was conscious. His smile was unmistakable. . . .

The morning coffee and cigarette were a motivation in themselves to get out of bed and go to work. Viljar enjoyed every second of the routine in the parking lot outside the newspaper building. He often went a little early to be quite sure to be alone out there. This morning ritual was so ingrained in him that he even missed it on weekends and vacations. Compensated then, of course, with corresponding doses of poison at home, but it didn't have the same calming effect. Viljar knew that he was the type who would never be able to quit smoking. He nodded in recognition at COPD patients who dragged their oxygen equipment coughing with them out in the "smoking garage" at Haugesund Hospital. Thought that he was just like that.

He let his thoughts wander back to the day before. In a casual attempt to find out what business Henrik Thomsen had with Hans Indbjo, he'd followed them in his car like a scruffy detective from a 1970s American TV series. Paranoid perhaps, he thought, but something didn't add up. Those two idiots well deserved each other's company, but from what he knew, they weren't on speaking terms otherwise.

Viljar had kept a discreet distance from the pair, but at the same time close enough that he could observe what they were up to. They stopped twice on the drive. Both times, Hans Indbjo stayed in the car while Henrik Thomsen waddled out of the tin can. The first stop was at the Shell station at Avaldsnes just on the other side of the Karmøy bridge. Then Thomsen had talked for a long time with a blond-haired girl in her early twenties. The second time, they stopped in Skåredalen. There Thomsen had given a ten-year-old a cell phone. Viljar could obviously not see it from far off, but guessed as much when he passed the kid a few minutes later and saw that he was coaxing a SIM card into a smartphone.

Viljar followed Thomsen home that afternoon. To the left on Strandgata right after Torgbakken, the man finally disappeared into an old wooden house. The doorplate showed that this was where Thomsen lived. Hans Indbjo had driven on. When Viljar passed the house on his way back from a soccer match at the Football Pub, Thomas was sitting in the same position inside the curtains, staring at a TV screen.

Viljar crushed out the second cigarette of the day in the saucer he'd brought with him, emptied the last drops of lukewarm coffee on the asphalt, sighed contentedly at the numbing sensation of nicotine in his veins, and added extra insurance with a stick of nicotine gum before wending his way to the other journalists in the cafeteria. It was buzzing in there as always first thing in the morning, but today it stopped when they caught sight of the nicotine wreck in the fluttering topcoat coming in from the light drizzle. Today's newspaper edition had left its mark. Viljar smiled to himself. This was if possible the greatest recognition a journalist could get in today's media world: his colleagues' envy and contempt.

Viljar went out and sat down at his workstation. Checked that no one had been in his computer since last time, and at the same time fished out the cell phone he'd forgotten on the desk the afternoon before. Seven unanswered calls. Five from Ranveig at various times during the afternoon and evening, and two from Øveraas quite late. Viljar guessed at what it was the boss wanted with him when it was almost midnight.

Over by Ingress, he could hear the editorial staff gathering for the morning meeting. Viljar stretched, took off his topcoat, and decided to meet the rest of the editorial team with a smile. He had a front-page feature today after all, and with that he could allow himself to bask in the glory for once. It had been ages since the last time.

Once again the murmur and talk stopped when they caught sight of him, but this time a smirking Johan Øveraas broke the silence by giving him the credit he actually deserved.

"See, here we have the hero of the day in the flesh. All of Norway is clicking on our website, and the servers can barely keep up with it. So far, *VG*, *Dagbladet*, TV 2, and NRK have all linked their stories to your article. We have to call that a scoop."

Øveraas rocked from side to side like an unbalanced bowling pin, and Viljar could actually take in only half of the boasting. The comic effect of Johan Øveraas's physical capers when he got excited distracted from what he had on his mind.

Viljar noticed that Ranveig's seat was empty. She was always one of the first to get to work. Viljar showed the editor-in-chief with a silent gesture that Ranveig was missing at the table as he was about to start. Øveraas looked over at the empty seat and wrinkled his eyebrows a little, as if there were something unpleasant he had to remove from his sight. He cleared his throat, but was interrupted by Viljar, who did not have the patience to wait on Øveraas's empty talk.

"Shouldn't Ranveig be here today, Johan?"

The editor nodded affirmatively and answered a little hesitantly, "Well . . . Yes, she should be, but . . ."

"But?"

Johan Øveraas sighed a little dejectedly before he explained the situation. "She may have overslept. She was out on a late assignment last night and probably didn't get too many hours of shut-eye."

"Overslept? Has Ranveig ever overslept in the years she's worked here? So what case was she covering last night?"

"She was supposed to cover the death of Stein Vikshåland."

The whole editorial team turned their heads toward the editor. The news landed like a bomb. Øveraas realized his blunder and raised both palms in front of him before he continued.

"Sorry, folks. *Alleged* death. Vikshåland is alive and in the best of health. Unfortunately, some will no doubt maintain. But last night the news desk received two phone tips that Vikshåland had been found dead in his own home. Ranveig drove out to check if there was any truth in that, which there wasn't. She called me from Tømmer-dalen around midnight, and it was dark and abandoned there then. It was the same on Salhusveien."

Viljar felt a shiver down his spine. There was something here that didn't add up. He tossed out a new question. "Why Ranveig? She doesn't cover news, and she didn't have a shift yesterday."

Viljar could see Johan Øveraas arch his back. He was about to get irritated now. Never liked it when anyone questioned his decisions.

"Do you know what? . . . It is and remains my decision and my responsibility, okay? First, the night-shift reporter was out on another assignment; second, I tried to call you without getting an answer; and third, Henrik Thomsen was in Stavanger to cover a concert. I had no one else to use, Gudmundsson. Is that answer good enough for you?"

Viljar was about to say something, but let it go. He simply got up and left.

"And where the hell do you think you're going?" Johan Øveraas called at Viljar's back.

Viljar stopped, turned around, and looked at the editor with an indulgent expression. "I can guarantee you one thing, and that is that Ranveig hasn't overslept. Since she's not here, I actually intend to go out and search. She would have called in if she was sick."

Johan opened his mouth to say something, but was at a loss for an answer and gave up. He sent Viljar off with a hand gesture that indicated that he was excused. Johan Øveraas had his human side, if he just thought about it.

Haugesund
Friday morning, October 17, 2014

Viljar was certain that something was amiss. Øveraas had avoided contacting Henrik Thomsen because he was in Stavanger last evening. As Øveraas said that, he'd shown them a feature from the culture pages with a review of yesterday's performance in the concert hall. A review Thomsen obviously had written without having been present himself.

Viljar was not the least bit surprised when a few minutes later with his own eyes he could see that Ranveig's car was gone from its regular parking space outside her building. As expected, no one answered when he rang the doorbell either. He tried for the fourth time this morning to call Ranveig's cell phone, but still with no answer. Based on a brief conversation they'd had the day before, he'd understood that she would be alone at home until the next day. Husband and child were with the parents-in-law in Grinde.

Viljar used the directory assistance app and found the cell phone number for Ranveig's husband. Hesitated calling for a long time, but knew he had to do it. She *might* have decided to drive to Grinde after the failed nocturnal assignment, but it wasn't very likely. When Rolf finally answered in a tired voice, Viljar chose the cowardly approach.

"Hi, did I wake you up, Rolf? Ranveig's cell phone must be on silent. Do you mind waking her up, I need to ask her something."

Viljar had a very guilty conscience about what he was doing, but he couldn't bear the thought of consoling a worried husband. He would rather take the heat later.

"Uh . . . Listen, Ranveig's at work. We're in Grinde, so I haven't seen her since yesterday. You'll get ahold of her if you call the office."

"Okay, sorry to bother you."

Viljar sounded nonchalant, but now felt worry raging inside him. Ranveig was gone, and neither work nor family had heard anything from her. He backed the car out on the street again and set a northeast course toward Tømmerdalen. Called Øveraas to hear if she had come to work, which she hadn't.

The air was stifling as a few minutes later he drove onto the little side road toward Skåredalen School by the entrance to Tømmerdalen. He parked in the lot outside the school. Quickly noted that Ranveig's car wasn't to be seen here either. Nonetheless, he chose to go up to the house to check a little around the Stein Vikshåland property.

The old house loomed dark and silent over him as he rang the doorbell. He could hear the echo from the doorbell inside in the hall. Not a sign of life. Not a movement. Everything was still. He put his head against the door to listen. Not so much as a creak in a floorboard. The house appeared to be unoccupied, and probably had been for several weeks. The mail carrier had clearly given up the fight, and the mailbox was overflowing with newspapers. Viljar looked at them. The oldest issue was over a week old. He turned toward the house again.

You were here last night, Ranveig. But where have you gone? . . . Viljar let the question hang in the air, turned around, and trudged down to the car again while he called Ranveig's number for the fifth time. Right there, in the gravel on the walk away from the house, time stopped.

The time it took from when he heard the sound until he actually interpreted what the sound meant was less than a second. For Viljar, that one second seemed like ten. Everything was in slow motion. He actually stopped and turned around in a single movement. With the phone clamped to his ear, he ran in long strides toward the place the sound came from. He knew Ranveig's ringtone as well as his own. The digital tones to "Angie" by the Rolling Stones were unmistakable.

Viljar grabbed the phone that was lying in the grass by the corner of the house. At the same time, he pressed the Off button on his own phone. "Angie" stopped its melodious journey in mid-refrain. Viljar looked around him. There was no doubt that something had happened to Ranveig, and it had happened here.

He looked at the phone. He was by no means the only one who had tried to get ahold of her in the course of the morning. Johan Øveraas, Rolf, a blocked number, and a call from Øystein Vindheim ten minutes ago. Viljar set the phone on silent and put it in his pocket.

He started moving along the wall of the house on the back side. Stopped and listened several times. Felt the whole time that he heard sounds from inside the house. A branch of a bare birch tree scratched on an old windowpane, making a whining sound. A cow mooed from a barn a little farther up. Viljar had not gone far before he caught sight of a broken cellar window. The opening was too small, however, for a person to get through. He continued on until he came to the deck that turned diagonally toward the back side. He had to either go back, or make his way up on the deck itself and move ahead from there. He chose the latter alternative.

With much effort, Viljar managed to hoist himself up over the railing and down on the other side. Tried to land softly on his feet so as not to make more sound than necessary. For all he knew, there might be someone inside who wasn't expecting him to come storming in.

Viljar raised his eyes and looked through the double picture window. His brain was unable to interpret the visual impression properly. There was a connection error somewhere along the way. Inside the window, he glimpsed a beautiful white angel who was looking at him. Viljar shook his head. Understood that he must have seen wrong and looked again. The recognition struck like a sledgehammer against his forehead. In the middle of the living room, only three meters from him, Ranveig was swaying, clad only in a white nightgown. The only thing that separated this angelic sight from the shepherds on the fields of Bethlehem two thousand years ago was that this angel was not hovering in the open air. She was hanging from the roof beam with a rope around her neck.

Four years earlier . . .
Samson Bar, Inner Pier, Haugesund
Tuesday afternoon, August 24, 2010

Besides a tall waiter who darted around wiping off tables, only a middle-aged married couple was sitting in the farthest corner of the outdoor restaurant Samson. Deeply engaged in conversation with clouds of cigarette smoke and half-empty beer glasses. Outside the fence, the Flaggruten express boat was docking, and a new load of people stepped out onto the cobblestone pier.

Jonas pushed a sun-bleached lock of hair from his face and looked at the people hurrying past. He felt naked and unprotected sitting there.

Ten minutes past the agreed time, Viljar Ravn Gudmundsson came strolling in and sat down beside him. With his emaciated body and long, stringy hair, he could easily have been mistaken for one of the city's many street people.

"I'd like to record the conversation if that's all right."

Jonas didn't like it, but nodded anyway. It was bad enough that he had to ask Viljar to take the illustration pictures himself. He didn't want a photographer to be in possession of the secret of who was behind it. Viljar had accepted this, if somewhat hesitantly.

"Are you alone? I thought there were two of you."

Jonas was stressed. On the phone, Gudmundsson had seemed so eager, but now Jonas felt like he was on trial.

"Fredric is coming in half an hour."

Viljar rolled a cigarette, fired up, and stuffed the tobacco pouch back in the front pocket of the denim jacket he had on. *Loose tobacco? Good Lord, is the man a holdover from the seventies, or what?* Gudmundsson blew smoke out his nose while the butt dangled from the corner of his mouth. Now and then he tilted it up, and the ember got new life. He smiled. Brushed off any lingering skepticism and let Jonas talk.

"If I understand you right, you maintain the Minister of Transport and Communications pays for sexual services from younger party members?"

"No, it's not payment for sex that this is about. He ingratiates himself with young boys and promises them a career in the party if they stay on good terms with him. At the same time, there's a hidden threat in what he says. If you refuse to be a 'friend,' then you're out in the cold."

"How young are the boys we're talking about here?"

"The *majority* are of legal age, to put it that way."

Viljar Ravn Gudmundsson opened his eyes wide and looked like a fish that was breaking the surface for the first time. The cigarette was dangerously close to falling out of the corner of his mouth.

"The majority are legal, you say. Does that mean not all of them are? Does Hermann Eliassen have sex with underage boys?"

"Yes, he has many times."

"These meetings between Eliassen and the young boys have gone on at various gatherings of New Voices in the Center Party, am I understanding correctly?"

Jonas took a breath. It was right before he dropped the bomb and admitted that it was in that context Eliassen had used him.

"Yes, unfortunately. One of the stories that has come to my attention is from a member of this group. What he has to tell is a lot like how I've experienced the minister privately, to put it that way, so the story is true."

"And you're one of those he has exploited?"

"Yes, systematically over a whole year. Until this summer, I thought I was in some kind of special position. That there were feelings involved in the game."

"Do you understand that this can be perceived as revenge from your side? That you want to get back at him for dumping you?"

With clenched teeth, Jonas answered Gudmundsson's frank question. "Would it make any difference in that case? He's used me and other teenagers quite deliberately to get access to sexual services. It's unheard of for a public official to act that way."

Jonas drew his index finger over his throat. Viljar picked up the recorder and turned it off.

"What the hell are you up to? I'm letting myself be interviewed, I'm not sitting in a courtroom."

Viljar Ravn Gudmundsson fired up another hand-rolled cigarette with the ember from the first one and looked at Jonas with a sly smile. "What I'm doing now, Jonas, is saving your ass. By my asking critical questions, the whole flock of Norwegian media people don't need to search you out to get answers. These are the kind of questions that must be both asked and answered before you can pounce on one of the country's foremost politicians." Viljar took a deep puff on the cigarette, and Jonas noted in amazement several seconds later that not so much as a wisp of smoke came out again between his lips.

"We want other journalists, and Eliassen's lackeys, to be looking for you somewhere other than in New Voices. We're doing this to protect the source, and even if it's on the borderline of what's ethically correct, it's something I choose to do to protect you. Do you understand that?"

Jonas nodded dejectedly. He completed the rest of the interview as best he could and agreed to the classic backlit pictures photographers prefer to use to conceal the identity of the interview subject. All that could be seen in the picture was the black shadow of a young man with sloping shoulders looking out over the sound.

Tømmerdalen, Haugesund
Late Friday morning, October 17, 2014

Alfred Isvik was the closest neighbor to Stein Vikshåland's house in Tømmerdalen. He was a part-time farmer, and had just sat down on the tractor when the first cries resounded through the air. He jumped off the tractor at once. The screams from the author's house persisted. People came running from the other neighboring houses too. The bellowing man standing on Stein Vikshåland's deck pounded and kicked at the living room window so it was heard in the whole valley. The heartrending cries and panicked bellowing bore witness to someone who had lost control.

When Alfred and another man from the neighboring farm climbed over the fence to help, they were met by a fury from another world. They had to use every ounce of force and muscle to tear the man away from the window, which had started to crack. He screamed, bit, and clawed in turn. The man was spindly and ungainly, but the terror and blackness in his eyes gave him a strength that could have over-turned a trailer load. After a while, Alfred got the man's hands firmly tethered to keep him from doing more damage. The neighbor still had to work to get his legs quiet under him. Gradually they managed to subdue him. Hysterical weeping turned into whimpering sobs. Alfred let go; another neighbor took over.

Never before had he been witness to such boundless despair.

He scratched his head and looked down at the man on the floor of the deck. The man was sobbing and staring stiffly ahead while he repeated the same thing over and over again. *Ranveig* . . .

Alfred followed the man's gaze. Then he saw her.

"Oh my God!"

Alfred's outburst made the other neighbors raise their eyes. The farmer's stomach contents came up without warning and struck the deck with a splash. The sight of the angelic woman dangling from a rope inside the living room was grotesque. The bloodshot eyes saw right through the window and cut into your soul like a projectile. The eyes were evidence of a death full of boundless anguish. The blue color of the face. The swollen tongue. Each detail evidence of a horrible death. Even so, the white was worst. White nightgown, white shoes, white belt, white hairband, white nail polish.

When the first ambulance came rolling onto Stein Vikshåland's yard, Alfred was still sitting beside Viljar. The neighbors had helped him get the desperate journalist to lie down on the lawn in front of the house. Viljar took frequent puffs on a cigarette while his hands trembled.

Tømmerdalen, Haugesund
Late Friday morning, October 17, 2014

The sight of Ranveig made Viljar black out completely. He couldn't remember what happened before he came to with a whole pile of people struggling on top of him. He could still see Ranveig from where he was lying, and he realized there was nothing he could do. This was not a bad dream he would wake up from. This was reality. So naked, so honest, so all-consumingly irrevocable. There were no pills for something like this. Nothing could reverse what had happened. Nothing could remove this awfulness. The darkness crept slowly into every nerve in his body. Settled like a veil over every single cell. Despondency and aversion hand in hand.

Does it have to hurt so much? The feeling lay there like a plague in his stomach. Seethed, ached, burned . . .

He lit another cigarette. Registered dimly that the ambulance personnel and others had come over to tend to him, were talking with him, shaking him. He answered them with apathy. Nothing was important any longer. Because of him, yet another innocent person had been deprived of life. He understood it now. He was an *angel of death*. It was best to keep your distance. Protect others.

It was only when a familiar face was standing in front of him shaking both his shoulders that he managed to move his gaze and attention out of the inner fog he found himself in.

"Damn it, Viljar! You have to wake up!"

He blinked . . . Looked inquisitively at Lotte Skeisvoll, who was standing over him. In the background, he could see that the ambulance personnel were getting a stretcher ready.

"Come on, Viljar! I don't have time for you to go cuckoo now. They're ready to roll you straight down to intensive care if you don't snap out of it. What happened here?"

Viljar took Lotte by the arm. Held on to her tightly before he nodded. He stared into Lotte Skeisvoll's determined dark brown eyes that were asking him to wake up.

Tømmerdalen, Haugesund
Late Friday morning, October 17, 2014

The headache threatened to burst through her skull. Lotte felt worn-out. Exhausted, tired, angry, afraid, and frustrated. All adjectives were suitable, and part of making Friday a true hell for the police detective. The dead seriousness was a lead blanket over everyone at the scene in Tømmerdalen. Nonetheless, she collected herself. Scraped up the last remnant of surplus energy to be able to look the rest of the team in the eyes and give them the necessary tasks. *Learn from the rain*, Ole Paus said in one of his songs. *There's always a drop left.* . . . She had to find that drop in each and every one of them.

It was as if only now did it occur to the folks around her that this was serious. Maybe because only now was it obvious that the perpetrator did not have the slightest sense of justice, even if that was what he cited in his emails. Maybe it was because everyone who worked with the investigation could see with their own eyes how unpredictable the killer was in the choice of his victims. But probably it was simply because the killer wanted it that way. He had staged the whole thing and left behind a trail of gloom and fear. This was a turning point. The gauntlet was thrown.

When Lotte Skeisvoll saw Ranveig hanging like a macabre decorative mannequin, a new reckoning of time started. She knew that the image would be there the rest of her life. She was hanging completely still, with her head bowed forward as if in reverence. All the white made her pure. The killer underscored that nothing was spared. The white reinforced the dramaturgy. A conscious choice from someone who knew exactly what he was doing. A provocation. A demonstration of strength: *If you haven't woken up before, you will now. . . .* Lotte barked out orders at the scene. Everything should be done by the book.

Not the slightest little detail should be overlooked. All traces the perpetrator left behind him had a purpose. It was not carelessness and nonchalance that meant that each crime scene had loads of traces of the perpetrator. These were guides. *He doesn't do anything that isn't calculated*, Lotte thought. What seemed banal and amateurish was a brilliant camouflage that gave him more latitude than he otherwise would have. Despite two murders, they really hadn't taken him completely seriously. There was an end to just that.

In front of her sat Viljar Ravn Gudmundsson, who had also shown signs of seeing the whole thing as an exciting game. If one were to believe a small fraction of the regurgitation he had written in today's *Haugesund News*, that is. The Norwegian crime press came completely unhinged after he had written about his mysterious letters from the murderer. From now on, the killer was referred to as "the Executioner" by the tabloid press. Crime journalists from far and near abandoned stolid courthouses and futile follow-up cases and instead took the shortest route to Haugesund. In the course of the afternoon, the number of media people in the City of Herring would increase by a factor of five. And every one of them would be calling her. . . .

After shaking Viljar awhile, it seemed like he was gradually starting to focus. She could sense a kind of decisiveness in his eyes.

Good, Viljar, I need you to roll up your sleeves now, she thought.

After a few minutes, she let him go and got him to talk. He told what had happened. She understood that Ranveig had been lured to Tømmerdalen through a news tipster sometime in the course of the night.

How could the tipster know that they would send her? She got up on stiff legs. Decided that the headache had if possible gotten even worse and rubbed her forehead with the back of her hand. Behind her and the police barricades, quite a few curiosity-seekers had started to gather. The homeowner, however, was conspicuous in his absence. They finally got hold of him through his agent. On a noisy phone line from Riga, the author could report that he hadn't been at home in Haugesund for over a week, which was also confirmed by the publisher. "The key is under the doormat," he said to the question of whether anyone had access to the house.

Lotte smoothed out the corner of her shirt collar and turned her gaze back to the mass of people below. Yet again, a sense of unreality came creeping in under her skin.

If this were a boring American detective series, the murderer would be in this crowd of people, she thought. He always returned to the scene of the crime. Unfortunately, real life was not so simple.

Requiem: Offertorium, Domine Jesu

I know I ought to take the pain medication the doctor prescribed for me before the weekend, but I don't want to. It will remove the pain, but it will also make me apathetic. Make me unable to act. Unable to observe. Unable to feel the music . . .

I feel the very *life* streaming through me like a kind of tingling lust. It pricks my fingers and toes. The major muscle groups flex. My blood pounds. The hair on my body stands up. Erection.

The police tape that runs along my stomach is a tingling caress. A feather-light touch from soft female fingers along my navel. Ranveig's fingers were soft. Even as they scratched me, they were soft. I have to hide the deep and bloody tears on my arms, but I feel them there. I get a surge in my belly every time I stroke my hand over the fresh scars. The same surge that I feel when the g-forces kick in on a roller coaster. Enjoyable, tingling, exciting.

The scratch marks are Ranveig's last remnant of living energy transferred from her fingers to my arms as I hung tightly entwined around the lower part of her body. Locked her arms and legs firmly with the weight of my own body dangling from hers. The double weight of two people made the rope around her neck tighten even more. Not so hard that the neck gave way, but hard enough that her life ended faster than it would have from her own weight alone.

I came while she was dying. Uncontrolled and sudden. That surprised me. I have never had any form of morbid sexual fantasies. Never associated death with anything sexual. My sexual advances have always been extremely ordinary. Not so much as one little forbidden fantasy has been allowed to climb to the surface. For that reason this came, literally speaking, suddenly to me. The feeling of power over life and death. The excitement of doing something forbidden, combined with having a trembling body in my arms . . . The sudden orgasm can be explained that way. Though it can't really be called an orgasm. . . . Not the kind that washes over you as a climax to a burning desire. This was more like a sudden trickling emptying. The kind you often wake up from at night as a teenager.

The delightful feeling is a tender memory as I'm standing here watching the police run around like confused little mice. They don't see the cat, but perhaps sense that he's in the vicinity? I see that Lotte Skeisvoll is studying us.

Does she know something? Does she understand what is in the process of happening around her?

I don't know. Can't know with certainty. Nonetheless, I'm quite sure of what she's thinking about right now. Probably reproaching herself because she hasn't taken me seriously earlier. She is angry at herself. Angry because she hasn't understood that it all goes much deeper than the emails have expressed. In despair because she wasn't able to protect Ranveig. Didn't discover in time what was going on.

She is going to wonder how I could know whom the newspaper would send out last night. The funny thing is that I couldn't know that. Only hope, and otherwise arrange everything so that other journalists were *burningly* occupied with other things.

I had the key to Ranveig's apartment in reserve in case the original plan didn't work.

The only thing I don't understand is why the police didn't put measures in place to protect Ranveig. It seems as if they work slower than I've foreseen. No problem, it does make my job easier, but it's an offbeat that doesn't belong. It's important that the instruments play together. Most of all, I want them to follow the recipe to the letter, but I can't do anything about what's happened so far. There isn't much that has to be changed, just some small adjustments to the score. Nothing that will create consequential errors toward the transition to my *Domine Jesu*.

I see Viljar Ravn Gudmundsson get up. It's about time. I have to watch myself a little so he doesn't collapse completely. We're not there in the score yet. In due time, he will get to meet himself and his actions at the door. But for now, I need him as first violinist. Seen that way, it's too bad that he was the one who found her, but good grief . . . That does increase the drama.

I slip away so he doesn't see me. If he had, he would have become suspicious. I am balancing on a knife edge now. I know that, but I've known all along that when the turning point comes, the border between success and fiasco will be just as thin and delicate as a bridal veil.

Viljar is a wounded animal. Dangerous, but not really capable of protecting himself. It was this state I had in mind when I was composing, and now it's only a matter of moving the baton properly, the rest will arrange itself.

The pain pounds in the back of my head while I babble with one of the neighbors as I walk away from the area. I use the real pain to show my sincere anguish. I know that it will be interpreted as sympathy and empathy, and that amuses me.

I turn around when I hear the murmur that goes through the crowd. I raise my eyes to find out what is causing their reaction. Out the door comes the stretcher with Ranveig. Naturally, she is covered by a white cloth. More white . . . Only white, actually. Just as white as Ranveig herself was. Innocent white. Guilty or not . . . It's utterly unimportant to me.

If I could do anything over, it would be the next email that will be sent. Pathetic when both sender and recipient know that it's bullshit, but so it must be. Every piece has its necessary place in the artwork, even if after the fact I see that perhaps it's slightly misplaced.

I think about what my old art teacher taught me in middle school. That Edvard Munch painted many versions of his pictures. Every time he was finished with a picture, he found something he was dissatisfied with, and so he made a new version. There are many different examples of *Madonna* and *The Girls on the Bridge*. Edvard Munch was privileged. I have just this one chance to make this complete. I can't do it over. There is only one *Scream* in me. . . .

Tømmerdalen, Haugesund
Late Friday morning, October 17, 2014

Lotte Skeisvoll turned in place, taking mental pictures. Tried to fix her gaze on small details. Things that in some way or other could tell a story about what had happened in here, and preferably also why. What was left behind in this room after Ranveig was carried out was here because she was *supposed* to find it.

At the previous crime scenes, the technicians had spent an enormous amount of time and resources securing physical and biological traces that could nail the perpetrator to the scene. Obviously that had to be done here too, but Lotte asked them to expend less energy on that and instead concentrate on finding other things in the room that could lead them further. This order sounded extremely unusual to Åse Fruholm, and she asked Lotte why she wanted to prioritize that way. Lotte looked at her a long time before she decided to be honest.

"If this person is ever in a courtroom, he's going to tell the whole story from start to finish. Then it will be enough to place him at the scene purely technically. We don't need to make a latticework of biological traces for every little move he's made."

Åse Fruholm looked grim and offended as she threw up her hands, but she capitulated. "By all means. You're saving me a lot of time-consuming work. But this is your responsibility. The hell if I'm going to be caught with my ass offside if it turns out you're wrong. Then you'll have to take the heat."

Lotte nodded, and twenty minutes later, she had the room to herself. She was just about to start fine-combing it when her cell phone rang. It was an agitated Knut Veldetun on the other end. She had to calm the rookie policeman down and ask him to start over. It helped a little.

"I've checked up the backstory to Ranveig Børve the way you said I should early this morning. . . ." He stopped.

"Tell me!"

"Well, I've found the connection, but I don't understand what you were thinking."

"What do you mean?"

Lotte noticed that her voice was a little harsher than she wanted it to be. Knut was young and didn't need to be put in his place for asking questions, but it was easy to get defensive. *Did I forget something?*

"I see from the registers that Ranveig Børve was charged with driving under the influence in a fatal accident back in 2004, but was acquitted when it couldn't be proved that she was the one who'd been driving. She herself maintained the whole time that a friend of hers was at the wheel, while she was asleep in the front seat after a party where the alcohol flowed a bit too freely." Knut made a brief dramatic pause before he continued.

"I mean, shouldn't we have checked?"

"We damn well have checked! Every single damned judgment and acquittal all the way back to 1995!"

She heard Knut clear his throat repeatedly. A sign that his nervousness hadn't subsided.

"Oh well. But what happened then? Why didn't anyone . . . I would have thought at least, but . . . Who was it who checked the lists?"

The last sentence struck down like a lightning bolt on a power substation. Scheldrup Hansen! That damned dinosaur!

"Damn it, Knut! It was Scheldrup Hansen who checked the lists. He must have been sloppy, because he emailed me the list of acquittals last evening, and Ranveig wasn't on it. That's quite certain, in any event."

Lotte stood there looking suspiciously down at her own phone. The thought of what could have been done for Ranveig if she'd gotten the complete list raced through her, and she felt a despair she hadn't felt since that time she found her sister lifeless on the street and thought she was dead. She pushed away the awful memory. There was no place for anger, despair, or guilty conscience in this room now. She would surely seal Olav Scheldrup Hansen's fate at the next crossroads.

Lotte breathed in and out calmly a few times with her eyes closed. Emptied her head completely of thoughts. Let a few seconds pass in a dark and solitary stillness before she slowly opened her eyes and focused. Let her gaze meet object after object. Associated and analyzed. Most of it was here already and was untouched. That had a thin veil of dust on it. Other things had either been used or brought into the room.

The box of zip ties on the coffee table was one of these things. This tallied well with the injuries Ranveig had on her wrists and ankles. Trying to pull or tear yourself loose from tight plastic strips makes them cut into the skin. She could see that the technicians had found fingerprints on the shiny plastic box.

Alongside it was a half-eaten apple. Oxidation showed that it had been a few hours since it was bitten into. It was gnawed off midway with an exact precision that could indicate compulsive behavior in the person who had done it. She could remember having done similar things herself.

On the floor below where Ranveig had been hanging, there was a vertical stripe of urine, which indicated that she had probably swayed back and forth like a pendulum at the moment of death. It also indicated that she had not broken her neck in a vertical fall, but was suffocated by the noose while she swayed. This was odd. Normally someone would squirm so that the urine that came out would splatter in a big circle, but here the puddle was vertical and even. Thus the body had been at rest, even though she was dying?

Lotte let her gaze sweep farther around the room. An apparent chaos that told her everything and nothing. An overturned chair. Ironing board and iron in the kitchen. Obviously used to smooth the white nightgown Ranveig was wearing. Newspapers, magazines, and books. What about the bloodstains on the floor? Was it important that they were right there? Was it important whether it was her blood or his? Was it actually important *how* Ranveig had dangled when she died? Was it of any importance whatsoever to note all the data from this crime scene and the other two? Would they find anything at all that the murderer didn't *want* them to find?

No, it struck her that she would have to search for what the killer hadn't planted. Everything else would only lead them a step closer to where *he* wanted them. It was time to break the pattern. Do the unexpected. She let the rest of the crime scene go and left the room. On her way out of the cordoned-off area, the flashbulbs hailed at her. She stopped and answered questions.

Then everyone is in place, she thought. *You've got what you wanted.*

Haugesund Police Station
Friday afternoon, October 17, 2014

Five minutes after Lotte got a phone call from Lars Stople, she was on her way to his office in the police building. Everything else would have to wait. She swept in and plopped down on the visitor's chair.

"Tell me!"

Lars Stople looked up over his square eyeglass frames. Cleared his throat briefly before he threw out his arms.

"What should I say? I told you most of it on the phone. Stein Åmli decided to change email provider yesterday. This created some problems for us, since we'd developed a good cooperation with the Google team, and we could get a localization from them in less than an hour. Now Åmli jumped over to Hotmail instead. That meant we couldn't get the sender localization tracked until this morning. Hotmail wasn't so eager to cooperate as Google was, as long as Interpol wasn't brought in. Fortunately at last we got them started anyway."

"And you got a location, but what does that actually mean? He's evidently wandering around on open networks."

Lotte looked at Stople. Could see that he too was starting to get bloodshot eyes and that his hands were trembling slightly. Signs of stress and lack of sleep. Lars Stople hemmed and hawed. . . .

"Well . . . What does it mean? The message was sent from the *Haugesund News* server located in the newspaper building. They don't have an open network, which means that the email was sent from one of the desktop computers connected to the office network in the editorial offices, marketing department, or at Radio 102, but which computer was used is hard to figure out, according to the experts. The only thing we can say with certainty is that the perpetrator was in the media building at 12:30 A.M. and that he was logged onto an office computer."

Lars Stople sighed. Leaned back in the office chair, took off his glasses, and rubbed his eyes.

"It won't stop here, will it? . . ."

"No, Lars, it won't stop here. I'm really afraid that it won't stop until we find him." She gave him a slightly dejected look.

The killer was too quick. They weren't able to move on from crime scene investigations and preliminary investigation before new emails and new murders dropped down into their laps. She looked over at Lars, who was staring vacantly into space.

"What are you thinking about, Lars?"

He turned, about to say something, but finally just shook his head.

"Come on, Lars. What are you brooding about?"

"It's not my job. Then it's just as well to keep your mouth shut, isn't it?"

"Stop fooling around. I've known you since my first day here in the building. No matter what you're thinking, you can come to me with it."

"Oh, well. That's fine, but you aren't exactly a world champion in not taking things personally, and I'll ask you not to take this wrong."

Lotte was about to respond to what he'd said, but he interrupted her by raising his palm.

"Listen here. I know you're not particularly fond of Olav Scheldrup Hansen, and God only knows he's not the sharpest knife in the drawer despite his position, but now I actually think you ought to let bygones be bygones for a moment and meet with him. We need him and his expertise."

Lars Stople could hardly have found a worse time to make his move. He was blissfully ignorant of what had happened concerning Scheldrup Hansen in the past few hours.

Lotte boiled over and stood up so quickly, the visitor's chair toppled to the floor. "You know what? You can damn well forget about sticking your nose into how I lead my investigation! Hansen is possibly the most incompetent person I've ever met. The fact that you and other old hermits think his methods are best is only because you're a bunch of flipping fossils with your asses buried in 1973. Earth to Lars! Have you ever taken off your glasses and seen that investigation methods have long passed by you and Hansen and all the other old farts?"

She went out the door at warp speed and slammed it behind her so that the knickknacks in Stolpe's office rattled. Several faces came into view along the row of offices in the corridor.

"Go to hell!" She howled so that it reverberated in the halls in the whole building.

Two minutes later, a red-faced Lotte Skeisvoll stormed right into the office of Police Chief Arnstein Guldbrandsen without knocking. He looked up in surprise. It was not daily fare that someone came into his office like that.

"What in the—?"

"I want to submit an official complaint against Olav Scheldrup Hansen for negligence in duty!" Lotte was clear and definite. The decision had been made hours ago, but she hadn't really intended to present it this way.

Guldbrandsen did not seem particularly surprised by this demand. He remained calm. "I see. . . . And on what grounds, if I dare ask?"

"He is hindering the investigation, playing the group against me to undermine my authority, and he's not doing the tasks he's assigned. Most recently yesterday, negligence that cost Ranveig Børve her life last night."

Guldbrandsen raised his eyebrows and asked her to sit down. After a few ifs and buts he was served her version of the story. He sat quietly and thought awhile before he answered her in a calm voice.

"I assume that you haven't talked with Olav about this and gotten his explanation of the matter?"

"No, I can't take any more of that guy. He's got to go!"

"That, Skeisvoll, is actually not for you to decide. In contrast to you, I *have* talked with Olav today. He's been in my office along with Kripos director Ove Fiskaa for several hours."

Lotte's face lost its color.

"Let it be said right off, Lotte. Olav Scheldrup Hansen is an arrogant sack of shit with an overly high opinion of himself and his own excellence. You and I are in agreement on that. He came here along with Fiskaa because the Kripos director had heard that the cooperation between you and Hansen wasn't working."

"That should damned well be certain—"

"Stop!" Guldbrandsen banged his palm on the desk and drilled his eyes into Lotte Skeisvoll. "Now, that's enough! Do you understand that? We have three homicides in a row, but you and Scheldrup Hansen are evidently far more occupied by showing who has the biggest balls than in solving the case. That is goddamned disrespectful to the victims and their families. We're a *police agency*, damn it! The point is that we should work together."

Lotte held her breath while she counted to ten.

"God knows I've tried to get some cooperation, Guldbrandsen."

"No, you damn well haven't. I've been at the meetings you've led. What I've seen there is pathetic. You've been using despicable domination techniques from the first moment. Don't you think those of us who've been in the room have seen the condescending looks you give him? That you never let him have the floor when he asks for it. That you never engage with the suggestions he makes. Irony and sarcasm at his expense. And now, yesterday . . . Then you went way over the line in your ridicule. You gave him a task that the office assistant could just as well have done, while the rest of the group was given police assignments! Are you aware of how embarrassing that was to witness?"

Lotte had listened throughout the monologue, but was not yet ready to call a truce.

"Office assistant, yes. I wish I'd given her that task, then perhaps Ranveig Børve would be alive now, but he couldn't even manage such a simple task."

"Quite correct, Lotte. If you'd given the task of checking the lists to the office assistant, Ranveig would be alive. But you chose not to do that. You chose to give it to someone else. *You* chose to give the task to someone who felt it was beneath his dignity to do such things. That's *your* responsibility! Think a little about the following scenario, Lotte. . . . If I had given you the task of going through all passports issued the past year to find out which of them had a slight error in a bar code. How precisely would you have done that job?" Lotte had no answer. She suddenly realized how furious she would have been at Guldbrandsen if he'd done something like that. If she had even completed the task, the work would have been done superficially. Her cheeks were redder than ever, but now mostly because she was blushing.

"Sorry, I see that," she admitted. "But I just get so incredibly angry at that guy. I'm not able to cooperate with him."

"You have to!"

"Excuse me, but what did you just say?"

"You have to, I said. From now on, I want the two of you to cooperate. What I've seen of you as an investigation leader so far is downright poor. Far from what I expect of my middle managers. For two days, Scheldrup Hansen has asked you to get ahold of the legal documents to find a connection to Gudmundsson's cases as a journalist. I can't see from your reports that you've actually done this. I expect you to start doing capable police work. You have a day or two to prove that you're able to not take things personally and to collaborate with Kripos in the way we intend it. Hansen is an idiot, but he is a resource. Start using him for what he's *good* at."

Lotte nodded curtly to her boss, turned on her heels, and left the office. First on the agenda was a sincere apology to Lars Stople. Then a meeting with Olav Scheldrup Hansen.

Media House *Haugesund News*
Friday afternoon, October 17, 2014

Viljar sat in the media house conference room without noticing his surroundings or colleagues. Stared out into space, but his pupils did not fasten on anything other than bare walls. Gathering at work this way only hours after Ranveig had been taken from them seemed meaningless. The others didn't think so. For them it was good to gather, light candles, and hug each other. Viljar just wanted to be alone. Taking part in this mourning choir was not on the agenda. Going around hugging people he otherwise hardly greeted in the hall was stepping far inside his intimacy zone.

When Øveraas had talked and wiped away tears in what seemed like the Hungarian entry in a film festival, Viljar stood up. Went over to the picture on the table, looked at the burning wax candle for a few seconds before he turned on his heels and strode out of the room.

At the exit, he was met by Henrik Thomsen, who stopped him. Viljar tried to clear a path forward, but Thomsen was no racing buoy.

"Viljar . . . Sorry! I know you were close to each other. It must suck to be you right now."

Viljar stared at Thomsen in disbelief. "Suck? . . . Excuse me, but did you say 'suck'? How brain-dead are you really? Ranveig was perhaps the finest person in the whole city. Have you asked her little girl, Victoria, if she thinks this 'sucks' a little? What about her husband, have you asked him whether it sucks?"

"No . . . I . . ."

"You sound like you care, while deep down you don't feel anything other than a little discomfort that something like that could happen to us in this little media house. You have never ever shown empathy to other people, Henrik. Not in your columns, not at work, not privately."

"Damn it, Gudmundsson. Do you even hear yourself talking? I was just trying to say to you that I'm sorry about what happened. I wish I could have been there when he took her. Taking the life of innocent, defenseless girls in that way . . . Fucking cowardly!"

"So where were you?" Viljar looked into Thomsen's guppy eyes with aggression in his gaze. The question had been milling in his head after Øveraas shared that Thomsen couldn't be used on the story, because he was in Stavanger at the concert house. Which he hadn't been.

"What do you mean?" Henrik Thomsen's eyes wandered. Clearly uncomfortable.

"Where were you last evening?"

"I was in Stavanger. Covered the concert with—"

"No!"

"What do you mean by no? I was there."

"No, you weren't in Stavanger yesterday. I saw you in Haugesund."

Henrik Thomsen's whole body squirmed; he looked around in panic and cleared his throat nervously several times. "You must have seen someone else. Read my review, damn it. You'll see that I was there."

"I'll be happy to read that concert review, Henrik, but it doesn't change the fact that you and Hans Indbjo were out on a joy ride all afternoon, and that you were getting cozy with chips, beer, and the last season of *Desperate Housewives* when I passed your apartment a few hours later."

With a resolute hand movement, Henrik Thomsen shoved Viljar away and went into the building.

For a moment, Viljar considered following Thomsen to force an answer out of him, but changed his mind. It was unimportant. Here and now, actually everything was unimportant. He fished out the pouch of tobacco. Observed his weeping colleagues, who were wandering around the room aimlessly.

This is a good image of the whole case, thought Viljar. *The perpetrator has created a universe where everyone passes each other without knowing what they're doing or where they're going.* A decision was suddenly growing in him. He had to get out. Not to satisfy the growing need for a smoke. Not to be alone. He had to get out of this building for good. What had once been his lifeblood no longer existed here.

He moved through the empty office landscape. Looked the other way as he passed Ranveig's desk, but stopped after a step or two, turned, and went over to the desk. He could barely detect a slight hint of her perfume from a forgotten blouse that was hanging over the chair, and the melancholy seized him with powerful claws. He struggled against the lump that sat in his throat, and had to steel himself yet again so as not to fall apart. The workplace still bore marks of the living Ranveig. The family picture smiled at him from the desk. Small Post-it notes where she'd written down tasks she had to remember. Her handwriting, the white wool slippers she bought at the winter Christmas market, the pencil with bite marks, IFA lozenges on the desk. Objects and traces of anything other than what had happened last night.

The computer screen was not turned off as it should be when you left work for the day. It was in sleep mode and showed a little ball that jumped from side to side on the screen, leaving a pattern of colors behind it.

Viljar knew instinctively that he did not have permission to touch anything in here, barely even to be here. Nonetheless, curiosity overtook common sense. He pressed the mouse alongside the keyboard. The ball stopped its restless journey immediately, and in a flash the last document Ranveig had been working on appeared on the screen. The library article. He had skimmed it in the newspaper's print edition before the morning meeting. A smiling Øystein alongside a stack of books.

Viljar was torn out of his speculations when he heard someone clear his throat behind him. Well aware that he had no business at this workstation, he turned around quickly. Behind him stood editor Johan Øveraas along with Lotte Skeisvoll.

"What the hell are you doing?"

Lotte Skeisvoll took a step forward to grab him by the arm. Viljar twisted away. Pushed his way between the two and then ignored all attempts to call him back. Down in reception, he picked up an envelope, put the ring of work keys in it, sealed it, and wrote the editor's name on the outside. He was through with this job. For good.

Haugesund Police Station
Friday afternoon, October 17, 2014

The aroma of Kripos director Ove Fiskaa's sweet aftershave lingered in the tiny temporary office that Olav Scheldrup Hansen had been assigned. The same applied to the smell of sweat. It felt stuffy, and Olav studied his own hands. His fingers still trembled slightly from the adrenaline that had pumped while he got the boss's rebuke served in plain terms. Scheldrup Hansen had chosen to crawl. He ate humble pie to be on good terms with the police chief, but also in a brief conversation with Lotte Skeisvoll a few minutes later. She didn't seem as embarrassed as he, but gave him her hand and asked him to engage in what was his special competence. Profiling.

He sat down and opened the tool on the computer. Plotted in everything they had in the way of facts so far. Changed a few parameters, considering that Lotte was of the clear understanding that the traces were planted at the crime scenes, not left behind carelessly. He entered the victims' data, the murder weapons, time parameters, an endless series of witness descriptions and degree of violence used in the homicides. Spent time entering his own observations and the investigation group's thoughts and theories. The two preliminary autopsy reports and the three crime scene reports followed into the FBI-developed software for use in homicide investigation.

Scheldrup Hansen knew from experience that the profile he would get out of this was in itself not even close to being reliable. Software reads only what is plotted in, and gives answers based on a preprogrammed system. It doesn't think logically. It doesn't take feelings, argumentation, and coincidences into account. He had caught killers who were as far from the perpetrator profile as you could possibly get, but it had also taught him to use the program for what it was meant to be. It was supposed to give the investigator new angles and ideas, hopefully also pick up details that had been overlooked in the huge quantity of data that was always collected in such cases.

It took a couple of hours to get everything into place. Even so, data was lacking from a good number of the interviews, and also the preliminary autopsy report for Ranveig Børve. It would be a while before he got that. He went to get coffee from the vending machine in the hall while the computer worked out the profile.

Afterwards, he let the coffee cup rest in his hand while he studied the results. Felt the heat spread out from his palms and throughout his body. He made himself more comfortable in the chair, and gradually, as he read the document closely, his mouth formed into a broad smile. *Wonder if this isn't the first smile I've allowed myself since I came to town on Wednesday?* Deep down, he knew that he ought to have seen this without a computer having to remind him of what was right before everyone's eyes, but that was just what this software was designed for.

The software had somewhat unexpectedly focused on a man with an eye for detail. An analytical person. This tallied little with the thoughts he'd had. A man was far more inclined both to plan and carry out serial killings. But that the man was analytical was not so easy to see in the chaos he left behind him at the crime scenes.

The killings bore the mark of a perpetrator who was careful about the details in everything he did. In any event, if you took into account that the form and message of the emails was significant, and that the chaotic crime scenes were not a result of carelessness, but of objects and traces that were planted intentionally. Producing this and at the same time misleading the police to think he was careless obviously assumed detailed planning that required above-average analytical abilities.

The perpetrator is not simply planning how he will carry out the killings, but also how he wants us to respond, thought Scheldrup Hansen, pounding a pen on the desk.

That way he can control both sides of the chessboard. Like a practiced player who always knows what move his opponent will be forced to make, and that way can also plan his next move based on this.

Scheldrup Hansen turned slightly on the swivel chair. Fished up a Post-it pad and wrote a word on top: *Policeman?*

Why he wrote this, he didn't know, but there was something about the pattern of action that fit. Policemen know how other policemen think and act in an investigation.

The rest of the information on the laptop created a gloomy picture. According to the software, it was highly probable that the man was solitary, childless, had grandiose ideas about his own excellence, and would not let himself be stopped except by force. This was a "stayer." The only positive thing was that he would probably not disappear from the surface the way other perpetrators had done in previous cases.

The probability was great that the person in question had an IQ well above average, and therefore probably had higher education and an occupation where he could work with something that was of academic interest. Doctor, lawyer, teacher, architect, journalist, editor, or some form of management position. There were plenty of college graduates with a law background in the police.

The most interesting thing, however, was at the end of the document. Based on the profile, the software gave credible tips about what weak points such a perpetrator might have.

Lack of flexibility. Lack of ability to adapt to sudden changes. Lack of ability to improvise, Olav read, nodding to himself as if he had gotten an oracle's answer from the computer screen. *Obviously it must be that way.* So long as everything went as the perpetrator expected, he was unbeatable. *We have to make an amateur move,* Olav thought, going over to the printer to pick up a copy of the profile. The story of the chess master who is knocked off his perch by the amateur who doesn't make the obvious and "formulaic" moves is a familiar one. If the amateur followed the book, he wouldn't have a chance, but when he makes unexpected moves, the master has to start improvising, and the amateur's big chance lies in the chaos that then arises.

Downtown Haugesund
Friday evening, October 17, 2014

Captain's Cabin was a home for worn-out souls. Their bodies had checked out long ago, leaving only the souls behind in empty, wrinkled skulls. Not to say that this was a place for drunks and dallying ladies only, that would be going too far, but they were certainly there. Many of them were fixtures. Others made more sporadic visits to Captain's. One of these was Viljar.

He was younger than his drinking companions, but he didn't care. According to Viljar, you would have to search far and wide for a place where loyalty and true friendship were more highly prized. Maybe you couldn't trust everyone who frequented the bar, but you could count on honesty. It was nailed into the walls. What was said at Captain's definitely did not stay at Captain's, but it was passed on with sincerity. So there was always something.

Viljar had strolled in the doors at three o'clock after wandering aimlessly around on Haraldsgata. His thoughts were a confused mess. Again and again, he had to exert himself to keep the anxiety from getting the best of him. The third time it swept over him, he saw no recourse other than to drown his nerves in alcohol. Not the world's best idea, common sense told him, but as things were now, that was secondary. He chose Captain's for one simple reason. No one knew that he occasionally frequented the bar with the somewhat sleazy reputation. The bartenders and regulars never asked intrusive questions. For them it was enough that he drank.

Four hours later, the anxiety was gone, even if the sorrow was still there. It had settled in his chest like a sinker. Viljar realized that he'd lost the only person that with a little goodwill he could call a close friend. Ranveig wouldn't have used that word herself, but for Viljar that was what she'd been. A friend. Never anything romantic or sexual. Just friendship, and a kind of mutual understanding.

Now she was gone, and Viljar knew very well that he had played a decisive role in the jigsaw puzzle that led to her death. This *must* have something to do with the Jonas case. He was up to his neck in misery, and he didn't believe in coincidences. This whole case revolved around him. That conviction would no doubt pursue him the rest of his life, but right here and now, there was no room for those thoughts. Now there was only sorrow. Sorrow and anger. Once again, the tears came, and one of the female regulars in the house stroked a wrinkled hand across his cheek. Her hand smelled strongly of loose tobacco, with a hint of something that might indicate she hadn't washed her hands after using the toilet. He wrinkled his nose, but did not remove the hand. The touch did something to him.

The woman, with the dignified name of Magda, snuffled slightly impudent overtures into Viljar's ear. The finger, which a moment ago had stroked him lightly across the cheek, was now doing the same exercise over his crotch. That part of him had a life of its own, and Magda grunted contentedly when she noticed that he was not unmoved by the touch. The alarm bells, however, were ringing full blast. This was not a woman he wanted to wake up with tomorrow.

Viljar got up with a jerk and stumbled over to the men's room. He double-checked the lock before he placed himself by the urinal. Magda might be expected to come after him.

When he came out again a few minutes later, Magda was gone. He noticed that his table had been occupied by a group from East Norway and Bergen. Viljar didn't have the energy to discuss seating arrangements, so he turned his nose toward the bar. A few unsteady steps later, the waitress had already taken his order, shown by raising one index finger in the air. The half liter came sliding toward him just as he reached the bar. Viljar knew he'd already had too much to drink, but this particular day did not allow for any more feelings. He saw no way out other than to seek oblivion in a serious bender. Tomorrow would have enough torments of its own.

In the morning edition of *Haugesund News*, he had appeared cool and balanced. The story about his private correspondence with the first serial killer in West Norway had a mark of sensationalism about it. The reportage, or commentary if you will, could very well have been written on glossy paper. The advantage was that he stood out as someone who had control of the situation. Someone who knew more than anyone else. The disadvantage was that the desk had used a number of pictures, which meant that Viljar was recognized everywhere, and just on that day in his life when he mostly wanted to tell the world to go to hell, and then sit down in the wagon along with them.

A little later, Viljar was scooped up from the bar by the group from East Norway and Bergen. They got him on his feet, and with some effort maneuvered him to a place at their table. Viljar was so far into the land of fog and mist that they had to supply him with three cups of coffee before he noticed he had company. He snuffled something unintelligible. Then suddenly he called loud and clearly out into the room.

"Journalists!"

The merry voices around the table turned their heads toward him at once.

"In the name of Jesus, is there life in the hero of the day?" said one of the journalists, who had evidently taken it upon himself to be the evening's master of ceremonies. He had an innate compulsion to talk a few decibels louder than what was strictly speaking pleasant, interrupt his associates with long discourses on this and that, and at any moment tell an even more amusing anecdote or story than the previous speaker. In that way, he guided the whole party as he wanted. Now he'd set his eyes on Viljar, and it was evident that he was enjoying himself.

"Of course we had to rescue you over there at the bar. You were about to collapse *under* the bar, but the bartender still kept serving you. Funny place, this," the man said, turning from right to left to see whether he had the full attention of his journalist colleagues. He did.

Viljar tried to say thank you, but his tongue seemed to have curled up, and it came out more a grunt than a word.

The man from East Norway changed position and sat cross-legged on a chair across from Viljar. "Since you evidently know all about this case, and carry on correspondence with Jack the Ripper, do you by any chance know what happened early today?"

"Yes." Viljar tried to smile, which turned into a distorted grimace.

The man from East Norway winked at the other journalists around the table and pulled his chair right next to Viljar. He leaned forward to pick up everything. One of the other dogs started fumbling feverishly with the recording function on his cell phone. They probably sensed easy prey and were ready to go on the attack. Viljar's peculiar smile had stiffened, and he looked dully at the attentive group.

"Yes, tell us then . . ." The man from East Norway shook his shoulder to get him started.

"What happened early today," Viljar began, but then it seemed as if the words stopped in his mouth.

He collected himself and opened his mouth again. "What happened was that I, in my fucking egotism, was blind that I was putting others in danger."

The man from East Norway and the other four around the table looked a little uncertainly at each other. *Was there something we didn't catch earlier today?*

"The woman who was killed was my very best friend for several years. She was an amazingly good person and . . . and . . ."

Viljar choked up again. The tears came, filling his eyes, and the words wouldn't come in the right order.

"She worked with Viljar as a journalist at *Haugesund News*."

A loud and clear voice made itself known from behind them. A moment later, the person in question was standing in front of the journalists. He placed a big, sturdy fist on Viljar's shoulder and looked down at the group sitting around the table. "Viljar here is in fucking bad shape, as you see. He lost a close colleague and friend today, and I think it's completely shameless of you to start pumping him for information in the state he's in now."

The man from East Norway stood up and was about to take hold of the uninvited guest.

"Take it easy, damn it. I can smell a rat, and just because you have a byline on the TV 2 News Channel doesn't mean you can carry on like this. One phone call from me, and your boss will find out that you're sitting here drunk, luring information out of a witness who is dangerously close to being in a coma. That sort of thing isn't nice, and you and the rest of your wolf pack know that perfectly well."

Viljar felt himself being lifted up from the chair. He looked like a cat that had been picked up by the scruff of its neck.

"Now, I'm taking young Ravn Gudmundsson here with me," said a dark voice. "He's had enough, and suffered enough for today. If you want to know anything, you can ask him tomorrow morning. Right now, there's as much credibility in what he's saying as there is at an after-party in a hotel room after a rock concert."

Outside Captain's, Viljar was lying in the ditch, moaning. He didn't seem to notice that he had his hands in his own vomit as he tried to stand up. Finally he got help from his rescuer. They moved on. Arm in arm down the steep hill on Strandgata from the IMI cemetery to the crossing at Kaibakken. They even walked past a police car parked outside the Egon restaurant without the policeman recognizing the dead-drunk figure. He was on the lookout for a killer, not a drowned doormat being dragged through the streets by a buddy.

Four years earlier . . .
Torvastad, Karmøy
Wednesday, August 25, 2010

It was when his father was silent and serious that Jonas felt afraid. Although he was almost always silent, he usually had a sense of piety about him. A gentle expression, and kind, friendly eyes. On rare occasions, dead seriousness took over. Then he got a distant expression, as if he weren't present in the room. The bushy eyebrows turned down and settled ominously close to his eyelids. His face turned gloomy and strained, and he moved with abrupt, staccato movements. At these moments, the family knew that they would be wise to keep their distance. It was like that too this particular day. His mother quickly started to take her precautions, and asked Jonas and his little sister, Ine, to go with her into Haugesund to shop. His father hadn't said anything, but with a firm movement, he held Jonas back when he was about to go out the front door.

"Not you," he said. "Not anymore."

His mother looked anxiously at Jonas, and Jonas himself wanted more than anything to run out the door before it was too late. His father's hand on his shoulder and those two simple words made that choice an impossibility. He was the head of the family. There was nothing to discuss. When his mother and sister had left, his father let go of Jonas's shoulder. Without saying anything, he went into the living room and sat down on the armchair. Demonstratively picked up the Bible and his reading glasses. Jonas did not let himself be affected by the scene. Instead he waited patiently on a spindle-backed chair over by the window.

After a while, André Ferkingstad got up from the chair. Reserved and sullen, he walked calmly over to the veranda door. Locked it. Then he did the same with the hasps in the kitchen window. Turned without giving his son a single glance and went out in the hall. Jonas could hear the front door being locked. His heart became a hammer. It thundered in his chest. Something was about to fall to pieces. The taste of blood in his mouth. He bit his tongue, but felt no pain. *What the hell do I do now?*

His father stopped by the door between the hall and the living room. He spoke quietly, but the silence around them was so complete that Jonas would have heard him if he'd whispered.

"The house is locked. We are alone. Everything that happens in here has only one witness, and that is God. Is there anything you want God and me to know, Jonas? You can get it off your chest now, because God looks with mercy on those who repent, and I will too."

Jonas gasped involuntarily. There was something threatening about his father's apparent calm and self-control. He observed Jonas at a distance and did not move his gaze. Tilted his head a little to one side, like a watchdog who expects that the intruder will make an attack. It was impossible to act as if he wasn't afraid. Everything about his father's figure radiated a calculating predator. Jonas would not get away. At last he managed to clear his throat enough to get out a word or two. Not exactly well chosen, but hopefully redeeming where figuring out what it was his father knew was concerned.

"What are you talking about, Dad? Have I done something you think is wrong?"

His father came closer. Still silent, but now he had clenched his fists. Jonas could see that the knuckles were white. He moved his head calmly from side to side as if he had a kink in his neck. "I'm not the one who decides what is wrong, Jonas. It's God. Have you done anything that violates His law? Have you, Jonas?"

Jonas noticed that he was about to empty his bladder. It was his father's insane calm that frightened him. If he had screamed, shouted, hit the table . . . Yes, anything at all. Those were normal reactions that could be dealt with.

"I have a clear conscience with respect to God, Father. I haven't sinned against a single one of His Ten Commandments, if that's what you mean."

André Ferkingstad stopped his son from saying anything else by holding an index finger in front of his mouth. The word "mean" came as a mumble.

"You know what we say in Abraham about the Ten Commandments, Jonas. Those were simplifications. Made so that small children could remember and understand them. You're grown now. Why should God dictate a whole book if ten simple commandments were enough?"

His father came a step closer, and Jonas could feel his warm breath against his face as he spoke.

"What is sin, Jonas? Yes, sin is breaking the law of God. Have you ever sinned against God? If you have taken something that doesn't belong to you, then you're a thief. If you have ever hated someone, then Jesus says you have committed murder in your heart. If you have looked at a person with sexual desire, then you've been unfaithful in your heart. Am I to understand that you are without sin in this world, Jonas? Is that the lie you stand in front of your father and say?"

The treacherous tears came without Jonas's being able to stop them. He knew what his father was capable of when he was like he was now. That submission was the only way out to get mercy, but he couldn't ask for that. Not this time.

"What have I done? I don't understand what you're talking about, Dad."

A little streak of doubt passed over his father's eyes, as if a spirit had passed through the room. It was only a flash, but enough to ignite hope in Jonas. His father didn't know anything for sure. He only assumed.

"There are those in the congregation who say I should pray for you, Jonas. That I ought to recite for you. They say that perhaps you haven't taken in what it says in the first letter to the Corinthians. In chapter six, verses nine to ten. Do you know what it says there, Jonas?"

The boy shook his head. A reflex of denial, even if he knew it perfectly well.

"Do you know what it says there?"

His father roared so that drops of saliva struck Jonas in the face. The calm mask was gone. Now both desperation and anger were seen in his face. For Jonas that was a relief. His father's unpredictable anger was easier to handle than his calculating coldness.

His father took him by the shirt collar and pressed him up against the wall.

"These are the words of the Lord. 'Or know ye not that the unrighteous shall not inherit the kingdom of God? Be not deceived: neither fornicators, nor idolaters, nor adulterers, nor effeminate, nor abusers of themselves with men, nor thieves, nor covetous, nor drunkards, nor revilers, nor extortioners, shall inherit the kingdom of God.'"

Jonas grasped the straw his father had given him by reciting the verses.

"Yes, Dad. I repent. I shouldn't have drunk alcohol at that class party. I know it was wrong. I know I've sinned. I've prayed to God for forgiveness for my sins."

Where the crocodile tears came from, he had no idea. Probably a result of pure terror.

The grip around his shirt loosened. His father suddenly looked surprised, just as Jonas had hoped. By admitting a different sin, perhaps he could get out of what his father thought he'd done.

"You . . . You drank alcohol? Was that what they meant?"

"Who are 'they,' Dad? *The congregation?* You know just as well as anyone that the congregation will wrench a sin out of every single word you say, out of every single thing you do. Do you remember what they said about Mom last winter? Do you remember? That she committed adultery because she went to the Christmas lunch at work without you?"

Jonas knew what he was doing now. The whole family was close to being excluded from Abraham when his father chose to defend his mother.

"Mother didn't do anything wrong. I have. I had a drink, but I've prayed for forgiveness from God. I can't let what the congregation might think about that bother me. I have to be called to account by Him, not them."

His father was looking furtively at him now. It was as if all the bundled-up energy had suddenly run out of him. He looked tired. Worn out. He cleared his throat.

"Go, my son, and sin no more."

Jonas backed out of the living room. Could almost not believe that he had gotten away. But someone in the congregation knew, and it was only a matter of time before the congregation stopped hinting to his father what he had done and instead said it flat out. When that happened, there would no longer be forgiveness or pardon in his father's eyes. Then there would only be damnation.

Austmann high-rises, Haugesund
Saturday morning, October 18, 2014

The sun struck Viljar in the eyes, and he twisted and turned to find a position where the rays didn't reach him. Quickly realized that it was useless. He wasn't lying in his bed, and he couldn't move in any direction. A heavy, syrupy brain mass tried in vain to make any connections. Viljar tried opening his eyes in the hope that it would cast light over the mystery. He regretted it immediately. Shooting pain rushed through his nerves from his eyeballs up to his head. He closed them again at once.

In despair, he tried to go back to sleep, but now the rest of his body had discovered that he was awake, with crystal clear messages on three primitive needs. A full bladder that must be emptied. A body that needed water, and last but not least . . . His back was about to seize up. In other words, he had to get up, and posthaste at that.

Viljar tried to open his mouth, but in the course of the night, saliva had glued his lips together, and he felt his lips crack when he forced them open with his jaw muscles. Laboriously he managed to get up into a sitting position, still with his eyes closed. Slowly Viljar got to his feet. Noted with some surprise that he was still dressed in yesterday's clothes and shoes, and that he had spent the night on the overly short couch in the living room.

Then I'm at home anyway, he thought, staggering into the bathroom. He had to hold firmly on to the sink while he emptied his bladder. His knees were dangerously close to giving way. A quick look in the mirror confirmed what he had suspected. He had a big lump on his forehead, but he couldn't remember what had caused the injury. When the trickling finally ended, he became aware of the rank smell of piss in the tiny bathroom. It didn't take more than that for the vomiting reflex to take over and turn him over with his head in the toilet. With his pants to his knees and a convulsive hold around the sides of the porcelain bowl, yesterday's final remnants came up. He noted that today would be considerably worse than previous blue Mondays. Next stop would undoubtedly be the bed.

On his way into the bedroom, Viljar became aware of something in the corner of his eye. A detail that had no business in his living room. He stopped and turned around slowly. By the black leather armchair in the living room, a pair of big shoes were sticking out from under a blanket. There was someone there! A person was lying in the chair. Completely motionless.

Viljar felt the hairs on the back of his neck stand up, and wondered for a moment whether he shouldn't take another turn over the porcelain in the adjacent room. Instead he steeled himself and approached the body under the blanket. All he could see were some thin strands of hair on top, and the shoes sticking out at the opposite end. The body was in a distorted and unnatural position. Some signals in Viljar's brain reported that what was lying under the blanket was a sight he did not want to see. Nonetheless, he removed the blanket. He plopped down on the couch across from the body and shook his head.

What the hell happened? Once again, Viljar looked at the person beside him. He sighed heavily and gingerly touched the bump on his forehead. Viljar had an explanation problem, and he knew it. He looked around desperately. Dryly noted that there was little point in keeping things hidden any longer. The body was lying there, and soon he would have to account for himself. Suddenly the lifeless carcass started mumbling incoherently. Viljar shook his colleague a little.

Henrik Thomsen opened first one eye, then the other. In contrast to Viljar, it did not seem as if Henrik was equally surprised or tormented by the state of things. He even managed to produce an ingratiating grin before he sat up. The old armchair complained in protest under his weight. Thomsen looked at Viljar and shook his head. "Jesus . . . has the ghost come back from the dead? Is there any coffee to be had for a gentleman who spent the night in the world's most uncomfortable armchair?"

"Spare the wisecracks, Henrik. I feel more sorry for the chair than for you. What the heck are you doing here?"

Henrik Thomsen looked at Viljar with feigned offense. "Now, then . . . Ingratitude is the wages of the world, I understand. For your information, you were so dead drunk last night that if I hadn't picked you up, you would have woken up in the gutter instead of here at home. God knows if you would have woken up at all."

Viljar observed his colleague with suspicion. Staggered out to the kitchen and started the coffeemaker with trembling hands. Back in the living room, he delivered a cup of steaming pitch-black coffee to Henrik, while he patted his pockets in search of a cigarette.

"Here," said Henrik, handing him the tobacco pouch. "You lost it on the way up the stairs last night. I brought it in. Figured you would need something to calm your nerves with today."

Viljar took it, found a half-full ashtray that was under the table, and lit an old butt that was in the pouch. The first deep drag produced a coughing fit worthy of an eighty-year-old COPD patient.

"And the experts think that's unhealthy. I just don't understand it," Henrik said sarcastically.

Viljar did not laugh.

They drank coffee in silence. It didn't seem as if either of them had any particular desire to talk about the unavoidable. They squinted at each other like two cowboys ready for a showdown at sunup. In that case, Henrik assumed the role of Bud Spencer. Viljar was probably a trifle slower than Terence Hill, but he fired off nonetheless.

"Can you explain to me why you bothered to drag me home from the ditch last night?"

Henrik sighed heavily, as if it were a burden he had borne for a long time and which he could now finally lift from his conscience. "I know you won't believe me, but it was actually a coincidence. I made an outing to Captain's Cabin last night. Not because I personally frequent that place to any great extent, but my sister does from time to time, and she was the one I was looking for."

He made a dramatic pause. Slurped down a little coffee before he continued.

"In there, I found you in poor condition, to put it mildly, and well on your way to shouting out all the secrets of the world to the assembled Norwegian tabloid press. I thought it was best to rescue you from the situation, and dragged you out of the place and back here. At first I intended to leave you in the stairwell, but when you fell over and hit your head on the flagstones, I realized that you probably needed help and supervision. So I got you in and tossed you down on the couch."

"And then you discovered all this," said Viljar, pointing toward the coffee table. The table was overflowing with papers that no one other than Viljar should have seen.

Henrik nodded thoughtfully and stroked his thin gray hair back. "Then I discovered this," he confirmed.

Viljar shook his head and looked down at the floor. Avoided Thomsen's gaze. He knew that Thomsen was as tight as a coarse-meshed fishing net when it came to keeping secrets, so there was little doubt that this would end in tabloid saturation coverage.

"So . . . What thoughts do you have?" Viljar mumbled, and if it hadn't been for the already oppressive silence in the room, Henrik probably wouldn't even have heard the question.

"I think you have a serious problem, and that you've behaved like an idiot. What's lying on the table here is not only flammable material, it's self-igniting, damn it."

Viljar nodded, but didn't say anything. All the clippings and notes he had saved from the Jonas case four years ago were not meant for eyes other than his own. Especially not the letter Jonas had written to him.

"How you've managed to keep this hidden from the editors and the general public for so long, I don't know, but there's little doubt that it will go off like a grenade in your hands."

Viljar had a good enough understanding of people that he could see that deep down, Thomsen was delighted by the situation.

"My journalistic career is over regardless. I don't care about that, to put it bluntly. I can't go on after what happened yesterday, and I think it's time that the truth comes out where my involvement with the Jonas case is concerned."

Henrik Thomsen squinted and looked at the wreck sitting in front of him. "That's where you're mistaken, Gudmundsson. Only you and I know anything about this for the time being, and now it's high time we scratch each other's backs here."

Viljar raised his eyes. *What is it that hagfish wants now?*

"You need to keep this hidden. I have my secrets too, which you, without knowing it, started to get dangerously close to the day before yesterday. Hans Indbjo and I have arranged things so that we can take some well-paid time off now and then. A concert in Stavanger, a festival in Denmark, a cultural evening in Stord. Overtime pay and comp time afterwards."

Henrik Thomsen scratched himself absentmindedly in the bristly beard that tickled him in the folds of skin under his chin.

"You see, we have a couple of young helpers who are more than willing to accept the task of taking some pictures, describing a concert, or making a few expert recordings. All for five hundred kroner and a free ticket to something they like. It's win-win, don't you think?

"We can help each other out of a jam here, Viljar. If you keep your mouth shut about my fake music review from Stavanger, I'll keep quiet about what's on the table here. No one needs to find out that I take such liberties now and then at the newspaper, and no one ever needs to know what really led to everything going to hell in the Jonas case four years ago."

Viljar shook his head. This must be bullshit! He had little faith that this was how it fit together. It was enough now. Enough lies. Enough secrets. Enough creeping anxiety. It had to stop here. Henrik Thomsen sighed. He squeezed his fingers around the bridge of his nose. Massaged his head behind the ear. Viljar was certainly not the only one with a headache in this room.

"Besides," he said, "I have a little ace up my sleeve. You see, I think I've discovered something where the case of the serial killer is concerned. Something that can lead the police a step closer to a solution. If you promise to keep your mouth shut, I'll share it with you. If not, I don't care that they're on the wrong track in the investigation."

Henrik had tossed out the line, and Viljar bit on it.

"What the heck, Henrik! If you know something, you have to say it. This concerns Ranveig, after all."

The words did not appear to have any effect on Henrik Thomsen.

He shrugged his shoulders indifferently.

Viljar was skeptical, but he could not let the chance get away. He had no real interest in telling Øveraas that Thomsen took liberties in his job, and that he probably leaked like a sieve to that nitwit in Radio 102. Seeing it that way, Viljar had nothing at all to lose by entering into an agreement with Thomsen.

He looked at the mountain of flesh awhile before he sighed in resignation.

"Fine, Henrik. I have everything to gain by following you in this. What have you discovered that the police wouldn't have seen already? You may think so yourself, but you're not really that ingenious."

"Fine, Viljar. Try to connect that sluggish brain of yours, and follow along with what I have to say. Don't interrupt me before I'm done. Okay?"

Viljar did not reply. Simply nodded curtly to his colleague, and fired up the little stub that was left of the butt in the ashtray.

"The killing of Ranveig. I've understood that she was hung for display in the living room in a completely white nightgown. What makes me wonder is that no one at the media house appears to see the obvious reference in having her hang that way. The police detectives don't appear to be noticeably interested in the manner in which she was hanging either. They're just digging away at her relationship to you, and if anyone may have had revenge motives against her."

"Her relationship to me?" Viljar squinted at the beast in the armchair with newly won interest.

"Well, forget about that. They're on a wild-goose chase, the whole lot of them. The question is, why don't they see the connection to the movie?"

Viljar leaned forward on the couch. Felt that the headache threatened to crawl out of his temples. He really had no idea what Thomsen was babbling about. "Movie? . . . What movie?"

Thomsen looked at Viljar in amazement a brief moment, before he leaned forward, found the cell phone on the table, and searched for the film trailer for *Fallen Angels*, a Varg Veum production from a few years earlier.

Varg Veum as played by Trond Espen Seim unfolded on the little screen in front of Viljar, and in small clips he sensed the outlines of what he understood must be a connection. The white gowns. The hanging women. The killer had copied a horror scenario from one of the most widely seen movies in Norway, and no one appeared to see the connection. No one, it should be noted, other than the numbskull Henrik Thomsen.

Haugesund Public Library
Saturday morning, October 18, 2014

Haugesund Public Library. Old and venerable and baked into the landscape on the upper side of magnificent Our Savior's Church right in central Haugesund. Viljar still felt the headache from the drunken bump pressing down on him, and he was nervous about going in. Stopped outside the main entrance and indulged in the third cigarette of the day. Noticed that people glowered at him on their way into the library. Wondered a moment about which smelled worse, the smoke or the sweaty clothes he'd slept in. Probably it was the combination that made people react with a frown.

Right then, the door opened behind him, and a tall, ungainly fellow barely stuck his head out the doorway. "Listen, smoking is actually prohibited here by the entry, could you go down to the parking lot, do you think?"

"Hi, Øystein!"

The head behind the door stuck a little farther out. More inquisitively now. "Oh, hi . . . Is that you, Viljar? Didn't recognize you in passing. Do you mind?"

The voice was neither friendly nor inquisitive. There are people who have that character trait. They ask but commandeer at one and the same time. In the same sentence.

Viljar did not respond, but instead flipped the half-smoked cigarette in an arc over the dry bushes and down onto the asphalt. He turned around and followed Øystein into the building.

"Nice that you're here, Øystein."

Viljar cleared his throat before he continued.

"Do you remember that evening we ended up at Bestastuå after we met Henrik Thomsen down at the pier?"

Øystein Vindheim looked at Viljar a moment before he nodded cautiously. "Hmmmm . . . That wasn't that long ago. What amazes me is that you remember it! You were drinking with both fists!"

Viljar waved him away. He had enough drunken anxiety already and didn't need to be reminded of previous liquor-soaked evenings too. "I talked with Henrik Thomsen about something today. If he'd taken any pictures of us in the course of the evening at Bestastuå. He hadn't. Did you?"

Øystein Vindheim raised his eyebrows high over the edge of his glasses. "Did I take pictures? I went home after ten minutes, Viljar. I don't care for that mountain of flesh, and had zero interest in spending a free evening with that idiot."

"So you left?"

"Ha-ha . . . That's what I thought. You don't remember a thing. You even followed me up the steps after I'd called for a taxi. Although I guess you stopped halfway when you ran into some ladies you knew, if I remember correctly."

Viljar could vaguely recall an episode where he was standing on the stairs with Øystein, but they were flimsy fragments of a memory that had never taken hold. He let it be, and instead proceeded to the real reason for his visit to the library.

"Oh well, it's not the first time Thomsen's made things up. But that wasn't why I came. You see, I need a little help with something, and I suspect you're the right man to ask."

Viljar stopped by the counter and waited until Øystein had made his way around carts and bookshelves and was securely behind the desk. He looked up at Viljar and gave him a smile.

"I see. If it has to do with books, then I'm sure I can help you, but it's a question of whether I want to."

Viljar pasted on a smile and looked stiffly back at his buddy. "What the hell . . . ?"

Viljar stared at him uncomprehendingly. Øystein Vindheim had always been friendliness itself. They were buddies. Where did this sudden animosity come from?

"Just today I don't know how much time I care to spend on *Haugesund News*. I have a bone to pick with the reporter who wrote about us yesterday. She misquoted me, and now she's so arrogant that she doesn't bother to answer when I call her. You don't exactly stand out as serious in the daylight, Viljar."

Viljar stood there without a word. He got a distant expression, which Øystein evidently made note of.

"What is it? Did I say something wrong, or what? You must take a little criticism when you—"

The librarian got no further before a fist pounded on the counter in front of him. A stack of returned books threatened to topple, but reconsidered at the last moment. Now it was Vindheim's turn to open his eyes wide.

"The reporter who interviewed you was killed last night, Øystein. I am reasonably certain that she would have picked up the phone and apologized for the misquotes if it wasn't for the fact that she was hanging from a noose."

"Oh, good Lord, Viljar. Was it Ranveig who—?"

"Yes!"

Viljar cut him off and covered his face with his hand. Struggled energetically with himself so that he wouldn't lose his composure. Øystein's face had lost all color. His customary smile vanished in a second, and the man clung to the library counter with white knuckles.

"Sorry if I was a little abrupt. I actually need help."

Øystein was as if frozen solid for several seconds before he snapped back to life . "Of course, of course . . . Anything at all . . . I'm truly sorry. It must have been too awful. . . ."

He tried in a slightly awkward way to pat his friend on the shoulder. Viljar gently removed the hand.

"It actually concerns this case. I've got a tip that indicates that the killer uses books or movies as models for his murders."

"Books . . . ? You mean like a copycat?"

Viljar looked up at the tall librarian. He hadn't used the word himself, but it was absolutely precise. *Copycat* . . . Someone who copies what others have done. Or in this case, if he was to take Henrik Thomsen's word, what others have *written*.

"Ranveig was hanging by a noose in the living room dressed in a white nightgown. Does that say anything to you?"

Viljar knew the answer, but wanted Vindheim to confirm it. Øystein looked at him in dismay. He wouldn't have been the person he was if he hadn't reacted to the details. This was not information the police had released to the media.

Øystein shook his head, then stopped a moment before he nodded. Viljar could see that it had not taken Øystein more than ten seconds or so to come to the same conclusion he and Henrik had. The similarity was striking. Nonetheless, it had been over twenty-four hours without the police having seen the connection. At least that he knew of . . .

"Yes . . . You're thinking of Gunnar Staalesen. *Fallen Angels*.

There the victims are hung up after they've been killed. All in white garments." Øystein nodded in confirmation of his own conclusion.

"So we obviously have the first murder too."

Viljar stared at Øystein without saying anything. The starter cables in his head were a bit sluggish this morning. It took time to get the right connections made. His inquisitive expression made the librarian continue where he'd left off.

"Yes, I mentioned it to Ranveig Børve too. . . . The first killing with the woman who fell out of the high-rise. Somewhat the same there too." Finally Viljar's brain connected. He understood that this was important. In other words, Ranveig had known about this connection already on Thursday.

"In what way? Is that killing also taken from a book or a movie?"

He did not answer. Simply turned around and went over to the bookshelves to the right of the reception counter. Accustomed fingers quickly made their way to a book on the shelf. He handed it to Viljar. Unni Lindell. *Man of Darkness*. Viljar turned it over and realized from what was on the back cover that it was a bull's-eye.

"The novel starts with a woman being thrown from the balcony of her own high-rise apartment. I thought about it at once when I read about the killing in the newspaper, but I thought it was a coincidence."

"You thought that, but didn't say anything about it to the police?"

"Ha-ha . . . I understand your reaction, but all murders that are committed in Norway have many similar features with some crime novel or other. Authors do research, you see. But, this is completely sick. . . ."

Øystein Vindheim stood and looked straight ahead. His hands hung limply by his side. Looked like he was hanging to dry on a rack.

Viljar summarized the facts about the second murder. The car salesman who'd been shot in the head from a distance on the steps outside his own residence. Vindheim shook his head. There wasn't anything from that murder he immediately recognized from the literature. Viljar was about to give up when Øystein asked him to wait a moment.

Two minutes later, he had fetched the two other librarians who were at work this Saturday. He outlined the sequence of events and asked them if they recalled having read anything like that recently.

The discussion went back and forth before one of the three, a short, dark, bubbly lady, spoke the triggering words that made Viljar rise up from his seat.

"Can it be Jo Nesbø? Wasn't it in one of his books that a slimy lawyer or something like that was shot on his steps with a single shot from a long distance? The murderer had been lying in wait all night. He used a kind of old rifle from the Second World War. . . ."

Øystein lit up. "Of course! There we have it. It's from the first book in the Oslo trilogy about Harry Hole. The one about the old front fighter. What was it called again? *Nemesis*? No . . . The one that came before . . ."

"*The Redbreast*?" The clever dark lady struck again.

"Yes! *The Redbreast*. Thanks, Ruth. It's a shot in the dark, but it may be that's the one we're searching for."

He went over to the bookshelves again and took it out.

"Seem to recall that the murder came quite late in the book. Not right at the end, but in any case more than halfway." Øystein handed Viljar the copy. Viljar thanked him curtly. Took the books under his arm and made his way toward the door. The alarm started to beep infernally at the same moment. Øystein ran over and turned off the mechanism.

"Library card?"

"I don't have one," Viljar mumbled, looking uneasily down at the floor. It was a little embarrassing to admit to his friend how unfamiliar he actually was with the library.

"Then damn it, it's high time! Come here," Øystein ordered him, and set about preparing Viljar Ravn Gudmundsson's library card.

Outside, Viljar stopped a moment and let his gaze travel down the central core of the City of Herring. In the parking lot for Europark, he caught sight of a figure he'd been together with barely an hour ago. Henrik Thomsen was on his way toward his car with a man Viljar recognized.

Viljar had interviewed the man once several years ago in connection with a theft. Inheritance, something or other. He couldn't remember his name, but the guy was a known face in town. Henrik opened the trunk of his car so that the man could set down the large case he was carrying.

Viljar stood there in his own thoughts and watched the car as it passed the library. The county musician who was sitting in the passenger seat was not to be mistaken. He had played in the North Rogaland Symphony Orchestra since Viljar was a teenager.

Typical Thomsen. Only high culture is good enough.

The Courthouse in Haugesund
Saturday morning, October 18, 2014

Every time Lotte Skeisvoll stood in front of the new courthouse in Haugesund, the same childhood memory came back to her. She and Anne are on the floor in the living room in their old house at Solvang. Dressed only in tights. Around them flows a tsunami of Lego pieces. She remembered that she always made sure that Anne had the nicest, best blocks to build with, while she took the leftovers. Pieces that were almost impossible to put together into a house. The result was a peculiar construction with bare poles at one end and narrow, oblong windows of various sizes at the other. Anne always started to laugh when she saw the strange buildings Lotte had scraped together with the leftover blocks.

The white courthouse in Haugesund resembled her childhood building projects. Normally it was closed on Saturday morning, but Lotte knew there was a commitment hearing going on inside, and she took the chance that she might get to speak with an executive officer.

There was a moderate gale, and the rain beat on the asphalt as she crossed Knut Knutsen OAS street from Rådhusplassen to the court-house. She found safety under the overhang in front of the entrance and cupped her hands around her face to peer into the windows along-side the entry door. She had guessed correctly. The executive officer, André Ferkingstad, was standing right inside, talking with one of the city's most recognizable defense attorneys.

She tapped lightly on the window to get his attention and was immediately recognized by Ferkingstad, who came over to open the door. The attorney removed himself as she stepped inside and stomped off the rain.

"I don't think you need to appear at this commitment hearing, Skeisvoll. You're not on my list."

"No, no . . . It's not that. I have a couple of questions that I was wondering if you or someone else here can answer for me. It's concerning the homicide cases we're working on."

She could see that the sober-minded prayer house man turned pale, and he looked nervously around.

"I don't know anything about that!"

Lotte was taken aback. She wasn't there to accuse him of anything. At the same time, the memory of a rejoicing Ferkingstad watching his own house burn down made her skin crawl. She shuddered at the thought. The man did not seem entirely of sound mind.

She did not comment on his reply, but instead took out her note-pad. It had gotten wet on one corner, and her irritation made itself known immediately.

I've gotten sloppy. There's no order in even the simplest things.

"I don't know how much you've picked up from the newspapers, but this concerns a killer who clearly has access to information from court documents. What I'm wondering is who, other than the police and you here at the courthouse, might have access to details from various court cases."

André Ferkingstad looked at her in astonishment. "All judgments are public, so in theory it can be anyone at all."

Lotte sighed. Ferkingstad was evidently not particularly quick on the top floor. She didn't need tautologies.

"Yes, I do know that. That wasn't what I meant, but both you and I know that it's not possible to do an internet search to find out whether your neighbor has been convicted of drunk driving or if he's a sex offender. Who, other than the police or you in here, can get to such information? Attorneys, journalists, security firms?"

"Not security guards. The press and law firms can probably dig out such information if they wish, but . . ."

"But?"

André Ferkingstad scratched his bushy beard thoughtfully before he threw out his hands in a gesture of resignation. "You have to come here and ask for access to the judgments. It's only the most recent court cases that are out on our systems. If you're going to find documents from older cases, you have to contact us directly. Us, or you . . . All the papers are archived in the police building."

"Do people often ask about this?"

"No, almost never. But if you think about the case in the newspaper, that journalist was one of our most frequent visitors a few years back. A coarse fellow, and a real nuisance."

"Gudmundsson?"

"Yes . . . He's plastered on every single newspaper stand in town with that self-glorifying smile of his. He's a hyena who smells blood and shit a mile away!"

Lotte noticed inflamed roses on Ferkingstad's cheeks. He was not the only one who had reacted with disgust to Viljar's tasteless feature in yesterday's paper. People were dismayed by the tabloid angle.

"Do you keep a log of such inquiries? Is it possible to see who has looked at which judgments?"

Ferkingstad nodded in confirmation. "Yes, but I must have the case numbers it concerns, and it will take a few days to come up with a complete list. We don't have it digitally, anyhow, not for cases from before 2010."

Lotte closed her eyes. Yet another locked door in this case. They didn't have several days at their disposal. The killer had such short intervals between homicides that it gave them minimal playing room with investigation tactics.

Probably that was also part of the plan. He wanted to keep them in high gear so they couldn't think about it.

"Okay. Do that as quickly as you can," said Lotte, giving the three case numbers to the executive officer.

As Ferkingstad opened the door to let her out, a tall figure came toward them. He walked with head lowered and his hands in front of his face to protect himself from the driving rain. It was Øystein Vindheim.

Ferkingstad indulged himself in a broad grin and patted the new arrival on the shoulder as he came up to them. "You're not at the library, brother?"

Vindheim tossed his wispy hair a little to shed the rain. "Early lunch break. Thought I should get my raincoat, which I forgot here last Thursday. Looks like I need it today."

"Are you brothers? You have two different surnames."

Vindheim turned toward Lotte and grinned. "Don't you see the similarity?" Øystein Vindheim placed himself right next to Ferkingstad. "We're half brothers. Same mother, different fathers. I'm the beauty, he's the beast."

Øystein poked his brother amiably in the side. André Ferkingstad seemed able to control his reaction to his brother's wisecracks.

Lotte wanted to ask him about the meeting with Ranveig Børve two days ago, but did not want to mention it with Ferkingstad as an audience.

She went out the door, and was closing her notepad when she discovered to her surprise that she had written only one word on it from the meeting with Ferkingstad: *Police?*

I have to pull myself together. Now I'm not doing my job.

She smoothed out the paper, which had curled up at the corner, let the door close behind her, and trotted down toward the police building. She had made it no farther than to the Old Slaughterhouse when a police car with blue lights stopped abruptly ahead of her. Out jumped Knut Veldetun. It was obvious that he was worried.

"Damn it, Lotte! Do you have it on silent, or what?" He ran over to her. "Jump into the car, I'll drive you up to the hospital. It's Anne. Overdose."

Lotte Skeisvoll grabbed Knut by the arm. Her legs buckled under her, but the sturdy policeman held her upright.

"Come on, Lotte, get in. Olav has taken over the case. We have to get you up to the hospital."

Right there and then, no police investigation in the world held any significance for Lotte. In one short minute, the world was turned on its head. Anne had been found unresponsive, Knut told her. If she was still alive, he didn't know.

Four years earlier . . .
McDonald's, Oasen Norheim
Late Saturday morning, August 28, 2010

His hands were shaking, but Jonas kept them hidden under the table. He had trouble breathing. The restaurant reeked of greasy, sticky, frying odors. His palpitating heart would not settle down. In front of him was the extensive feature in *Haugesund News*. Five pages inside the paper. Besides a two-page spread for him, there was one full page with Hermann Eliassen and two pages of political denunciations. All written under Gudmundsson's byline. In principle, this was everything he had dreamed of. The ultimate revenge. A solid nail in Eliassen's political coffin. The follow-up cases would seal it once and for all.

Yet everything had gone completely wrong. Gudmundsson had overlooked a tiny little detail. A little stroke that felled a great oak. In the illustration picture, it wasn't possible to identify him, but in the left-hand corner of the picture, you could see the table where Jonas and Viljar had sat and talked. On the table was an open interview pad. Invisible to the naked eye, but with a magnifying glass the details in the picture came out more clearly.

INTERVIEW WITH JONAS FERKINGSTAD it said in capital letters at the top of the pad. The rest was illegible. Viljar Ravn Gudmundsson had thus unwittingly revealed his name. He had been careless about the most important thing of all: protecting the source.

As if that weren't enough, Viljar refused to pick up when he called. Only voice mail. So far, he had to hope that no one at home or in his social circles read the newspaper with a magnifying glass. If he could have, he would have collected all the newsstand copies from every single store and burned them. This was a total nightmare. He felt that people were staring. That they were whispering behind his back. He got up so suddenly that the soda cup crashed to the floor. He didn't notice it, just sprinted out of the fast-food restaurant. Had to get air. Had to think.

Shaking, he sat down on a bench alongside Norheim Church. Tried to make out the writing on the pad without a magnifying glass. It was impossible. He crossed his fingers that the journalists in Oslo wouldn't reveal his name. That they took into account that he was a victim. But that was a lost hope.

Just then, a text message came in from an unknown number. Someone who said he was a reporter on TV 2 wanted to give him the opportunity to comment on the statements from Hermann Eliassen that this was a fabrication and purely an act of revenge from a candidate for New Voices. Someone who felt offended because he hadn't been selected for the core of youth they would be grooming in the party.

Since TV 2 had discovered his name in the picture, Jonas realized that it was only a question of time before the whole world would collapse around him.

There was no way back. It would come out this evening. *I have to take hold of the situation myself. I have to buy myself time. I need until tomorrow to get away.*

Jonas took the phone and browsed back to the TV journalist's first call. With shaking hands, he pressed the Reply button, and made a silent prayer that this would work.

"Sandgren, TV 2."

"Yes, this is Jonas Ferkingstad calling. I have an offer for you. If you wait to release my name until tomorrow night, you will get an exclusive, candid interview with me in the evening. Only TV 2, no one else gets to talk with me."

Haugesund Hospital
Late Saturday morning, October 18, 2014

The room was white. White walls, white ceiling, white linens, white skin. For once, Anne looked as if she had peace. The light hair waved nicely down her cheeks and shoulders. Pale and lifeless. All the small wrinkles and furrows in her face were whisked away. It was like looking at a beautiful little doll. A doll who might suddenly decide to open her eyes and burst out a mechanical "Mama!" Anne didn't do that. There was no button on her back that could make her wake to life in a moment. The batteries were run down.

Lotte looked at her sister with different eyes. For the first time in many years, she saw the defenseless little girl. The girl who had always been the happy, bubbly one. The girl who was always ready with a joke or an amusing story. The girl who always wondered how things really fit together. Curious about life, without a thought that the world also offered danger and wickedness. When she was little, she was fragile as a baby bird in the nest. It took nothing to disappoint her, hurt her, or make her angry. Anne always thought well of others, and never understood that anyone could deceive her. When their parents died, life struck Anne with full force. Like a car that at high speed smashes skin, bone, and flesh into a bloody, lifeless mass. It happened right in front of Lotte's eyes without her noticing it. Anne had slipped out of her hands. Little by little. Small, trivial problems. Then slightly bigger, but obviously understandable problems. Gradually major, dangerous problems that made the warning lights blink.

It wasn't until she saw the needle marks that she became aware of the decline, and realized that her sister had gone under. Since that day shame had pounded on the door, and there were no more excuses and rationalizations. Lotte had used most of her strength to defend herself. Not her sister. She had hidden away the despair, sorrow, and powerlessness in a corner of her brain that was locked with a chain and double padlocks. No one would get to see that space.

Only now, in all this whiteness and cleanliness, did it come to the surface. She let it happen. The tears ran while she whispered her sister's name again and again. Lotte realized that this was a turning point. Never again would she act indifferent to what happened with Anne. There was no longer any point in pretending that it didn't affect her.

The doctors had barely managed to bring Anne back to life. Her heart had stopped, and it had been awhile before the ambulance personnel got it started with resuscitation.

"We still don't know if there will be damage from the cardiac arrest," a nurse explained. "But it seems as if it's going better than we feared. She's breathing on her own, and she has sensitivity in her extremities. We'll keep her sedated for the time being. Until we wake her, we can't say anything more about the state of things."

The happiness that she was actually alive was overshadowed by this uncertainty. Could Anne be confined to a bed for the rest of her life? Lotte was ashamed that her train of thought also touched on the fact that she didn't have time or room for a sister requiring nursing care.

How egotistical can a person really be, she thought at the next moment, and gave herself an imaginary box on the ear.

While Lotte was absorbed in her own thoughts, her phone beeped again and again. She chose not to look at the messages while she was sitting beside Anne. There had to be an end to putting career ahead of family.

A short time later, a flock of white coats came gliding into the room. Lowered eyes. Mumbling. Glasses on the end of their noses. One of them came over to Lotte and asked her nicely to wait outside until the doctor visit was over. She could come back in again later, but they had decided to keep Anne sedated for another few hours, so she would probably not have contact with her sister until then at least. This sort of thing could take time.

Lotte went out and sat in a little group of sofas located right outside the patients' common room. She took out her cell phone and started browsing through the messages. There were considerably more well-wishers than she would have thought, and actually no one who questioned that she wasn't steering the boat at the moment.

Have I started to get a cynical image of human nature?

She smiled a little at herself. Opened message after message and felt on the verge of tears. Suddenly a message from Viljar leaped out at her. She had obviously noted that he had called a couple of times too, but she couldn't bear to get involved in his problems right now.

When she read the message, that view changed almost immediately.

Hi, Lotte. I've found out something important. The guy we're chasing copies murders from crime novels. I've been at the library and got help. We found all three murders in different books. Call me soon!

Was that possible?

Lotte sighed dejectedly and tried to recall whether she had heard of anything similar before. The murderer must think they were a flock of birdbrains in the department who hadn't discovered this before now. She called Viljar. He answered on the first ring.

"Is it possible for you to stop by, Lotte? It will be hard to do this over the phone. You have to see this with your own eyes."

Lotte bit her lip. She shouldn't. Anne needed her here. It would be much better if she sent Scheldrup Hansen or one of the others.

"Listen, I'm actually pretty occupied now. My sister is in the hospital. Is it okay if I send the Kripos investigator?"

"Only if that means I get to give him a kick in the balls. . . ."

She sighed heavily. There were evidently others who had a strained relationship with the Kripos investigator.

Lotte gave up. Maybe it was best if she did this herself. She felt guilty as she made her decision, but she couldn't let this wait either. She confirmed that she would be there in half an hour.

Lotte took a deep breath and then slowly let it out again. A trick she had learned at yoga class. It was supposed to empty the body of worries, thoughts, and bad feelings. Lotte talked to herself.

"Now, it's crucial to focus. Maybe Anne won't wake up until tomorrow. She won't even notice that I'm here. I'll go see Viljar and hear what he has to say. After that I'll contact the department physician and go on family leave immediately. It's impossible to lead an investigation at the same time as I have to get Anne on her feet again."

Viljar's apartment on Austmannavegen, Haugesund
Late Saturday morning, October 18, 2014

After the visit to the library, Viljar let apathy surround him again. He hadn't said anything to Lotte on the phone, but there was an unopened email in his in-box. The subject line of the message left little doubt about the contents.

Pronouncement of judgment #4

Viljar did not want to open it. Had no desire whatsoever to read another one of these bizarre messages. The last one had been about Ranveig. Portraying her as a kind of lawbreaker who deserved the death penalty was just as hair-raising as it was bloody unjust. That action had convinced Viljar of one thing anyway. This was not about finding offenders who deserved punishment. This was about finding offenses in those whom the killer had decided to kill.

The Oslo media had woken up from its slumber. The tabloid press was hysterical in its headlines. In the newspapers he had grabbed on the way, the pictures from Tømmerdalen leaped out at him. *VG* enticed with THE EXECUTIONER'S LATEST VICTIM and a large picture of Ranveig. *Dagbladet* went for the more "serious" variation. NEW

KILLING IN HAUGESUND—PEOPLE LEAVE TOWN. Every single news broadcast and current events program was about "the Executioner." Implicit in this was that Ranveig had done something criminal.

Ranveig had told him the story at a staff party with an open bar. She had fallen asleep in the passenger seat of a car and woke up only after the accident had happened, and the driver had fled the scene. The keys were still in the ignition. The car owner even maintained that she had stolen the car. She was indicted for drunk driving, but acquitted because of the state of the evidence. No one could prove that she was the one who'd been driving.

Using the incident as an excuse that she deserved to die was just laughable, and deep down, the killer knew that too. Ranveig was chosen to affect him personally.

This case is about me. Lotte can believe what she wants. This is a vendetta. If I disappear, it will stop.

When Lotte showed up, he was about to open the email for her, but from now on, she would have to read them herself. He had no plans to stay in the city much longer. She would get an insight into the theories he and Øystein Vindheim had come up with. She and the rest of the police would have to take on the rest. This game had gone too far.

I have more than enough with my own ghosts, he thought as the doorbell rang.

Outside stood Lotte. Or more precisely, what was left of her. They didn't say anything to each other. Viljar simply opened the door wide to let her past. He could see she'd been crying. Her cheeks were streaked, and her eyes red-rimmed and sore. She was unkempt and tousled.

She passed him and hurried right into the living room without taking off her coat. Plopped down in the nearest armchair and let out a deep, heartfelt sigh. It was as if someone had vacuumed all the identity and personality out of her. Left behind was a zombie in full daylight. Viljar sat down on the couch and pushed the laptop toward her. Pointed at the email.

A tinge of despair came over her eyes. She fixed her gaze on the screen and opened the email. Read it carefully.

Lotte shook her head with a grieved expression when she was through reading. For the first time since she came to Viljar's apartment, she opened her mouth.

"Oh my God . . . Have you read the message?"

Viljar shook his head. Fished out a pouch of tobacco and at the same time couldn't care less about Lotte's warning gaze. His house, his rules. If it was unpleasant, she could leave. Lotte cleared her throat, looking around for a window she could open. She slipped out of the armchair and trudged over to the window by the kitchen nook.

"He's after smugglers this time. Uses the same name, but has changed email provider again." She picked up the phone and called the police station with the information. Promised to forward the email to Olav at once. Viljar waited to say anything till she was done.

"That means nothing," Viljar said. "You won't find him based on the information he provides. It may limit the search somewhat, but he's going to succeed. What is interesting is the letters and numbers in small type at the bottom. What does it say?" Lotte looked inquisitively at him before she turned her eyes toward the screen again. She scrolled down until she found what she was looking for.

"AH 1-2."

"Great. Then we'll know very soon how the murder is going to be committed," said Viljar. The whole case was so exhausting that he felt no satisfaction in being in possession of part of the solution.

"I'm about as fond of guessing games as I am of secretive, over-the-hill journalists. If there's anything we don't have here, it's plenty of time."

"The code refers to an exact murder in a crime novel. More precisely, a crime novel written by an author with the initials AH. It will be the second murder in his or her first book."

"Anne Holt?"

"For example, but there might be others, and that has to be checked. If it's Anne Holt, you're fortunate. I have her whole collection on the shelf here."

Viljar pointed with his thumb behind him, where an enormous bookcase covered the whole wall from floor to ceiling. Even if the rest of the apartment was messy as a drug den, there was order there.

"Didn't think you read books . . ."

Viljar brushed aside the comment with a hand gesture. "Left behind by the ex."

Lotte got up and went over to the shelves. She ran her index finger carefully over the spines of the books.

"Which is number one?"

"*Blind Goddess*. They're in the right sequence on the shelf."

Lotte didn't answer. Only nodded thoughtfully and pulled out the mentioned title from the shelf. She started to browse, but stopped after a few pages.

"Do we have to read, or do you know the answer?" She turned her head away from the bookshelf and toward Viljar on the couch.

"No idea. You'll have to search for yourself."

Lotte went over to the armchair again. With the book in her hands. "The other three, then. Which books?"

"The first was from Unni Lindell's *Man of Darkness*. A lady gets thrown off the balcony in her high-rise apartment. The second was the most difficult. Jo Nesbø's *The Redbreast*. An attorney is shot on his doorstep with a rifle. The last one I hardly need to say. We've all seen the movie. . . ."

"*Fallen Angels* . . ."

Lotte whispered the words out in the air. The scenes with the angelic murder victims hanging from the ceiling in white nightgowns was one of the most frightening ever in Norwegian cinema. Gunnar Staalesen's horror script had become unpleasantly lifelike on film.

Viljar looked away. The memory of Ranveig would always be nailed to that scene.

The awkward silence lasted no more than a few seconds. He reached his hand toward her. Not to have someone to hold on to, but to get the book she had in her hands. She took the hint. Gave him the book, and made another call to the police station.

Ten minutes later, he was sitting with the answer before him.

"Here it is. . . . A guy is shot at close range with a high-caliber pistol at the front door of his own home. Short and brutal. A shot in the head, and game over. If Anne Holt is the right author, here's your answer."

"Can there be any others?"

Lotte looked from Viljar to his bookcase.

"You'll have to check thoroughly, but I think it's Holt. All three others have been well-known Norwegian crime writers. Gunnar Staalesen, Unni Lindell, and Jo Nesbø."

Lotte nodded. In that case, they had the answer to both what and how.

The problem was that they were lacking *who, where,* and *when.*

Viljar stole a glance at Lotte as she sat with her own thoughts. He felt sorry for her. She had responsibility for a case that wouldn't let itself be solved. The killer was too quick for that.

Haugesund Police Station
Saturday afternoon, October 18, 2014

Three hours after the meeting between Lotte and Viljar, the atmosphere was focused in the operations center inside the police station. Olav Scheldrup Hansen had been briefed by Lotte after her visit with Viljar, but now she wasn't here. That her thoughts were with her sister at the hospital was inopportune, but he had decided to leave her alone. He was just happy that he got to steer the ship alone for the time being. It was clear to him what had to be done, and he tried to give concise and direct orders to the group.

"Knut . . . You are responsible for coughing up acquitted smugglers at Haugesund District Court from 2002 until now. You'll take two constables from the station with you of your own choosing. All weekend leaves are withdrawn, so you'll have a few folks to pick from. I've made an agreement with executive officer André Ferkingstad that you can meet him at the courthouse. He'll help you locate the right judgments more quickly."

Olav then looked over at Lars Stople.

"Lars! You know the people on the street after having walked a beat for years. I assume that you also know some of the men behind smuggling. Forget about drug dealers. The email gives a clear impression that this concerns smugglers who shirk their civic responsibility for taxes and fees by selling alcohol and tobacco. You know who I'm talking about. Try to have a chat with some of them. See if you can produce some interesting names. Take a couple of constables with you who know the milieu in the city, okay?"

The Kripos investigator did not take time to wait for a confirming nod or yes from Lars Stople. He expected that the man would do as he was told.

"I'll take responsibility for meeting with a team from Kripos in Oslo and briefing them thoroughly about the case. The rest of the group will concentrate on investigation of the murders that have been committed, but be ready to take part in operations later this evening if anything should turn up."

Everyone around the table nodded, and the assembly left with their own assignments.

Two hours later, Olav Scheldrup Hansen had the list in front of him. Seven names and addresses. Seven potential victims.

I have to eliminate some of these, we can't be in seven places at once, he thought, and waved Lars Stople over to him. Perhaps the old policeman could help him.

"We have seven names, Lars. Can you tell me a little about what challenges we face in terms of protecting them?"

Lars scratched his head and looked over the address list. He took his time. Thorough, as always. Olav wanted to shake him. Just as he was about to lose control and scold the policeman, Lars cleared his throat.

"This will be simple," he said, pointing at the third name on the list. Johan Gundersen. Fjellvegen 8H in Haugesund. Olav exhaled and waited for an explanation. After a few seconds, it came.

"Johan lives on the eighth floor in the high-rise where Rita Lothe lived. There's only one exit from the high-rise, and a patrol of two men could easily stop people on their way in and out of there."

"Good, Lars. That's exactly how I wanted you to think. With that said, I think we can remove Gundersen from this list with certainty. He can sleep securely tonight."

"I see . . . ?" Lars looked skeptically over at his superior.

Olav smiled. "Our man isn't stupid. No one ever uses the same crime scene twice. He knows that the residents in that area are nervous and on their guard. They will be observant and curious about people who come and go. The risk is too great."

Lars Stople nodded. "This one," he said, putting his finger on the last name. "Ivar Staurseth. You can delete him too. He's gone underground."

"Underground, what do you mean?"

"We've had a search warrant out on him for the past two weeks. He showed up in a narcotics case, but disappeared from his residence before we got ahold of him. We've had the whole building under observation, and he's not there anyway. The guy I talked with in the environment thought that 'Ivers' had fled and was now enjoying tropical drinks at some warmer place on the globe."

The investigator nodded contentedly. Maybe the old man was a little sluggish on the trigger, but he shot with high caliber. This was beyond all expectation. Five names left.

"Reidun Samland . . . Even if we can't delete her, we can protect her easier than the others anyway."

Lars pointed at the address behind her name. "Røvær, where's that?"

"A little island community ten kilometers west of the city. He would have to take a coastal steamer or have his own boat to get out there, and it would be impossible to anchor without being observed. We could stop him by having a couple of observers keep an eye on her out there, who can warn us if anything happens."

"Does that mean that by sending two men out to this island, we can use the rest of the corps for the remaining four addresses?"

Lars nodded. Made a check mark by the four names that remained. "I assume that we'll have flashing lights and visibility this time?"

Even Olav Scheldrup Hansen knew that the safest approach this time was to be visible. Nothing would be worse than if the killer was able to get to the victim unseen. A visible police presence would scare him off.

"Yes, we'll do that. All patrols should position themselves in the vicinity of the residences we've checked off."

Lars nodded again. Olav wondered for a moment whether that was a rehearsed movement in any conversation with a superior. First a cautious question, then a nod . . .

"So you're not evacuating? No police inside?"

"If we do that, he'll be forced to wait. All opportunities are closed. By being present the way we're doing it now, we allow for his big ego to take the chance to try to fool us. He feels self-confident, and he will try if he glimpses a slight hope of succeeding."

Lars seemed indisposed. Coughed and cleared his throat before he asked yet another question.

"What you are saying is that these four people will be used as bait? I have a problem believing that Lotte has approved this."

Olav led him away from the others. He refused to tolerate that the old man stuck his nose into his tactics and plans. He chose to give him a reminder.

"Listen here, Lars . . . Lotte and I are in agreement about how to proceed. What you're doing is sowing doubt about that. It's just these kinds of things that obstruct an investigation. Negative focus and lack of coordinated action. Do you understand?"

Olav waited for a response from old Stople, but this time there was no nodding, but no more questions either.

Requiem: Offertorium, Hostias

All I feel is my calm pulse. Slight electrical jolts that throb. I am present in my own body. Feel every single nuance in the changes in my surroundings. The sea breeze that tickles the back of my neck. The odor of people passing me on Haraldsgata. Kebab, sausage, and garlic dressing. Every single impulse is reinforced. Nothing gets past me. A predator on the hunt. Sensing the prey ahead.

The final preparations were made early today. Then an almost unbearable ten-hour waiting period followed. In the beginning, I enjoyed this pocket of time. It gave me an excitement I'd never felt before. Now this feeling is replaced by impatience and restlessness. I don't want to wait. Just want to feel yet another life go out between my hands.

Today's chosen one will be the simplest. It will all be over in three seconds. A door opens, the pull of a trigger, and the subsequent shot. Pistols are the simplest.

The police are still blissfully unaware of who I am, and so far I've kept myself under their radar. Something that in itself is quite laughable. Yet no one has asked a single critical question or raised an eye-brow. The birdbrains are behaving like . . . Well, confused, headless chickens.

This unforeseen incompetence in the opposing party entails added work. I have to adjust the score again. Add to and take away. It works in a way, but I liked the original better.

It was not so predictable. It had elements of surprise.

I smile a little at myself while I have these thoughts. I've prepared myself for this. These are *people* I'm working with. People aren't marionettes in a puppet theater. They do unexpected things. Make irrational choices. Act with their heart instead of their head. Nonethe-less, I must say I'm satisfied. If everything doesn't go according to plan, the notes are still just as predictable in harmony as the pattern of moves in a master chess game. I can lead the pieces where I want them to be. Places where I can take them one by one. When the game is over, the moves will remain in the history books. Unchange-able for all eternity.

Arnfred Simonsen's residence is as if created for my task. At the bottom of a grove of trees above Our Savior's cemetery. It is playfully easy to slip unseen both in and out from the lot through the grove. From the walking path two hundred meters farther up, I can easily disappear without anyone being able to see what's happening. No one will notice a jogger along the path, and the view into the grove of trees is hidden by the underpass along Karmsundsgata.

I look over my shoulder as the underpass approaches. No one in the vicinity. Jog calmly down toward the underpass and sprint toward the grove of trees as soon as I'm out of sight from the path. In among the trees, I lie down in the dry fall leaves and wait. Five min-utes slip away without anyone passing. The forest is not very dense, and it's easy to move ahead toward the house. I can see the red roof reflected in the light from the streetlamps on Salhusveien. Once at the end of the grove of trees, I stop. Get down on my knees and breathe deep and long. Crawl soundlessly back, because I'm not alone. I feel the sweat beading on my forehead, and my heart rate increases.

Two police cars with rotating blue lights are parked on the road down by the cemetery. This is definitely not part of the plan, and I feel panic taking hold of me. The calm I have felt has been closely connected with control. In less than a second, it's gone. I am irritated. Not at the police, they're just doing their job, but at myself. I should have waited with the email until this afternoon, the way I'd planned. *I got too eager!* Now the police have had enough time to take their precautions. I am starting to get careless. Overeager. Impatient and incautious. Everything I promised myself not to be.

I lay my head down in the leaves and breathe out. Exhort myself to an even pulse and even breathing. My brain needs oxygen in order to think clearly. I must think clearly in order to regain control. I must regain control in order to get the mission accomplished. I must complete the mission so as not to ruin the artwork. Simple. Logical. Rational. I look down at the police cars again. Two men in each car. Passersby will perceive it as police cars waiting to stop a drunk driver along Salhusveien. I know better. They are here to scare me away from the house. To prevent Arnfred Simonsen from becoming the next victim.

I am tempted to execute the original plan, but that's my heart talking. A few breathing exercises later, I have turned my thoughts onto the right frequency. The strategy is clear. When the police are here, they are also at other possible locations. It's time for plan B. I smile as I stand up and stroll back. I love plan B. . . .

Central Haugesund
Saturday evening, October 18, 2014

Lotte Skeisvoll felt uncomfortable. Squeezed into the backseat of a police car, she sat looking out a steamed-up window that had to be constantly wiped off. The climate control system had evidently called it a day, and was barely able to keep the windshield clear. She poked Scheldrup Hansen, who was sitting in the front seat.

"Can you quickly go through the operation one more time? There were a couple of details I didn't understand."

He showed no sign of turning around, but cleared his throat a little before he repeated himself from the briefing a few minutes earlier. Slower this time, as if Lotte were less intelligent and needed time to take in the points.

"We've limited the surveillance to four possible sites. The surveillance is not concealed, but made visible by using rotating lights. This is done to frustrate his plans so that he might start improvising. Do you follow so far?"

Olav barely looked over his shoulder. Lotte nodded in confirmation.

"The four addresses we're monitoring are two addresses here in the center of town, one on Salhusveien out by the cemetery, and one in Skudeneshavn. In addition, we've sent two men out to Røvær to babysit a lady who may also be in the killer's crosshairs.

"In the city center, we're talking about the old building we see on the other side of the street, right by the entry to the Palestine Restaurant. Jomar Palsgård lives there. "Jompa" to his friends. Age fifty-five. Alcoholic. Multiple convictions, but also acquitted on a few occasions. Has a fondness for Polish liquor and cigarettes. There's one more car in the city center. It's up by Haugesund Stadium. An immigrant lives there. His name is . . . Wait a moment. . . ."

Olav Scheldrup Hansen fished a phone out of his jacket pocket and browsed in his notes. He found the name.

"That's it! Heilu Manstrawi. Age forty. Was indicted for unlawful import and sale of cigarettes from Nigeria . . . Who the hell wants to smoke Nigerian cigarettes? Whatever . . . He was acquitted of illegal selling because he managed to convince the court in some strange way that it was only for his own use. Forty-two cartons, actually . . . He was fined for unlawful import, but thus acquitted of selling, so he avoided prison."

Lotte felt a little surprised by the tactic, but didn't quite know how far she could stretch the cord without Scheldrup Hansen getting obstinate.

"Out of pure curiosity, why have you chosen the strategy of monitoring? I mean . . . wouldn't the first instinct be to protect the possible victims inside the buildings, or evacuate them to a safe place?"

Scheldrup Hansen straightened up in the seat. She knew from experience that he disliked such questions, but in any event, she got a complete answer without his getting angry.

"He has to be stressed. By being visible at the scene, we force him to act irrationally. Then he'll be out of his comfort zone and have to play on our territory. We simply turn the tables on him."

Lotte saw the logic in Olav's line of argument, but didn't like it. This was a game of chance where they couldn't afford to make a mistake. She was about to ask more questions, but decided against it. She was simply too tired.

She looked down at her hands. They were shaking a little. The worry. The anxiety. The shame. Only hours after they had revived Anne at the hospital, Lotte did what she had promised herself she would stop doing. She had prioritized her job ahead of her family. *Why is it that way?* she thought. *It doesn't make any difference whether I'm here or not this evening.*

The tears came without warning, and she had to turn away so that neither the constable nor Scheldrup Hansen would see it in the rear-view mirror. There and then, she felt that her sister was much closer to the pearly gates than she herself would ever get. On a day like this, Lotte chose the adrenaline kick over concern. She had little faith that He up there had much use for that line of thought.

She dried the tears with the back of her hand. Promised herself to stop by the hospital as soon as the action was over. She had to. She couldn't desert Anne completely. Right now it was important for her to show Anne that she could be trusted. The question was whether that was really true.

The constable and Olav were talking so quietly together that Lotte couldn't make out what they were saying. It almost seemed like they were doing it deliberately. She felt ignored in the backseat. Involved, but it doesn't count . . . The fragile child's voice from her inner-most childhood memories echoed in her ears. She said it every time they were out on the street and played hide-and-seek or war. She didn't want to really be involved. Then she might lose, and she didn't like that. Was it that way now too? Had she taken herself out of the investigation as soon as she met a little resistance? Was it safest to let the big, tough boys take the lead, so she could just be there without having it count? Lotte shook off that thought. Of course it wasn't that way. She still had control. She was the leader. It was just that she was sitting in the backseat. . . .

Her line of thought was broken when the police radio started to crackle. One of the other patrols was calling them.

"We hear shots! I repeat. We can hear shots. Not here by the stadium, but up toward Fjellvegen, I think. We heard the shots down here. Two shots. I repeat . . . Two shots. Should we leave our position, or send other patrols up there?"

"Are you sure those were shots?" the Kripos investigator asked. "You say Fjellvegen. . . . Isn't that where those confounded high-rises are?"

"That's confirmed. We don't know yet if the shots came from there, but it tallies with both direction and distance."

"All patrols . . . I repeat . . . All patrols! Drive to the high-rises on Fjellvegen. Shots have been fired. We have a potential victim living in apartment 8H."

Lotte stared openmouthed from the backseat. A probable victim in the high-rises?

Unprotected?

"What the hell are you doing, Olav?"

"We removed that victim from our list. He lives on one of the top floors in the high-rise, and it was quite improbable that the killer would venture back to the same crime scene he's used before, while he is sure to be observed both on the way in and coming out of the high-rise. After shots were fired, that is."

"You are, God help me, the biggest idiot I have ever met!" Lotte screamed out the words, and then gave him a smack on the back of the head that he definitely felt. The sirens could be heard from all directions shortly after they took off toward Fjellvegen.

Two police cars screeched into the parking lot in front of the high-rises simultaneously. Right behind, they could see the blue lights from the other cars that had been sent out. A handful of residents had huddled together outside the entryway to one of the high-rises. Lotte, Scheldrup Hansen, and the constable were quickly out of the car and barricaded themselves behind it. The Kripos investigator shouted to people that they should get away from the building, but they stood as if paralyzed.

One minute later, all three police cars were at the scene, and they could hear that several sirens were on their way farther down Fjellvegen. Knut Veldetun had been in car number two, and he now called on the megaphone that everyone should remove themselves from the high-rise. Slowly the mass of people broke up, but there was no hint of either panic or fear. One of the spectators came sauntering toward the police cars without showing any sign of haste. Lotte was about to get up, but was brusquely pulled down again by Scheldrup Hansen.

She felt it in her body. There was something that didn't add up. Ordinarily, people would have run to safety if there was danger afoot, but here there was nothing to see but curiosity. The way in which the man came toward them signaled the same. He stopped right before them and looked down at the police officers behind the car.

"He took off," he said dryly, pointing toward the student housing alongside the high-rise.

Lotte made a fresh attempt to stand up, and this time no one tried to prevent her.

"What happened, and who is it who took off?" she asked while she made signs to the others that they should follow her. The man looked back toward the entry to the high-rise.

"There was a guy in here who fired two shots, and then disappeared on a bicycle that way," he said, pointing once again toward the spot where Fjellvegen turns past the student housing and farther down toward Geitafjellet. Lotte took him by the arm and led him a bit to the side.

"Did you see him?"

"Well . . ." He hesitated a little. "I got a slight glimpse of his back as he left on the bike, but he was already a good ways down the street when I came out on the pavement here. Black clothes, in any event, and a jacket with a hood."

"So how do you know it was a man?"

"No, did I say . . . ? That I don't really know. I just thought it was."

"Do you know if anyone in there is injured?"

The man's pupils widened when it occurred to him that of course that was a possibility. "Oh dear . . . Good Lord, that may be, but . . ."

"But?"

"No, I don't know. People streamed out of the apartments, so I don't think that happened. Then someone would have called for help, or we would have seen if someone had been hit."

"You stay here. I need to talk more with you as soon as we've checked out the apartments. Could you hear from which floor the shots came?"

The man was apparently confused. He shook his head and looked at Lotte questioningly. "Floor? No, I don't think it came from any floor. More from the exit here. I live on the first floor, and I ran out at once. Then he was already on his bicycle, so he can't have been farther inside than the entry."

Lotte didn't understand a thing. If the man who fired the shot had only been in the entry, it couldn't have been the goal to hit anyone. She jogged across the parking lot toward the entry, where several constables were already busy checking whether anyone had been wounded. Scheldrup Hansen stood by the entry and called to them.

"Go to apartment 8H first. Check if anyone's there."

"Who lives there?" Lotte asked.

"Johan Gundersen. Loner, age forty-three. Acquitted of smuggling four years ago. He was on our list."

"And despite that, he was unprotected here this evening?"

The Kripos investigator looked uncomfortable. His facial expression alternated between fury and uncertainty. Lotte could not understand that he'd made such a mistake. She thought he had learned from the episode with Ranveig.

"It's stupidity to try to shoot someone on the eighth floor. You would definitely be observed on the way down again."

"No, Olav! Stupidity is assuming that our man thinks rationally and reasonably, and basing our actions and people's safety on what we might think. We're police officers, Olav. We are here to protect people, not put them in danger. Damn it all!"

She pushed past Scheldrup Hansen and took the stairs up to the eighth floor. Bitterly regretted it when she was halfway. There was an elevator in this building after all. She sighed and continued up the last flights of stairs. Passed police officers who were on their way to other residents in the apartments above. Outside 8H stood Knut Veldetun. He was talking with a man who could be none other than Johan Gundersen.

The stench of alcohol from Gundersen reached her already on the landing below, and the man's face showed that it was not the first drink of the evening. Or the first in his life either. A tattered knit jacket hung loosely around a bare torso and a potbelly that bulged in all its glory and suggested that it had been a while since Johan last saw his penis. Whatever . . . The man was alive, and that was the most important thing. Lotte shook her head. Gave a sign to Knut that she was going down again.

The projectiles from the shots were evident on the white brick wall between the first and second stories. The whole thing seemed completely unmotivated. Lotte tried to think through what made the guy act this way. Did he want to scare them? Show that he still had power and the possibility to take out his victims?

She walked back toward the police cars. Felt that she was inexpressibly tired. Maybe it wasn't their man who had shot in the entry? Maybe the whole thing was a weird coincidence? The answer came two minutes later when she had settled into the front seat of the police car. *I'll be damned if Scheldrup Hansen is going to sit there one more second*, she thought as the police radio crackled.

"Emergency response center here. Can anyone answer me?"

Lotte sighed and picked up the intercom microphone from the holder on the dashboard. "This is car 554 here. Skeisvoll. What's this about?"

"We've just gotten a message about a shooting on Djupaskarsveien right by the stadium. Are you in the vicinity?"

The blood left her head, and she turned cold. The police patrol had been there all evening, but not now. With all police resources up here, the killer obviously had free rein wherever he wanted in the city. It would surprise her if the immigrant at Djupaskarsveien 21B was still alive. She got on the horn to summon the others, even though she already knew it was too late.

As the sirens finally reached the address three minutes later, the scene outside Manstrawi's house was quite different from the one they had seen at the high-rises. Here too people had gathered, but these people were afraid. Someone screamed. Another was crying, while the others stood apathetically and stared into space. The door into the single-family house was wide open, and in the hallway lay a dead Nigerian cigarette smuggler.

Lotte gave up. She gave word to Lars Stople that she was not reachable by phone, and left the scene without any further explanation. Right then and there, she couldn't care less about the whole job. Anyone who wanted it could have it. *Dereliction of duty is not great, but regardless, the police chief will have someone and something to blame when he is covering his ass in front of an assembled national press corps tomorrow,* Lotte thought, going toward the footbridge. The hospital was only a two-minute walk away, and someone was waiting for her there. Someone who was still alive, if only just barely . . .

Viljar's apartment on Austmannavegen, Haugesund
Saturday evening, October 18, 2014

Holed up inside the apartment, Viljar had the company of Johnnie Walker this evening. Boring guy: doesn't say much and smells a little like an old man. After Lotte left the apartment in a hurry a few hours before, Viljar had done what he'd decided to do earlier in the day. He called his psychologist at the district psychiatric center. He needed to know what she had told the police, but she flatly denied having said anything at all. They hadn't even called her. The psychologist understood in the course of the call that something was terribly wrong, and a quick explanation resulted in a four-week medical leave due to long-term mental stress.

The all-encompassing darkness had been a torment in Viljar's life in recent years, but he had always dragged himself out of it by pure mental force. Besides, he had to. Viljar had Alexander to think about too. Even if the boy lived with his mother, he couldn't just go to seed. He longed for an inner voice that could tell him that everything was going to be fine. That it would soon be over.

The moment with Ranveig's white figure dangled before his eyes over and over again, and it didn't seem as if all the whiskey in the world could conjure that image away. A tableau in his mind stamped ETERNITY.

Viljar emptied another brimful of whiskey in the glass. A water glass.

Like a damned alkie, he was sitting here downing whiskey from a water glass while feeling sorry for himself. He decided to take care of what he had to do. The email to the editor with the password to the mailbox was at the top of the list. After that, pack up . . .

When Viljar sat back on the couch twenty minutes later, everything was done. Two suitcases of capriciously chosen clothes were on the living room floor. Passport and wallet with bank card and credit cards were packed. The email was sent. The only thing that remained was figuring out where he should go.

He searched for various travel destinations with seats available the next day. He had not really traveled to speak of, and actually it was utterly immaterial where he ended up. He just wanted to get away from everything. A place where it fazed no one that he had stiff drinks in the morning and a tendency to be antisocial. *Alicante? Why not?*

Viljar paid, printed out the ticket, and put it along with the passport and wallet in the one bag. Then he leaned back on the couch. Found the alarm clock on the cell phone and set it for ten o'clock the next day. Then he would have plenty of time to get a few more drops of liquid in him before he had to take the Coast Bus to Stavanger. Before he fell asleep, he made a silent prayer that there wouldn't be anyone he knew on the flight. He just wanted to get away. Forget. Get some distance from all the problems here at home.

Jonas sought him out in the state between dream and reality. That young, innocent, and beautiful face. The blond, shoulder-length hair. The cautious smile that Viljar had misunderstood when he received the letter. He had seen him on only two occasions, but Jonas had followed him like an incubus every single night in his dreams. He would never let go, and this time he was closer than ever. He was standing outside Viljar's front door with a new letter in his hands. Not the same one as last time. This letter had a pink envelope. Viljar gradually became aware that Jonas was not alone. By his side, Ranveig was standing, holding him by the hand. She was beautiful, but the sight of the white gown made his heart hammer wildly in Viljar's throat.

He woke up with a start when the doorbell buzzed. He was in a cold sweat. Viljar felt more than heard that he had screamed loudly when he saw Ranveig and Jonas by the door in his dream.

Half unconscious, he staggered to the front door. Still caught between dream and reality. In a daze, he almost expected to see Jonas and Ranveig standing outside. They weren't. . . .

If Viljar had been wide awake, perhaps he would have been more on his guard. Maybe . . . Before he could open his mouth, the person in the doorway was inside. With violent force, the figure struck his head against the wall beside the door. A second later, his brain was disconnected from all physical pain.

Four years earlier . . .
Torvastad, Karmøy
Late Sunday morning, August 29, 2010

Doubt held Jonas back. He knew he should go, or even better run, now when he had the chance, but he was unable to tear himself away from the house.

"Hurry up, Jonas! We don't have all fucking morning. Your dad can get here at any moment." Fredric was shifting from one foot to the other alongside him.

"He never gets here until after church coffee is finished, you know that."

"There isn't anyone who hasn't heard the rumors, Jonas. He's going to drive home as soon as someone or other talks with him on the church steps."

Jonas hesitated. He knew that Fredric was right, but the house that he had hated more than anything on earth suddenly seemed so much safer. It was as if it were leaning toward him, whispering that in here nothing could go wrong.

He clung to the bag he had packed. Looked at the letter he had written to his sister and mother. He had asked for forgiveness. Asked them to treasure the good memories. Asked them to remember all the nice things there were before the congregation swallowed them up with its doomsday prophecies, before the fear of sin took over and removed every trace of human warmth.

He had even asked them to take care of his father. Try to get him to understand. He knew deep down that it would be of no use. That his own son chose sin and damnation, before His safe and protective embrace, would not be forgiven.

There was no way out other than to run away. When his father came home from church, it would be with the assuredness of what had gone on behind his back. Jonas stood there on the yard in front of the old house after the last bag had been thrown into the back of Fredric's car. He had a desire to pray to God, but at the same time felt that there had to be a limit to hypocrisy, so he let that be.

The stunt with TV 2 the day before had bought him the time he needed. He had promised them an exclusive interview on Sunday evening in exchange for their withholding any information that might reveal his identity. *"I need time to prepare the family,"* he'd said. And they fell for it.

This evening, there would be hell to pay when they found out they'd been fooled. They would probably question his credibility, but there he'd received unexpected help in the morning hours. A young man from Surnadal had contacted Norwegian Radio and told about his experiences when as a sixteen-year-old and an elected representative in the party, he'd been seduced by the current Minister of Transport and Communications. True enough, at that time Eliassen was only county leader, but still. The story confirmed who Eliassen was, and what skeletons were hanging in his closet.

Now it was about getting away before his father found out about it in town. Probably he already knew, and Fredric might well be right that he was already on his way home.

"Damn it, Jonas! We have to split!"

The motor was running and he waited impatiently for his friend. Jonas stood as if frozen, looking at the house. He didn't react to Fredric's exhortation. Only when Fredric put his hand on his shoulder did he seem to come back to life.

"What are you up to, Jonas? We have to get out of here. They'll be here at any moment."

"Ine . . . Little Ine. She'll be all alone in here, Fredric. Alone with Dad. She only has me, and the little that's left of Mom. She'll be so lonely."

Jonas struggled with the tears. The concern for his little sister had always been the glue that held him to his childhood home.

"She'll manage, Jonas. You, on the other hand, are through if he gets hold of you, you know that. You have to come now. Please!"

Jonas looked over at his lover, almost surprised. Like the living dead, he let himself be led to a seat in the car. Fredric jumped in and stepped on the gas so the gravel sprayed higher than the foundation of the house. He barely managed to clear the gate on the driveway when the car skidded.

They hadn't gone more than a hundred meters before what mustn't happen, happened. His father's black Opel Corsa turned onto the same gravel road and was headed right toward them. There wasn't room for two cars if you didn't make use of the field alongside. Fredric braked suddenly and hit the steering wheel.

"Damn it! Damn it!"

He screamed for all he was worth. Now there was no way around it. They had to face André Ferkingstad's anger. They saw the door on the driver's side open, and Jonas's father get out. He stood there a moment by the car with clenched fists along his sides before he slowly started moving toward them.

Time slowed down. The seconds had a whole eternity of broken dreams in them. They sat paralyzed, waiting for the unavoidable. His father's figure grew with each step. There was no doubt. He knew. His face was stone, his gaze implacable. A crow screeched and flapped past, but otherwise it was quiet. Nonetheless, Fredric barely heard the words that Jonas whispered to him. An almost soundless hissing. An exhalation.

"Drive, Fredric."

"What?" Fredric couldn't believe what he was hearing.

"Drive!"

Jonas said it considerably louder now. "Drive! Drive! Drive! Go to the left. There's room on the ground alongside. Just drive!"

Fredric reacted immediately. Pressed the gas to the floor and released the clutch. Sped past his father and over on the left side of the car ahead. They could hear Jonas's father screaming, and what was probably a blow with a fist against the trunk as they passed him at high speed.

It was only when they came alongside the Opel, and the wheels grabbed hold of the grass on the ground, that they realized the catastrophe. The back door of his father's car was open, and right ahead of them stood a little girl, screaming. Neither of them had time to react. They heard the blow only when the car struck her and sent her in an arc against the windshield. She hit it with a thud, continued over the roof, and landed in a twisted position behind the car before Fredric could step on the brake pedal. The car skidded across the ground before it stopped. The silence was total for a few seconds. Then came the screams. Jonas's mother was out of the car and running toward the unmoving figure on the ground. The blood formed a pool under her. His father roared as he ran. Not at the girl, but at them.

Fredric put the car in gear and accelerated. Jonas sat quite calmly beside him. Didn't protest. Didn't scream. No tears could convey the despair he felt. As the car rushed out on the road again, they could see in the rearview mirror that his father finally stopped. He waved his fists and shouted something they couldn't hear. Jonas paid no notice to what his friend was doing. He sat with a stiff gaze and stared into space. All color had vanished from his face, and without warning, he threw up over his shirt and lap.

Fredric wiped away tears and moaned while he drove faster and faster on the road toward the Karmsund Bridge. A woman who was about to cross the road at Bø Middle School leaped back in terror. Fredric didn't notice her. There was no way back. Nothing they did could help Ine. Nothing could help them.

Djupaskar, Haugesund
Saturday night, October 18, 2014

Olav Scheldrup Hansen felt unbelievably tired. Almost borderline apathetic. He had to realize that he and the whole investigation team had been made fools of. They totally fell for it. The simplest diversion trick in history. Not a single one of them had even thought this might be trickery. They'd walked into the trap and jumped into their cars as soon as there was gunfire up at the high-rises. The way was clear for the killer after that maneuver. One shot in the head from close range in the doorway. The Nigerian didn't know what hit him before his brain was disconnected for good.

There was little blood, which showed that his heart stopped beating the moment the bullet penetrated the brain mass.

This death is on my shoulders, he thought.

What irritated him most of all was that he was right. He had pointed out one of the most likely victims. He had also foreseen that killing Johan Gundersen would entail such a great risk for the murderer that he would choose someone else. All this added up, but they'd let themselves be deceived, and right now there was little doubt that most of the decisions made that evening were incorrect assessments.

One man posted at the high-rises would have been enough. Police in the apartments instead of on the outside would have fooled the killer into striking against a victim with police protection. Evacuation of potential victims would have saved a human life. All this could have been done on his orders, but he chose blue lights, deterrents, and stress theory. Thought that the police presence would stress the killer into committing fatal errors. Errors he hadn't made. Two shots in a stairwell, and presto! . . . . The whole police corps was put out of play.

It was embarrassing and degrading, but Scheldrup Hansen refused to do as Lotte had. He would stand in the storm. Not chicken out with his tail between his legs as soon as things got a little hot. Did she really think she could take a leading role in a team and then run away from the responsibility when they committed an error? The captain stays with the ship, but Lotte Skeisvoll had shown what she was made of when she was the first man in the lifeboat this evening.

That part about stressing the killer had produced some results, and they had a number of pieces of information about him. He was observed on the bicycle by two witnesses, and the nearest neighbor to the house in Djupaskar actually saw the killing from his living room window. Thus the killer had been observed for the first time. Not just once, but three times! He was incautious and took chances. In addition, they now knew a number of other things that could be of use in the investigation. Two solid footprints in the moist sand outside the Nigerian's house gave them shoe size, and after a little searching probably also type of shoe. They could establish approximate height and weight based on the witness accounts.

Both were very useful pieces of information that narrowed down the list of suspects considerably. As he understood it, there could not be more than five or six persons left among those who'd been at the media building when the third email was sent, and who in addition matched the killer's shoe size, height, and weight.

There should be cause to demand DNA samples of the rest who are in the searchlights, thought Scheldrup Hansen. He looked at the chaos around him. Inspected the curiosity-seekers who stood in large numbers outside the police barricades. Most of them were on their way home after a night of drinking at the Inner Pier. Their voices buzzed, but it was low-pitched. They talked to each other as if they were afraid of disturbing the dead.

While he stood there letting his thoughts wander, he became aware of a man standing just behind the crowd of people. A man in a black jacket with a bicycle. The thought struck the investigator at once.

Can it be him? It's a laughable crime cliché, of course, that the offender returns to the scene of the crime, but everything about this case was like a copy of a crime plot by a rejected, used-up author. Olav turned calmly around toward one of the crime scene investigators and asked if he'd taken pictures of those who stood outside the barricades watching. The CSI looked up at him and furrowed his bushy eyebrows. A comic awning of hair settled over the bridge of his nose.

"No. Should I?"

"Yes, but do it discreetly. Don't let them realize that you're taking a picture of them. Make sure to include that guy with the bicycle who's standing at the back, ten meters away from the others, to the right. We have a witness description that resembles him."

The bushy eyebrows settled down again where most people have them. The Kripos investigator placed his hand on the arm of the CSI and barely managed to stop him from turning around toward where the man was standing.

"Don't!"

The CSI nodded curtly to Olav. A little later, he was strolling around behind the crowd of people snapping pictures, apparently of footprints that were close by the barricades. He didn't go to where the bicyclist was standing, but Olav assumed that he used the tele-photo lens, sweeping the camera toward the other side while he changed sitting position.

A few minutes later, the CSI was back. He pointed toward the area where the footprints had supposedly been, and gestured with his arms while he showed the digital screen on the camera to Olav. The series of pictures showed clear and sharp pictures of everyone who was standing by the barricades. Also of the cyclist, Olav noted contentedly.

The face of the person in question was completely hidden under the hood, but there was something about the figure itself that seemed familiar. If it was the way he moved, how he was standing, or some-thing else, he couldn't say for sure. There was no doubt anyway. He had met the person in question in another context, but where?

Olav Scheldrup Hansen moved cautiously in the direction of the man, but was not even close to getting there before the man got on his bicycle and hurried around the crossing to Karmsundsgata. He disappeared in the direction of Flotmyr. The investigator called one of the patrols to pick him up, but ten minutes later, the man was still at large. Olav Scheldrup Hansen cursed out loud.

"Damn it! Is it possible?"

He struck his fist on the siding of the house. *The hell if I'm going to tell this to Lotte Skeisvoll. She'll strangle me*, thought the Kripos investigator.

Haugesund Police Station
Sunday morning, October 19, 2014

Less than a week ago, everything was in shining order at the police station. No one suspected danger. A peaceful Sunday drive in secure surroundings. Then came a semitrailer at full speed out of a hairpin curve. Police Chief Arnstein Guldbrandsen cleared his throat slightly before he sighed, shook his head, and handed the doctor's certificate back to Lotte Skeisvoll.

"You're my best detective, Lotte. I can't really do without you. But you make it terribly difficult for me by proceeding in the manner you have in this case. That slip of paper saves your hide and prevents me from suspending you, but both you and I know that what happened last night was actually unforgivable. You don't leave the scene of a crime like that."

"I had a medical emergency, Arnstein. . . ." Lotte didn't let herself undermine her own doctor's certificate. That was the only thing that meant she still had a justified hope of having a job to come back to.

The police chief sighed again. "Great . . . I understand that you're sticking to the official version. That's all well and good. I can hide behind it too when I let you continue, but you should know that everyone, and by that I mean everyone involved, is going to understand that this is bullshit."

"I can't act based on what people think. I was sick and needed immediate medical care. If someone believes otherwise, so be it. Rumors, assumptions, and backbiting are not something either you or I can base decisions on."

The corner of Arnstein Guldbrandsen's mouth quivered a little, and he looked at Lotte over the top of his glasses. "If you weren't so damned capable, Lotte."

He sent her out of the office and gave Olav Scheldrup Hansen word to update Lotte on the developments in the case.

Lotte exhaled once she was safely out of Guldbrandsen's office. It hadn't been a sure thing that he would accept either the explanation or the doctor's certificate. He surely knew that Lotte could get a doctor at the hospital to cough up a medical certificate for anything, considering that she'd been there to take care of her sister.

The hours after she left the crime scene the night before were a haze for Lotte. Anne had gradually woken up, and all the tests turned out to be fine. They'd had some brief conversations during the night, but Lotte struggled to remember what had been said. The shame blocked her from being able to capture the essence of what they'd talked about. Lotte fell asleep in the chair around three o'clock and didn't wake up until with trembling hands and puppy-dog eyes Anne was sitting on the edge of the bed getting dressed in the rags she wore out on the street.

Nothing stops an addict faced with abstinence. Gone were the tears, the regret and despair. Gone were all the promises that she would get sober and back on her feet. Gone was the need to have Lotte around. Now there was only one thing that could heal her, and that wasn't found at the hospital.

The night's small glimpses of golden moments were gone. From the radio in the waiting room she could hear the well-known lines from Johnny Cash like an omen through the corridors as she walked:

The needle tears a hole—the old familiar sting . . .

Haugesund Police Station
Late Sunday morning, October 19, 2014

Olav Scheldrup Hansen had never felt small. His ego occupied a bit
too much of his body weight for that. Nonetheless, it was just that
feeling that crept under his skin as he trotted behind Knut Veldetun's
back. The man was truly abnormal. He looked almost strange. Like
a Florentine Renaissance sculpture. Despite his size, the man's movements seemed almost feline. Olav caught himself missing his vanished youth as he studied the man who was now unnecessarily holding
the door open for him, as if he himself were missing both arms.

"Have you tried all channels for getting hold of Gudmundsson,
Knut? What did they say at the media house?"

The young policeman glanced quickly over his shoulder before he
answered. "He's taken four weeks of sick leave and isn't at work."

They got into one of the police cars outside the station. Olav was
glad the handsome policeman didn't prefer hoofing it, but he couldn't
help thinking that the whole thing was a bit comical. The big constable almost didn't have room for his legs when he got in on the driver's side. He looked just as misplaced behind the steering wheel as

the massive Bubba Smith did in his role as Moses Hightower in the first *Police Academy* movie.

In front of the Austmanna high-rises, they attracted curious looks. It was Sunday, and the high-rise residents were for the most part outside in the pleasant fall weather. Children were playing in the grassy areas to the left of the B Building, and parents sat patiently watching their offspring. The two policemen struggled out of the car and pretended not to notice they were being observed. All movements the police were making now during the day were put in direct connection with the "Executioner Case." The whole city was swarming with reporters and TV cameras.

Knut Veldetun and Olav went up to the entry where Viljar Ravn Gudmundsson lived and rang the bell. After having tried this a couple of times without success, Olav did the old "getting into the building without keys trick." He rang all the doorbells in the entry. Very soon the door buzzed once and even twice, and they had free passage in. Viljar lived on the second floor. Olav breathed out in relief. *Knut would not likely take the elevator, and there are twenty-five floors*, he thought dryly.

They could hear the doorbell buzzing inside the apartment, but no one answered. Knut pounded on the door so that it echoed in the stairwell. Still no response. They were about to leave with unfinished business when a woman stuck her head out the door right across the hall from Viljar's.

"He's not home."

She didn't say anything else. Just looked at the two policemen. When she very clearly had no intention of saying anything more on her own initiative, the Kripos investigator took command.

"I see . . . How do you know that? Have you seen him go out today?"

She cocked her head. Her eyes were fixed on Knut and not on Olav. There was something hungry in her eyes that she was unable to conceal. She hesitated. . . .

"No . . . I don't know if he's been here today, that is. Haven't seen or heard anything from there anyway. But he was home yesterday. There was a terrible racket in the hall. It woke me up, and when I'd put on some clothes and went to the door to see whether everything was okay, I just got a glimpse of his back as he went out the door downstairs."

"Great. You're sure it was him? I mean, since you only saw his back?"

"Well, who else would it be? I heard the row from his apartment, and after he left, it was completely quiet in there."

"What kind of clothes did he have on, can you say anything about that? Or whether he was drunk or anything?"

The lady in the doorway tossed her head and grinned. "Whether he was drunk? It would surprise me if he was sober, put it that way. It's probably not that often that sober folks knock over the coat stand on their way out the door and don't set it back up again."

"Did you say he knocked over the coat stand? I thought you said you only saw his back on the way out the door below?"

She sighed dejectedly and now came all the way out on the stairwell. At the same time, a pair of slender, bare thighs appeared under a silk top. Knut rolled his eyes and looked shyly anyplace other than at her.

"See here," she said, looking demonstratively through the little peephole in the door. "Here you see the coat stand at an angle over by the wall." She waved them over and took the opportunity to have plenty of body contact as Knut leaned over to look through the hole.

"Did you go over here after he'd left?"

The lady in the silk top observed the investigator as if he were an idiot. "Of course I did. I had to see that everything was all right. There was a lot of commotion in there, you see."

Olav Scheldrup Hansen suspected the helpful neighbor of being a touch more curious than she tried to appear. "You go over and look in the peephole to see whether everything is okay with Viljar *after* you've seen him go out the door below?"

She got a sullen look on her face, sighed, and started speaking with clearer diction, as if she were talking to a deaf person. "I don't know whether it was Viljar who went out the door. I just assume it was him. I saw a man in a black jacket and hood. He walked as if he was carrying a sack in his arms. There's garbage pickup tomorrow, so I assume he had a garbage bag with him."

Scheldrup Hansen tugged on his colleague's shirtsleeve and gave him a signal that they had to leave.

Knut looked at the Kripos investigator with surprise and followed him down the stairs. He blushed a little when the lady sent him a look of clear invitation.

Out in the sun, Olav took Knut aside and gave him instructions to get ahold of the janitor or building manager. "I don't like this. Gudmundsson has been securely lashed to this case like the string around a Sunday pot roast since day one.

"We'll need a search of the apartment. Should go fine, considering the neighbor's observations in addition to the overturned coat stand and the fact that we haven't had any response from him. If you can try to find someone who has keys, I'll arrange the formalities."

Knut jogged over to the group of dads and moms who were sitting on the bench. One of them ought to know who had master keys.

When half an hour later they stood in front of the door to Viljar's apartment for the second time, they had company from the police department technicians. A clearly nervous janitor opened the door for them. It slid open a few centimeters, and then stopped. Something heavy was blocking the way. Olav did not have the patience to wait and pressed on. At last, he managed to make his way through the opening. Three seconds after he went in, he stuck his head out again. A brief order was enough for everyone to understand the seriousness.

"Sound a full alarm, Knut! Full alarm . . ."

Haugesund
Late Sunday morning, October 19, 2014

The room still had a hint of tar-stained ship's floor, salt sea, kelp, and freshly cleaned fish. Memories from the sun-filled, peaceful existence of childhood.

There was the creaking of old woodwork. From outside, the gentle lapping of waves was heard. Quiet creaking from rope struggling against the tide. A two-cycle engine chugged past at a leisurely tempo. Loud screeches from gulls cut through from time to time. *A moored boat?*

He was lying completely still. The floor did not rock. In this room, you could both smell and hear the sea, but not feel it. *Solid ground, in other words.*

His subconscious picked up something that his brain registered without having it reach the processing center. A hint of sweat. A sound. Heat radiation, as if someone was right next to him. *There's someone here!* The smell of desire . . . or fear?

A modern human is basically robbed of these instincts. They show up only in a few situations in life when you are deprived of one of your senses. Sight, for example. Or . . . Perhaps mainly then. Sight is our strongest sense, and we are so dependent on it that a person has to reinforce what's already there in order to survive. Read with your fingers. Interpret body language with hearing. Calculate distances by resonance and echo. Recognize people by the sense of smell. Become aware of danger through feeling.

An animal will always camouflage its handicap if that is possible. Conceal how vulnerable it is. With a blindfold over your eyes, it is difficult for a person to camouflage that he cannot see. The waiting predator is completely aware of the prey's handicap and is convinced of its own invincibility.

In many ways, this certainty was harder for Viljar Ravn Gudmundsson to handle than the fact that he couldn't see. The certainty that there was someone in the room observing him. A silent stranger, but he was there. . . . Someplace between the creaking woodwork and the smell of tar, he was there.

He also suspected who it was. It was his turn now. Fate had finally picked him up and made him ready for the ultimate journey. Deep down, he'd seen it coming. The past had caught up with him.

The pain in his head was unbearable, and did not get any better from the aftereffects of yesterday's whole bottle of whiskey. As if that weren't enough, he was lying on his stomach on a hard wooden floor with his arms and legs tied behind his back. He had almost as much pain in his ribs after hours on his stomach as he had in his head. But just almost.

Viljar had thought that the anxiety would grab him, overpower and paralyze him, but not this time. The reality was much worse than all the fears he could imagine. The physical pain was so intense that it forced away all thoughts about what might be coming. Right now a shot in the forehead would be true liberation, and then he would no longer have anything to fear. For the first time, he had encountered something that overcame the anxiety.

Viljar was silent. Lay quietly. Breathed softly. Did not want the person in the room to realize that he was awake. Had to buy himself time. *Time for what?* Someplace or other in all this pain and in the total darkness around him, there was a solution. There had to be. If he just lay there a little longer, it would come to him.

It always had. Through his entire life, the solution was always served up nonchalantly on a platter, and he got out of the problem. Or . . . That is . . . Almost always. *Not with Jonas.* Not when he needed it the most.

With the blindfold over his eyes, it was impossible to know whether it was night or day or how long he'd been in the room. No voices could be heard outside. No cars. No sounds from a pulsating small town. He was probably in a boathouse. But it couldn't be one along the Inner Pier in Haugesund. Then he would have heard sounds from people. Even at night, he would have heard both people and cars. In other words, this boathouse was in an isolated location. For that matter, it could be anywhere at all. He had been transported here, but he'd been unconscious during the trip.

He tried to remember something from the seconds before everything turned black in the hall in the apartment, but it was foggy and unclear. He produced the face, but realized that it might be a face he had conjured forth from his memory simply because it was the most probable attacker.

Viljar could remember hearing the doorbell. He also recalled that he went to answer the door. Then it turned black. There was actually no face. He could see it now. The face was wrapped in a black bandanna or scarf. A black hood over his head concealed the rest. The next memory was lapping waves, the smell of tar, and intense pain.

While his thoughts wandered around in circles, he became aware of a new sound in the room. Steps. Someone was walking across the floor. He had to struggle against the compulsion to scream. The steps were almost soundless, but they were there. He had been right. There was another person in the room. Now the steps were moving away from where Viljar lay. There was creaking from rusty door hinges.

Viljar waited a couple of minutes. Then he took the chance to move as best he could. He felt a sharp stab in his foot when he tried to move his legs. He ran his foot over the same place again. Could feel the outline of what might be a nail sticking out from the wall behind him.

Centimeter by centimeter, he crawled backwards and finally managed to twist his back next to the place where he'd felt the nail against the ball of his foot. Felt the sharp metal against his fingers. He breathed out in relief. Hoped intensely that what bound his hands and feet together was made of a material that would give way with a combination of precision and friction. For a brief moment, he lay still and listened. This was going to take time.

Finally he managed to get one end of the rope between his index finger and thumb. The rope was probably the kind you tie a turkey up with before roasting. He penetrated the skin just as often as he got hold of a thread. Several times he was about to give up. The sweat poured down his back. Long strands of hair were plastered to his face. He forced himself to maintain focus. Whittled, sweated, and cursed. As he felt that the rope was giving a little in the bindings, he heard the creak from the door hinges again. Like a spider, he froze his position, even as he pushed the back of his hands apart. The sound of steps that hurried toward him made him pull all he could with his hands. The twine did not give way.

Viljar screamed as the man lifted him up in a sitting position, as if he weighed five kilos and not seventy-five. The familiar sound of a zip tie that was tightened behind his back killed all hope. Next it was his legs' turn. The man in the dark breathed out. Viljar felt the heat from his body as he sat down close beside him.

"I've been waiting a long time to get you alone, Viljar. It's time to settle up for old sins, don't you think?"

Four years earlier . . .
Viljar's apartment, Haugesund
Tuesday evening, August 31, 2010

Viljar Ravn Gudmundsson could not let go of the thought that it was the newspaper interview on Saturday that made Jonas flee head over heels on Sunday along with his friend. He could not understand what had come over the boys.

First came the shock over what had happened at Torvastad, then a new shock when he realized that prior to what happened, Jonas had decided to go out in the media with his full name. What was the point of making him anonymous in Saturday's paper if he intended to be interviewed by TV 2 the next day? And why run away from his family if he'd planned to come forward anyway?

Two full days had passed, and no one had yet been able to track down the two boys. The car had been found in the parking lot at Amanda Shopping Center a few hours after the accident, but after that, it was as if Jonas and Fredric had been lifted to heaven by angels. Not a single trace. No witness reports. Fruitless searches on cell phone tracking. They had evaporated.

For Viljar, it had been a double-edged sword, sitting in London and following Norwegian news broadcasts on the internet. The long weekend with Alexander had not turned out the way he'd pictured it. A furious Johan Øveraas wanted him home to cover what had happened, but he could live with that. It was worse to think about the young boy who in a way had placed his life in his hands and who was in flight from everything and everyone. Viljar understood that it wasn't his fault, it just couldn't be, but nonetheless, it felt like it was his responsibility. From London, he couldn't do anything. He had to focus on making the holiday into the dream weekend his son had awaited for so long.

He had done his best, but even in the roar of exultation at Stamford Bridge, when Alexander threw himself around his neck, Viljar's thoughts had been in Norway. With a completely different boy, who didn't care in the least that Chelsea had just beaten Stoke 2–0. And with a little nine-year-old girl who was no more. Whose last thought in life, according to her parents, had been to try to stop her brother from running away from home.

When Viljar's flight landed at Haugesund Airport in the afternoon that Tuesday, he knew what he would encounter at work the next day. The entire Norwegian press corps and an impressively large police force were on an English foxhunt, and Viljar was sought after wildly in the news broadcasts. He was the expert who could tell about which boys they were dealing with. After all, he had met them. Talked confidentially with them. Heard their story.

Viljar was deep into the thought process about what he should tell the media the next day, and almost didn't hear that his doorbell was ringing. It took a few seconds before he collected himself and stumbled out in the hall in his slippers to answer. He was completely unprepared for what met him when the door was opened. A skinny, ungainly figure, with hair wet from rain in strips down his face, stood in the hall and handed him a letter. Once again, Viljar was slow to make the connection. He stood there with the letter in his hands for some time before it occurred to him what had happened.

"Jonas!"

Viljar called after the spindly back that was already far down the stairs. He was about to run after the boy, but happened to think that if he let go of the door, it would close behind him, and he would be locked out. Quickly he ran in, put on shoes, grabbed his keys, and took the stairs three at a time. When he burst out the front door on the first floor, it was like running right into a brook. The rain was pouring down, and he got soaked to the skin. He looked around in all directions, but Jonas was nowhere to be seen. *Where did he go?* Viljar hadn't taken more than half a minute to find shoes and keys. *He can't be far away, can he?*

He called to Jonas a few times, but the boy was gone. For that matter, it was no challenge to hide in the confusion of high-rises, cars, cellar stairs, and paths in this area. And right behind the high-rises, there was a forested recreational area. Viljar realized that it was useless. He trudged back to the apartment and slammed the door behind him as he went into the hall. The letter he had gotten from Jonas was on the floor. It was in a simple, unsealed envelope, and Viljar could see that the letter was handwritten. He plopped down on the black armchair in the living room and unfolded the letter. His head was empty, and he fished out a cigarette and fired it up with the ember from the one he'd been smoking when the doorbell rang two minutes earlier.

Viljar felt a little prick of guilty conscience because he didn't call the police first of all. Nonetheless . . . There was something in Jonas's eyes that stopped him. It was a wounded animal in flight who'd been standing outside.

Viljar read slowly. Stopped several times to see that what was there was really true. That he wasn't misinterpreting the bad handwriting. He wasn't. At the back of the letter there was a newspaper clipping of the picture he had taken at the outdoor restaurant at Samson, and which he had approved in passing before he left to make the Ryanair flight to London. *Can this be true?* He looked again and again at the picture, but was unable to see what Jonas alleged was there. At last he took out his reading glasses, which an overeager optician's employee had palmed off on him after a free vision test. Used them as a magnifying glass and with his own eyes could see himself sliding down into an inferno that could only be the outer court of hell.

The evidence, along with the final words in the letter, made Viljar clutch his chest. He could feel the pain radiate out to his arms. The blood disappeared from his head, and his throat constricted. He couldn't breathe, while the chest pains only increased in intensity. In a final spasm, he grabbed the phone and called 911.

While Viljar lay on the floor waiting for the ambulance, the final words from Jonas buzzed around in his head again and again. There was nothing more to say. He truly deserved to die from this heart attack. He almost hoped that the men in yellow would come too late.

You promised to protect me. You didn't. My sister is dead. Soon I will be too.

Austmannavegen, Haugesund
Sunday afternoon, October 19, 2014

In six days, the number of police, Kripos investigators, technicians, and constables had tripled, so Lotte Skeisvoll had to force her way up to the high-rise apartment. The press corps grew with every passing day, and to her surprise, she noted that it actually said BBC on one camera that captured her movements toward the entry to Viljar's apartment.

She avoided any contact with the press, and the more of them there were, the less they got out of her. Hans Indbjo had been in his element all week, and of course had redone the broadcast schedule to fill it with six hours of live coverage every day. But for once, it wasn't Indbjo standing with microphone in hand. A pimply teenager who could barely have finished the media and communications program at Vardafjell High School had taken his place.

Lotte couldn't understand why Indbjo had let a whippersnapper handle a case like this, but the short-statured radio journalist had become a national celebrity from all his "revelations" the past few days,

and probably had his hands full nursing his own ego. It wouldn't surprise Lotte if he showed up on a reality show next season.

Inside the doors, a slightly more subdued chaos prevailed. She
quickly made eye contact with Scheldrup Hansen.

He waved at her. "We don't think he left the apartment of his own
free will. There's a lot that suggests he was attacked right by the door
and then carried out of the building."

Lotte gave Scheldrup Hansen a searching gaze. "Carried . . . ?"

"Yes. We have a witness statement from a neighbor who saw the
back of a man who was probably carrying something heavy out the
door down in the entry last night."

Lotte felt a stab in her chest. *If a person is carried out like that,
that person is either unconscious or dead. Either one gives Viljar very
poor odds.*

"So . . . We have the witness statement. Time established at about
ten o'clock last night. We have to check if any other neighbors
observed him. It was early enough that someone must have seen
something."

Scheldrup Hansen looked down at his notes before he continued.

"If we assume that it's our man who struck again, he would have
managed to carry out this, the shooting at the high-rises, and the murder at the stadium. The question is, how did he do such quick work,
and why was it important to remove Gudmundsson, dead or alive?"

Lotte didn't say anything, but gave him a sign to continue.

"There was a minor scuffle at the front door. An overturned coat
stand and a heavy vase were lying on the floor, and some blood has
been found on the flooring." Scheldrup Hansen sighed a little and
shook his head.

"Is there more?" asked Lotte.

"Hmmm . . ."

She looked at her colleague.

He pointed at the rest of the apartment. "We have the computer here, for example. It was logged in. We found a folder where he had lots of notes about our case. It turns out that he's been holding some things back from us, and that he has had suspicions about why he was involved in the case."

"I see. . . ." Lotte went over to the computer that was on the table over by the window.

"Look at this," Scheldrup Hansen said, and double-clicked on a folder. A series of image files and Word documents appeared on the screen.

"Pictures . . . ?"

"Well, not that interesting. Mostly screenshots of the emails he received, besides the picture of him and Rita Lothe at the bar. What gets me is what he writes in the documents. These are his thoughts about why things are happening around him. Here, for example, he's figured out where and when the picture was taken, and who was with him."

"Are you kidding?" Lotte asked, leaning closer to the screen. Viljar hadn't said a thing to them about this.

"He thinks that the picture was taken at the Bestastuå night-club on Strandgata in September, and that he and a buddy went there, accompanied by Henrik Thomsen. If I recall correctly, that's one of the names we're starting to look at closer, isn't it? The big journalist?"

"Yes, it sure is. He's an arts reporter at the newspaper."

" 'Don't remember anything,' it says here, and a little farther down, 'Who were the dames we checked out?' I think we need to have a chat with this Thomsen, because he had opportunity, in any event, to take the picture that we found on the fake Facebook profile for Rita Lothe."

"Anything else?"

Olav aimed his index finger at another document in the folder. "Here," he said, opening it.

Lotte looked down at the screen again and registered the name, but was unable to glean anything from it. It just said *Jonas*.

It was only when she opened the folder that it occurred to her. It was the case with Jonas Ferkingstad he referred to.

She tugged on Olav's shirt collar. "Here is the last puzzle piece in the picture, Olav. This case may explain why Gudmundsson is linked so closely to the murders. We have to talk with Jonas's father, André Ferkingstad, and very soon. He has a motive to avenge himself on Viljar."

"Ferkingstad? The one you talked with at the courthouse?"

"Executive officer. He works at the courthouse, and he behaved strangely, to put it mildly, on Thursday when his old house was in flames at Torvastad. The guy is not completely balanced. He was clearly nervous when I talked with him too."

"Excuse me, Lotte. . . . Why hasn't anyone told me about this before? Shouldn't he have been checked out days ago?"

Lotte Skeisvoll's mouth tightened, and she took Olav Scheldrup Hansen aside outside hearing range of the others. "Now, you back off, Hansen. You were the one who in no uncertain terms wanted to check out the Eliassen lead. Do you mean to say you haven't done that?"

Scheldrup Hansen looked at Lotte Skeisvoll in surprise. Shook his head, and seemed to have problems starting the sentence. "No, now . . . What do you mean? I *have* checked out Eliassen. He's still in prison for the assaults, but what does his case have to do with this Ferkingstad?"

Lotte stood there by the one armchair, puzzled. She mostly had a desire to sink down in it. She'd been careless again. Took it for granted that Scheldrup Hansen had been told of the connection between the Eliassen case and the Jonas case. It was obvious, of course, for everyone here in Haugesund that they were linked, but not for a Kripos investigator from East Norway with minimal interest in anything that happened outside Ring 3 in Oslo.

She patted him on the shoulder and nodded quietly. The furthest she could extend herself to make a confession. "Fine, Olav. Fine . . ."

Lotte had a patrol sent out to pick up Ferkingstad, while she studied the rest of the clippings, the pictures, and the Word files more closely.

There was no doubt. It fit together. *It has to,* she thought.

"God damn you, Viljar!" she said out loud as she slammed the cover on his laptop.

Requiem: Sanctus

I love Sundays. They are so innocently pure. So white. So refreshingly naïve. But . . . I know it's getting closer now! It can't be long before they have the whole score. I went too far in my eagerness to get them on the right track, and now the tempo has to slow down. What until now have been small adjustments have become more time consuming and extensive. There are false notes in my requiem, and they must be removed. Cleared away. The orchestra must be tightened up before the remaining movements.

The sweat is collecting at the base of my spine and under my arms. Small hints of doubt and fear make my body react irrationally. I spend time on the adjustments, and that means less time for preparations. In the next round, this means greater risk. The thought of making a mistake now when I'm so close to the goal is unbearable. I'm restless and impatient. Two things I had promised myself I wouldn't be. Time should be my best friend, not my enemy. I need a perfect glissando toward a change in tempo. It must go faster to create chaos and desperation, but I hadn't thought that this also leads to less foreseeability and therefore bigger adjustments. To get a combined orchestra together in a crescendo is demanding, and it increases the danger that someone will play wrong, that strings break.

I observe the final changes in the artwork, and consider myself satisfied for now. The certainty that it won't be the last time I'll have to change it annoys me more than I like. What in principle was the whole point behind the actions has become a distraction. I ought to have been happy every time I raised the conductor's baton. Been happy that they are following my instructions. I am driven by something else now. The urge toward a climax where everything melts together to a heavenly unison tone. The execution will give me so much more than the preparations. The electrical impulses that glide through my body as I inhale the last breaths of my chosen ones are an erotic experience. A rush that surpasses anything else I have experienced. My restlessness increases at the very thought.

I can do it here and now. All I need is ready on the table before me. I have access to the chosen one. He is in the same room. If it hadn't been that the artwork still has perfection in itself, and that I still have a trace of self-control, I would have done it now. Let all inhibitions loose and simply felt the rush, the lust, and the glow in the final exhalation. It strikes me in the fraction of a second that this is madness, but my defenses hold up. It is the art that forces me to be rational and perform my actions out of necessity, not lust. I force the thoughts back where they should be. Focus. The time schedule must be observed, even if I feel that my senses are failing. Everything moves more sluggishly. Movements, reasoning, memory, like measure after measure of whole notes. Probably due to lack of sleep after having to be on the move during the night, but sleep will have to wait. Now the email must be sent. I can't delay it any longer.

I place the laptop in the backpack along with the rest of the equipment I need. Think through what I have to do one last time before I

leave the room. Everything is in place. New sender and new recipient. Both are arranged, and this time it won't help the police that they
manage to narrow down possible victims. He is already taken care
of. A little, ingenious trick that will surprise them. It wasn't part of
the original plan to do it this way, but now it is. It lacked a trill. Now
it's there. I can no longer risk them getting involved in my selection,
so it's nice to be out in front. They won't know what hit them until
it's too late.

I walk quietly across the creaking floor and out the door. Take in
fresh sea air as I look over the water of Smedasundet. I feel safe and
secure. The chosen one knows what is coming. I could actually feel
the scent of pure terror. It was pleasant and liberating.

Now, a few hours later, the smell has evaporated, and another,
more penetrating odor has entered the room. He has evidently relieved the pressure of his bladder. The bait is set, and out here the
air is fresh and new. As if it too is cleaned and ready for a new day
with new sins. I set a course for the Inner Pier. A long series of unprotected networks stands in line, waiting for me in the sunshine.

I love Sundays. They are so innocently pure. So white. So refreshingly naïve.

Gjøvik
Sunday, October 19, 2014

The publisher Harald Madsen stretched on the couch and concluded that the coffee was done brewing in the kitchen. It was not long since the final sputtering sounds had come from the Moccamaster. He had great plans for enjoying the last day of autumn vacation to the fullest. His body still felt the jet lag after journeying home from rainy Scotland, but a few hours of sleep in his own bed had done him good.

He had actually intended to travel to more southerly regions, but didn't get around to ordering tickets in time. At last he gave up the attempt to get some cheap sunrays and instead pounced on a theme vacation to Scotland in the fall. Whiskey tour . . .

Scotland was damp. Both he and his wardrobe screamed for a spin in the dryer, and he hoped that his bloodshot eyes would stop watering before he had to be at work the next day. He had this one day for recuperation, and now his body was crying for industrial-strength coffee and a solid quantity of Tylenol.

A pale sun struggled with the cloud cover. The temperature was quite satisfactory. Sixteen degrees Celsius was much warmer than what he'd experienced for over a week in windblown northern Scotland. He looked out at the farms. If he'd owned a fraction of such a farm, he would have multiplied many times over what he made in salary from the publishing company he started in Gjøvik ten years ago. He had dreamed of big money. Finding a Harry Potter out there, or a Dan Brown. Something that took the market by storm and got rid of his financial worries for all time. The reality was mournful. Every time he got wind of something that might be big, the major Norwegian publishers had already signed the joker. There was only pocket lint left over for him and his three employees at Alfa Madsen Publishing in Gjøvik.

They kept it going, and the ship afloat, even though it could have used a thorough floor coating. Mainly due to a lucky signing the second year they were in business. Then they had received a manuscript from a first-time author who actually had followed the advice of not submitting to more than one publisher at a time. Ridiculous advice, but for Alfa Madsen, it was worth gold. They were first on all the alphabetical lists. The author had long since moved to Aschehoug with his next books, but the debut book still sold by the bucketload, and it also kept finding new markets abroad. This revenue stream meant that the liquidity was good enough, but didn't allow for any risk-taking or major investments. Two times Aschehoug and the author had tried to buy back the rights to the book, but Harald Madsen knew better. The money they got out of something like that would be like pissing in your pants to stay warm. Good finances for a couple of years, and then . . . end of the line if no new golden manuscripts dropped down in the mailbox.

Harald Madsen settled down comfortably on the couch. Supported himself with pillows behind his back, the cup of coffee, cigarettes, and ashtray within reach. In his hands he had his iPad, which he had written off as a business expense, but seldom used for anything other than a little free-time surfing on various websites. He had been in a kind of haze for a whole week. Starting the day with four whiskies at some isolated farm meant that the rest of the day flowed by in a mist he could barely recall. No more than waking up in another hotel every morning with the same travel companions on their way to new distilleries.

As usual, he opened the news sites first, and could quickly establish that Norway had been turned on its head while he tippled whiskey on the other side of the sea. The ultra-bold fonts screamed at him and made it impossible to go past them in silence. He sipped at the coffee while he read. After the first article, he lit a cigarette. Something about the case excited him. A little thread far back in his head was calling for his attention, but he was unable to get hold of it.

Four homicides in one week committed by what must be the same man. After having skimmed the first few articles from the national papers, he started to read carefully. *There is something here. . . .* Something he recognized. Something from the past, but he couldn't pin it down just yet. Harald Madsen raised himself up and immediately felt the hangover still lurking by the bridge of his nose. He knocked back yet another Tylenol from the package on the coffee table before he leaned toward the screen again. The whole thing was presented in such tabloid fashion that he couldn't make out the essence. The fear propaganda that made people worried and nervous.

Harald abandoned the Oslo press and concentrated on the local web paper, *Haugesund News*. It was when he opened it that it occurred to him. *How could I know that the local newspaper was called* Haugesund News? He started reading the articles, but quickly made his way to an overview story instead. Here all four murders were listed. Place, date, victim, and method of killing were all presented. Harald Madsen stopped in mid-summary. He got goose pimples all over his body. The truth struck him with full force. He tried to convince himself that this couldn't be true, but as quickly as that thought tried to take root, more images showed up steadily in his mental photo album.

Gradually, as Harald read article after article, his suspicions were confirmed. He was right. Toward the end, he knew what was going to be in the various articles before he'd read them. What Harald could not understand, however, was why no one had gone to the police with this earlier. It was so obvious that even a listless, hungover Norwegian with a fog of whiskey before his eyes saw it at once.

What the hell are the police up to when they haven't managed to catch this? he thought, sitting back on the couch.

With trembling hands, he fished a cigarette out of the pack.

He didn't need to read any more articles. He knew perfectly well what was in them. He also knew very well what was going to be in the news tomorrow, and the day after that. He picked up the iPad again and connected it to the work server. A brief search later gave him the answer he knew was in the database at the publishing house.

Harald Madsen picked up his phone and found the number to Haugesund Police Station. After three ringtones, a voice came on the other end who claimed she could help him.

"Can you transfer me to a detective by the name of Skeisvoll? I have a tip in the case you're investigating."

"Yes, right now there are a lot of people calling and wanting to give us tips, and the investigation team can't take all the tips themselves. Could you say what your name is and what the tip concerns?"

There was silence for a moment. Madsen thought a little about how he should formulate this without being perceived as some kind of idiot. He went for the hard-line version. Right to the point.

"My name is Harald Madsen, and I think I have the name of the killer you're after."

Haugesund
Sunday afternoon, October 19, 2014

Viljar felt the surge of nausea again and again. At last it was impossible to stop. The taste of bile that seeped up through his esophagus and settled like moldy water in his mouth was too much. It felt as if the entire contents of his stomach came out at one time. He didn't have a chance to turn his head to the side, reach a sink or a toilet. He was tied up to one of the structural beams in the room where he was imprisoned. His arms around the beam. His head was held up by another strap, which was attached under his chin, just tight enough that it didn't slide down around his throat. . . . His legs were taped together at the ankles. The only route the vomit could take was over his chest and lap.

The acrid smell that struck him seconds after the first wave came immediately started another, more powerful wave of vomiting. The strap under his chin moved backwards a little, toward his Adam's apple. The stomach cramps did not let up until the last remnant of bile and acid was out in the open air. Viljar felt helpless sitting there in his own vomit, waiting for the final judgment. He tried to hang on to a final scrap of dignity by refusing to think about how he looked, and about the yellow pools that he could feel were bathing his lap. That it should all end like this came as a surprise. Despite his anxiety problems, he had pictured a dignified finish for himself.

The pieces of the puzzle had fallen into place when he confirmed who was in the room with him. At least three, and probably four, people had to pay with their lives simply so that the perpetrator could have his great, grandiose finish with Viljar. The killer could have made it much simpler, sparing innocent lives along the way, but he didn't want that. Evidently he wanted Viljar to have more blood on his hands than he already did. Simply so that Viljar would feel regret. Feel what he had really done that time he betrayed Jonas.

Why couldn't he have stepped forward and taken the hit back then? Why couldn't he have admitted all the guilt and let the damned newspaper job go? Then this wouldn't have happened. Then Ranveig would still be alive.

Viljar tried to shove all the negative thoughts out of his head. Regardless of how hopeless that was, he had to keep his courage up. He knew he couldn't get himself loose, but he was alone. The kidnapper had gone out. It was quiet. Several times Viljar tried to shout. Only three times had he heard signs of what might be human activity outside. He'd shouted himself hoarse, but to no avail.

If Viljar were to get help, it had to happen now. He needed the last remnant of his voice in case he heard someone outside. He had to make a sound another way. A way that didn't wear him out. The way he was sitting now, the solution presented itself. He had to call with his legs. Three short thumps. Three long ones. Three new short ones. Pause . . . Repeat . . . Pause . . .

Viljar focused a hundred percent on the Morse code signal. It seemed completely idiotic, but in a way, it gave him new hope and new courage. If someone walked past, they would hear it. The SOS signal was known by everyone, even children. . . . He encouraged himself to continue even if his legs got tired. The small thumps were his last wisp of hope, and it gave him something to think about other than what was waiting. Maybe it would be over in a few minutes or a few hours. Maybe this evening. He didn't know, and in a sense he was happy about that. Knowing would be worse. Now he had at least a straw of time, and a regular, thumping communication out toward the world.

Viljar went into a kind of self-hypnosis. The thumps became more and more distant from him, like echoes from a parallel world that didn't concern him. For that reason, he didn't notice the first sounds outside. Strolling steps in the gravel that stopped and listened.

It was only when the steps in the gravel were heard again that Viljar was torn out of his trance. All the nerve endings in his body reacted at the same time. His body tensed and he roared as loud as he was able. The steps in the gravel continued. The person out there could not help hearing him now, yet the steps became more distant. He screamed again and again. When he had no breath left, he listened. Outside, it was completely quiet.

He was unable to stop the sobbing that welled up through his sore throat. Not until a few minutes later did he hear a click in what must be a lock from the floor below. His heart was racing. Viljar roared. Steps were heard on the stairs. There was creaking in every single step. The straps around his chin prevented him from turning his head toward the stairs.

The steps stopped at the doorway. Viljar was sobbing more than shouting now. Why didn't the person standing there come over to him? He got the answer three seconds later. The person who stood in the doorway started laughing out loud.

Viljar collapsed, and in a way that was fine. Now it was finally over. It was the beginning of the end, and it was what he deserved. Only the judgment awaited; then his soul would be free. That freedom no one could take from him. . . .

Media House *Haugesund News*
Sunday afternoon, October 19, 2014

Olav Scheldrup Hansen wiped the sweat from his forehead with the back of his hand. Even if the new *Haugesund News* building had a well-functioning air-conditioning system, the sun sneaked through the window where he was sitting. The investigator was taking saliva samples from the employees. After yesterday's fiasco, the prosecutor's office had also gotten stressed and impatient. The press was screaming at them from magazines and websites. Getting permission to obtain DNA samples from those who'd been in the newspaper building on Thursday was suddenly unproblematic. The cotton swabs were lined up like soldiers before him. One holder with marked swabs, and one for unused ones. Scheldrup Hansen focused on the task. Registered employees one by one as they came in, and had their mouths scraped with the cotton swab. Exchanged a few words with each of them to write down where they were at the relevant time, and if they had heard or seen anything. There was nothing new that could illuminate the dark tunnel they found themselves in.

Right before the two final samples were to be taken, editor Johan

Øveraas came into view in the doorway. He showed signs that he wanted to have a word with the investigator. The man looked nervous and uncomfortable. Scheldrup Hansen decided to finish the last two samples first, so he signaled to the editor to wait outside. The man sat down on a chair and started tapping on his phone.

When he was finished ten minutes later, he followed Øveraas into his office. He was placed in the editor's chair with Johan standing behind him. In front of him was a sizable computer screen. The screen saver sent figures back and forth. A psychedelic pattern of shapes. Øveraas touched the mouse slightly and then clicked on the mail icon for Outlook.

With practiced fingers, he went to an email with a familiar heading. It was him. A new judgment was pronounced in front of the eyes of Olav Scheldrup Hansen and Johan Øveraas.

He had read it so many times now that the only thing that was of interest was which "sin" was to be punished, and the letter and number code at the bottom that could tell how the whole thing would happen. Scheldrup Hansen scrolled down until he found what he needed.

The code was HM-5-1. He wrote it down on a note on his cell phone. The mortal sin was laughable.

The investigator shook his head before he looked up at Johan Øveraas. "You're kidding me now. . . . Lies! . . . *Lies!* He can't very well send folks to the boatman because they've lied on some occasion or other? This is completely over the top!" Olav cleared his throat. Thought about it.

"I don't know if you've thought about this before, but this doesn't look genuine at all. It doesn't seem as if he bothers to ever put any weight behind his arguments. It looks as if the guy is *bored* while he writes."

"What you're saying there is a bull's-eye," said Scheldrup Hansen.

"We have *no* faith at all that this is a man with the slightest trace of morals. The fictional judgments are a pretext . . . I—"

Olav Scheldrup Hansen bit off his own sentence when he noticed the oily grin of the editor.

"Damn it, you can't use what I said in your newspaper! You don't dare!"

Scheldrup Hansen overturned the office chair as he left Øveraas in fury. He called Lotte as soon as he came out in the hall.

"Olav here. Has the patrol gotten hold of Ferkingstad yet? In that case, they should check whether he has cell phone or Wi-Fi in the vicinity. You see, we just got a new email. Øveraas is the recipient this time."

"And? . . . You can forget Ferkingstad. I have something much better. I have a name."

"A name?"

"Yes, I know who we're searching for. I have his name right in front of me."

Haugesund Police Station
Sunday afternoon, October 19, 2014

The phone call from the publisher Harald Madsen had cut the Gordian knot. It was the kind of call every investigator dreams of, but unfortunately happens only once in a blue moon. An outsider who has the answer and the solution. A little, random detail that makes everything fall into place. She had always had faith that they would find the killer, but not this way. Not because a person from somewhere else suddenly called and gave them the name. It was unbelievable, and pleasant. She breathed out slowly. There had been enough fiascos. They had underestimated him at every turn, but now they knew who was sitting on the other side of the table.

Her phone rang. It was Madsen again. This time from a taxi en route from Helganes to Haugesund. She'd asked him to jump on the first flight from Gardermoen as soon as he'd said what he had on his mind. In his baggage, he had with him what would hopefully give them all the answers they were waiting for. *The manuscript.* Obviously it would have been simplest to email the manuscript, but it had been submitted in paper form. The company computer register showed only the filing number, title, and author.

What they struggled to understand had been written down three years ago. Harald Madsen had recognized the sequence of events once he'd read through the newspaper articles. It all added up. The killings were performed in the same way and in the same sequence as in a manuscript his publishing house had received. A very poor manuscript, to be sure. Harald Madsen had not hesitated to refuse the "mess," as he put it. It was a barely believable story, written with a weak pen. The clichés were like snails in a rain-filled pasture, Madsen said.

Lotte was not entirely able to see what was banal about what had gone on in the city the past week. It was bloody, ghastly, and genuine. As far as she could see from searches on the internet, the book and the author were not anywhere to be found. The book must not have been published. Madsen, in other words, was not the only one who had rejected the manuscript. The killer had evidently decided to show the world that his crime story measured up. He was *his own* copycat, with an unknown recipe in his hands. But . . . thanks to Alfa Madsen Publishers' filing procedures, the manuscript would soon be in her hands too. This was something the killer had not expected. *That will give us an advantage*, thought Lotte.

As far as Madsen could recall, the manuscript and the events were very coincidental, both in dramaturgy and time interval. In practice, almost a carbon copy.

When half an hour later Harald Madsen was in Lotte's office at the police building and rattling off how he had just barely managed to both book a seat on Norwegian Air's afternoon departure and get to Gardermoen in time, Lotte Skeisvoll listened with half an ear. The only thing that meant anything was in the bag he had over his shoulder.

She'd gotten the name on the phone, but it was the details in the manuscript she needed now.

Besides herself and the editor from Gjøvik, she had managed to get hold of Olav, Knut, Lars, and the police chief. That would have to do for now. Besides the fact that it would have required some logistics to call in the whole team, which now was made up of seventeen men, there was a rationale for keeping this information internal. The press must not get hold of what Madsen had. The killer must not for anything in the world know that they knew who he was.

Besides, he probably had Viljar at an unknown place, and for that reason, he hadn't been arrested yet, but was under constant and precise monitoring.

Plainclothes policemen were placed no more than fifty meters from him at any time. In his house, which had been searched in total secrecy, Lotte hoped they would find Viljar, but the house was empty of anything that could expose him. He must have access to another place from which he could operate.

Madsen was duly placed on a stick-back chair with a cup of coffee in his hand, and he was just about to take the manuscript out of his bag when a constable from the team stuck his head in the door. The same stripling who had been with her up to Fjellvegen less than a week ago, she noted.

"Listen, Lotte, can I have two words with you?"

She sighed, but managed to paste on a fake smile before she answered. "As perhaps you see, we're a little busy here. Can it wait, do you think?" Lotte was unable to conceal the sarcasm.

The constable looked around a little in confusion at the people who were sitting like herring in a can inside the little office, nodded in recognition to Lars and Knut, before he replied. "I think the meeting room down the hall is free if you need it. . . ." The constable got no further. He quickly noticed that the gaze of both Lotte and the police chief had blackened. "Whatever . . . It probably can't wait. I think we've solved the code in the email we got from Øveraas, and then we know how . . ."

Lotte softened up a little. This was good news. She nodded curtly at him to continue. He cleared his throat a few times.

Clearly nervous.

"Uh . . . It took a little time, because we didn't find any Norwegian crime author with the initials HM. It may be that he doesn't just use Norwegian ones, and in that case, we think that HM stands for Henning Mankell."

Once again, he looked around at the gathering in order to get confirmation that he was on the right track. Everyone except for the worn-out guy with the bag in the middle nodded.

"The code refers in that case to Henning Mankell's fifth book. The first murder. We have proceeded based on his crime novel bibliography, because that's what's used in the others. The fifth book is titled *Sidetracked*, and the scene being referred to is—"

"The fire in the rape field." The man with the bag had interrupted the constable before he got to the point.

"That's right. A girl burns herself to death in the middle of a rape field."

Lotte felt her heart sink like a stone in her chest. Of all the ghastly ways to die, this was one of the worst.

"He can't mean that seriously, can he? Does he intend to set fire to someone?" Knut Veldetun's outburst was an echo of the others' thoughts.

The only one who wasn't shocked was Harald Madsen. "I'm afraid that's exactly what he intends to do. He wrote this," said Madsen, lifting a bundle of paper tied together with string out of his back-pack. He set it on the table. Everyone's eyes were fixed like flies to flypaper on the first page of the manuscript, where the title and author were written in capital letters:

MAESTRO by GEIR TANGEN

Haugesund Police Station
Sunday evening, October 19, 2014

Everything suddenly seemed so common now that they had a name to relate to. An ordinary name. An ordinary man with a completely ordinary job. An elementary-school teacher. Nowhere near the profile Olav Scheldrup Hansen had drawn up for him. A family man with a wife and kids. A known, humor-filled face in the local community. Recognized soccer supporter, former politician, and someone constantly seen on local TV.

"He must have lost his mind."

It was Lars Stople who broke the silence in the room after Harald Madsen placed the printout of the manuscript on the table. Only two of those in the room looked inquisitively at Lars. Olav Scheldrup Hansen and Harald Madsen obviously didn't know who this guy was. For them, it was just a name on a piece of paper.

"Does that mean you already know who he is?"

Harald Madsen gave Lotte a look of surprise. He obviously could not know that this was a name many people in the city recognized.

"Yes, Tangen is a familiar name here in Haugesund," Lotte replied.

"We've followed Geir Tangen closely all afternoon since we got the name from you. We hope that he'll lead us to where he's keeping the journalist hidden," Knut Veldetun added.

Harald Madsen suddenly looked embarrassed, and he cleared his throat several times before he said anything.

"I think you can release him. . . . Didn't you hear what I said when I spoke with you on the phone, Skeisvoll?"

"What do you mean?"

"I said that your killer had submitted a manuscript to us under the *pseudonym* Geir Tangen."

"And that means . . . ?"

"A pseudonym is a false name that some authors use when they publish books in order to conceal their real identity. Maria Amelie was in the air a few years ago, but that's not her real name. In the classic literature, we find pseudonyms like George Orwell, for example. His real name was Eric Arthur Blair."

Lotte felt her cheeks turning red. This was not just embarrassing. This was downright catastrophic.

"Are you telling me that we really don't know the name of the killer anyway? Are we shadowing an innocent guy out there, while the one we want to get ahold of is probably about to set fire to someone in some field or other?"

Harald Madsen held her gaze a long time, but lowered it at last, even if he wasn't the one who had lost the battle. It was decidedly she.

"Uh . . . Yes."

"Damn it all to hell! Are you an idiot? You must have realized that it was the *real* name of the killer I wanted, not a fucking pen name!"

Lotte was yelling. Everyone in the room hunched up. The seconds dragged by in silence. She looked at the tabletop for a while, straightened out a corner of the tablecloth before she took a breath and decided. A few minutes later, the room was almost empty. The police chief left the office after having assured himself that Lotte had control. Left behind was a bewildered Harald Madsen and a worn-out edition of Detective Inspector Lotte Skeisvoll.

"I'm sorry, but I thought you knew. . . ."

Harald Madsen didn't say anything else for a while, before he cleared his throat. He saw that the investigator was still struggling to get control of her own frustration, and decided that there was no point in embroidering on the misunderstanding. He chose a different strategy.

"We can find out who was behind the pseudonym if I have access to my old emails. Tomorrow is Monday, and then our office assistant will be at work, so perhaps—"

Lotte threw herself over the phone. Here it wasn't relevant to wait for any tomorrow. If the office assistant was holding things up, the Gjøvik police could pick her up with flashing lights.

"Great, Madsen. As you know, we don't have until tomorrow to rescue the next victim in this case. We'll send a patrol and pick up your office assistant."

"In Spain . . . ?"

"Spain . . . What do you mean?"

"She's on a fall vacation in Albir with her grandchildren. Comes home early tomorrow."

Lotte looked up at him with tired eyes. They had been jerked back to the start. The killer was still a ghost who was moving in the shadows. *Maybe a name tomorrow . . .*

Lotte struggled to gather both courage and energy. She had to think differently. They would soon have him now. They were getting close; there was no doubt of that.

"I think we need to look in this guy's manuscript a little. Has he described the murder of this woman in the field such that we can trace her and rescue her?"

"Not her. Him. In this manuscript, the killer copies Mankell's suicide from *Sidetracked*, but in the killer's version, it's a man who is killed, not a woman who commits suicide. If I don't remember completely incorrectly, it was a journalist who had spread lies and half truths for years."

Lotte had had a secret hope when she heard that the victim in Henning Mankell's book was a woman. In that case, it would have meant that Viljar Ravn Gudmundsson was temporarily out of danger, but now that little scrap of hope flickered out like a tealight on a back burner. It was Viljar's turn this time.

Harald Madsen appeared to have read her thoughts.

"You should read the chapter. So far, the killer has been very occupied with being correct when it comes to places. Although, at the last murder. The pistol killing . . . It should have happened down toward something he calls Karmsundet, but it didn't, as I understand it from the news sites?"

"What is it you're telling me now? Is it that detailed? So that you can recognize places and such?"

"Put it this way," Madsen answered. "I was sitting with the manuscript in one hand and my iPad with the news on the other the whole way here to Haugesund. Almost everything tallies. Crime scenes. Victims. Names. Methods—"

"Names? Are you kidding me? Has the guy used real names?"

Harald Madsen broke into a smile. "That's probably why he uses a pseudonym. He knows you, or at least knows who you are. If he'd used his own name and had this published, he would've had his head bitten off by everyone. Now he's hiding behind a name that everyone knows, but that no one can attack."

Lotte shook her head. She'd been so sure they had him, but now he was slipping out of their hands again. "Is such a thing even legal? Can authors write about whomever they want under a false name?"

"Don't forget that this is an amateur when it comes to publishing,

Skeisvoll. You have no idea how many manuscripts we get every year where it turns out that the author has used the names of real people. It does make it easier for the author to write when he knows who the various characters are, but we take that sort of thing out as soon as we start editing."

Harald stood up, took the first pages of the manuscript with him, and browsed up to the first section at the beginning. "Look here," he said, pointing.

Lotte felt herself turning cold. The words flickered before her eyes. This was unbelievable:

On the morning, four days before the light went out, the journalist Viljar Ravn Gudmundsson stood proudly in the conference room, enjoying the atmosphere around him. Big smiles, hungry eyes, and arrogant laughter filled the room. This was how things should be.

"Good Lord! This is completely crazy! Is there more?"

A few seconds later, Harald Madsen had browsed up to what was the first murder a few pages later. Lotte held her hand in front of her mouth as she read her own name and the victim Rita Lothe's name. It felt as if a rubber band were about to break inside her head. *This isn't possible.*

"How can this be? Is he psychic? He's planned every slightest little detail? This is completely cuckoo!" With the exception that the weather was wrong, that Lars Stople wasn't present, and that she had an experienced, older investigator with her instead of an unseasoned constable, this was almost an exact copy of the events that morning.

Harald Madsen took the pages back and turned them. Pointed at the title.

"Why do you think the title is *Maestro*?"

Haugesund Police Station
Sunday evening, October 19, 2014

After the meeting in the cramped office, the next step was to start contacting publishers all over the country. If the guy sent the manuscript to a tiny little publisher at Toten, he must have sent it to others too. No publisher would accept a pseudonym without correct name and address being listed as contact information.

Hopefully not all the office assistants are in Spain, thought Lotte. There was a reasonable hope that someone besides Alfa Madsen Publishers had saved both the manuscript and the contact info, according to Harald Madsen. He'd been sent with Lars Stople to get the names of publishing people he knew whom they could contact at home on a Sunday evening.

She stayed behind in her office. Her first priority was to read the manuscript in detail. See if it might lead them to the next victim, and where according to the recipe he would be killed. How, they already knew. She knew she was short on time and had to focus on the pages that concerned this murder. Lotte shuddered as she browsed ahead in the manuscript. Recognized names, places, crime scenes. Knew she shouldn't, but stopped when she saw the depiction of the murder of Ranveig Børve. The whole thing was so calculated. So consistent. Everything was described, giving answers to several questions in the investigation. She herself was the protagonist, and the person behind the pseudonym must have frighteningly good insight into her psyche, because the accounts of her thoughts in the book tallied quite well with what she was thinking at the scene. Where she thought she was ingenious when she decided to drop the details and concentrate instead on everything the murderer hadn't deliberately left behind, the killer described how she thought along similar lines. Not verbatim, obviously, that would be too much, but similar enough that it was nonetheless frightening. For a moment the thought struck her: Was she herself a victim later in the action? Lotte was afraid to look.

A feeling of being observed crept down her spine. Reading this. All the details. Even her own thoughts and actions. It was impossible to imagine that it was real.

Has he been observing me over time? Three years ago? Is he still doing it?

Lotte refused to accept her own paranoia. It must simply be an almost autistic insight into the work and mentality of the police.

Or was it that every detail was placed like that deliberately to force her to think along the lines she did? Do the things he wanted her to do? Make the choices he'd written in advance that she should make?

The words of Harald Madsen echoed in her head.

"Why do you think the title is Maestro?*"*

A maestro. An orchestra conductor. Someone who directs everything and everyone in the orchestra to get them to follow his instructions, and in that way achieve musical art.

He is going to exert himself to the utmost to follow the given notes. Any break will frustrate him, and he must make corrections to get us on his tracks again. In other words, he will not deviate from the manuscript so long as he has a chance to do it just as it says. There is our chance to stop him, she thought.

She quickly browsed to what was to come. The time for the murder was late in the afternoon, or early evening. The author hadn't used exact time designations. Didn't give the name of the victim this time.

"Damn it!"

She saw Harald Madsen out in the hall and called him in.

"Do you remember who it was who was killed in that field? Was it Viljar? Is it toward the end of the manuscript, maybe?"

Lotte flapped the manuscript in front of the publisher's eyes.

"No, it's just that . . . This is not exactly a stroke of genius as a novel. Then we would have published it. It is crawling with loose threads toward the end. Maybe it says that somewhere, but I seem to recall that one of these logical faults is *who* gets set on fire out on that field. Hopelessly weak for a crime writer, but the guy doesn't have an ounce of talent, so—"

Lotte sighed. Was no longer able to control herself.

"Yes, I've understood that, but now we have to act. We're fighting against time. Your literary observations will unfortunately have to wait." She could hear how that sounded, but didn't really care. "Is Viljar there toward the end?"

Madsen put on an offended expression. "Listen, it's three years now since I read this manuscript. I don't remember all the details."

She stood up, waved him out the door as if he were a cat that had done its business indoors. Slammed the door behind him and sat down with the manuscript. All the stress delayed her. It was as if she were living in a nightmare where she couldn't leave the spot.

"Focus, Lotte," she said sternly to herself. She read about how he would transport the victim in a boat from a boathouse in the vicinity of town to an open field right behind the small-boat harbor on the island of Lindøy. There, according to the manuscript, he would carry the victim out in the field and tie him up to a fencepost. Afterwards he would douse the victim and a wide area around him with gasoline. Enough to create a fire that would cause a sensation and attract attention from people in the vicinity. He himself would already have passed through Røyksundet and be on his way back to the city in the boat when the homemade fuse reached the stripe of gasoline and set off the inferno.

There was only one thing to do to rescue Viljar, and that was to frustrate the author's plan. Set out some mines that would obstruct him from following the book, but at the same time without revealing that they knew the sequence of events. The problem was that perhaps they were already too late. Perhaps Viljar Ravn Gudmundsson was already tethered firmly to a fencepost on Lindøy at that moment. If they were unable to rescue Viljar, then at least they had the killer now. The boat would be stopped when it came to the pier in Haugesund.

Lotte picked up the intercom and told everyone in the group to come back at once. This time she chose to follow the newbie's well-intentioned tip. The meeting room on the west side could serve as an operations center for the final hunt.

Requiem: Benedictus

I feel his wheezing breath against my throat while I carry him. He's heavy, and he is constantly squirming. I don't care. I have an iron grip around his waist that he won't get out of. He's hog-tied besides and can't do any great harm with his outbursts. The panic is noticeable. The anxiety, despair, and fear. I know how bad it is to feel these things, but nonetheless, the worst is hope. That little sprout that everything will work out in the end. That you'll be rescued. That you'll get away. That death isn't awaiting you up ahead after all. Hope creates panic. The adrenaline makes the blood pump with unreduced force. Fortunately for him, I have everything required to take away the panic. Everything that's needed to replace the frightening hope with far more pleasant resignation.

It's only then, while the last shreds of hope die, that I find peace among those who must be sacrificed. Then calm settles like the silence when the first snow falls against the ground on Christmas Eve. Before the bells chime. Quietly and softly. The certainty is like that too. Quiet and soft. The pulse that gets slower. The gaze that is slowly lowered toward the ground. Resignation . . .

In a few minutes, that is where we are. When he finally understands that help isn't coming. When he realizes that he won't get loose. When at last he grasps that this is happening to him, and that I'm not going to grant him amnesty. Then comes resignation.

Screams are replaced by sobbing. Stiff muscles relax. I know this, because I've seen it before. Ranveig was like that. . . . A feverish struggle against death, until she quite suddenly collapsed in total apathetic resignation. Surrender . . . I savor the word. Whisper it in his ear while I carry him up toward the goal. *Surrender.*

He's not there yet, but soon.

The sound of the lapping water against the stones on the shore rinses my thoughts away for a second or two. It's so peaceful here. Quiet. No worry that ruins the picture. Just me and the water. He's tied up. The whimpering no longer reaches me. I don't hear the protests, the oaths, and the spite. Mostly thanks to the muzzle, of course, but all the same . . . I don't think I would hear him if he shouted either. If he screamed, or blew on all the trumpets on Judgment Day. He can't reach me. I am out of range. It's just me and the whispering of the water on the beach rocks. The thumping from the gas can I'm carrying. I am. He isn't. It can be that simple.

"It is written in the Scriptures," I whisper to him as I come up to the stake for the second time. He sees my red gas can, and I realize from his look that he understands the scope of what is coming. Not a peaceful death. No, not this time. Not a sleeping fall from the seventh floor, no exploding bullet that turns everything black in a hundredth of a second, no blackout after insufficient oxygen supply to the brain . . . No, this time there will be pain. Skin that slowly melts in the flames and that implodes the body in a hell of agony. Blood that boils, the smell of singed flesh, before the brain collapses from all the nerve endings shrieking out in a simultaneous scream of pain. A short time later, death occurs, when the flames pass the skin and all blood circulation stops. Minutes later, all that remains is carbon and ash. What before were thoughts, feelings, smells, tastes, and urges will turn into what they arose from. Carbon and ash.

I feel my fingers prickling from getting to be a witness to this step into eternity. Getting to see a person leave the body in his final moment. A bit stupid that I can't be standing right there. I regret writing the scene that way. I see now that I wouldn't have had any problem witnessing the event before I take the boat back, but I'm sticking to the plan. My requiem must be completed to the letter. I sprinkle and sprinkle. Over him and around him. In spirals around the stake. I am overjoyed by the dry grass around my feet. This will be a spectacular sight. Even out from sea.

I wait for the resignation, but it is long in coming. Maybe it's not so easy to let go when the outcome involves so much pain? I think about my own pain. It's going to hurt indescribably toward the end. I know that. But it will be worth it. When that happens, people will have seen me. Seen my talent. My exit will happen in the certain knowledge that I won't be forgotten. It's close now, but still there is no one who knows. No one who understands. No one who sees the picture the way I've drawn it. That will come only when all the bridges are burned, and the final tone in the piece slips out of the melancholy oboe. Piano pianissimo . . . One last beat with the baton, and everything that is and will be is gone.

The white, homemade fuse is the last thing that will draw into itself the potential energy of 95-octane fossil fuel. Not really necessary. Fuses don't burn faster for that reason, but the danger that it will go out on the way toward the spiral in the dry grass is slightly less. That was what was described in the recipe anyway. I lift it up so that he can see it. He feverishly shakes his head and tries to shout. It sounds like a low rutting roar from a moose. Anger. Desperation. Fear. Still no resignation. That irritates me. Are journalists tougher than others? Do they have more undone in life than most people? Do they have a built-in faith that everything can be changed at the last second? That a deadline is something that can be postponed? I smile a little at my own thought.

"Deadline. That's exactly what this is," I mumble to myself. A line of death. I raise the fuse in the air one more time and call to him, "This is the deadline!"

He stiffens. A swelling pride expands in my chest. I can see the head being lowered. The shoulders shaking. He is crying. *Finally*, I think. Finally he got peace.

I ignite the lighter and let it work the end of the fuse. He doesn't react. Arches his back as far as possible. Sinks down on his knees. Some sparks come before the fuse starts to crackle. A shimmering white light. I set it down and turn my back to the scenario. Walk toward the boat. Know I have about two minutes to board the boat and get myself around the cape. Too bad that I don't get to see the high point itself, but I suspect I'll hear it.

I have just come on board the little dinghy, and at first I don't notice what is happening behind me. I turn around one last time and see to my amazement that there is activity out in the field. I don't understand how that's possible. Two police cars have swerved in by the small-boat harbor, and while I am approaching the narrow sound between the north side of Lindøy and Røyksund, I see people running down toward the stake in the field. They can't possibly reach it. In that case, it will be fatal. I am forced to slow down. I must see the outcome before I round the cape.

They are only fifty meters away now, but I feel my own pulse lowering. The fuse has reached the goal, and the flame erupts. In less than five seconds, it's done. The flames stand several meters in the air as the body is ignited. The hellfire reaches out toward the police, who almost reach him. But only almost . . . An unearthly scream is heard over the roar of the engine. Clean, pure, and delightful pain resounds through the air.

Small-Boat Harbor, Lindøy
Sunday evening, October 19, 2014

The flames were almost five meters in the air from the stake. Lotte could hear the deranged scream of pain all the way up at the command car where she was sitting. She turned away. There was nothing they could do to rescue him. The scream turned into a kind of bellowing howl before it was cut off. It was over in just a few seconds, but for Lotte it felt endlessly longer. Standing by the car and seeing the man be consumed by the flames was a definitive defeat.

No matter how this ends, we've lost, she thought as she slowly sank into a crouch and hid her head in her hands. Despair and hopelessness washed over her while people shouted and screamed in all directions. When she raised her eyes later, she could see that someone had managed to overturn the stake where the body was tied and that they were vainly trying to pour seawater over it. She herself turned toward the car. Didn't want to see any more. Didn't want to hear. With trembling hands, she took out the microphone for police coordination and reported the incident. She asked them to send an ambulance, crime scene investigators, and firemen. It all happened mechanically. Action without thought.

She stood there watching the three police officers who were still running around like confused lice down on the field. *What is it they're stressing about? It's too late anyway.*

After a few moments, she understood that there was something going on down there. A guy who came running from the harbor was pointing and gesturing wildly to two of the constables. Lotte forced herself out of her apathy and slowly started moving toward them.

"He was out by the point over there when it started to burn," she heard the man say loudly as she approached. He showed them the place by pointing over toward the approach to the breakwater. She jogged the last stretch down to the three who were talking together.

"Who is he? Did you see someone here?" Lotte's piercing voice made the men flinch.

The boat owner turned toward her and repeated what he had just said to the two constables. He had seen a man take off in a dinghy around the point more or less at the same time as it started burning.

"He took the route through Røyksundet," he specified.

"And this happened five minutes ago, you say?" Lotte had subdued herself a little so as not to scare the pants off the poor guy.

He nodded. "Less than that . . . Three, maybe. He must have come down from the shore, because otherwise I would have noticed him from my boat."

Lotte called the others to her. Here they had to pivot quickly. There was still hope they'd be able to stop that bastard. If he was on his way to town in the dinghy, at any rate.

"Knut, you go with me in the car. The two of you stay here and watch the crime scene. Don't let anyone else wander in before the CSIs are on-site. Okay? Not the ambulance personnel either if it's possible to stop them. Viljar is dead, and right now we don't need twelve men tramping down the field around him."

She jogged back up to the car. The energy came as soon as she glimpsed a hope of getting ahold of the killer. She threw herself into the driver's seat and barely waited for Knut to get his long limbs in place before she screeched off on the narrow road while gravel sprayed around the car. The undercarriage scraped as she flew over the first bump. She had Knut call the response center and ask them to be on the lookout for a white dinghy, with one man on board, on its way north in Karmsundet.

"Damn it that we don't have a police boat here! Then we could have cut him off before he made it to land."

They had to hope and believe that he was following his own manuscript. In that case, he would have a bit of a welcoming committee. She called the police station and asked to be transferred to Harald Madsen, who had been allowed to use her office and quickly made himself comfortable in her chair.

"Harald! Lotte here . . . Double-check the killer's escape route from Lindøy. What does he do, and where does he come ashore? We know it said Haugesund, but look over the details." Harald cleared his throat and she heard the sound of loose pages being turned right by the phone.

It took a few endless seconds before Harald cleared his throat yet again. He'd found something.

"In the book, he leaves the victim before it starts burning, and takes his boat back to the pier in Haugesund to a place he calls . . . Wait a moment . . . the Bakarøy breakwater."

Lotte knew it was risky business to bet everything on one card, but she had no other choice, the way things were now. An emergency response team could be ready to take him if he followed his own recipe. He would need over thirty minutes on the trip north in a little dinghy, she thought. If he deviated from his own writings, they would lose him. Again!

Lotte drove even faster. She scraped bushes and the edge of ditches before she threw the car out on the main road by the entrance to the new subway connection. Knut Veldetun gave her a frightened look from where he was hanging on to the seat belt, trying to steady himself with one hand on the strap above the passenger door.

Cars moved over to the side of the road in all directions, and new routes constantly opened up where before there was traffic. Only when the car just barely managed to stay on the road in the roundabout at Raglamyr did Lotte seem to realize that there were limits to speed even in a police response. BMW M3 was not the standard police vehicle, after all. Between the many roundabouts leading into the city center, she stepped on the gas anyway, far beyond what was reasonable driving. This time nothing would stop her. For the first time since the whole thing started, they were ahead of him. For the first time, she was the one who was the hunter and he was the prey.

Over the police radio, she arranged full call-out to the Bakarøy breakwater, but discreetly so that lights and sirens could not be seen from the sea. The police should park nearby and keep out of sight. Everyone should be armed. The killer should be overpowered as he came on land. This was the only chance they had to stop him, the way Lotte saw it. If he discovered them, it was guaranteed that he would deviate from the original plan. The trump card they had by knowing about the unpublished manuscript would be lost if he discovered them before the arrest and had the opportunity to get away.

At the roundabout at Flotmyr, she turned the car toward the city center, while she turned off the rotating blue lights. She hadn't used the siren since she passed the city line. Two minutes later, she parked the police car by the Billed Gallery and unlocked the gun from the car. Put on bulletproof vest and helmet. She checked Knut's equipment, and he checked hers, before they made their way down toward the bridge that led over to Hasseløy. They crouched down while they ran across the bridge so they wouldn't be visible from the sound. For the time being, there was no boat to be seen on its way in toward the breakwater, and the two police officers were quickly waved over to the side of the response force. If the perpetrator came in here, he wouldn't have a chance.

Hasseløy, Haugesund
Sunday evening, October 19, 2014

The little dinghy was not moving very fast. For those who were waiting on land, it seemed like an eternity from when the first reports came in from the operations post until they could see the outlines of the boat that kept an even speed toward land. In an ideal world, there wouldn't have been any other boats on the sea, but it just wasn't like that. A warm autumn evening in Haugesund obviously enticed boat owners out, even if a good many had put their boats into winter hibernation. It was Sunday, and weekend sailors were gradually turning their noses homeward toward the pier.

What Lotte in her confusion had thought would be a simple task turned out to be a rare test of patience. Time estimates showed that the dinghy ought to have been in the harbor at least ten minutes ago, but it wasn't. Many boats had come and gone, but none that matched the description from the man on Lindøy. Not until now. She'd felt frustration seething again and again. She called the officers who were on Lindøy to get a more precise description of the boat they were hunting. The man maintained that it was white with a horizontal dark gray stripe. The boat had a small outboard motor, and there was certainly not room for more than three or four people on board. That was all. Strictly speaking, that description fit half a dozen boats that had been on Karmsundet the past half hour, but none of them had set a course toward the Bakarøy breakwater. This one, on the other hand, had.

There was a crackle in the receiver she had in her ear. The observation post up by the bridge was calling her.

"Sierra One, two persons have been observed on board. I repeat . . . Two persons on board the object."

Lotte was about to stand up from her hiding place, but she restrained herself. She wouldn't be able to confirm the observation from here anyway. She asked the ops post to verify, and immediately got confirmation.

"There is no doubt, Sierra One. There are two persons on board. One steering the boat, and a figure who is sitting in the bow." Lotte cursed out loud and got a surprised look from Knut, who was lying beside her on the rock-covered slope. She didn't understand a thing. Was it the wrong boat? Had they failed again, or did he have his next victim with him in the boat already? The questions were piling up, but there was little she could do about it. They just had to wait and see. The problem was that the arrest would be much more difficult now, as the man had a potential hostage. They couldn't risk putting the other person in danger by moving in the way they'd planned.

A new scenario struck her. *What if it turns out to be two perpetrators who are working together?* She dismissed that as quickly as she thought it. For one thing, it would be too improbable that there would be two such perpetrators in the same city and, as if that weren't enough, who worked together besides. For another, there was nothing in the book that referred to more than one perpetrator. "Maestro" worked alone. There was no doubt whatsoever about that. Which might mean that the other person in the boat was either blissfully ignorant of what danger he or she was in, or else the person was a captive.

Lotte turned to the side and called the police station. She hadn't read the scene where the killer puts to shore by the breakwater. Only Harald Madsen had. The joker hadn't forgotten to inform them that there were two in the boat, had he? She was transferred at once.

"No, Lotte, there's nothing about that here anyway. He's alone when he comes to shore. But having said that, not everything matches a hundred percent here. He has deviated from the original plan a few times. He's not psychic."

Lotte felt a headache coming on. She must have answers. The others waited for her commands now as the situation had suddenly changed.

"Is Scheldrup Hansen there with you?"

Harald Madsen answered affirmatively and handed the phone to the Kripos investigator.

"Olav, I need answers quickly. Based on this guy's psyche, how probable is it that he has picked up a hostage that he's dragged with him on the boat?"

There was silence a few seconds before he answered the question.

"Based on his profile, I can't get it to add up. In any event, if what Harald says is true, he hasn't written anything about it in the manuscript. The guy seems almost manic about getting things to match the script. He evidently has a very clear intention of re-creating his own book, and the way I see it, he wants to exert himself very far to avoid major changes. Taking another person with him on the boat doesn't seem very likely in that scenario. Having said that, he must have noticed us when we almost caught him at Lindøy, so he may well have put two and two together and realized that we know about the manuscript. In that case, it would be madness to stick to it."

"Madness, damn it? The guy is crazy!"

"Yes, of course, but not in the sense that he doesn't know what he's up to. He's not irrational and unbalanced. He apparently has full control, and seen that way, he would never think of ruining the rest of his plot by ending up in a hostage situation. Are you sure that it really is him on his way into the breakwater? That it's not just someone who's been out on a pleasure cruise in this nice weather?"

Lotte hung up. She didn't need Scheldrup Hansen's overbearing truisms. In rapid succession, she called up the three groups of police. Asked them to hold off and not follow the original plan of arrest in case he came ashore. She asked them to wait until they had a closer observation of who was in the boat, any weapons, and if the other person was in any form of danger.

Out on the sound, the dinghy approached the breakwater. Everything appeared normal. Nothing indicated that it was a man under pressure who was guiding the boat, or that the passenger felt threatened in any way.

"Sierra One, there are two men in the boat. We have not observed any form of weapon. Neither of the two appears to be threatened by the other in any way."

Lotte now had a clear view to the boat as it slowly moved toward land. She put the binoculars to her eyes and focused. A brief cry came from her lips before she collected herself. The skipper had a bearskin cap pulled down over his head and was impossible to identify through the binoculars. An older man around sixty, she guessed. But it wasn't the skipper who made her break her sound protocol. It was the sight of the slightly uncomfortable passenger. A worn, thin, and stoop-shouldered figure. Lotte held her breath. Looked again and again. There was no doubt. The passenger in the boat was Viljar Ravn Gudmundsson.

Four years earlier . . .
Stemmen, Haugesund
Tuesday evening, August 31, 2010

Fredric Karjoli turned away. Crawled on his knees farther in under the trees. What he had seen wasn't real. It couldn't be. The scream from the bridge still echoed in his ears. *This isn't true. This isn't happening.*

The terrifying sight from the bridge whisked away the last little scrap of hope. There was no way back.

Fredric tried to stand up. He had to get away. He had solemnly promised to stay away from Eivindsvatnet, but he hadn't been able to. He wanted to be there. Make sure that nothing went wrong. Warn Jonas of the threat if the police were waiting for him up there. He realized suddenly how naïve he'd been. Jonas must have known what could happen. There was no other reasonable basis to refuse to let Fredric be present. All of Norway knew they were on the run together. He didn't need to hide it. Not even from his family.

"I can't travel with you without apologizing to Mom," Jonas had said.

Travel . . . As if it were only a vacation trip. As if what had happened wouldn't lead to a manhunt all over the world.

"She's not coming alone, Jonas. For God's sake, we killed your sister. Do you think she'll go there without taking the police with her?"

"I don't know, Fredric. That's why you shouldn't be there. If Mom reports me, that's great. No matter what, I won't be able to go on living without having talked with her."

Speak of the devil, thought Fredric.

Jonas hadn't said anything more to him before he left him in the grove of trees down by Haraldsvang and started walking up toward Stemmen, where he and his mother had agreed to meet. None of Fredric's protests had helped. Instead it meant that he couldn't keep his promise. As the rain picked up, he followed his friend at a safe distance to avoid being discovered. Once there, he had hidden by the boathouse. With a clear view to the bridge, he could see everything. Including the inconceivable, which was never meant for his eyes.

The whole thing happened so fast that Fredric had no time to react. Mother and son in a tight embrace at one moment. The next moment, Jonas's legs disappeared over the edge. A horrible scream as the woman who gave him life also took life from him.

When five minutes later Fredric ventured out from his hiding place on wobbly legs, the bridge was abandoned. No one was in sight. He was shaking like an aspen leaf. His knees were about to buckle. Fredric held on hard to the railing while he looked down into the abyss. Spied for his lover. It was much too dark. After shouting himself hoarse, he sank down on his knees and cried. He vaguely glimpsed that there was a person standing over him.

Fredric couldn't bear to see whether it was her. It was all over regardless. It was only when the person started talking to him that he realized that others had ventured out in the storm.

"Do you need help?"

Fredric nodded. Sobbed out some words that were so unclear, he had to say them again.

"Call the police. I'm Fredric Karjoli. I think they're searching for me."

The man stood up abruptly and walked away from him, but Fredric could hear him mumbling on the phone farther away. Minutes later, he sensed a blue shimmer from a police car in his peripheral vision. No sirens. Just blue lights. Through the small glimmers of cold blue light, he could see the bottom of the dam. Jonas's red T-shirt showed where he had landed.

Hasseløy, Haugesund
Sunday evening, October 19, 2014

On their way in toward the breakwater, Viljar had a strange sensation of being observed by a thousand eyes. He shook off the feeling and stared at André Ferkingstad, who was sitting in the stern, steering the dinghy. The old churchman had been seconds from breaking the fifth commandment. If everything had gone according to plan, Viljar would have been in the company of a cement block, down in the depths outside Røvær. Jonas's bitter father had come to his senses, however. Listened to him. Heard his plea.

The moment when he was standing there in the door to the boathouse, he had given no sign of a man who would relent. The tall, broad-shouldered man stood ramrod straight and observed Viljar. No Bible in the world could convert him. Nevertheless, it had happened. Viljar didn't know what changed his mind, but he thought it was the sincerity. The honesty. The repentant sinner.

Viljar had seen the hatred in the eyes of the aging man. The desperation. The sorrow. The despair . . . All the pain. This was the hour of reckoning, and even if Viljar was aware that it would probably end with his own death, it felt good anyway. He should have had this reckoning long ago. Then perhaps both of them could have moved forward with their grief.

André Ferkingstad sat down on one of the herring barrels right across from Viljar. Demanded answers. It was like opening a floodgate. Viljar talked and talked. Didn't conceal anything. Described what he'd been thinking. What he'd done. Why he'd made the choices he had. The whole time with the certain knowledge that this was probably the last chance to tell it the way it really was.

As the details of the story slowly unfolded, the gaze of the old man softened. What was hard and hateful disappeared. Only the mournful expression remained on his face. Perhaps he understood that this had also marked Viljar for life. A fatal misjudgment, which had destroyed life for so many. Viljar remembered everything that happened. He could recall the smells. Hear the sounds. Even relived the intoxicating feeling he'd had from the praise before it all fell apart. Before it unraveled.

Viljar had been negligent in his work, and the consequence was that two young people were torn out of time. Two others were in prison. Viljar had gotten off too easy. But the very worst was the thought that he had indirectly taken the life of an innocent nine-year-old girl. It was her blood he felt he had on his hands.

In the time after the Jonas case, the desire to write, investigate, and expose disappeared. Anxiety tore him to pieces, and the scoop journalist gradually became a shadow of himself. Allowed to stay on the job based on mercy and old achievements. Burned out, tired, and with no drive.

He had always expected that the fateful error would come out in the media storm that arose. That he would be exposed and put up against the wall. First by colleagues in the Oslo press who had discovered the oversight—but they had placed their protective hand over him. Next he expected that local gossip would catch up with him. That sooner or later, Johan Øveraas would call him into his office. It was a mystery, but the confrontation never came. Not even during the trial of Jonas's mother.

In her testimony, she had touched on the revelation several times, but what was behind Jonas's desperate choices those last few days never came out.

Viljar fooled himself into thinking that he was the only one who knew that he was the cause of the tragic deaths. Not even Jonas's father knew it. At least that was what he'd believed until now. Then the whole thing ended in an inferno of even more death and suffering. He had confronted André Ferkingstad about the madness of killing other people simply to get at him. Asked him why. What was the purpose of all this violence?

Then suddenly the table turned. . . . Ferkingstad looked at him with gentle eyes and said the words that made Viljar's framework of logic and context collapse.

"It wasn't me. I'm no killer. Don't you see that? I should kill the one person that I've hated more than anything on earth the past four years, and I couldn't even manage that. I have God's light in me, Gudmundsson. I cannot kill."

"But then who is it who . . . ? This must have something to do with Jonas and me?"

Once again, Ferkingstad looked at him with steady calm. Made room for the silence.

"No, Viljar, as far as I can see, none of those killed have any connection to Jonas. This is a product of your guilty conscience, nothing else. Isn't it perhaps time that you turn your face toward God and pray for forgiveness? Perhaps then you will have peace from your demons."

Viljar suddenly collapsed in tears. From exhaustion. From relief. From regret.

André Ferkingstad had gradually learned to live with the sorrow, the loss, and the shame. He had come to terms with the fact that Viljar made a professional error that he couldn't be blamed for. That the regret and conviction about what had happened were punishment enough. That the shame in itself was a lesson. For four years, this was something he had come to accept. On Friday, that changed. Then he read Viljar's bantering reportage in consternation, where he made fun of his own contact with a simple murderer. A journalist who very clearly hadn't learned anything from what happened to Jonas and Ine.

It was at that moment André Ferkingstad decided that Viljar Ravn Gudmundsson himself should feel what it was like to be a victim. He wanted to see Viljar suffer. See him feel regret. After striking him down and securing him in the boathouse by his cabin on Røvær, he actually thought about killing him.

It wasn't until he saw how despondent the journalist was that he settled down. Viljar was, like himself, a marked man. He himself had lost everything. His children were dead; his beloved wife was in prison. All he had left was a congregation that clearly claimed its distance from all that had happened. He was a wounded animal, but no killer.

Without any more words, they got in the boat and silently chugged back to the city in the belief that everything that had happened between them went unnoticed.

Requiem: Agnus Dei

I see them standing there, all together. My characters, all lined up.
What they're doing here on the breakwater, I don't know, but I have
an idea that they must have known something. One way or another,
they've figured out what is happening, but I don't understand how.
No one but me has access to all the details. There is only one possible
solution, and that is that they've seen me and know my identity. That
someone is shadowing me. Following my movements. But then why
don't they stop me? Why do they let me commit more murders?
That would be madness, right?

It can't be that way. They may have had suspicions, but they can't
possibly have known. It wasn't quite according to the notes that the
police should come to Lindøy, but even so, they did. I was only minutes away from being caught. Perhaps they noticed the boat and followed its journey toward land? But then they should have stayed
hidden and waited for me here! Not stood there echoing each other
right out in the open as if they were on an outing. Was it my little
stop at the pier on Litlasund that confused them? Was it the case that

they really did wait for me, but now the operation ended because I should have been on land long ago if I sailed straight to the Bakarøy breakwater? Yes, that's probably how it was.

It was a rare stroke of luck that I swept the area with the binoculars before I took off on the last stretch in toward land. If not, it would have stopped here. The masterwork would have been unfinished.

There is a shiver down my spine. That *must not happen*! For everything in the world, that must not happen. Fortunately, they know nothing about what is coming. *Requiem: Communio*. The final movement. Now it's all about staying out of sight. They evidently know who I am, but not what I'm doing.

When the police leave, it's crucial to be careful. I can't risk anything now. They've gotten too close. I must find another way to a different place. With dawning curiosity, I turn my gaze the opposite way. Toward the island group that is bobbing on the surface of the water to the northwest. Espevær.

No one will suspect a boat on its way out there. From there, I can operate in peace. No police will look in that direction. I can prepare the finale leisurely. The only problem is the manuscript. I look down in the red backpack. All I need is on the laptop computer. It will take a whole night to rewrite it, but it will be worth it. So far everything tallies. There have been fewer rewrites than I feared. I need a space with electricity and a bed. The little island community out there has that, and I know exactly where I can get the peace I require to complete what is waiting tomorrow.

Under cover of the skerries, I set out from the boathouse and point the boat toward Espevær. The night sky is coal black, and the sea is dead calm. The calm before the storm.

Haugesund Police Station
Sunday night, October 19, 2014

Olav Scheldrup Hansen looked over at Lotte Skeisvoll where she sat with her head in her hands.

"Are you joking with me? Gudmundsson denied that he'd been kidnapped?"

Lotte Skeisvoll mumbled a "Yes, why is that?" down into her coffee cup. She did not raise her eyes. When there was no response from the Kripos investigator, she sighed and explained the whole thing to him.

"It seems our dear friend Viljar Ravn Gudmundsson has been on a daylong fishing trip with his 'new friend' André Ferkingstad. He picked Viljar up at home on Saturday night, and they've been blissfully unaware out there on the island. That Viljar was both bloody and injured was from a nasty fall on the slippery rocks."

Scheldrup Hansen shook his head. This was as believable as a Russian professional cyclist with clean blood tests. He let it go. The killer must have been in another boat in any case, which in some peculiar way or other, they'd managed to let slip between their fingers. How that happened, only God must know. Now, however, they had more important things to focus on than Gudmundsson's fairy tales.

Lotte had come to life again, and she stood up from the chair.

"We have to know who the incinerated corpse on Lindøy is, because it's not Gudmundsson."

She'd been saying such things for two hours now. Truisms and empty phrases. She had Harald Madsen copy the last forty-five pages of the manuscript for the team, and they'd all read it. There was no doubt about what was going on, but they had one night at their disposal if the killer stuck to the text. Nothing would happen before early tomorrow morning, but then on the other hand, it would happen incredibly fast.

Scheldrup Hansen looked at the others on the team. Worn-out, broken-down faces. They let themselves be influenced by a leader who had more or less given up. He decided to take hold of the situation and stood up abruptly. The chair scraped behind him and made a loud, piercing sound. He had their attention from the first second, so it was actually superfluous to clear his throat loudly and say that he wanted to say something. No one nodded or smiled. Only vacant or skeptical gazes were seen.

"Listen here . . . It's leading us nowhere to sit and stare down at the tabletop. Even if the maniac obviously didn't follow the plan by coming ashore at the breakwater, that doesn't mean he's discovered that we know about his plans. He may have changed them a little in the approach. Don't forget that he wrote this years ago. Nevertheless, he has tried all along to stay close to the original manuscript. The guy must have uncommonly good intuition or insight into how police think. We'll have to hope and believe that he hasn't changed too much."

Scheldrup Hansen stopped briefly. Took a slurp from his coffee cup before he again let his gaze sweep across the gathering. He could see some of the faces had woken up. Lotte too. She sent him a grateful look from her seat at the end of the table. Lars Stople showed with a finger in the air that he wanted to say something.

"In that case, the manuscript shows whom we have to bring in protection for. We've received the last email, and we've all read what it involves in the manuscript. An awful scene where Lotte's head is found on a stake up by the outdoor café at Haraldsvang. I assume that we'll keep guard over her here, so he doesn't get ahold of her?"

Olav nodded, but looked thoughtfully at his colleague beside him. "Yes, of course we have to protect her, but we mustn't forget either that the author has failed seriously at one point in his predictions."

He looked around and could see for the first time some who were humming and smiling around the table. Lotte, on the other hand, hid her reddening cheeks in her hands. Some levity was created amidst all the tragedy in that the manuscript described a passionate love scene between Lotte and Viljar right before he disappeared from the story. That the scene referred to a number of kinky details didn't make matters any better for Lotte. Olav Scheldrup Hansen could see that if she'd had a sinkhole available, she would happily have made herself disappear. He continued before anyone got a chance to comment.

"That's not important in this instance, but what that scene shows is that we're dealing with a person. A person who makes mistakes. Who thinks wrong. Not a psychic divinity who knows all. But at the same time, the simple fact that we know how he's going to act is our only trump card. If he starts to improvise, we're through. It will be even worse if he isn't able to track down Lotte tomorrow. Then he will undoubtedly become both desperate and unpredictable. Then we will lose the slight advantage we have."

All attention was directed toward Scheldrup Hansen now. What he said made sense, but at the same time was so unheard of that it was on the edge of being pure madness.

Lotte raised her head and looked him right in the eyes. "Are you insinuating that I shouldn't have protection? Use me as a kind of decoy? Put my life at risk? It's not enough that police regulations strictly prohibit this, it's also completely indefensible."

The Kripos investigator sighed. He knew he was on very thin ice now, but collected himself to explain what he'd been thinking.

"The answer is both yes and no, Lotte. We can let you be *apparently* unprotected. We know both where and how the killer intends to strike at you. We have a pack of police officers ready at every conceivable corner so that we can strike so quickly, the killer won't know what's going on before he is overpowered. Then we'll manage to avoid the whole tragic scene he wants to play out in Haraldsvang an hour later."

Everyone's eyes turned toward Lotte. When all was said and done, this decision was hers. They knew that.

She held both arms up in front of her. "You know . . . the arrangement is pure systematized madness, but this will have to be the police chief's decision. If he's in agreement with you, Olav, then I'll back down. I just hope you've thought through the consequences better this time. You've already calculated his thoughts and actions wrong on more than a few occasions."

Austmannavegen, Haugesund
Monday morning, October 20, 2014

Lotte Skeisvoll was no coward by nature, but now she was scared. If this case had proved anything the past week, it was that this killer was capable of surprise every single time the police thought they would get the better of him. For that reason, she had also tried to protest when the police chief hesitantly went along with Scheldrup Hansen's hypothesis.

It was only when she got the police chief face-to-face and he explained what made him give in that she realized she couldn't say no. One thing was that everything about this guy showed that he always had a plan B if the main one failed. In plain terms, that meant that if he didn't attack Lotte, he would find another woman to take her place. They didn't know who that would be, but it was someone the killer definitely already had in reserve. A woman they could not possibly protect. Another thing was that purely tactically, this was the last possibility they had to take him out. After this scene, the manuscript was almost unusable, as it didn't give the reader any information about where the killer would be before it was too late to intervene.

Lotte probably seemed much more confident on the outside than she was inside. Even though it was a mild autumn morning, she felt cold, and her legs were shaking as she jogged on her regular route, the way she did every morning from six to seven. An hour of asphalt before the city woke up was the closest she came to comprehending the dependency that her sister Anne talked about. She still had a short stretch left before she reached what the author had pointed out in the manuscript as the scene of the crime. The underpass at the Opel Building just west of the high-rises where Viljar lived.

Lotte had done as she was asked. Left her apartment in Ramsdalen at the usual six o'clock, the way she always did. The run was such a transparent routine that the killer had written it down years ago. She had to honestly admit that she hadn't changed her behavior pattern noticeably. People could set their watches by her, and today they were literally doing just that.

Down by the underpass, she knew that it was apparently deserted. But it wasn't. A total of ten police officers were placed in the area around the tunnel, and they could probably both locate and take out the killer long before she herself arrived. If not, they would be ready regardless as soon as the man had intervened and taken her with him. According to the manuscript, it would happen by the entrance to the tunnel, and the killer would do it by knocking her out with an electric stun gun, and then carry her with him the ten meters up to a parked car by Opel. Now they knew this, however, and for that reason, the arrest itself didn't involve any great risk, Olav thought. Even if it went so far that the killer used the stun gun, a bruise would be all Lotte needed to be afraid of.

All this was fine. Lotte understood the logic. The problem was that this man had fooled them completely so many times now that she didn't feel the least bit secure as she was running. In case the whole thing broke down, she had been supplied with a can of powerful pepper spray in one pocket.

In principle, this self-defense measure was probably meant to make Lotte more confident, but it had the exact opposite effect on her. It meant, of course, that the police chief had a gap in his theories; this could go wrong. The thought was worrisome, but the assurance that at least ten pairs of eyes would be following her on her way into the little tunnel helped, and was the very reason she had chosen to go along with the plan. She had seen enough examples of the response force's enormous effectiveness previously.

Her heart rate increased as she crossed the road by the nearest high-rises. The tunnel was fifty meters farther ahead. It was a matter of seconds. Lotte took herself by the scruff of the neck. Didn't want to seem uncertain and hesitant. She jogged nimbly toward the opening while her gaze searched across the area. Farther ahead, she could see the figure who stood and waited. The adrenaline pumped through her body, and she noticed that her legs threatened to buckle under her. The outline of the figure in the tunnel got sharper and sharper. A recognizable figure. Lotte knew who was standing there, but she couldn't believe it was true. The person in question had hardly been in the crosshairs through the entire investigation. In astonishment, she ran the final steps toward the man while she surreptitiously stuck one hand into her pocket to take out the pepper spray. The man had a broad, self-satisfied smile as she came up to him, but only for a fraction of a second. Just as Lotte reached him, all hell broke loose around them.

A crazy bang and a sharp flash sent them right to the ground. Lotte was blinded and stunned. Her ears were ringing. A burning pain shot from her neck and down toward her chest. She couldn't breathe. Completely paralyzed, she was lifted up from the ground and roughly thrown into the cement wall. She could hear tramping steps that echoed in the tunnel walls and intense shouting. Gradually she discerned figures running around her. A woman was lying on the ground farther away, screaming hysterically. Lotte tried to raise her hands to her head, but they didn't obey. She tried to get her legs under her, but a foot struck her in the temple with great force, and everything disappeared around her.

Haugesund Police Station
Monday morning, October 20, 2014

The cameras clicked like machine gun fire as Lotte Skeisvoll and Olav Scheldrup Hansen turned past the press gathered at the police station. Fortunately, they could drive right into the parking garage below police headquarters. No journalists were allowed in there. Lotte registered a TV camera with the CNN logo sweep by as they passed. That was frightening. It was bad enough that Norwegian media closely followed what you did, but when the world's leading news channel had its Argus eyes on you, you knew that everything you did and said from here to eternity would have your name on it.

The police station was thronged with people, even though it was just past seven thirty in the morning. Kripos had sent over two full teams on Saturday and Sunday, and now reinforcements were brought in from all possible departments in the district. Five homicides in seven days was the total so far, and today a sixth was supposed to happen. Now it had been prevented. They'd arrested him. That was probably what the press had gotten wind of. The killer was placed in a bed in the emergency ward at the hospital, and heavily guarded. She had personally asked the response team members to proceed carefully during the arrest, but they didn't. If the treatment the man got went under the designation of "careful," she would prefer not to see the rough-handed variety. He'd been beaten black and blue even though he must have lost consciousness the moment he hit the asphalt in the underpass. A deep cut in his head testified to a hard encounter with the pavement.

Things hadn't gone much better with her. One of the police officers who stormed the tunnel from the west had mistaken which of the two was lying there, and gave her a solid kick to the head when she showed signs of trying to get up. Fortunately, it was something she could remedy with an ice pack. Foggy and bruised, but alive. That was more than she would have been if they hadn't managed to stop the killer.

She was groggy. Staggered a little and needed help on the stairs. She probably should have been in the hospital too. *It feels like a concussion*, Lotte noted on her way up the first stair steps. She waited. Scheldrup Hansen took hold of her arm and gave her a little extra support. Whether it was the pressure from the shock grenade or the well-aimed kick that made Lotte hazy was not easy to say, but her face was a hardly becoming shade of gray, and she looked like she was about to throw up at any moment.

"Will you manage? Are you okay?"

Lotte didn't answer, but nodded affirmatively. They went into her office and each took a seat. A little later, Lars and Knut came in and placed themselves by one wall. The police chief came in right after them. He had a stick-back chair with him from the hall. A couple of curious souls hung around outside, so Olav went over and closed the door.

The police chief got right down to business.

"Do we know him? The man in the tunnel?"

Lotte nodded and cleared her throat. "We know him very well. He's someone we've had on the radar at the newspaper. We have DNA samples from him, but the results from the lab won't get here until tomorrow."

The four others in the room looked at one another. This was what they had hoped would happen. That there was a clear connection between the person they'd arrested in the tunnel and something to do with the case. An employee at the newspaper was perfect in that respect.

Olav Scheldrup Hansen asked the burning question. "Who is it?"

Lotte looked up at them. Peered at four faces that for the first time in a week had traces of energy and enthusiasm. So this was how it felt to succeed in bringing in a killer. They looked like a hunting party that had just shot the royal stag.

"It's Henrik Thomsen. The arts reporter."

Lotte had recognized him at once. The man was enormous. She had run into Thomsen a number of times before.

Scheldrup Hansen seized the chance that came in the silence after the name had sunk in among the three others. "This Thomsen . . . Did he say anything? Did he do anything when you came into the tunnel?"

Lotte sighed and shook her head. "No, there was an explosion, and then it was all just chaos."

There was silence in the room. All five appeared to be lost in their own thoughts. The adrenaline that had raced through their bodies the past few hours had kept them alert and on edge. Now fatigue came creeping in. They finally knew who he was, and they had him under control. Thomsen would have to force his way past no fewer than ten policemen to escape from the hospital. Regardless of how much intended mayhem this man had prepared, he probably didn't have a plan B for this scenario.

They were roused from their reveries by a knock at the window. Outside stood a fresh and cheerful Harald Madsen. The publisher was smiling from ear to ear. He was let in.

"I've been talking with several of the other publishers today, and now I just had a phone call from Arno Vigmostad at Vigmostad and Bjørke. He had the name and address of the man behind the pseudonym Geir Tangen."

Harald Madsen threw the paper he had in his hand on the table. The others smiled at him. So they'd figured out the name too.

The police chief patted Madsen on the shoulder. "Well done. Fortunately, we got hold of him in a maneuver up in the city earlier today. Henrik Thomsen is in our custody at the hospital. It's over now."

Harald Madsen smiled back at the tall police chief. He nodded, but evidently had a question on his mind. His gaze wandered among the five others in the office.

The police chief looked at him. "Is there anything else you're wondering about in this connection?"

"Uh . . . No. Now, of course, I'm not completely updated on everything in this case, but who is Henrik Thomsen?"

Requiem: Communio

The police cars roar past along Kirkegata. I am amused. Once again, it was a close call. Much too close, actually. I understand it now, what was tormenting me all last night. How could they know? How could they be in the vicinity two times in a row? They actually must have been able to solve the case and found the manuscript.

In that case, it's only a matter of time before they know who I am. I'm gambling that I still have time. Half an hour is all I need for the finish. Nevertheless, I notice that it is unpleasant to have them so near me now when I can see the final stretch and the finish line in front of me. I have only one plan B, and it involves a major risk that they will be faster than I.

For that reason, I'm standing by the window, so that I can see. Be aware if someone were to suddenly come to get me. In that case, a rapid retreat through the emergency exit in the basement is the only alternative.

My body is racked with impatience. The work computer has always been sluggish, but never so bad as today. I notice that the tiredness is seizing hold of me now. There was no sleep at the boathouse last night. I got a call from André. He had to confess his sins, he said. He had to tell what had happened that day out at Røvær. That he'd almost killed Viljar, but changed his mind. It amused me that he didn't have the slightest idea what I'd been up to the past week.

André's unexpected intervention in my story about Jonas was an interesting twist. It *must* be written into the manuscript. I noticed that it was just the little sequence that was missing to make the piece of music complete. The Jonas story got its worthy ending.

While the computer trudges through the start-up programs, I look down at the street below me. Everything appears normal. People are scurrying to and fro, and the cars maneuver around all the illegally parked vehicles on the streets surrounding the prayer meeting house in the city center. I marvel at how they can live their normal lives completely unaffected by everything that has happened in the past week. What will happen when they read about Hans Indbjo, who stood in the bright flames on Lindøy last evening, I don't know, but it will undoubtedly speed up the media circus, which has already gone completely off the rails. I allow myself a smile. It was a delightful feeling to hear the screams of pain echoing between the skerries.

Half an hour ago, I witnessed the drama over by the Opel Building. I felt it physically as I approached the place that something was wrong. A tingling sense of worry in my body. A feeling that something wasn't normal. More rapid breathing. An incipient anxiety that pinched me in the ribs. Ten minutes before the scheduled time, I was standing at the crossing by the old power station trying to make up my mind. The manuscript I had edited in the little summerhouse at Espevær gave me directions about what I should do, but back in town, it was as if everything suddenly was wrong. I had a creeping suspicion that the police knew more than I thought. I could not meet Lotte in the tunnel.

While I was standing there, a familiar figure appeared before me, and right then I understood that this must be fate. A hundred and thirty kilograms of walking negativity was exactly what I needed there and then. Henrik Thomsen nodded in recognition and shook my hand. I fired off a couple of dry polite phrases before I asked if he could do me a favor.

"Lotte Skeisvoll is coming in five minutes, and I was supposed to give her this flash drive down in the tunnel on my way to work, but now something has come up, so I can't wait. Could you wait here for her, do you think? It's extremely important. . . ."

"Why in the tunnel?" Thomsen had looked a bit skeptical. Certainly not happy to be inconvenienced.

"No, we just agreed on there. She usually jogs that route, and I go past here on my way to work."

Henrik Thomsen nodded and took the flash drive. "I won't wait long, just so you know. Maximum five minutes."

I nodded and left him.

I got in my car by the Austmann high-rises, started it, and rolled a short way in the opposite direction before I turned around. Just then, I caught sight of Lotte, who came running. From my vantage point I took in the whole episode. It didn't take more than half a minute from when she passed me before there was an explosion. At the same time, the place was swarming with police, and I understood that I had been quite right in my suspicions. I jumped out of the car and ran over to take in the details. When a flock of police was carrying a bloody and unconscious Henrik Thomsen from the tunnel, I knew that I still had some time. Not much, because he would blab as soon as they started asking questions. But that wouldn't happen right away. Now the man needed medical attention, and he was out cold besides.

I make a name change and amend the scene by the tunnel. Lotte Skeisvoll got away. I chuckle a little at the thought of something Hans

Olav Lahlum said at a crime festival one time: *"It's frustrating when my characters suddenly start living their own lives. One time, one of the main characters decided that he should come out of the closet as gay in the middle of a book. Incredibly irritating. That created a lot of trouble for me."* In my book, it's a bit different. The characters have their own free will in reality too, and I'm the one who has to change the story so that it will be correct. Unfortunately, reality can't be changed.

I am approaching the final sequence. Soon it will actually be over. Before I write my *manu propria*, my final words, I go to the email list of all the Norwegian literary publishers. Paste them in and get ready to send. If the police come now, I'll manage to press Send before I run away. This time I won't get a single rejection. There will be seventeen publishers, all of whom have permission to argue till the fur flies about who will get the rights. The answer is in my will, in the event I don't live that long. The tumor in my head is knocking steadily louder on the door. Just a pity that I won't be able to see the success of the book itself. That is my great sorrow. Still, it's enough to know it. Mozart didn't get to hear his Requiem, after all. Wergeland never got to see "To a Nightingale" in print. It will probably be that way with my masterwork.

I sigh in relief. Know I'm going to make it now. In a short while, I can pick up my last victim. She is sitting ready in reception. Happily ignorant of her own fate. Half an hour ago, she had her life ahead of her. Now I'm writing her in as dead. I actually couldn't have found a better stand-in for Lotte. She actually should have been plan A, but I hardly knew about her three years ago when I wrote the first draft. She was a minor character. I'm giving her the place she deserves. I will take time to write the afterword too. Without that in place, no one will understand what *really* happened.

Everything is written. Everything is in place. I study the details one last time before I tap the baton. The curtain goes up. Enjoy the feeling when everyone *finally* sees me. I'm the one who is the masterwork.

I am Maestro. . . .

Haugesund Police Station
Late Monday morning, October 20, 2014

Lotte tossed the sheet of paper with the name down on the table. Everything that made it look like "case closed" a minute ago was suddenly turned on its head again. The name that was written in red marker on the paper Harald Madsen had with him glared at the five officers in the room.

"What the hell is going on?"

Lotte Skeisvoll collapsed like a sack of potatoes in the chair. She looked up in despair at the publisher in the hope that he would reveal what would have been the worst, most subtle joke of all time, but the publisher just looked at them uncomprehendingly.

"Well, that was the name I got from Vigmostad, anyway. They've cataloged all submitted manuscripts digitally since the company started, and it was an easy matter to search the contact information behind the pseudonym."

"Øystein Vindheim, isn't that the librarian that Ranveig interviewed the day before she was killed?" Scheldrup Hansen stood with the paper in hand and looked over his glasses at the others.

Lotte nodded weakly in confirmation.

"Damn it! I knew there was something familiar about that figure on the bicycle at Djupaskar. I talked with him about those confounded codes in the emails that same day."

The police chief had collected himself and took control of the situation. "Great. That's the way it is. What Henrik Thomsen was doing in the tunnel we'll know soon enough. Now we just have to get ahold of this librarian before he finds some random victim or other that he takes with him."

Everyone stood up, except for Lotte. The others stopped and looked at her. She looked tired. As if all the energy had left her. In slow motion, she turned her gaze toward the inquisitive faces before her. The words were stuck in her throat. They wouldn't come out. At last she managed to whisper what she had to say. What struck her the moment the police chief had spoken.

"It's not a random victim."

The five in the room did not say anything. They looked at her with greater puzzlement. The silence had settled around them like a vacuum.

"It's Anne . . . my sister," she added. "She was given an offer from NAV for subsidized work at the library. Part of the new municipal arrangement where they try to place drug abusers during the day. It was Øystein who arranged it. Anne told me when she woke up at the hospital on Saturday. I couldn't understand what use the library could have for a worn-out addict, but never asked her about it. She was supposed to start today, she said."

"Damn! Is there a single scenario this man hasn't thought out in advance?"

Olav Scheldrup Hansen was furious and struck a clenched fist into the wall in frustration.

Lotte did not react. She sat as if paralyzed, looking down at the table. This time, there was nothing left of her. She remained a passive witness as the police chief and Olav took charge. Everything was arranged over her head. Together with a confused publisher, she remained sitting at her desk while all the others were running around in the corridors. As the first sirens were heard, she came around.

"I can call . . ."

She fumbled in her pockets for her phone, but her fingers and hands wouldn't obey. Only on the third try did she find where it should be. In the clip on her uniform belt.

"No answer," she called. "Pick up, damn it!"

Harald Madsen stood up carefully and left the room.

Lars Stople came in right after that. He went over and put his arms around Lotte. She resisted while she howled out new oaths. Lars hushed and consoled her, and then it was as if something shook loose. Lotte placed her head against the shoulder of the old policeman. There was nothing to do now other than hope. Hope that the killer wasn't one step ahead of them, but that they would find him where he should be. At the library. Nevertheless, it struck them both in the midst of their embrace. If there was a sign of how Øystein Vindheim had operated the past week, then it was that he was always one step ahead.

Confirmation came on a crackling intercom system two minutes later. An out-of-breath Knut Veldetun reported in.

"He's not here. Left ten minutes ago, the woman behind the counter said. He was going to buy office supplies and took the new assistant from NAV with him. I expect they're not at Staples shopping. . . ."

Lotte straightened the earbud and the microphone. She cleared her throat a few times so as not to give away her tear-filled voice.

"No, Knut. They're probably on their way to Haraldsvang. The cards are dealt now. The only thing to do is go all in. We no longer have anything to lose." There was silence for a moment at the other end before Knut came back.

"You're wrong there. We have everything to lose, Lotte. If we fail this time, you no longer have a sister."

Lotte turned off the microphone and murmured quietly, "I've lost my sister many times before."

Haraldsvang Café, Haugesund
Late Monday morning, October 20, 2014

A gentle breeze made the dry birch leaves rustle slightly by the playground in Haraldsvang. Otherwise, it was completely still. Not a single screaming child. No voices. No cars in the parking lot. The café at the end toward the water was dark and the blinds were lowered. No joggers on the paths around the open area. No one walking with a stroller. Nothing.

It was as if the whole world were holding its breath. In the summer, the place was crawling with teenagers on the diving platform and families with small children in peaceful play in the spot in front of the café. But today no one was to be seen.

That is, almost no one was to be seen. On a bench in the park, a man sat quietly observing the surroundings. The whole setting in the park was arranged for a re-creation of the opening scene in *The Night Man* by Jørn Lier Horst. With the exception of the man himself, the bench, and the fact that they were in a peaceful park in the forest in nice weather. Not on a busy shopping street in the middle of the city while fog placed its veil over the inconceivable.

The sound of the sirens increased in strength, and the blue lights shimmered among yellow autumn leaves in the forest.

Lotte Skeisvoll had thrown herself into one of the first cars. She wanted to be there. If she wasn't there, Anne would have no one she knew around her. Lotte knew very well what it would lead to if everything went the way it was written, but the alternative was to let Anne stand there alone.

Lotte looked in panic out the window of the police car as they screeched into the lot by Haraldsvang Café. Time stopped as she raised her eyes and saw what Øystein Vindheim had managed to stage in the barely ten minutes he had on them. The cars came in a line behind them. The sirens were turned off. Doors opened, police threw themselves down into position, and commands flew through the air for a few seconds. Then suddenly it was as if the entire scenario turned into a tableau.

If it hadn't been for the all-encompassing silence, everything would have been seemingly normal. The metal slides of the playground equipment glistened in the sun. The shells of car tires swung cautiously back and forth in the wind. One of the suspension chains was rusty and creaked every time the wind put the tire into motion. You could hear the water lapping the stones at the water's edge. Everything was exactly the way he wanted it. Him alone on the bench. The police in position in front of him. Anne standing by his side.

Lotte opened the door of the police car in a continuous slow movement. She stood up. Clung to the doorframe so she wouldn't fall. The policemen in the response team had lowered their weapons a few centimeters. All of them looked apprehensively over at her. She stroked a brown shock of her hair to the side. Noticed that she was hyperventilating. Her hands were shaking. Her legs struggled to support her. She whispered to her sister first.

"Anne . . ."

Her sister could not hear her. The words did not reach her. They were ten meters apart, but Lotte couldn't reach her. She called to her sister. Louder and louder.

"Anne! . . . *Anne!*"

She did not answer. Anne stared vacantly over the parking lot.

From the treetops, a light rustling could be heard from the remnants of what had been fresh, green foliage a month earlier. A chilly breeze crept over the hills from the waters of Skeisvannet. Settled like a layer of ice over the people standing there. Everything that was normal and everyday was whisked away by this one thing in front of them. High over the man on the bench, Anne wobbled with her head fastened to a two-meter-long pole. Where had the rest of her body gone? Only the contented man sitting on the bench knew that. *The Maestro.*

Requiem: Manu propria

Why? . . .

For a week they've been asking me that question. There is no "why." What, who, where, and how are good words. Words I can relate to. But "why"? . . .

I answer that it had to be done. They ask whether it was a compulsive act. No. I could have chosen not to. Could have gone quietly out of time with a two-column obituary on a back page in the local paper. Prayed to a God that doesn't exist that someone would pick up the manuscript and let it have a life after me. That someone, against all odds, would see the words I have written, and give me a name postmortem. I could have done that. Lived my final days in the hope that someone would discover me, and see me. But I didn't do that. I chose to turn the words into action. The interplay to music.

A game with mirrors. A Mass for the dead. A requiem. A swan song over ice-covered water. I don't get how it's so difficult to understand.

They shake their heads. Mumble to each other. Turn toward me again. Ask more "why" questions. I squirm on the stick-back chair. Don't comprehend what the point is with this wordplay. Mozart wrote symphonies. No one asked him "why"!

"I wanted people to see this story. That it wouldn't disappear with me."

A moment later, I wonder whether I said that out loud, or if I just thought those sentences. There is no response from the two policemen, so I don't know. I can't keep track of how many times I've repeated myself in answer to their questions. I am an echo of myself. An echo in the white-plastered walls.

Why did you write that story? Because I wanted to. Because I'd lived a whole life of wandering among bookshelves and never found myself. Because I knew I could do it better. Because I had a story I wanted to share.

Why did you use real persons in a novel? Idiotic question. Everyone who knows anything about books knows that the characters must be genuine so the story will be believable. Genuine characters, genuine persons, genuine names. You don't get closer to reality. As I said, it's a game with mirrors. Using my friends and other known faces the way *I* see them. Letting them be themselves in a role. Let them live their life in my story. Or die . . . Someone always has to die.

The man from Oslo. Olav Scheldrup Hansen. The man that I had to write into the story along the way turns toward me. Tries to stare me down with tired eyes. Peeks down at his notes.

Asks the endless question again.

"*Why* did they have to *die*? *Why* did you choose these victims, and not others?"

It should be obvious. I didn't choose them; they chose me. Like one of the judges in court, I was there when they were acquitted against my will, and I was there when they got their rightful judgment. A circle completed. I saw them on the witness stand, and heard all their little lies. It was *there* the seed was sown. That someone let them get their punishment nevertheless? That was the crime plot I'd waited for. The story of the genius who in his madness took out his revenge on those who avoided their punishment. "Maestro" was a shadow of me, written into a book. He came alive through me. When the Mass for the dead was to be performed, they *had* to die. That wasn't my wish. It was just the way it was written in the notes. You can improvise over a composition, but the leading tone must be the same.

"You killed them because you had written in this novel that this would happen?"

Scheldrup Hansen again. Monotonous voice. Tired type. Finally a question I can answer. A precise, concise answer coming from me:

"Yes."

The Kripos investigator shakes his head. Looks at his colleague and whispers something to her. She nods. This isn't Lotte Skeisvoll. I haven't seen her since the final note faded out in Haraldsvang a week ago. She is still one of the meaningless questions. Why just her? I answered them truthfully.

Why not? . . .

She was too good not to be used in a novel. Her little peculiarities that I had studied in the courtroom again and again. *OCD, wasn't that the abbreviation for this diagnosis?* Small, meaningless compulsive actions that make the character different. Brilliant but insecure. Confident but afraid. Steady but unstable. I understood it as soon as I started on *Maestro*. It had to be Lotte. I tarry a little on the good memories from all the times I studied her predictable habits and routines. Who else shops for milk, bread, sliced ham, and cheese every day at exactly 5:05 P.M.?

"*Why* this hatred toward Viljar Gudmundsson? I thought you were friends."

The man from East Norway is clearly not through wondering yet.

They definitely have a hard time with that. Don't they understand yet? *I don't hate Viljar.* He's my hero. He's the one who plays the main role. My first violinist. My soloist. I love Viljar. That's why I let him live. All heroes have their problems on the way toward the resolution; otherwise, it wouldn't be exciting. Yes, I let him suffer for the weak job he did with Jonas, my delightful nephew. But I don't hate him for that reason. It just gave me an excellent reason to get to tell Jonas's story too. No one has written it down before. Not the *actual*, true story. The one Jonas and Fredric told me when I hid them in my house after what happened with Ine.

A mirror in a mirror. That's the way it is.

Or . . . that's the way I *hope* it will be as I sit alone at the library, listening for sirens that still seem to be waiting. Fantasize about how this scene will play out. I have written the last movement from Haraldsvang. I see before me that this is the way it *must* end. That I succeed, and that the story ends there. But I don't know where the mirror captures and reality ends. Thus I see myself sitting in a chair in a week, where they ask me why, and I answer with my soundless thoughts. They *are* going to do that, aren't they?

In any event, that is how it shall be, if it goes the way I've written. Then this will happen. Then the world will see me shine. Then the period will be set here. Anne dies. I will also die at last, but *Maestro* will live forever. Here at the library in Haugesund, in the center of the endless magic of the books, like a mirror in a mirror for all eternity.

October 29, 2014
Øystein Vindheim